The Art of Disappearing

John Talbot Smith

ESPRIOS DIGITAL PUBLISHING

THE ART OF DISAPPEARING

By John Talbot Smith

AUTHOR:

"SARANAC" "HIS HONOR THE MAYOR," "A WOMAN OF
CULTURE," "SOLITARY ISLAND," "TRAINING OF A PRIEST,"
ETC., ETC.

NEW YORK, CINCINNATI, CHICAGO :

BENZIGER BROTHERS.

PRINTERS TO THE HOLY APOSTOLIC SEE.

THE ART OF DISAPPEARING

By John Talbot Smith

AUTHOR:

"Saranac" "His Honor the Mayor," "A Woman Of Culture,"
"Solitary Island," "Training of a Priest," Etc., Etc.

1902

CONTENTS.

THE TEST OF DISAPPEARANCE.

DISAPPEARANCE.

CHAPTER I.

THE HOLY OILS.

Horace Endicott once believed that life began for him the day he married Sonia Westfield. The ten months spent with the young wife were of a hue so roseate as to render discussion of the point foolish. His youth had been a happy one, of the roystering, innocent kind: noisy with yachting, baseball, and a moderate quantity of college beer, but clean, as if his mother had supervised it; yet he had never really lived in his twenty-five years, until the blessed experience of a long honeymoon and a little housekeeping with Sonia had woven into his life the light of sun and moon and stars together. However, as he admitted long afterwards, his mistake was as terrible as convincing. Life began for him that day he sat in the railway carriage across the aisle from distinguished Monsignor O'Donnell, prelate of the Pope's household, doctor in theology, and vicar-general of the New York diocese. The train being on its way to Boston, and the journey dull, Horace whiled away a slow hour watching the Monsignor, and wondering what motives govern the activity of the priests of Rome. The priest was a handsome man of fifty, dark-haired, of an ascetic pallor, but undoubtedly practical, as his quick and business-like movements testified. His dark eyes were of fine color and expression, and his manners showed the gentleman.

"Some years ago," thought Horace, "I would have studied his person for indications of hoofs and horns—so strangely was I brought up. He is just a poor fellow like myself—it is as great a mistake to make these men demi-gods as to make them demi-devils—and he denies himself a wife as a Prohibitionist denies himself a drink. He goes through his mummeries as honestly as a parson through his sermons or a dervish through his dances—it's all one, and we must allow for it in the make-up of human nature. One man has his parson, another his priest, a third his dervish—and I have Sonia."

1

This satisfactory conclusion he dwelt upon lovingly, unconscious that the Monsignor was now observing him in turn.

"A fine boy," the priest thought, "with *man* written all over him. Honest face, virtuous expression, daring too, loving-hearted, lovable, clever, I'm sure, and his life has been too easy to develop any marked character. Too young to have been in the war, but you may be sure he wanted to go, and his mother had to exercise her authority to keep him at home. He has been enjoying me for an hour.... I'm as pleasant as a puzzle to him ... he preferred to read me rather than Dickens, and I gather from his expression that he has solved me. By this time I am rated in his mind as an impostor. Oh, the children of the Mayflower, how hard for them to see anything in life except through the portholes of that ship."

With a sigh the priest returned to his book, and the two gentlemen, having had their fill of speculation, forgot each other directly and forever. At this point the accident occurred. The slow train ran into a train ahead, which should have been farther on at that moment. All the passengers rose up suddenly, without any ceremony, quite speechless, and flew up the car like sparrows. Then the car turned on its left side, and Horace rolled into the outstretched arms and elevated legs of Monsignor O'Donnell. He was kicked and embraced at the same moment, receiving these attentions in speechless awe, as he could not recall who was to blame for the introduction and the attitude. For a moment he reasoned that they had become the object of most outrageous ridicule from the other passengers; for these latter had suddenly set up a shouting and screeching very scandalous. Horace wondered if the priest would help him to resent this storm of insult, and he raised himself off the Monsignor's face, and removed the rest of his person from the Monsignor's body, in order the more politely to invite him to the battle. Then he discovered the state of things in general. The overthrown car was at a stand-still. That no one was hurt seemed happily clear from the vigorous yells of everybody, and the fine scramble through the car-windows. The priest got up leisurely and felt himself. Next he seized his satchel eagerly.

"Now it was more than an accident that I brought the holy oils along," said he to Horace. "I was vexed to find them where they shouldn't be, yet see how soon I find use for them. Someone must be badly hurt in this disaster, and of course it'll be one of my own."

"I hope," said the other politely, "that I did you no harm in falling on you. I could not very well help it."

"Fortune was kinder to you than if the train rolled over the other way. Don't mention it, my son. I'll forgive you, if you will find me the way out, and learn if any have been injured."

The window was too small for a man of the Monsignor's girth, but through the rear door the two crawled out comfortably, Monsignor dragging the satchel and murmuring cheerfully: "How lucky! the holy oils!" It was just sundown, and the wrecked train lay in a meadow, with a pretty stream running by, whose placid ripplings mocked the tumult of the mortals examining their injuries in the field. Yet no one had been seriously injured. Bruises and cuts were plentiful, some fainted from shock, but each was able to do for himself, not so much as a bone having been broken. For a few minutes the Monsignor rejoiced that he would have no use for what he called the holy oils. Then a trainman came running, white and broken-tongued, crying out: "There was a priest on the train—who has seen him?" It turned out that the fireman had been caught in the wrecked locomotive, and crushed to death.

"And it's a priest he's cryin' for, sir," groaned the trainman, as he came up to the Monsignor. The dying man lay in the shade of some trees beside the stream, and a lovely woman had his head in her lap, and wept silently while the poor boy gasped every now and then "mother" and "the priest." She wiped the death-dew from his face, from which the soot had been washed with water from the stream, and moistened his lips with a cordial. He was a youth, of the kind that should not die too early, so vigorous was his young body, so manly and true his dear face; but it was only a matter of ten minutes stay beside the little stream for Tim Hurley. The group about him made way for Monsignor, who sank on his knees beside him, and held up the boy's face to the fading light.

3

"The priest is here, Tim," he said gently, and Endicott saw the receding life rush back with joy into the agonized features. With something like a laugh he raised his inert hands, and seized the hands of the priest, which he covered with kisses.

"I shall die happy, thanks be to God," he said weakly; "and, father, don't forget to tell my mother. It's her last consolation, poor dear."

"And I have the holy oils, Tim," said Monsignor softly.

Another rush of light to the darkening face!

"Tell her that, too, father dear," said Tim.

"With my own lips," answered Monsignor.

The bystanders moved away a little distance, and the lady resigned her place, while Tim made his last confession. Endicott stood and wondered at the sight; the priest holding the boy's head with his left arm, close to his bosom and Tim grasping lovingly the hand of his friend, while he whispered in little gasps his sins and his repentance; briefly, for time was pressing. Then Monsignor called Horace and bade him support the lad's head; and also the lovely lady and gave her directions "for his mother's sake." She was woman and mother both, no doubt, by the way she served another woman's son in his fatal distress. The men brought her water from the stream. With her own hands she bared his feet, bathed and wiped them, washed his hands, and cried tenderly all the time. Horace shuddered as he dried the boy's sweating forehead, and felt the chill of that death which had never yet come near him. He saw now what the priest meant by the holy oils. Out of his satchel Monsignor took a golden cylinder, unscrewed the top, dipped his thumb in what appeared to be an oily substance, and applied it to Tim's eyes, to his ears, his nose, his mouth, the palms of his hands, and the soles of his feet, distinctly repeating certain Latin invocations as he worked. Then he read for some time from a little book, and finished by wiping his fingers in cotton and returning all to the satchel again. There was a look of supreme satisfaction on his face.

"You are all right now, Tim," he said cheerfully.

4

"All right, father," repeated the lad faintly, "and don't forget to tell mother everything, and say I died happy, praising God, and that she won't be long after me. And let Harry Cutler"—the engineer came forward and knelt by his side—"tell her everything. She knew how he liked me and a word from him was more——"

His voice faded away.

"I'll tell her," murmured the engineer brokenly, and slipped away in unbearable distress. The priest looked closer into Tim's face.

"He's going fast," he said, "and I'll ask you all to kneel and say amen to the last prayers for the boy."

The crowd knelt by the stream in profound silence, and the voice of the priest rose like splendid music, touching, sad, yet to Horace unutterably pathetic and grand.

"Go forth, O Christian soul," the Monsignor read, "in the name of God the Father Almighty, who created thee; in the name of Jesus Christ, Son of the living God, who suffered for thee; in the name of the Holy Ghost, who was poured forth upon thee; in the name of the Angels and Archangels; in the name of the Thrones and Dominations; in the name of the Principalities and Powers; in the name of the Cherubim and Seraphim; in the name of the Patriarchs and Prophets; in the name of the holy Apostles and Evangelists; in the name of the holy Martyrs and Confessors; in the name of the holy Monks and Hermits; in the name of the holy Virgins and of all the Saints of God; may thy place be this day in peace, and thy abode in holy Sion. Through Jesus Christ our Lord. Amen."

Then came a pause and the heavy sigh of the dying one shook all hearts. Endicott did not dare to look down at the mournful face of the fireman, for a terror of death had come upon him, that he should be holding the head of one condemned to the last penalty of nature; at the same moment he could not help thinking that a king might not have been more nobly sent forth on his journey to judgment than humble Tim Hurley. Monsignor took another look at the lad's face, then closed his book, and took off the purple ribbon which had hung about his neck.

"It's over. The man's dead," he announced to the silent crowd. There was a general stir, and a movement to get a closer look at the quiet body lying on the grass. Endicott laid the head down and rose to his feet. The woman who had ministered to the dying so sweetly tied up his chin and covered his face, murmuring with tears, "His poor mother."

"Ah, there is the heart to be pitied," sighed the Monsignor. "This heart aches no more, but the mother's will ache and not die for many a year perhaps."

Endicott heard his voice break, and looking saw that the tears were falling from his eyes, he wiping them away in the same matter-of-fact fashion which had marked his ministrations to the unfortunate fireman.

"Death is terrible only to those who love," he added, and the words sent a pang into the heart of Horace. It had never occurred to him that death was love's most dreaded enemy,—that Sonia might die while love was young.

CHAPTER II.

THE NIGHT AT THE TAVERN.

The travelers of the wrecked train spent the night at the nearest village, whither all went on foot before darkness came on. Monsignor took possession of Horace, also of the affections of the tavern-keeper, and of the best things which belonged to that yokel and his hostelry. It was prosperity in the midst of disaster that he and Endicott should have a room on the first floor, and find themselves comfortable in ten minutes after their arrival. By the time they had enjoyed a refreshing meal, and discussed the accident to the roots, Horace Endicott felt that his soul was at ease with the Monsignor, who at no time had displayed any other feeling than might arise from a long acquaintance with the young man. One would have pronounced the two men, as they settled down into the comfort of their room, two collegians who had traveled much together.

"It was an excellent thing that I brought the holy oils along," Monsignor said, as if Endicott had no other interest in life than this particular form of excellence. To a polite inquiry he explained the history, nature, and use of the mysterious oils.

"I can understand how a ceremony of that kind would soothe the last hours of Tim Hurley," said the pagan Endicott, "but I am curious, if you will pardon me, to know if the holy oils would have a similar effect on Monsignor O'Donnell."

"The same old supposition," chuckled the priest, "that there is one law for the crowd, the mob, the diggers, and another for the illuminati. Now, let me tell you, Mr. Endicott, that with all his faith Tim Hurley could not have welcomed priest and oils more than I shall when I need them. The anguish of death is very bitter, which you are too young to know, and it is a blessed thing to have a sovereign ready for that anguish in the Sacrament of Extreme Unction. The Holy Oils are the thing which Macbeth desired when he demanded so bitterly of the physician.

Canst thou not minister to a mind diseased,
Pluck from the memory a rooted sorrow?

That is my conviction. So if you are near when I am going to judgment, come in and see how emphatically I shall demand the holy oils, even before a priest be willing to bring them."

"It seems strange," Horace commented, "very strange. I cannot get at your point of view at all."

Then he went on to ask questions rapidly, and Monsignor had to explain the meaning of his title, a hundred things connected with his priesthood, and to answer many objections to his explanations; until the night had worn on to bedtime, and the crowd of guests began to depart from the verandahs. It was all so interesting to Horace. In the priest and his conversation he had caught a glimpse of a new world both strange and fascinating. Curious too was the profound indifference of men like himself—college men—to its existence. It did not seem possible that the Roman idea could grow into proportions under the bilious eyes of the omniscient Saxon, and not a soul be aware of its growth! However, Monsignor was a pleasant man, a true college lad, an interesting talker, with music in his voice, and a sincere eye. He was not a controversialist, but a critic, and he did not seem to mind when Horace went off into a dream of Sonia, and asked questions far from the subject.

Long afterwards Endicott recalled a peculiarity of this night, which escaped his notice at the time: his sensitiveness to every detail of their surroundings, to the colors of the room, to the shades of meaning in the words of the Monsignor, to his tricks of speech and tone, quite unusual in Horace's habit. Sonia complained that he never could tell her anything clear or significant of places he had seen. The room which had been secured from the landlord was the parlor of the tavern; long and low, colonial in the very smell of the tapestry carpet, with doors and mantel that made one think of John Adams and General Washington. The walls had a certain terror in them, a kind of suspense, as when a jury sits petrified while their foreman announces a verdict of death. A long line of portraits in oil produced this impression. The faces of ancient neighbors, of the Adams, the Endicotts, the Bradburys, severe Puritans, for whom the name of priest meant a momentary stoppage of the heart, looked coldly and precisely straight out from their frames on the Monsignor. Horace fancied that they exchanged glances. What fun it would have been to see the entire party move out from their frames, and put the wearer of the Roman purple to shameful flight.

"I'll bet they don't let you sleep to-night," he said to the priest, who laughed at the conceit.

A cricket came out on the window-sill, chirped at Horace's elbow, and fled at the sound of near voices. Through the thick foliage of the chestnut trees outside he could see stars at times that made him think of Sonia's eyes. The wind shook the branches gently, and made little moans and whispers in the corners, as if the ghosts of the portraits were discussing the sacrilege of the Monsignor's presence. Horace thought at the time his nerves were strung tight by the incidents of the day, and his interest deeply stirred by the conversation of the priest; since hitherto he had always thought of wind as a thing that blew disagreeably except at sea, noisy insects as public nuisances to be caught and slain, and family portraits the last praiseworthy attempt of ancestors to disturb the sleep of their remote heirs. When he had somewhat tired of asking his companion questions, it occurred to him that the Monsignor had asked none in return, and might waive his right to this privilege of good-fellowship. He mentioned the matter.

"Thank you," said Monsignor, "but I know all about you. See now if I give you a good account of your life and descent."

He was promenading the room before the picture-jury frowning on him. He looked at them a moment solemnly.

"Indeed I know what I would have to expect from you," he said to the portraits, "if you were to sit upon my case to-night. Your descendant here is more merciful."

They laughed together.

"Well," to Horace, "you asked me many questions, because you know nothing about me or mine, although we have been on the soil this half century. The statesmen of your blood disdain me. This scorn

9

is in the air of New England, and is part of your marrow. Here is an example of it. Once on a vacation I spent a few weeks in the house of a Puritan lady, who learned of my faith and blood only a week before my leaving. She had been very kind, and when I bade her good-by I assured her that I would remember her in my prayers. 'You needn't mind,' she replied, 'my own prayers are much better than any you can say.' This temper explains why you have to ask questions about me, and I have none to ask concerning you."

Horace had to admit the contention.

"Life began for you near the river that turned the wheel of the old sawmill. Ah, that river! It was the beginning of history, of time, of life! It came from the beyond and it went over the rim of the wonderful horizon, singing and laughing like a child. How often you dreamed of following it to its end, where you were certain a glory, felt only in your dreams, filled the land. The fishes only could do that, for they had no feet to be tired by walking. Your first mystery was that wheel which the water turned: a monstrous thing, a giant, ugly and deadly, whose first movement sent you off in terror. How could it be that the gentle, smiling, yielding water, which took any shape from a baby hand, had power to speed that giant! The time came when you bathed in the stream, mastered it, in spite of the terror which it gave you one day when it swallowed the life of a comrade. Do you remember this?"

Monsignor held up his hand with two fingers stretched out beyond the others, and gave a gentle war-whoop. Horace laughed.

"I suppose every boy in the country invited his chums to a swim that way," he said.

"Just so. The sign language was universal. The old school on the village green succeeded the river and the mill in your history. Miss Primby taught it, dear old soul, gentler than a mother even, and you laughed at her curls, and her funny ways, which hid from child's eyes a noble heart. It was she who bound up your black eye after the battle with Bouncer, the bully, whose face and reputation you wrecked in the same hour for his oppression of the most helpless boy in school. That feat made you the leader of the secret society which met at awful hours in the deserted shanty just below the sawmill. What a creep went up and down your spine as in the chill of the evening the boys came stealing out of the undergrowth one by one, and greeted their chief with the password, known by every parent in town. The stars looked down upon you as they must have looked upon all the great conspirators of time since the world began. You felt that the life of the government hung by a thread, when such desperate characters took the risk of conspiring against it. What a day was July the Fourth—what wretches were the British—what a hero was General Washington! What land was like this country of the West? Its form on the globe was a promontory while all others lay very low on the plane."

"In that spirit you went to Harvard and ran full against some great questions of life. The war was on, and your father was at the front. Only your age, your father's orders, and your mother's need held you back from the fight. You were your mother's son. It is written all over you,—and me. And your father loved you doubly that you were his son and owned her nature. He fell in battle, and she was slain by a crueller foe, the grief that, seizing us, will not let us live even for those we love. God rest the faithful dead, give peace to their souls, and complete their love and their labors! My father and mother are living yet—the sweetest of blessings at my time of life. You grieved as youth grieves, but life had its compensations. You are a married man, and you love as your parents loved, with the fire and tenderness of both. Happy man! Fortunate woman!"

He stopped before the nearest portrait, and stared at it.

"Well, what do you think of my acquaintance with your history?" he asked.

"Very clever, Monsignor," answered Horace impressed. "It is like necromancy, though I see how the trick is done."

"Precisely. It is my own story. It is the story of thousands of boys whom your set will not regard as American boys, unless when they are looking for fighting material. Everything and anything that could carry a gun in the recent war was American with a vengeance. The Boston Coriolanus kissed such an one and swore that he must have come over in the Mayflower. But enough—I am not holding a brief for anybody. The description I have just given you of your life and mine is also——"

"One moment—pardon me," said Horace, "how did you know I was married?"

"And happy?" said Monsignor. "Well, that was easy. When we were talking to-night at tea about the hanging of Howard Tims, what disgust in your tone when you cried out, there should be no pity for the wretch that kills his wife."

"And there should not."

"Of course. But I knew Tims. I met him for an hour, and I did not feel like hanging him."

"You are a celibate."

"Therefore unprejudiced. But he was condemned by a jury of unmarried men. A clever fellow he is, and yet he made some curious blunders in his attempt to escape the other night. I would like to have helped him. I have a theory of disappearing from the sight of men, which would help the desperate much. This Tims was a lad of your own appearance, disposition, history even. I had a feeling that he ought not to die. What a pity we are too wise to yield always to our feelings."

"But about your theory, Monsignor?" said Horace. "A theory of disappearing?"

"A few nights ago some friends of mine were discussing the possible methods by which such a man as Tims might make his escape sure. You know that the influences at his command were great, and tremendous efforts were made to spare his family the disgrace of the gallows. The officers of the law were quite determined that he should not escape. If he had escaped, the pursuit would have been relentless and able. He would have been caught. And as I maintained, simply because he would never think of using his slight acquaintance with me. You smile at that. So did my friends. I have been reading up the escapes of famous criminals—it is quite a literature. I learned therein one thing: that they were all caught again because they could not give up connection with their past: with the people, the scenes, the habits to which they had been accustomed. So they left a little path from their hiding-place to the past, and the clever detectives always found it. Thinking over this matter I discovered that there is an art of disappearing, a real art, which many have used to advantage. The principle by which this art may be formulated is simple: the person disappearing must cut himself off from his past as completely as if he had been secretly drowned in mid-ocean."

"They all seem to do that," said Horace, "and yet they are caught as easily as rats with traps and cheese."

"I see you think this art means running away to Brazil in a wig and blue spectacles, as they do in a play. Let me show some of the consequences a poor devil takes upon himself who follows the art like an artist. He must escape, not only from his pursuers—that's easy—but from his friends—not so easy—and chiefly from himself— there's the rub. He who flies from the relentless pursuit of the law must practically die. He must change his country, never meet friend or relative again, get a new language, a new trade, a new place in society; in fact a new past, peopled with parents and relatives, a new habit of body and life, a new appearance; the color of hair, eyes, skin must be changed; and he must eat and drink, walk, sleep, think, and speak differently. He must become another man almost as if he had changed his nature for another's."

"I understand," said Horace, interested; "but the theory is impossible. No one could do that even if they desired."

"Tims would have desired it and accomplished it had I thought of suggesting it to him. Here is what would have happened. He escapes from the prison, which is easy enough, and comes straight to me. We never met but once. Therefore not a man in the world would have thought of looking for him at my house. A week later he is transferred to the house of Judy Trainor, who has been expecting a sick son from California, a boy who disappeared ten years previous and is probably dead. I arrange her expectation, and the neighbors are invited to rejoice with her over the finding of her son. He spends a month or two in the house recovering from his illness, and when he appears in public he knows as much about the past of Tommy Trainor as Tommy ever knew. He is welcomed by his old friends. They recognize him from his resemblance to his father, old Micky Trainor. He slips into his position comfortably, and in five years the whole neighborhood would go to court and swear Tims into a lunatic asylum if he ever tried to resume his own personality."

The two men set up a shout at this sound conclusion.

"After all, there are consequences as dark as the gallows," said Horace.

"For instance," said the priest with a wave of his hand, "sleeping under the eyes of these painted ghosts."

"Poor Tim Hurley," said Horace, "little he thought he'd be a ghost to-night."

"He's not to be regretted," replied the other, "except for the heart that suffers by his absence. He is with God. Death is the one moment of our career when we throw ourselves absolutely into the arms of God."

The two were getting ready to slip between the sheets of the pompous colonial bed, when Horace began to laugh softly to himself. He kept up the chuckling until they were lying side by side in the darkened room.

"I am sure, I have a share in that chuckle," said Monsignor.

"Shades of my ancestors," murmured Horace, "forgive this insult to your pious memory—that I should occupy one bed with an idolatrous priest."

"They have got over all that. In eternity there is no bigotry. But what a pity that two fine boys like us should be kept apart by that awful spirit which prompts men to hate one another for the love of God, and to lie like slaves for the pure love of truth."

"I am cured," said Horace, placing his hand on the Monsignor's arm. "I shall never again overlook the human in a man. Let me thank you,

Monsignor, for this opening of my eyes. I shall never forget it. This night has been Arabian in its enchantment. I don't like the idea of to-morrow."

"No more do I. Life is tiresome in a way. For me it is an everlasting job of beating the air with truth, because others beat it with lies. We can't help but rejoice when the time comes to breathe the eternal airs, where nothing but truth can live."

Horace sighed, and fell asleep thinking of Sonia rather than the delights of eternity. The priest slept as soundly. No protest against this charming and manly companionship stirred the silence of the room. The ghosts of the portraits did not disturb the bold cricket of the window-sill. He chirped proudly, pausing now and then to catch the breathing of the sleepers, and to interpret their unconscious movings. The trained and spiritual ear might have caught the faint sighs and velvet footsteps of long-departed souls, or interpreted them out of the sighing and whispering of the leaves outside the window, and the tread of nervous mice in the fireplace. The dawn came and lighted up the faces of the men, faces rising out of the heavy dark like a revelation of another world; the veil of melancholy, which Sleep borrows from its brother Death, resting on the head which Sonia loved, and deepening the shadows on the serious countenance of the priest. They lay there like brothers of the same womb, and one might fancy the great mother Eve stealing in between the two lights of dawn and day to kiss and bless her just-united children.

When they were parting after breakfast, Monsignor said gayly.

"If at any time you wish to disappear, command me."

"Thanks, but I would rather you had to do the act, that I might see you carry out your theory. Where do you go now?"

"To tell Tim Hurley's mother he's dead, and thus break her heart," he replied sadly, "and then to mend it by telling her how like a saint he died."

"Add to that," said Horace, with a sudden rush of tears, which for his life he could not explain, "the comfort of a sure support from me for the rest of her life."

They clasped hands with feeling, and their eyes expressed the same thought and resolution to meet again.

CHAPTER III.

THE ABYSSES OF PAIN.

Horace Endicott, though not a youth of deep sentiment, had capacities in that direction. Life so far had been chiefly of the surface for him. Happiness had hidden the deep and dangerous meanings of things. He was a child yet in his unconcern for the future, and the child, alone of mortals, enjoys a foretaste of immortality, in his belief that happiness is everlasting. The shadow of death clouding the pinched face of Tim Hurley was his first glimpse of the real. He had not seen his father and mother die. The thought that followed, Sonia's beloved face lying under that shadow, had terrified him. It was the uplifting of the veil of illusion that enwraps childhood. The thought stayed his foot that night as he turned into the avenue leading up to his own house, and he paused to consider this new dread.

The old colonial house greeted his eyes, solemn and sweet in the moonlight, with a few lights of human comfort in its windows. He had never thought so before, but now it came straight to his heart that this was his home, his old friend, steadfast and unchanging, which had welcomed him into the world, and had never changed its look to him, never closed its doors against him; all that remained of the dear, but almost forgotten past; the beautiful stage from which all the ancient actors had made irrevocable exit. What beauty had graced it for a century back! What honors its children had brought to it from councils of state and of war! What true human worth had sanctified it! Last and the least of the splendid throng, he felt his own unworthiness sadly; but he was young yet, only a boy, and he said to himself that Sonia had crowned the glory of the old house with her beauty, her innocence, her devoted love. In making her its mistress he had not wronged its former rulers, nor broken the traditions of beauty. He stood a long time looking at the old place, wondering at the charm which it had so suddenly flung upon him. Then he shook off the new and weird feeling and flew to embrace his Sonia of the starry eyes.

Alas, poor boy! He stood for a moment on the threshold. He could hear the faint voices of servants, the shutting of distant doors, and a hundred sweet sounds within; and around him lay the calmness of the night, with a drowsy moon overhead lolling on lazy clouds. Nothing warned him that he stood on the threshold of pain. No instinct hinted at the horror within. The house that sheltered his holy mother and received her last breath, that covered for a few hours the body of his heroic father, the house of so many honorable memories, had become the habitation of sinners, whose shame was to be everlasting. He stole in on tiptoe, with love stirring his young pulses. For thirty minutes there was no break in the silence. Then he came out as he entered, on tiptoe, and no one knew that he had seen with his own eyes into the deeps of hell. For thirty minutes, that seemed to have the power of as many centuries, he had looked on sin, shame, disgrace, with what seemed to be the eyes of God; so did the horror shock eye and heart, yet leave him sight and life to look again and again.

In that time he tasted with his own lips the bitterness which makes the most wretched death sweeter by comparison than bread and honey to the hungry. At the end of it, when he stole away a madman, he felt within his own soul the cracking and upheaving of some immensity, and saw or felt the opening of abysses from which rose fearful exhalations of crime, shapes of corruption, things without shape that provoked to rage, pain and madness. He was not without cunning, since he closed the doors softly, stole away in the shadows of the house and the avenue, and escaped to a distant wood unseen. From his withered face all feeling except horror had faded. Once deep in the wood, he fell under the trees like an epileptic, turned on his face, and dug the earth with hands and feet and face in convulsions of pain.

The frightened wood-life, sleeping or waking, fled from the great creature in its agony. In the darkness he seemed some monster, which in dreadful silence, writhed and fought down a slow road to death. He was hardly conscious of his own behavior, poor innocent, crushed by the sins of others. He lived, and every moment was a dying. He gasped as with the last breath, yet each breath came back with new torture. He shivered to the root of nature, like one struck fatally, and the convulsion revived life and thought and horror. After long hours a dreadful sleep bound his senses, and he lay still, face downward, arms outstretched, breathing like a child, a pitiful sight. Death must indeed be a binding thing, that father and mother did not leave the grave to soothe and strengthen their wretched son. He lay there on his face till dawn. The crowing of the cock, which once warned Peter of his shame, waked him. He turned over, stared at the branches above, sat up puzzled, and showed his face to the dim light. His arms gathered in his knees, and he made an effort to recollect himself. But no one would have mistaken that sorrowful, questioning face; it was Adam looking toward the lost Eden with his arms about the dead body of his son. A desolate and unconscious face, wretched and vacant as a lone shore strewn with wreckage.

He struggled to his feet after a time, wondering at his weakness. The effort roused and steadied him, his mind cleared as he walked to the edge of the wood and stared at the old house, which now in the mist of morning had the fixed, still, reproachful look of the dead. As if a spirit had leaped upon him, memory brought back his personality and his grief together. Men told afterwards, early laborers in the fields, of a cry from the Endicott woods, so strange and woful that their hearts beat fast and their frightened ears strained for its repetition. Sonia heard it in her adulterous dreams. It was not repeated. The very horror of it terrified the man who uttered it. He stood by a tree trembling, for a double terror fell upon him, terror of her no less than of himself. He staggered through the woods, and sought far-away places in the hills, where none might see him. When the sun drifted in through dark boughs he cursed it, the emblem of joy. The singing of the birds sounded to his ears like the shriek of madmen. When he could think and reason somewhat, he called up the vision of Sonia to wonder over it. The childlike eyes, the beautiful, lovable face, the modest glance, the innocent blushes—had nature such masks for her vilest offspring? The mere animal senses should have recognized at the first this deadly thing, as animals recognize their foes; and he had lived with the viper, believing her the peer of his spotless mother. She was his wife! Even at that moment the passionate love of yesterday stirred in his veins and moved him to deeper horror.

He doubted that he was Horace Endicott. Every one knew that boy to be the sanest of young men, husband to the loveliest of women, a happy, careless, wealthy fellow, almost beside himself with the joy of life. The madman who ran about the desolate wilds uttering strange and terrible things, who was wrapped within and without in torments of flame, who refrained from crime and death only because vengeance would thus be cheaply satisfied, could hardly be the boy of yesterday. Was sin such a magician that in a day it could evolve out of merry Horace and innocent Sonia two such wretches? The wretch Sonia had proved her capacity for evil; the wretch Horace felt his capabilities for crime and rejoiced in them. He must live to punish. A sudden fear came upon him that his grief and rage might bring death or madness, and leave him incapable of vengeance. *They* would wish nothing better. No, he must live, and think rationally, and not give way. But the mind worked on in spite of the will. It sat like Penelope over the loom, weaving terrible fancies in blood and flame! the days that had been, the days that were passing; the scenes of love and marriage; the old house and its latest sinners; and the days that were to come, crimson-dyed, shameful; the dreadful loom worked as if by enchantment, scene following scene, the web endless, and the woven stuff flying into the sky like smoke from a flying engine, darkening all the blue.

The days and nights passed while he wandered about in the open air. Hunger assailed him, distances wearied him, he did not sleep; but these hardships rather cooled the inward fire, and did not harm him. One day he came to a pool, clear as a spring to its sandy bottom, embowered in trees, except on one side where the sun shone. He took off his clothes and plunged in. The waters closed over him sweet and cool as the embrace of death. The loom ceased its working a while, and the thought rose up, is vengeance worth the trouble? He sank to the sandy bed, and oh, it was restful! A grip on a root held him there, and a song of his boyhood soothed his ears until it died away in heavenly music, far off, enticing, welcoming him to happier shores. He had found all at once forgetfulness and happiness, and he would remain. Then his grip loosened, and he came to the surface, swimming mechanically about, debating with himself another descent into the enchanted region beneath.

Some happy change had touched him. He felt the velvety waters grasp his body and rejoiced in it; the little waves which he sent to the reedy bank made him smile with their huddling and back-rushing and laughing; he held up his arm as he swam to see the sun flash through the drops of water from his hand. What a sweet bed of death! No hard-eyed nurses and physicians with their array of bottles, no hypocrites snuffling sympathy while dreaming of fat legacies, no pious mummeries, only the innocent things direct from the hand of God, unstained by human sin and training, trees and bushes and flowers, the tender living things about, the voiceless and passionless music of lonely nature, the hearty sun, and the maternal embrace of the sweet waters. It was dying as the wild animals die, without ceremony; as the flowers die, a gentle weakening of the stem, a rush of perfume to the soft earth, and the caressing winds to do the rest. Yes, down to the bottom again! Who would have looked for so pleasant a door to death in that lonely and lovely pool!

He slipped his foot under the root so that it would hold him if he struggled, put his arms under his head like one about to sleep, and yielded his senses to that far-off, divine music, enticing, welcoming.... It ceased, but not until he had forgotten all his sorrows and was speeding toward death. Sorrow rescued sorrow, and gave him back to the torturers. The old woman who passed by the pond that morning gathering flowers, and smiling as if she felt the delight of a child—the smile of a child on the mask of grief-worn age—saw his clothes and then his body floating upward helpless from the bottom. She seized his arm, and pulled him up on the low bank. He gasped a little and was able to thank her.

"If I hadn't come along just then," she said placidly, as she covered him decently with his coat, "you'd have been drownded. Took a cramp, I reckon?"

"All I remember is taking a swim and sinking, mother. I am very much obliged to you, and can get along very well, I think."

"If you want any help, just say so," she answered. "When you get dressed my house is a mile up the road, and the road is a mile from here. I can give you a cup of tea or warm milk, and welcome."

"I'll go after a while," said he, "and then I'll be able to thank you still better for a very great service, mother."

She smiled at the affectionate title, and went her way. He became weak all at once, and for a while could not dress. The long bath had soothed his mind, and now distressed nature could make her wants known. Hunger, soreness of body, drowsiness, attacked him together. He found it pleasant to lie there and look at the sun, and feel too happy to curse it as before. The loom had done working, Penelope was asleep. The door seemed forever shut on the woman known as Sonia, who had tormented him long ago. The dead should trouble no one living. He was utterly weary, sore in every spot, crushed by torment as poor Tim Hurley had been broken by his engine. This recollection, and his lying beside the pool as Tim lay beside the running river, recalled the Monsignor and the holy oils. As he fell asleep the fancy struck him that his need at that moment was the holy oils; some balm for sick eyes and ears, for tired hands and soiled feet, like his mother's kisses long ago, that would soothe the aching, and steal from the limbs into the heart afterwards; a heavenly dew that would aid sleep in restoring the stiffened sinews and distracted nerves. The old woman came back to him later, and found him in his sleep of exhaustion. Like a mother, she pillowed his head, covered him with his clothes, and her own shawl, and made sure that his rest would be safe and comfortable. She studied the noble young head, and smoothed it tenderly. The pitiful face, a terrible face for those who could read, so bitterly had grief written age on the curved dimpled surface of youth, stirred some convulsion in her, for she threw up her arms in despair as she walked away homeward, and wild sobs choked her for minutes.

He sat on the kitchen porch of her poor home that afternoon, quite free from pain. A wonderful relief had come to him. He seemed lifted into an upper region of peace like one just returned from infernal levels. The golden air tasted like old wine. The scenes about him were marvelous to his eyes. His own personality redeemed from recent horror became a delightful thing.

"It is terrible to suffer," he said to Martha Willis. "In the last five days I have suffered."

"As all men must suffer," said the woman resignedly.

"Then you have suffered too? How did you ever get over it, mother?"

She did not tell him, after a look at his face, that some sorrows are indelible.

"We have to get over everything, son. And it is lucky we can do it, without running into an insane asylum."

"Were your troubles very great, mother?"

"Lots of people about say I deserved them, so they couldn't be very great," she answered, and he laughed at her queer way of putting it, then checked himself.

"Sorrow is sorrow to him who suffers," he said, "no matter what people say about it. And I would not wish a beast to endure what I did. I would help the poor devil who suffered, no matter how much he deserved his pain."

"Only those who suffered feel that way. I am alone now, but this house was crowded thirty years ago. There was Lucy, and John, and Oliver, and Henry, and my husband, and we were very happy."

"And they are all gone?"

"I shall never see them again here. Lucy died when I needed her most, and Henry, such a fine boy, followed her before he was twenty. They are safe in the churchyard, and that makes me happy, for they are mine still, they will always be mine. John was like his father, and both were drunkards. They beat me in turn, and I was glad when they took to tramping. They're tramping yet, as I hear, but I haven't seen them in years. And Oliver, the cleverest boy in the school, and very headstrong, he went to Boston, and from there he went to jail for cheating a bank, and in jail he died. It was best for him and for me. I took him back to lie beside his brother and sister, though some said it was a shame. But what can a mother do? Her children are hers no matter if they turn out wrong."

"And you lived through it all, mother?" said the listener with his face working.

"Once I thought different, but now I know it was for the best," she answered calmly, and chiefly for his benefit. "I had my days and years even, when I thought some other woman had taken Martha Willis' place, a poor miserable creature, more like the dead than the live. But I often thought, since my own self came back, how lucky it was Lucy had her mother to close her eyes, and the same for poor Henry. And Oliver, he was pretty miserable dying in jail, but I never forgot what he said to me. 'Mother,' he said, 'it's like dying at home to have you with me here.' He was very proud, and it cut him that the cleverest of the family should die in jail. And he said, 'you'll put me beside the others, and take care of the grave, and not be ashamed of me, mother.' It was the money he left me, that kept this house and me ever since. Now just think of the way he'd have died if I had not been about to see to him. And I suppose the two tramps'll come marching in some day to die, or to be buried, and they'll be lucky to find me living. But anyway I've arranged it with the minister to see to them, and give them a place with their own, if I'm not here to look after them."

"And you lived through it all!" repeated Horace in wonder.

Her story gave him hope. He must put off thinking until grief had loosened its grip on his nerves, and the old self had come uppermost. He was determined that the old self should return, as Martha had proved it could return. He enjoyed its presence at that very moment, though with a dread of its impending departure. The old woman readily accepted him as a boarder for a few days or longer, and treated him like a son. He slept that night in a bed, the bed of Oliver and Henry, — their portraits hanging over the bureau — and slept as deeply as a wearied child. A blessed sleep was followed by a bitter waking. Something gripped him the moment he rose and looked out at the summer sun; a cruel hand seized his breast, and weighted it with vague pain. Deep sighs shook him, and the loom of Penelope began its dreadful weaving of bloody visions, while the restful pool in the woods tempted him to its cool rest. For a moment he gave way to the thought that all had ended for him on earth. Then he braced himself for his fight, went down to chat cheerfully with Martha, and ate her tasty breakfast with relish. He saw that his manner pleased the simple heart, the strong, heroic mother, the guardian of so many graves.

CHAPTER IV.

THE ROAD TO NOTHINGNESS.

"Whatever trouble you're a-sufferin' from," said Martha, as he was going, "I can tell you one sure thing about it. Time changes it so's you wouldn't think it was the same trouble a year afterwards. Now, if you wait, and have patience, and don't do anything one way or another for a month, you'll be real glad you waited. Once I would have been glad to die the minute after sorrow came. Now I'm glad I didn't die, for I've learned to see things different somehow."

His heart was being gnawed at that moment by horrible pain, but he caught the force of her words and took his resolve against the seduction of the pool, that lay now in his vision, as beautiful as a window of heaven.

"I've come to the same thought," he answered. "I'll not do anything for a month anyway, unless it's something very wise and good. But I'm going now to think the matter over by myself, and I know that you have done me great service in helping me to look at my sorrows rightly."

She smiled her thanks and watched him as he struck out for the hills two miles away. Often had her dear sons left the door for the same walk, and she had watched them with such love and pride. Oh, life, life!

By the pool which tempted him so strongly Horace sat down to study the problem of his future.

"You are one solution of it," he thought, as he smiled on its beautiful waters. "All others failing to please, you are here, sure, definite, soft as a bed, tender as Martha, lovely as a dream. There will be no vulgar outcry when you untie the knot of woe. And because I am sure of you, and have such confidence in you, I can sit here and defy your present charm."

He felt indeed that he was strong again in spite of pain. As one in darkness, longing for the light, might see afar the faint glint of the dawn, he had caught a glimpse of hope in the peace which came to him in Martha's cottage. It could come again. In its light he knew that he could look upon the past with calmness, and feel no terror even at the name of Sonia. He would encourage its return. It was necessary for him to fix the present status of the woman whom he had once called his wife. He could reason from that point logically. She had never been his wife except by the forms of law. Her treason had begun with his love, and her uncleanness was part of her nature; so much had he learned on that fearful night which revealed her to him. His wealth and his name were the prizes which made her traitor to lover and husband. What folly is there in man, or what enchantment in beauty, or what madness in love, that he could have taken to his arms the thing that hated him and hated goodness? Should not love, the best of God's gifts, be wisdom too? Or do men ever really love the object of passion?

Oh, he had loved her! Not a doubt but that he loved her still! Sonia, Sonia! The pool wrinkled at the sound of her name, as he shrieked it in anguish across the water. There was nothing in the world so beautiful as she. Her figure rose before him more entrancing than this fairy lake with its ever-changing loveliness. Its shadows under the trees were in her eyes, its luster under the sun was the luster of her body! Oh, there was nothing of beauty in it, perfume, grace, color, its singing and murmuring on the shore, that this perfect sinner had not in her body!

He steadied himself with the thought of old Martha. A dread caught him that the image of this foul beauty would haunt him thus forever, and be able at any time to drive joy out of him and madness into him. Some part of him clung to her, and wove a thousand fancies about her beauty. When the pain of his desolation gripped him the result was invariable: she rose out of the mist of pain, not like a fury, or the harpy she was, but beautiful as the morning, far above him, with glorious eyes fixed on the heavens. He thought it rather the vision of his lost happiness than of her. If she were present then, he would have held her under the water with his hands squeezing her throat, and so doubly killed her. But what a terror if this vision were to become permanent, and he should never know ease or the joy of living again! And for a thing so worthless and so foul!

He steadied himself again with the thought of old Martha, and fixed his mind on the first fact, the starting-point of his reasoning. She had never been his wife. Her own lips had uttered that sentence. The law had bound them, and the law protected her now. But she enjoyed a stronger guard even: his name. It menaced him in each solution of the problem of his future life. He could do little without smirching that honored name. He might take his own life. But that would be to punish the innocent and to reward the guilty. His wealth would become the gilding of adultery, and her joy would become perfect in his death. Imagine him asleep in the grave, while she laughed over his ashes, crying to herself: always a fool. He might kill her, or him, or both; a short punishment for a long treason, and then the trail of viperous blood over the name of Endicott forever; not blood but slime; not a tragedy, but the killing of rats in a cellar; and perhaps a place for himself in a padded cell, legally mad.

He might desert her, go away without explanation, and never see her again. That would be putting the burden of shame on his own shoulders, in exile and a branded man for her sake. She would still have his name, his income, her lover, her place in society, her right to explain his absence at her pleasure. He could ruin her ruined life by exposing her. Then would come the divorce court, the publicity, the leer of the mob, the pointed fingers of scorn. Impossible! Why could he not leave the matter untouched and keep up appearances before the world? Least endurable of any scheme. He knew that he could never meet her again without killing her, unless this problem was settled. When he had determined on what he should do, he might get courage to look on her face once more.

He wore the day out in vain thought, varying the dulness by stamping about the pond, by swimming across it, by studying its pleasant features. There was magic in it. When he stripped off his clothes and flung them on the bank part of his grief went with them. When he plunged into the lovable water, not only did grief leave him, but Horace Endicott returned; that Horace who once swam a boy in such lakes, and went hilarious with the wild joy of living. He dashed about the pool in a gay frenzy, revelling in the sensation that tragedy had no part in his life, that sorrow and shame had not yet once come nigh him. The shore and the donning of his garments were like clouds pouring themselves out on the sunlit earth. He could hardly bear it, and hung about listlessly before he could persuade himself to dress.

"Surely you are my one friend," he said to the quiet water. "Is it that you feel certain of giving me my last sleep, my last kiss as you steal the breath from me? None would do it gentlier. You give me release from pain, you alone. And you promise everlasting release. I will remember you if it comes to that."

The pool looked up to him out of deep evening shadows cast upon it by the woods. There was something human in the variety of its expression. As if a chained soul, silenced forever as to speech, condemned to a garment of water, struggled to reach a human heart by infinite shades of beauty, and endless variations of sound. The thought woke his pity, and he looked down at the water as one looks into the face of a suffering friend. Here were two castaways, cut off from the highway of life, imprisoned in circumstances as firmly as if behind prison grills. For him there was hope, for the pool nothing. At this moment its calm face pictured profound sadness. The black shadow of the woods lay deep on the west bank, but its remotest edge showed a brilliant green, where the sun lingered on the top fringes of the foliage. Along the east bank, among the reeds, the sun showed crimson, and all the tender colors of the water plants faded in a glare of blood. This savage brilliance would soon give way to the gray mist of twilight, and then to the darkness of night. Even this poor dumb beauty reflected in its helplessly beautiful way the tragedies of mankind.

As before with the evening came peace and release from pain. Again he sat on Martha's porch after supper, and thought nothing so beautiful as life; and as he listened to further details of her life-story, imparted with the wise intention of binding him to life more securely, he felt that all was not yet lost for him. In his little room while the night was still young, he opened an old volume at the play of Hamlet and read the story through. Surely he had never read this play before? He recalled vaguely that it had been studied in college, that some great actor had played it for him, that he had believed it a wonderful thing; memories now less real than dreams. For in reading it this night he entered into the very soul of Hamlet, lived his tortures over again, wept and raved in dumb show with the wretched prince, and flung himself and his book to the floor in grief at the pitiful ending. He was the Hamlet; youth with a problem of the horrible; called to solve that which shook the brains of statesmen; dying in utter failure with that most pathetic dread of a wounded name.

> Oh, good Horatio, what a wounded name.
> Things standing thus unknown, shall live behind me.
> If thou didst ever hold me in thy heart,
> Absent thee from felicity awhile,
> And in this harsh world draw thy breath in pain,
> To tell my story.

For a little he had thought there could not be in the world such suffering as his; how clear now that his peculiar sorrow was strange to no hour of unfortunate time; an old story, innocence and virtue— God knew he had no pride in his own virtue—preyed upon by cunning vice. He read Hamlet again. Oh, what depth of anguish! What a portrayal of grief and madness! Horace shook with the sobs that nearly choked him. Like the sleek murderer and his plump queen, the two creatures hatefulest to him lived their meanly prosperous lives on his bounty. What conscience flamed so dimly in the Danish prince that he could hesitate before his opportunity? Long ago, had Horace been in his place, the guilty pair would have paid in blood for their lust and ambition. Hamlet would not kill himself because the Almighty had "fixed his canon 'gainst self-slaughter;" or because in the sleep of death might rise strange dreams; he would not kill his uncle because he caught him praying; and he was content with preaching to his mother. Conscience! God! The two words had not reached his heart or mind once since that awful night. No scruples of the Lord Hamlet obscured his view or delayed his action.

He had been brought up to a vague respect of religious things. He had even wondered where his father and mother might now inhabit, as one might wonder of the sea-drowned where their bodies might be floating; but no nearer than this had heaven come to him. He had never felt any special influence of religion in his life. In what circumstances had Hamlet been brought up, that religious feeling should have so serious an effect upon him? Doubtless the prince had been a Catholic like his recent acquaintance the Monsignor. Ah, he had forgotten that interesting man, who had told him much worth remembrance. In particular his last words ... what were those last words? The effort to remember gave him mixed dreams of Hamlet and the Monsignor that night.

In the morning he went off to the pool with the book of Hamlet and the echo of those important but forgotten words. The lonely water seemed to welcome him when he emerged from the path through the woods; the underbrush rustled, living things scurried away into bush and wave, the weeds on the far bank set up a rustling, and little waves leaped on the shore. He smiled as if getting a friend's morning salute, and began to talk aloud.

"I have brought you another unfortunate," he said, "and I am going to read his thoughts to you."

He opened the book and very tenderly, as if reciting a funeral service, murmured the words of the soliloquy on suicide. How solemnly sounded in that solitude the fateful phrase "but that the dread of something after death!" That was indeed the rub! After death there can be anything; and were it little and slender as a spider's web, it might be too much for the sleep that is supposed to know no waking and no dreams. After all, he thought, how much are men alike; for the quandary of Hamlet is mine; I know not what to do. He laid aside the book and gave himself to idle watching of the pool. A bird dipped his wing into it midway, and set a circle of wavelets tripping to the shore. One by one they died among the sedges, and there was no trace of them more.

"That is the thing for which I am looking," he said; "disappearance without consequences ... just to fade away as if into water or air ... to separate on the spot into original elements ... to be no more what I

31

am, either to myself or others ... then no inquest, no search, no funeral, no tears ... nothing. And after such a death, perhaps, something might renew the personality in conditions so far from these, so different, that *now* and *then* would never come into contact."

He sighed. What a disappearance that would be. And at that moment the words of the Monsignor came back to him:

"If at any time you wish to disappear, command me."

A thrill leaped through his dead veins, as of one rising from the dead, but he lay motionless observing the pool. Before him passed the details of that night at the tavern; the portraits, the chirping cricket, the vines at the window, the strange theory of the priest about disappearing. He reviewed that theory as a judge might review a case, so he thought; but in fact his mind was swinging at headlong speed over the possibilities, and his pulses were bounding. It was possible, even in this world, to disappear more thoroughly behind the veil of life than under the veil of death. If one only had the will!

He rose brimming with exultant joy. An intoxication seized him that lifted him at once over all his sorrow, and placed him almost in that very spot wherein he stood ten days ago; gay, debonair, light of heart as a boy, untouched by grief or the dread of grief. It was a divine madness. He threw off his clothes, admired his shapely body for a moment as he poised on the bank, and flung himself in headlong with a shout. He felt as he slipped through the water but he did not utter the thought, that if this intoxication did not last he would never leave the pool. It endured and increased. He swam about like a demented fish. On that far shore where the reeds grew he paddled through the mud and thrust his head among the sedges kissing them with laughter. In another place he reached up to the high bank and pulled out a bunch of ferns which he carried about with him. He roamed about the sandy bottom in one corner, and thrust his nose and his hands into it, laying his cheek on the smooth surface. He swallowed mouthfuls of the cool water, and felt that he tasted joy for the first time. He tired his body with divings, racings, leapings, and shouting.

When he leaped ashore and flung himself in the shade of the wood, the intoxication had increased. So, not for nothing had he met the priest. That encounter, the delay in the journey, the stay in the village, the peculiar character of the man, his odd theory, were like elements of an antidote, compounded to meet that venom which the vicious had injected into his life. Wonderful! He looked at the open book beside him, and then rose to his knees, with the water dripping from his limbs. In a loud voice he made a profession of faith.

"I believe in God forever."

CHAPTER V.

THE DOOR IS CLOSED.

Even Martha was startled by the change in him. She had hoped and prayed for it, but had not looked for it so soon, and did not expect blithe spirits after such despair. In deep joy he poured out his soul to her all the evening, but never mentioned deeds or names in his tragedy. Martha hardly thought of them. She knew from the first that this man's soul had been nearly wrecked by some shocking deviltry, and that the best medicine for him was complete forgetfulness. Horace felt as a life-prisoner, suddenly set free from the loathsomest dungeon in Turkestan, might feel on greeting again the day and life's sweet activities. The first thought which surged in upon him was the glory of that life which had been his up to the moment when sorrow engulfed him.

"My God," he cried to Martha, "is it possible that men can hold such a treasure, and prize it as lightly as I did once."

He had thought almost nothing of it, had been glad to get rid of each period as it passed, and of many persons and scenes connected with childhood, youth, and manhood. Now they looked to him, these despised years, persons, and scenes, like jewels set in fine gold, priceless jewels of human love fixed forever in the adamant of God's memory. They were his no more. Happily God would not forget them, but would treasure them, and reward time and place and human love according to their deserving. He was full of scorn for himself, who could take and enjoy so much of happiness with no thought of its value, and no other acknowledgment than the formal and hasty word of thanks, as each soul laid its offering of love and service at his feet.

"You're no worse than the rest of us," said Martha, "I didn't know, and very few of my friends ever seemed to know, what good things they had till they lost 'em. It may be that God would not have us put too high a price on 'em at first, fearin' we'd get selfish about 'em.

Then when they're gone, it turns our thoughts more to heaven, which is the only place where we have any chance to get 'em back."

When he had got over his self-scorn, the abyss of pain and horror out of which God had lifted him—this was his belief—showed itself mighty and terrible to his normal vision. Never would he have believed that a man could fall so far and so awfully, had he not been in those dark depths and mounted to the sun again. He had read of such pits as exaggerations. He had seen sorrow and always thought its expression too fantastic for reality. Looking down now into the noisome tunnel of his own tragedy, he could only wonder that its wretched walls and exit did not carry the red current of blood mingled with its own foul streaks. Nothing that he had done in his grief expressed more than a syllable of the pain he had endured. The only full voice to such grief would have been the wrecking of the world. Strange that he could now look calmly into this abyss, without the temptation to go mad. But its very ghastliness turned his thought into another channel. The woman who had led him into the pit, what of her? Free from the tyranny of her beauty, he saw her with all her loveliness, merely the witch of the abyss, the flower and fruit of that loathsome depth, in whose bosom filthy things took their natural shape of horror, and put on beauty only to entrap the innocent of the upper world. Yes, he was entirely freed from her. Her name sounded to his ears like a name from hell, but it brought no paleness to his cheeks, no shock to his nerves, no stirring of his pulses. The loom of Penelope was broken, and forever, he hoped.

"I am free," he said to Martha the next morning, after he had tested himself in various ways. "The one devil that remained with me is gone, and I feel sure she will never trouble me again."

"It is good to be free," said Martha, "if the thing is evil. I am free from all that worried me most. I am free from the old fear of death. But sometimes I get sad thinking how little we need those we thought we could not do without."

"How true that sounds, mother. There is a pity in it. We are not necessary to one another, though we think so. Every one we love dies, we lose all things as time goes on, and when we come to old age nothing remains of the past; but just the same we enjoy what we have, and forget what we had. There is one thing necessary, and that is true life."

"And where can we get that?" said Martha.

"Only from God, I think," he replied.

She smiled her satisfaction with his thought, and he went off to the pool for the last time, singing in his heart with joy. He would have raised his voice too, but, feeling himself in the presence of a stupendous thing, he refrained out of reverence. If suffering Hamlet had only encountered the idea of disappearing, his whole life would have been set right in a twinkling of the eye. The Dane had an inkling of the solution of his problem when in anguish he cried out,

> Oh, that this too, too solid flesh would melt,
> Thaw and resolve itself into a dew!

But he had not followed his thought to its natural consequence, seeing only death at the end of reasoning. Horace saw disappearance, and he had now to consider the idea of complete disappearance with all its effects upon him and others. What would be the effect upon himself? He would vanish into thin air as far as others were concerned. Whatever of his past the present held would turn into ashes. There would be no further connection with it. An impassable void would be created across which neither he nor those he loved could go. He went over in his mind what he had to give up, and trembled before his chum and his father's sister, two souls that loved him. Death would not be more terrible. For him, no; but for them? Death would leave them his last word, look, sigh, his ashes, his resting-place; disappearance would rob them of all knowledge, and clothe his exit with everlasting sadness. There was no help for it. Many souls more loving suffered a similar anguish, and survived it. It astonished and even appalled him, if anything could now appal him, that only two out of the group of his close friends and near acquaintances seemed near enough in affection and intimacy to mourn his loss. Not one of twenty others would lose a dinner or a fraction of appetite because he had vanished so pitifully. How rarer than diamonds is that jewel of friendship!

He had thought once that a hundred friends would have wept bitter tears over his sorrow; of the number there were left only two!

It was easy for him to leave the old life, now become so hateful; but there was terror in putting on the new, to which he must ally himself as if born into it, like a tree uprooted from its native soil and planted far from its congenial elements in the secret, dark, sympathetic places of the earth. He must cut himself off more thoroughly than by death. The disappearance must be eternal, unless death removed Sonia Westfield before circumstances made return practically impossible; his experience of life showed that disagreeable people rarely die while the microbe of disagreeableness thrives in them.

What would be the effect of his disappearance on Sonia and her lover? The question brought a smile to his wan face. She had married his name and his money, and would lose both advantages. He would take his property into exile to the last penny. His name without his income would be a burden to her. His disappearance would cast upon her a reproach, unspoken, unseen, a mere mist enwrapping her fatally, but not to be dispelled. Her mouth would be shut tight; no chance for innuendoes, lest hint might add suspicion to mystery. She would be forced to observe the proprieties to the letter, and the law would not grant her a divorce for years. In time she would learn that her only income was the modest revenue from her own small estate; that he had taken all with him into darkness; and still she would not dare to tell the damaging fact to her friends. She would be forced to keep up appearances, to spend money in a vain search for him, or his wealth; suspecting much yet knowing nothing, miserably certain that he was living somewhere in luxury, and enjoying his vengeance.

He no longer thought of vengeance. He did not desire it. The mills of the gods grind out vengeance enough to glut any appetite. By the mere exercise of his right to disappear he gave the gods many lashes with which to arm the furies against her. He was satisfied with being beyond her reach forever. Now that he knew just what to do, now that with his plan had come release from depression, now that he was himself again almost, he felt that he could meet Sonia Westfield and act the part of a busy husband without being tempted to strangle her. In her very presence he would put in motion the machinery which would strip her of luxury and himself of his present place in the world.

The process took about two months. The first step was a visit to Monsignor O'Donnell, a single visit, and the first result was a single letter, promptly committed to the flames. Then he went home with a story of illness, of a business enterprise which had won his fancy, of necessary visits to the far west; which were all true, but not in the sense in which Sonia took these details. They not only explained his absence, but also excused the oddity of his present behavior. He hardly knew how he behaved with her. He did not act, nor lose self-confidence. He had no desire to harm her. He was simply indifferent, as if from sickness. As the circumstances fell in with her inclinations, though she could not help noticing his new habits and peculiarities, she made no protest and very little comment. He saw her rarely, and in time carried himself with a sardonic good humor as surprising to him as inexplicable to her. She seemed as far from him as if she had suddenly turned Eskimo. Once or twice a sense of loathing invaded him, a flame of hatred blazed up, soon suppressed. He was complete master of himself, and his reward was that he could be her judge, with the indifference of a dignitary of the law. The disposal of his property was accomplished with perfect secrecy, his wife consenting on the plea of a better investment.

So the two months came to an end in peace, and he stood at last before that door which he himself had opened into the new future. Once closed no other hand but his could open it. A time might come when even to his hand the hinge would not respond. Two persons knew his secret in part, the Monsignor and a woman; but they knew nothing more than that he did not belong to them from the beginning, and more than that they would never know, if he carried out his plan of disappearance perfectly. Whatever the result, he felt now that the crisis of his life had come.

At the last moment, however, doubts worried him about thus cutting himself off from his past so utterly, and adopting another personality. Some deep-lying repugnance stirred him against the double process. Would it not be better to live under his own name in remote countries, and thus be ready, if fate allowed, to return home at the proper time? Perhaps. In that case he must be prepared for her pursuit, her letters, her chicanery, which he could not bear. Her safety and his own, if the stain of blood was to be kept off the name of Endicott, demanded the absolute cessation of all relationship between them. Yet that did not contain the whole reason. Lurking somewhere in those dark depths of the soul, where the lead never penetrates, he found the thought of vengeance. After all he did wish to punish her and to see her punishment. He had thought to leave all to the gods, but feared the gods would not do all their duty. If they needed spurring, he would be near to provide new whips and fresher scorpions. He shook off hesitation when the last day of his old life came, and made his farewells with decision. A letter to his aunt and to his friend, bidding each find no wonder and no worry about him in the events of the next month, and lose no time in searching for him; a quiet talk with old Martha on her little verandah; a visit to the pool on a soft August night; and an evening spent alone in his father's house; these were his leave-takings.

They would never find a place in his life again, and he would never dare to return to them; since the return of the criminal over the path by which he escaped into secrecy gave him into the hands of his pursuers. The old house had become the property of strangers. The offset to this grief was the fact that Sonia would never dishonor it again with her presence. Just now dabbling in her sins down by the summer sea, she was probably reading the letter which he had sent her about business in Wisconsin. Later a second letter would bear her the sentence of a living death. The upright judge had made her the executioner. What a long tragedy that would be! He thought of it as he wandered about the lovely rooms of his old home; what long days of doubt before certainty would come; what horror when bit by bit the scheme of his vengeance unfolded: what vain, bitter, furious struggling to find and devour him; and then the miserable ending when time had proved his disappearance absolute and perfect!

At midnight, after a pilgrimage to every loved spot in the household shrine, he slipped away unseen and struck out on foot over the fields for a distant railway station. For two months he lived here and there in California, while his beard grew and his thoughts devoured him. Then one evening he stepped somewhat feebly from the train in

New York, crawled into a cab, and drove to No. 127 Mulberry Street. The cabman helped him up the steps and handed him in the door to a brisk old woman, who must have been an actress in her day; for she gave a screech at the sight of him, and threw her arms about him crying out, so that the cabman heard, "Artie, alanna, back from the dead, back from the dead, acushla machree." Then the door closed, and Arthur Dillon was alone with his mother; Arthur Dillon who had run away to California ten years before, and died there, it was supposed; but he had not died, for behold him returned to his mother miraculously. She knew him in spite of the changes, in spite of thin face, wild eyes, and strong beard. The mother-love is not to be deceived by the disguise of time. So Anne Dillon hugged her Arthur with a fervor that surprised him, and wept copious tears; thinking more of the boy that might have come back to her than of this stranger. He lay in his lonely, unknown grave, and the caresses meant for him had been bought by another.

RESURRECTION.

CHAPTER VI.

ANOTHER MAN'S SHOES.

As he laid aside his outer garments, Horace felt the joy of the exhausted sailor, entering port after a dangerous voyage. He was in another man's shoes; would they fit him? He accepted the new house and the new mother with scarcely a comment. Mrs. Anne Dillon knew him only as a respectable young man of wealth, whom misfortune had driven into hiding. His name and his history she might never learn. So Monsignor had arranged it. In return for a mother's care and name she was to receive a handsome income. A slim and well-fashioned woman, dignified, severe of feature, her light hair and fair complexion took away ten from her fifty years; a brisk manner and a low voice matched her sharp blue eyes and calm face; her speech had a slight brogue; fate had ordained that an Endicott should be Irish in his new environment. As she flew about getting ready a little supper, he dozed in the rocker, thinking of that dear mother who had illumined his youth like a vision, beautiful, refined, ever delightful; then of old Martha, rough, plain, and sad, but with the spirit and wit of the true mother, to cherish the sorrowful. In love for the child these mothers were all alike. He felt at home, and admired the quickness and skill with which Anne Dillon took up her new office. He noted everything, even his own shifting emotions. This was one phase of the melancholy change in him: the man he had cast off rarely saw more than pleased him, but the new Arthur Dillon had an alert eye for trifles.

"Son dear," said his mother, when they sat down to tea, "we'll have the evenin' to ourselves, because I didn't tell a soul what time you were comin', though of course they all knew it, for I couldn't keep back such good news; that after all of us thinkin' you dead, you should turn out to be alive an' well, thank God. So we can spend the evenin' decidin' jist what to do an' say to-morrow. The first thing in the mornin' Louis Everard will be over to see you. Since he heard of your comin', he's been jist wild, for he was your favorite; you taught him to swim, an' to play ball, an' to skate, an' carried him around with you, though he's six years younger than you. He's goin' to be a priest in time with the blessin' o' God. Then his mother an' sister, perhaps Sister Mary Magdalen, too; an' your uncle Dan Dillon, on your father's side, he's the only relative you have. My folks are all dead. He's a senator, an' a leader in Tammany Hall, an' he'll be proud of you. You were very fond of him, because he was a prize-fighter in his day, though I never thought much of that, an' was glad when he left the business for politics."

"And how am I to know all these people, mother?"

"You've come home sick," she said placidly, "an' you'll stay in bed for the next week, or a month if you like. As each one comes I'll let you know jist who they are. You needn't talk any more than you like, an' any mistakes will be excused, you've been away so long, an' come home so sick."

They smiled frankly at each other, and after tea she showed him his room, a plain chamber with sacred pictures on the walls and a photograph of Arthur Dillon over the bureau.

"Jist as you left it ten years ago," she said with a sob. "An' your picture as you looked a month before you went away."

The portrait showed a good-looking and pugnacious boy of sixteen, dark-haired and large-eyed like himself; but the likeness between the new and the old Arthur was not striking; yet any one who wished or thought to find a resemblance might have succeeded. As to disposition, Horace Endicott would not have deserted his mother under any temptation.

"What sort of a boy was—was I at that age, mother?"

"The best in the world," she answered mildly but promptly, feeling the doubt in the question. "An' no one was able to understan' why you ran away as you did. I wonder now my heart didn't break over it. The neighbors jist adored you: the best dancer an' singer, the gayest boy in the parish, an' the Monsignor thought there was no other like you."

"I have forgotten how to sing an' dance, mother. I think these accomplishments can be easily learned again. Does the Monsignor still hold his interest in me?"

"More than ever, I think, but he's a quiet man that says little when he means a good deal."

At nine o'clock an old woman came in with an evening paper, and gave a cry of joy at sight of him. Having been instructed between the opening of the outer door and the woman's appearance, Arthur took the old lady in his arms and kissed her. She was the servant of the house, more companion than servant, wrinkled like an autumn leaf that has felt the heat, but blithe and active.

"So you knew me, Judy, in spite of the whiskers and the long absence?"

"Knew you, is it?" cried Judy, laughing, and crying, and talking at once, in a way quite wonderful to one who had never witnessed this feat. "An' why shouldn't I know you? Didn't I hould ye in me own two arrums the night you were born? An' was there a day afther that I didn't have something to do wid ye? Oh, ye little spalpeen, to give us all the fright ye did, runnin' away to Californy. Now if ye had run away to Ireland, there'd be some sinse in it. Musha thin, but it was fond o' goold ye wor, an' ye hardly sixteen. I hope ye brought a pile of it back wid ye."

She rattled on in her joy until weariness took them all at the same moment, and they withdrew to bed. He was awakened in the morning by a cautious whispering in the room outside his door.

"Pon me sowl," Judy was saying angrily, "ye take it like anny ould Yankee. Ye're as dull as if 'twas his body on'y, an' not body an' sowl together, that kem home to ye. Jist like ould Mrs. Wilcox the night her son died, sittin' in her room, an' crowshayin' away, whin a dacint woman 'ud be howlin' wid sorra like a banshee."

"To tell the truth," Anne replied, "I can't quite forgive him for the way he left me, an' it's so long since I saw him, Judy, an' he's so thin an' miserable lookin', that I feel as if he was only a fairy child."

"Mother, you're talking too loud to your neighbors," he cried out then in a cheery and familiar voice, for he saw at once the necessity of removing the very natural constraint indicated by his mother's words; and there was a sudden cry from the women, Judy flying to the kitchen while Anne came to his door.

"It's true the walls have ears," she said with a kindly smile. "But you and I, son, will have to make many's the explanation of that kind before you are well settled in your old home."

He arose for breakfast with the satisfaction of having enjoyed a perfect sleep, and with a delightful interest in what the day had in store for him. Judy bantered and petted him. His mother carried him over difficult allusions in her speech. The sun looked in on him pleasantly, he took a sniff of air from a brickish garden, saw the brown walls of the cathedral not far away, and then went back to bed. A sudden and overpowering weakness came upon him which made the bed agreeable. Here he was to receive such friends as would call upon him that day. Anne Dillon looked somewhat anxious over the ordeal, and his own interest grew sharper each moment, until the street-door at last opened with decision, and his mother whispered quickly:

"Louis Everard! Make much of him."

She went out to check the brisk and excited student who wished to enter with a shout, warning him that the returned wanderer was a sick man. There was silence for a moment, and then the young fellow appeared in the doorway.

"Will you have a fit if I come any nearer?" he said roguishly.

In the soft, clear light from the window Arthur saw a slim, manly figure, a lovable face lighted by keen blue eyes, a white and frank forehead crowned by light hair, and an expression of face that won him on the instant. This was his chum, whom he had loved, and trained, and tyrannized over long ago. For the first time since his sorrow he felt the inrushing need of love's sympathy, and with tear-dimmed eyes he mutely held out his arms. Louis flew into the proffered embrace, and kissed him twice with the ardor of a boy. The affectionate touch of his lips quite unmanned Arthur, who was silent while the young fellow sat on the side of the bed with one arm about him, and began to ply him with questions.

"Tell me first of all," he said, "how you had the heart to do it, to run away from so many that loved the ground you walked on. I cried my eyes out night after night ... and your poor mother ... and indeed all of us ... how could you do it? What had we done?"

"Drop it," said Arthur. "At that time I could have done anything. It was pure thoughtlessness, regretted many a time since. I did it, and there's the end of it, except that I am suffering now and must suffer more for the folly."

"One thing, remember," said Louis, "you must let them all see that your heart is in the right place. I'm not going to tell you all that was said about you. But you must let every one see that you are as good as when you left us."

"That would be too little, dear heart. Any man that has been through my experiences and did not show himself ten times better than ever he was before, ought to stay in the desert."

"That sounds like you," said Louis, gently pulling his beard.

"Tell me, partner," said Arthur lightly, "would you recognize me with whiskers?"

"Never. There is nothing about you that reminds me of that boy who ran away. Just think, it's ten years, and how we all change in ten years. But say, what adventures you must have had! I've got to hear the whole story, mind, from the first chapter to the last. You are to come over to the house two nights in a week, to the old room, you remember, and unfold the secrets of ten years. Haven't you had a lot of them?"

"A car-load, and of every kind. In the mines and forests, on the desert, lost in the mountains, hunting and fishing and prospecting; not to mention love adventures of the tenderest sort. I feel pleasant to think of telling you my latest adventures in the old room, where I used to curl you up with fright— —"

"Over stories of witches and fairies," cried Louis, "when I would crawl up your back as we lay in bed, and shiver while I begged you to go on. And the room is just the same, for all the new things have the old pattern. I felt you would come back some day with a bag of real stories to be told in the same dear old place."

"Real enough surely," said Arthur with a deep sigh, "and I hope they may not tire you in the telling. Mother ... tells me that you are going to be a priest. Is that true?"

"As far as I can see now, yes. But one is never certain."

"Then I hope you will be one of the Monsignor's stamp. That man is surely a man of God."

"Not a doubt of it," said Louis, taking his hat to go.

"One thing," said Arthur as he took his hand and detained him. He was hungry for loving intimacy with this fine lad, and stammered in his words. "We are to be the same ... brothers ... that we were long ago!"

"That's for you to say, old man," replied Louis, who was pleased and even flattered, and petted Arthur's hands. "I always had to do as you said, and was glad to be your slave. I have been the faithful one all these years. It is your turn now."

After that Arthur cared little who came to see him. He was no longer alone. This youth loved him with the love of fidelity and gratitude, to which he had no claim except by adoption from Mrs. Anne Dillon; but it warmed his heart and cheered his spirit so much that he did not discuss with himself the propriety of owning and enjoying it. He looked with delight on Louis' mother when she came later in the day, and welcomed him as a mother would a dear son. A nun accompanied her, whose costume gave him great surprise and some irritation. She was a frank-faced but homely woman, who wore her religious habit with distinction. Arthur felt as if he were in a chapel while she sat by him and studied his face. His mother did the talking for him, compared his features with the portrait on the wall, and recalled the mischievous pranks of his wild boyhood, indirectly giving him much information as to his former relationships with the visitors. Mrs. Everard had been fond of him, and Sister Mary Magdalen had prepared him for his first communion. This fact the nun emphasized by whispering to him as she was about to leave:

"I hope you have not neglected your religious duties?"

"Monsignor will tell you," he said with an amused smile. He found no great difficulty in dealing with the visitors that came and went during the first week. Thanks to his mother's tactful management no hitches occurred more serious than the real Arthur Dillon might have encountered after a long absence. The sick man learned very speedily how high his uncle stood in the city, for the last polite inquiry of each visitor was whether the Senator had called to welcome his nephew. In the narrow world of the Endicotts the average mind had not strength enough to conceive of a personality which embraced in itself a prize-fighter and a state senator. The terms were contradictory. True, Nero had been actor and gladiator, and the inference was just that an American might achieve equal distinction; but the Endicott mind refused to consider such an inference. Arthur Dillon no longer found anything absurd or impossible. The surprises of his new position charmed him. Three months earlier and the wildest libeller could not have accused him of an uncle lower in rank than a governor of the state. Sonorous names, senator and gladiator, brimful of the ferocity and dignity of old Rome! near as they had been in the days of Cæsar, one would have thought the march of civilization might have widened the interval. Here was a rogue's march indeed! Judy gave the Senator a remarkable character.

"The Senator, is it?" said she when asked for an opinion. "Divil a finer man from here to himself! There isn't a sowl in the city that doesn't bless his name. He's a great man bekase he was born so. He began life with his two fishts, thumpin' other boys wid the gloves, as they call 'em. Thin he wint to the war, an' began fightin' wid powdher an' guns, so they med him a colonel. Thin he kem home an' wint fightin' the boss o' the town, so they med him a senator. It was all fightin' wid him, an' they say he's at it yet, though he luks so pleasant all the time, he must find it healthy. I don't suppose thim he's fightin' wid finds it as agreeable. Somewan must git the batin', ye know. There's jist the differ betune men. I've been usin' me fists all me life, beltin' the washboord, an' I'm nowhere yet. An' Tommy Kilbride the baker, he's been poundin' at the dough for thirty years, an' he's no better off than I am. But me noble Dan Dillon that began wid punchin' the heads of his neighbors, see where he is to-day. But he's worthy of it, an' I'd be the last to begrudge him his luck."

In the Endicott circle the appearance of a senator as great as Sumner had not been an event to flutter the heart, though the honor was unquestioned; but never in his life had the young man felt a keener interest than in the visit of his new uncle. He came at last, a splendid figure, too ample in outline and too rich in color for the simple room. The first impression he made was that of the man. The powerful and subtle essence of the man breathed from him. His face and figure had that boldness of line and depth of color which rightly belong to the well-bred peasant. He was well dressed, and handsome, with eyes as soft and bright as a Spaniard's. Arthur was overcome with delight. In Louis he had found sympathy and love, and in the Senator he felt sure that he would find ideal strength and ideal manhood, things for the weak to lean upon. The young patrician seized his uncle's hand and pressed it hard between his own. At this affectionate greeting the Senator's voice failed him, and he had difficulty in keeping back his tears.

"If your father were only here now, God rest his soul this day," he said. "How he loved you. Often an' often he said to me that his happiness would be complete if he lived to see you a man. He died, but I live to see it, an' to welcome you back to your own. The Dillons are dying out. You're the only one of our family with the family name. What's the use o' tellin' you how glad we are that Californy didn't swallow you up forever."

Arthur thanked him fervently, and complimented him on his political honors. The Senator beamed with the delight of a man who finds the value of honors in the joy which they give his friends.

"Yes, I've mounted, Artie, an' I came by everything I have honest. You'll not be ashamed of me, boy, when you see where I stand outside. But there's one thing about politics very hard, the enemy don't spare you. If you were to believe all that's said of me by opponents I'm afraid you wouldn't shake hands with me in public."

"I suppose they bring up the prize-fighting," said Arthur. "You ought to have told them that no one need be ashamed to do what many a Roman emperor did."

"Ah," cried the Senator, "there's where a man feels the loss of an education. I never knew the emperors did any ring business. What a sockdologer it would have been to compare myself with the Roman emperors."

"Then you've done with fighting, uncle?"

There was regret in his tone, for he felt the situation would have been improved if the Senator were still before the public as a gladiator.

"I see you ain't lost none o' your old time deviltry, Artie," he replied good-naturedly. "I gave that up long ago, an' lots o' things with it. But givin' up has nothin' to do with politics, an' regular all my sins are retailed in the papers. But one thing they can never say: that I was a liar or a thief. An' they can't say that I ever broke my word, or broke faith with the people that elected me, or did anything that was not becoming in a senator. I respect that position an' the honor for all they're worth."

"And they can never say," added Arthur, "that you were afraid of any man on earth, or that you ever hurt the helpless, or ever deserted a friend or a soul that was in need."

The Senator flushed at the unexpected praise and the sincerity of the tone. He was anxious to justify himself even before this sinner, because his dead brother and his sister-in-law had been too severe on his former occupations to recognize the virtues which Arthur complimented.

"Whatever I have been," said the Senator, pressing the hand which still held his, "I was never less than a square man."

"That's easy to believe, uncle, and I'll willingly punch the head of the first man that denies it."

"Same old spirit," said the delighted Senator. "Why, you little rogue, d'ye remember when you used to go round gettin' all the pictures o' me in me fightin' days, an' makin' your dear mother mad by threatenin' to go into the ring yourself? Why; you had your own fightin' gear, gloves an' clubs an' all that, an' you trained young Everard in the business, till his old ... his father put a head ... put a stop to it."

"Fine boy, that Louis, but I never thought he'd turn to the Church."

"He never had any thin' else in him," said the Senator earnestly. "It was born in him as fightin' an' general wildness was born in you an' me. Look into his face an' you'll see it. Fine? The boy hasn't his like in the city or the land. I'll back him for any sum—I'll stand to it that he'll be archbishop some day."

"Which I'll never be," said Arthur with a grin.

"Every man in his place, Artie. I've brought you yours, if you want to take it. How would politics in New York suit you?"

"I'm ripe for anything with fun in it."

"Then you won't find fault, Artie, if I ask how things stood with you—you see it's this way, Artie——"

"Now, hold on, old man," said Arthur. "If you are going to get embarrassed in trying to do something for me, then I withdraw. Speak right out what you have to say, and leave me to make any reply that suits me."

"Then, if you'll pardon me, did you leave things in Californy straight an' square, so that nothin' could be said about you in the papers as to your record?"

"Straight as a die, uncle."

"An' would you take the position of secretary to the chief an' so get acquainted with everything an' everybody?"

"On the spot, and thank you, if you can wait till I am able to move about decently."

"Then it's done, an' I'm the proudest man in the state to see another Dillon enterin'——"

"The ring," said Arthur.

"No, the arena of politics," corrected the Senator. "An' I can tell from your talk that you have education an' sand. In time we'll make you mayor of the town."

When he was going after a most affectionate conversation with his nephew the Senator made a polite suggestion to Mrs. Dillon.

"His friends an' my friends an' the friends of his father, an' the rank an' file generally want to see an' to hear this young man, just as the matter stands. Still more will they wish to give him the right hand of fellowship when they learn that he is about to enter on a political career. Now, why not save time and trouble by just giving a reception some day about the end of the month, invite the whole ga—the whole multitude, do the thing handsome, an' wind it up forever?"

The Senator had an evident dread of his sister-in-law, and spoke to her with senatorial dignity. She meekly accepted his suggestion, and humbly attended him to the door. His good sense had cleared the situation. Preparation for a reception would set a current going in the quiet house, and relieve the awkwardness of the new relationships; and it would save time in the business of renewing old acquaintance. They took up the work eagerly. The old house had to be refitted for the occasion, his mother had to replenish a scanty wardrobe, and he had to dress himself in the fashion proper to Arthur Dillon. Anne's taste was good, inclined to rich but simple coloring, and he helped her in the selection of materials, insisting on expenditures which awed and delighted her. Judy Haskell came in for her share of raiment, and carried out some dread designs on her own person with conviction. It was pure pleasure to help these simple souls who loved him.

After a three weeks' stay in the house he went about the city at his ease, and busied himself with the study and practise of his new personality. In secret, even from Louis who spent much of his leisure with him, he began to acquire the well-known accomplishments of the real Arthur Dillon, who had sung and danced his way into the hearts of his friends, who had been a wit for a boy, bubbling over with good spirits, an athlete, a manager of amateur minstrels, a precocious gallant among the girls, a fighter ever ready to defend the weak, a tireless leader in any enterprise, and of a bright mind, but indifferent to study. The part was difficult for him to play, since his nature was staidness itself beside the spontaneity and variety of Arthur Dillon: but his spirits rose in the effort, some feeling within responded to the dash and daring of this lost boy, so much loved and so deeply mourned.

Louis helped him in preparing his wardrobe, very unlike anything an Endicott had ever worn. Lacking the elegance and correctness of earlier days, and of a different character, it was in itself a disguise. He wore his hair long and thick in the Byronic fashion, and a curly beard shadowed his lower face. Standing at the glass on the afternoon of the reception he felt confident that Horace Endicott had fairly disappeared beneath the new man Dillon. His figure had filled out slightly, and had lost its mournful stoop; his face was no longer wolfish in its leanness, and his color had returned, though melancholy eyes marked by deep circles still betrayed the sick heart. Yet the figure in the glass looked as unlike Horace Endicott as Louis Everard. He compared it with the accurate portrait sent out by his pursuers through the press. Only the day before had the story of his mysterious disappearance been made public. For months they had sought him quietly but vainly. It was a sign of their despair that the journals should have his story, his portrait, and a reward for his discovery.

No man sees his face as others see it, but the difference between the printed portrait and the reflection of Arthur Dillon in the mirror was so startling that he felt humbled and pained, and had to remind himself that this was the unlikeness he so desired. The plump and muscular figure of Horace Endicott, dressed perfectly, posed affectively, expressed the self-confidence of the aristocrat. His smooth face was insolent with happiness and prosperity, with that spirit called the pride of life. But for what he knew of this man, he could have laughed at his self-sufficiency. The mirror gave back a shrunken, sickly figure, somewhat concealed by new garments, and the eyes betrayed a poor soul, cracked and seamed by grief and wrong; no longer Horace Endicott, broken by sickness of mind and heart, and disguised by circumstance, but another man entirely. What a mill is sorrow, thus to grind up an Endicott and from the dust remold a Dillon! The young aristocrat, plump, insolent, shallow, and self-poised, looked commonplace in his pride beside this broken man, who had walked through the abyss of hell, and nevertheless saved his soul.

He discovered as he gazed alternately on portrait and mirror that a singular feeling had taken hold of him. Horace Endicott all at once seemed remote, like a close friend swallowed and obliterated years ago by the sea; while within himself, whoever he might be, some one seemed struggling for release, or expression, or dominion. He interpreted it promptly. Outwardly, he was living the life of Arthur Dillon, and inwardly that Arthur was making war on Horace Endicott, taking possession as an enemy seizes a stubborn land, reaching out for those remote citadels wherein the essence of personality resides. He did not object. He was rather pleased, though he shivered with a not unwelcome dread.

The reception turned out a marvelous affair for him who had always been bored by such ceremonies. His mother, resplendent in a silk dress of changeable hue, seemed to walk on air. Mrs. Everard and her daughter Mona assisted Anne in receiving the guests. The elder women he knew were Irish peasants, who in childhood had run barefoot to school on a breakfast of oatmeal porridge, and had since done their own washing and baking for a time. Only a practised eye could have distinguished them from their sisters born in the purple. Mona was a beauty, who earned her own living as a teacher, and had the little virtues of the profession well marked; truly a daughter of the gods, tall for a woman, with a mocking face all sparkle and bloom, small eyes that flashed like gems, a sharp tongue, and a head of silken hair, now known as the Titian red, but at that time despised by all except artists and herself. She was a witch, an enchantress, who thought no man as good as her brother, and showed other men only the regard which irritates them. And Arthur loved her and her mother because they belonged to Louis.

"I don't know how you'll like the arrangements," Louis said to him, when all things were ready. "This is not a society affair. It's an affair of the clan. The Dillons and their friends have a right to attend. So you must be prepared for hodcarriers as well as aristocrats."

At three o'clock the house and the garden were thrown open to the stream of guests. Arthur gazed in wonder. First came old men and women of all conditions, laborers, servants, small shopkeepers, who had known his father and been neighbors and clients for years. Dressed in their best, and joyful over his return to life and home and friends, they wrung his hands, wept over him, and blessed him until their warm delight and sincerity nearly overcame him, who had never known the deep love of the humble for the head of the clan. The Senator was their benefactor, their bulwark and their glory; but Arthur was the heir, the hope of the promising future. They went through the ceremony of felicitation and congratulation, chatted for a while, and then took their leave as calmly and properly as the dames and gallants of a court; and one and all bowed to the earth with moist and delighted eyes before the Everards.

"How like a queen she looks," they said of the mother.

"The blessin' o' God on him," they said of Louis, "for priest is written all over him, an' how could he help it wid such a mother."

"She's fit for a king," they said of Mona. "Wirra, an' to think she'd look at a plain man like Doyle Grahame."

But of Anne Dillon and her son they said nothing, so much were they overcome by surprise at the splendor of the mother and the son, and the beauty of the old house made over new. After dark the Senator arrived, which was the signal for a change in the character of the guests.

"You'll get the aristocracy now, the high Irish," said Louis.

Arthur recognized it by its airs, its superciliousness, and several other bad qualities. It was a budding aristocracy at the ugliest moment of its development; city officials and their families, lawyers, merchants, physicians, journalists, clever and green and bibulous, who ran in with a grin and ran out with a witticism, out of respect for the chief, and who were abashed and surprised at the superior insolence of the returned Dillon. Reminded of the story that he had returned a wealthy man, many of them lingered. With these visitors however came the pillars of Irish society, solid men and dignified women, whom the Senator introduced as they passed. There were three emphatic moments which impressed Arthur Dillon. A hush fell upon the chattering crowd one instant, and people made way for Monsignor O'Donnell, who looked very gorgeous to Arthur in his purple-trimmed soutane, and purple cloak falling over his broad shoulders. The politicians bent low, the flippant grew serious, the faithful few became reverent. A successful leader was passing, and they struggled to touch his garments. Arthur's heart swelled at the silent tribute, for he loved this man.

"His little finger," said the Senator in a whisper, "is worth more to them than my whole body."

A second time this wave of feeling invaded the crowd, when a strong-faced, quiet-mannered man entered the room, and paid his respects to the Dillons. Again the lane was made, and hearts fluttered and many hands were outstretched in greeting to the political leader, Hon. John Sullivan, the head of Tammany, the passing idol of the hour, to whom Arthur was soon to be private secretary. He would have left at once but that the Senator whispered something in his ear; and presently the two went into the hall to receive the third personage of the evening, and came back with him, deeply impressed by the honor of his presence. He was a short, stocky man, of a military bearing, with a face so strongly marked as to indicate a certain ferocity of temperament; his deep and sparkling eyes had eyebrows aslant after the fashion of Mephisto; the expression a little cynical, all determination, but at that moment good-natured. The assembly fell into an ecstasy at the sight and the touch of their hero, for no one failed to recognize the dashing

General Sheridan. They needed only a slight excuse to fall at his feet and adore him.

Arthur was impressed indeed, but his mother had fallen into a state of heavenly trance over the greatness which had honored their festival. She recovered only when the celebrities had departed and the stream of guests had come to an end. Then came a dance in the garden for the young people, and the school-friends of Arthur Dillon made demands upon him for the entertainment of which his boyhood had given such promise; so he sang his songs with nerve and success, and danced strange dances with graceful foot, until the common voice declared that he had changed only in appearance, which was natural, and had kept the promise of his boyhood for gayety of spirits, sweet singing, and fine dancing.

"I feel more than ever to-night," said Louis at parting, "that all of you has come home."

Reviewing the events of the day in his own room after midnight, he felt like an actor whose first appearance has been a success. None of the guests seemed to have any doubt of his personality, or to feel any surprise at his appearance. For them Arthur Dillon had come home again after an adventurous life, and changes were accepted as the natural result of growth. They took him to their heart without question. He was loved. What Horace Endicott could not command with all his wealth, the love of his own kin, a poor, broken adventurer, Arthur Dillon, enjoyed in plenty. Well, thank God for the good fortune which followed so unexpectedly his exit from the past. He had a secure place in tender hearts for the first time since father and mother died. What is life without love and loving? What are love and loving without God? He could say again, as on the shore of the little pool, I believe in God forever.

CHAPTER VII.

THE DILLON CLAN.

After the reception Arthur Dillon fell easily into the good graces of the clan, and found his place quite naturally; but like the suspicious intruder his ears and eyes remained wide open to catch the general sentiment about himself, and the varying opinions as to his manners and character. He began to perceive by degrees the magnitude of the task which he had imposed upon himself; the act of disappearing was but a trifle compared with the relationships crowding upon him in his new environment. He would be forced to maintain them all with some likeness to the method which would have come naturally to the real Dillon. The clan made it easy for him. Since allowance had to be conceded to his sickly condition, they formed no decisive opinions about him, accepting pleasantly, until health and humor would urge him to speak of his own accord, Anne's cloudy story of his adventures, of luck in the mines, and of excuses for his long silence. All observed the new element in his disposition; the boy who had been too heedless and headlong to notice anything but what pleased him, now saw everything; and kept at the same time a careful reserve about his past and present experiences, which impressed his friends and filled Judy Haskell with dread.

"Tommy Higgins," she said, to Anne in an interval of housework, "kem home from Texas pritty much the same, with a face an him as long as yer arm, an' his mouth shut up like an old door. Even himself cudn't open it. He spint money free, an' av coorse that talked for him. But wan day, whin his mother was thryin' an a velvet sack he bought for her, an' fightin' him bekase there was no fur collar to id, in walked his wife an' three childher to him an' her, an' shtayed wid her ever afther. Begob, she never said another word about fur collars, an' she never got another velvet sack till she died. Tommy had money, enough to kape them all decent, bud not enough for velvet and silk an' joolry. From that minnit he got back his tongue, an' he talked himself almost to death about what he didn't do, an' what he did do in Californy. So they med him a tax-collecthor an' a shtump-speaker right away, an' that saved his neighbors from dyin' o' fatague lishtenin' to his lies. Take care, Anne Dillon, that this b'y o' yours hastn't a wife somewhere."

Anne was in the precise attitude of old Mrs. Higgins when her son's wife arrived, fitting a winter cloak to her trim figure. At the sudden suggestion she sat down overcome.

"Oh, God forgive you, Judy," said she, "even to mention such a thing. I forbid you ever to speak of it again. I don't care what woman came in the door, I'd turn her out like a thramp. He's mine, I've been widout him ten years, and I'm going to hold him now against every schemin' woman in the world."

"Faith," said Judy, "I don't want to see another woman in the house anny more than yerself. I'm on'y warnin' yez. It 'ud jist break my heart to lose the grandher he's afther puttin' on yez."

The two women looked about them with mournful admiration. The house, perfect in its furnishings, delighted the womanly taste. In Anne's wardrobe hung such a collection of millinery, dresses, ornaments, that the mere thought of losing it saddened their hearts. And the loss of that future which Anne Dillon had seen in her own day-dreams ... she turned savagely on Judy.

"You were born wid an evil eye, Judy Haskell," cried she, "to see things no wan but you would ever think of. Never mention them again."

"Lemme tell ye thin that there's others who have somethin' to say besides meself. If they're in a wondher over Artie, they're in a greater wondher over Artie's mother, buyin' silks, an' satins, an' jools like an acthress, an' dhressin' as gay as a greenhorn jist over from Ireland."

"They're jealous, an' I'm goin' to make them more so," said Anne with a gleeful laugh, as she flung away care and turned to the mirror. For the first time since her youth she had become a scandal to her friends.

Judy kept Arthur well informed of the general feeling and the common opinion, and he took pains not only to soothe his mother's fright but also to explain the little matters which irritated her friends. Mrs. Everard did not regard the change in Anne with complacency.

"Arthur is changed for the better, but his mother for the worse," she said to Judy, certain that the old lady would retail it to her mistress. "A woman of fifty, that always dressed in dark colors, sensibly, to take all at once to red, and yellow, and blue, and to order bonnets like the Empress Eugenie's ... well, one can't call her crazy, but she's on the way."

"She has the money," sighed Mona, who had none.

"Sure she always had that kind of taste," said Judy in defence, "an' whin her eyes was blue an' her hair yalla, I dunno but high colors wint well enough. Her father always dhressed her well. Anyhow she's goin' to make up for all the years she had to dhress like an undertaker. Yistherday it was a gran' opery-cloak, as soon as Artie tould her he had taken four opery sates for the season."

The ladies gasped, and Mona clapped her hands at the prospect of unlimited opera, for Anne had always been kind to her in such matters.

"But all that's nawthin'," Judy went on demurely, "to what's comin' next week. It's a secret o' coorse, an' I wudn't have yez mintion it for the world, though yez'll hear it soon enough. Micksheen has a new cage all silver an' goold, an' Artie says he has a piddygree, which manes that they kep' thrack of him as far back as Adam an' Eve, as they do for lords an' ladies; though how anny of 'em can get beyant Noah an' the ark bates me. Now they're puttin' Micksheen in condition, which manes all sorts of nonsense, an' plenty o' throuble for the poor cat, that does be bawlin' all over the house night an' day wid the dhread of it, an' lukkin' up at me pitiful to save him from what's comin'. Artie has enthered his name at the polis headquarthers somewhere, that he's a prize cat, an' he's to be sint in the cage to the cat show to win a prize over fifty thousand other cats wid piddygrees. They wanted me to attind on Micksheen, but I sed no, an' so they've hired a darky in a uniform to luk after him. An' wanst a day Anne is goin' to march up to the show in a different dhress, an' luk in at Micksheen."

At this point Judy's demureness gave way and she laughed till the tears came. The others could not but join.

"Well, that's the top of the hill," said Mrs. Everard. "Surely Arthur ought to know enough to stop that tomfoolery. If he doesn't I will, I declare."

Arthur however gave the affair a very different complexion when she mentioned it.

"Micksheen is a blooded cat," said he, "for Vandervelt presented it to the Senator, who gave it to mother. And I suggested the cat-show for two reasons: mother's life has not been any too bright, and I had a big share in darkening it; so I'm going to crowd as much fun into it as she is willing to stand. Then I want to see how Micksheen stands in the community. His looks are finer than his pedigree, which is very good. And I want every one to know that there's nothing too good in New York for mother, and that she's going to have a share in all the fun that's going."

"That's just like you, and I wish you luck," said Mary Everard.

Not only did he go about explaining, and mollifying public sentiment himself, he also secured the services of Sister Mary Magdalen for the same useful end. The nun was a puzzle to him. Encased in her religious habit like a knight in armor, her face framed in the white gamp and black veil, her hands hidden in her long sleeves, she seemed to him a fine automaton, with a sweet voice and some surprising movements; for he could not measure her, nor form any impression of her, nor see a line of her natural disposition. Her human side appeared very clearly in her influence with the clan, her sincere and affectionate interest in himself, and her appetite for news in detail. Had she not made him live over again the late reception by her questions as to what was done, what everybody said, and what the ladies wore? Unwearied in aiding the needy, she brought him people of all sorts and conditions, in whom he took not the slightest interest, and besought his charity for them. He gave it in exchange for her good will, making her clearly understand that the change in his mother's habits must not lead to anything like annoyance from her old friends and neighbors.

"Oh, dear, no," she exclaimed, "for annoyance would only remove you from our midst, and deprive us of a great benefactor, for I am sure you will prove to be that. May I introduce to you my friend, Miss Edith Conyngham?"

He bowed to the apparition which came forward, seized his hands, held them and patted them affectionately, despite his efforts to release them.

"We all seem to have known you since childhood," was her apology.

The small, dark woman, pale as a dying nun, irritated him. Blue glasses concealed her eyes, and an ugly costume concealed her figure; she came out of an obscure corner behind the nun, and fell back into it noiselessly, but her voice and manner had the smoothness of velvet. He looked at her hands patting his own, and found them very soft, white, untouched by age, and a curious contrast to her gray hair. Interest touching him faintly he responded to her warmth, and looked closely into the blue glasses with a smile. Immediately the little woman sank back into her corner. Long after he settled the doubt which assailed him at that moment, if there were not significance in her look and words and manner. Sister Magdalen bored him ten minutes with her history. He must surely take an interest in her ... great friend of his father's ... and indeed of his friends ... her whole life devoted to religion and the poor ... the recklessness of others had driven her from a convent where she had been highly esteemed ... she had to be vindicated ... her case was well on the way to trial ... nothing should be left undone to make it a triumph. Rather dryly he promised his aid, wondering if he had really caught the true meaning of the little woman's behavior. He gave up suspicion when Judy provided Miss Conyngham with a character.

"This is the way of it," said Judy, "an' it's aisy to undhershtan' ... thin agin I dinno as it's so aisy ... but annyway she was a sisther in a convent out west, an' widout lave or license they put her out, bekase she wudn't do what the head wan ordhered her to do. So now she's in New York, an' Sisther Mary Mag Dillon is lukkin afther her, an' says she must be righted if the Pope himself has to do it. We all have pity an her, knowin' her people as we did. A smarter girl never opened a book in Ameriky. An' I'm her godmother."

"Then we must do something for her," said the master kindly in compliment to Judy. After his mother and Judy none appealed to him like the women of the Everard home. The motherly grace of Mary and the youthful charm of beautiful Mona attracted him naturally; from them he picked up stray features of Arthur Dillon's character; but that which drew him to them utterly was his love for Louis. Never had any boy, he believed, so profoundly the love of mother and sister. The sun rose and set with him for the Everards, and beautiful eyes deepened in beauty and flashed with joy when they rested on him. Arthur found no difficulty in learning from them the simple story of the lad's childhood and youth.

"How did it happen," he inquired of Mary, "that he took up the idea of being a priest? It was not in his mind ten years back?"

"He was the priest from his birth," she answered proudly. "Just seven months old he was when a first cousin of mine paid us a visit. He was a young man, ordained about a week, ... we had waited and prayed for that sight ten years ... he sang the Mass for us and blessed us all. It was beautiful to see, the boy we had known all his life, to come among us a priest, and to say Mass in front of Father O'Donnell—I never can call him Monsignor—with the sweetest voice you ever heard. Well, the first thing he did when he came to my house and Louis was a fat, hearty baby in the cradle, was to take him in his arms, look into his face a little while, and then kiss him. And I'll never forget the words he said."

Her dark eyes were moist, but a smile lighted up her calm face.

"Mary," he said to me, "this boy should be the first priest of the next generation. I'll bless him to that end, and do you offer him to God. And I did. He was the roughest child of all mine, and showed very little of the spirit of piety as he grew up. But he was always the best boy to his own. He had the heart for us all, and never took his play till he was sure the house was well served. Nothing was said to him about being a priest. That was left to God. One winter he began to keep a little diary, and I saw in it that he was going often to Mass on week days, and often to confession. He was working then with his father in the office, since he did not care much for school. Then the next thing I knew he came to me one night and put his arms about me to say that he wished to be a priest, to go to college, and that this very cousin who had blessed him in the cradle had urged him to make known the wish that was in him, for it seems he discovered what we only hoped for. And so he has been coming and going ever since, a blessing to the house, and sure I don't know how I shall get along without him when he goes to the seminary next year."

"Nor I," said Arthur with a start. "How can you ever think of giving him up?"

"That's the first thing we have to learn," she replied with a smile at his passion. "The children all leave the house in time one way or another. It's only a question of giving him to God's service or to the service of another woman. I could never be jealous of God."

He laughed at this suggestion of jealousy in a mother. Of course she must hate the woman who robs her of her son, and secures a greater love than a mother ever knew. The ways of nature, or God, are indeed hard to the flesh. He thought of this as he sat in the attic room with his light-hearted chum. He envied him the love and reverence of these good women, envied him that he had been offered to God in his infancy; and in his envy felt a satisfaction that very soon these affectionate souls would soon have to give Louis up to Another. To him this small room was like a shrine, sacred, undefiled, the enclosure of a young creature specially called to the service of man, perfumed by innocence, cared for by angels, let down from heaven into a house on Cherry Street. Louis had no such fancies, but flung aside his books, shoved his chum into a chair, placed his feet on a stool, put a cigar in his mouth and lighted it for him, pulled his whiskers, and ordered the latest instalment of Dillon's Dark Doings in Dugout. Then the legends of life in California began. Sometimes, after supper, a knock was heard at the door, and there entered two little sisters, who must hear a bear-story from Arthur, and kiss the big brother good-night; two delicate flowers on the rough stem of life, that filled Horace Endicott with bitterness and joy when he gathered them into his embrace; the bitterness of hate, the joy of escape from paternity. What softness, what beauty, what fragrance in the cherubs! *Trumps*, their big brother called them, but the world knew them as Marguerite and Constance, and they shared the human repugnance to an early bed.

"You ought to be glad to go to bed," Arthur said, "when you go to sleep so fast, and dream beautiful dreams about angels."

"But I don't dream of angels," said Marguerite sadly. "Night before last I dreamed a big black man came out of a cellar, and took baby away," casting a look of love at Constance in her brother's arms.

"And I dreamed," said Constance, with a queer little pucker of her mouth, "that she was all on fire, in her dress, and——"

This was the limit of her language, for the thought of her sister on fire overwhelmed the words at her command.

"And baby woke up," the elder continued—for she was a second mother to Constance, and pieced out all her deficiencies and did penance for her sins—"and she said to mother, 'throw water on Marguerite to put her out.'"

"What sad dreams," Arthur said. "Tell Father O'Donnell about them."

"She has other things to tell him," Louis said with a grin. "I have no doubt you could help her, Artie. She must go to confession sometime, and she has no sins to tell. The other day when I was setting out for confession she asked me not to tell all my sins to the priest, but to hold back a few and give them to her for her confession. Now you have enough to spare for that honest use, I think."

"Oh, please, dear cousin Artie," said the child, thrilling his heart with the touch of her tender lips on his cheek.

"There's no doubt I have enough," he cried with a secret groan. "When you are ready to go, Marguerite, I will give you all you want."

The history of Arthur's stay in California was drawn entirely from his travels on the Pacific slope, tedious to the narrator, but interesting because of the lad's interest, and because of the picture which the rapt listener made. His study-desk near by, strewn with papers and books, the white bed and bookcase farther off, pictures and mottoes of his own selection on the white walls, a little altar in the depths of the dormer-window; and the lord of the little domain in the foreground, hands on knees, lips parted, cheeks flushed, eyes fixed and dreamy, seeing the rich colors and varied action as soon as words conveyed the story to the ear; a perfect picture of the listening boy, to whom experience like a wandering minstrel sings the glory of the future in the happenings of the past.

Arthur invariably closed his story with a fit of sighing. That happy past made his present fate heavy indeed. Horace Endicott rose strong in him then and protested bitterly against Arthur Dillon as a usurper; but sure there never was a gentler usurper, for he surrendered so willingly and promptly that Endicott fled again into his voluntary obscurity. Louis comforted those heavy moments with soft word and gentle touch, pulling his beard lovingly, smoothing his hair, lighting for him a fresh cigar, asking no questions, and, when the dark humor deepened, exorcising the evil spirit with a sprinkling of holy water. Prayers were said together—an overpowering moment for the man who rarely prayed to see this faith and its devotion in the boy—and then to bed, where Louis invariably woke to the incidents of the day and retailed them for an hour to his amused ear; and with the last word fell into instant and balmy sleep. Oh, this wonder of unconscious boyhood! Had this sad-hearted man ever known that blissful state? He lay there listening to the soft and regular breathing of the child, who knew so little of life and evil. At last he fell asleep moaning. It was Louis who woke with a sense of fright, felt that his bedfellow was gone, and heard his voice at the other side of the room, an agonized voice that chilled him.

"To go back would be to kill her ... but I must go back ... and then the trail of blood over all...."

Louis leaped out of bed, and lit the night-candle. Arthur stood beside the altar in the dormer-window, motionless, with pallid face and open eyes that saw nothing.

"Why should such a wretch live and I be suffering?—she suffers too ... but not enough ... the child ... oh, that was the worst ... the child ... my child...."

The low voice gave out the words distinctly and without passion, as of one repeating what was told to him. Rid of fear Louis slapped him on the shoulder and shook him, laughing into his astonished face when sense came back to him.

"It's like a scene, or a skene from Macbeth," he said. "Say, Artie, you had better make open confession of your sins. Why should you want to kill her, and put the trail of blood over it all?"

"I said that, did I?" He thought a moment, then put his arms about Louis. They were sitting on the side of the bed.

"You must know it sometime, Louis. It is only for your ear now. I had a wife ... she was worthless ... she lives ... that is all."

"And your child? you spoke of a child?"

Arthur shook with a chill and wiped the sweat from his forehead.

"No," he groaned, "no ... thank God for that ... I had no child."

After a little they went back to bed, and Louis made light of everything with stories of his own sleep-walking until he fell asleep again. The candle was left burning. Misfortune rose and sat looking at the boy curiously. With the luck of the average man, he might have been father to a boy like this, a girl like Mona with beautiful hair and a golden heart, soft sweet babies like the Trumps. He leaned over and studied the sleeping face, so sweetly mournful, so like death, yet more spiritual, for the soul was there still. In this face the senses had lost their daylight influence, had withdrawn into the shadows; and now the light of innocence, the light of a beautiful soul, the light that never was on land or sea, shone out of the still features. A feeling which had never touched his nature before took fierce possession of him, and shook him as a tiger shakes his prey. He had to writhe in silence, to beat his head with his hands, to stifle words of rage and hate and despair. At last exhausted he resigned himself, he took the boy's hand in his, remembering that this innocent heart loved him, and fell into a dreamless sleep.

The charm and the pain of mystery hung about the new life, attracting him, yet baffling him at every step. He could not fathom or grasp the people with whom he lived intimately, they seemed beyond him, and yet he dared ask no questions, dared not go even to Monsignor for explanations. With the prelate his relations had to take that character which suited their individual standing. When etiquette allowed him to visit the rector, Monsignor provided him with the philosophy of the environment, explained the difficulties, and soothed him with the sympathy of a generous heart acquainted with his calamities.

"It would have been better to have launched you elsewhere," he said, "but I knew no other place well enough to get the right people. And then I have the hope that the necessity for this episode will not continue."

"Death only will end it, Monsignor. Death for one or the other. It should come soon, for the charm of this life is overpowering me. I shall never wish to go back if the charm holds me. My uncle, the Senator, is about to place me in politics."

"I knew he would launch you on that stormy sea," Monsignor answered reflectively, "but you are not bound to accept the enterprise."

"It will give me distraction, and I need distraction from this intolerable pain," tapping his breast with a gesture of anguish.

"It will surely counter-irritate. It has entranced men like the Senator, and your chief; even men like Birmingham. They have the ambition which runs with great ability. It's a pity that the great prizes are beyond them."

"Why beyond them?"

"High office is closed to Catholics in this country."

"Here I run up against the mysterious again," he complained.

"Go down into your memory," Monsignor said after a little reflection, "and recall the first feeling which obscurely stirred your heart when the ideas of *Irish* and *Catholic* were presented to you. See if it was not distrust, dislike, irritation, or even hate; something different from the feeling aroused by such ideas as *Turk* and *atheist*."

"Dislike, irritation, perhaps contempt, with a hint of amusement," Arthur replied thoughtfully.

"How came that feeling there touching people of whom you knew next to nothing?"

"Another mystery."

"Let me tell you. Hatred and contempt of the Irish Catholic has been the mark of English history for four centuries, and the same feelings have become a part of English character. It is in the English blood, and therefore it is in yours. It keeps such men as Sullivan and Birmingham out of high office, and now it will act against you, strangely enough."

"I understand. Queer things, rum things in this world. I am such a mystery to myself, however, that I ought not be surprised at outside mysteries."

"I often regret that I helped you to your present enterprise," said the priest, "on that very account. Life is harsh enough without adding to its harshness."

"Never regret that you saved a poor fellow's life, reason, fortune, family name from shame and blood," Arthur answered hotly. "I told you the consequences that were coming—you averted them—there's no use to talk of gratitude—and through you I came to believe in God again, as my mother taught me. No regret, for God's sake."

His voice broke for a moment, and he walked to the window. Outside he saw the gray-white walls which would some day be the grand cathedral. The space about it looked like the studio of a giant artist; piles of marble scattered here and there gave the half-formed temple the air of a frowsy, ill-dressed child; and the mass rising to the sky resembled a cloud that might suddenly melt into the ether. He had seen the great temples of the world, yet found in this humbler, but still magnificent structure an element of wonder. From the old world, ancient, rich in tradition, one expected all things; centaurs might spring from its soil unnoticed. That the prosaic rocks of Manhattan should heave for this sublimity stirred the sense of admiring wonder.

"This is your child?" said Arthur abruptly.

"I saw the foundation laid when I was a youth, great boulders of half-hewn rock, imbedded in cement, to endure with the ages, able to support whatever man may pile upon them. This building is part of my life—you may call it my child—for it seems to have sprung from me, although a greater planned it."

"What a people to attempt this miracle," said Arthur.

"Now you have said it," cried the priest proudly. "The poor people to whom you now belong, moved by the spirit which raised the great shrines of Europe, are building out of their poverty and their faith the first really great temple on this continent. The country waited for them. This temple will express more than a desire to have protection from bad weather, and to cover the preacher's pulpit. Here you will have in stone faith, hope, love, sacrifice. What blessings it will pour out upon the city, and upon the people who built it. For them it will be a great glory many centuries perhaps."

"I shall have my share in the work," Arthur said with feeling. "I feel that I am here to stay, and I shall be a stranger to no work in which my friends are engaged. I'll not let the mysteries trouble me. I begin to see what you are, and a little of what you mean. Command me, for no other in this world to-day has any right to command me— none with a right like yours, father and friend."

"Thanks and amen, Arthur. Having no claim upon you we shall be all the more grateful. But in good time. For the present look to yourself, closely, mind; and draw upon me, upon Louis, upon your mother, they have the warmest hearts, for sympathy and consolation."

Not long before and Arthur Dillon would have received with the polite indifference of proud and prosperous youth this generous offer of sympathy and love; but now it shook him to the center, for he had learned, at what a fearful price! how precious, how necessary, how rare is the jewel of human love.

CHAPTER VIII.

THE WEARIN' O' THE GREEN.

By degrees the effervescence of little Ireland, in which strange land his fortune had been cast, began to steal into his blood. Mirth ruled the East side, working in each soul according to his limitations. It was a wink, a smile, a drink, a passing gossoon, a sly girl, a light trick, among the unspoken things; or a biting epigram, the phrase felicitous, a story gilt with humor, a witticism swift and fatal as lightning; in addition varied activity, a dance informal, a ceremonious ball, a party, a wake, a political meeting, the visit of the district leader; and with all, as Judy expressed it, "lashins an' lavins, an' divil a thought of to-morrow." Indeed this gay clan kept Yesterday so deeply and tenderly in mind that To-day's house had no room for the uncertain morrow. He abandoned himself to the spirit of the place. The demon of reckless fun caught him by the heels and sharpened his tongue, so that his wit and his dancing became tonics for eyes and ears dusty with commonplace. His mother and his chum had to admonish him, and it was very sweet to get this sign of their love for him. Reproof from our beloved is sweeter than praise from an enemy.

They all watched over him as if he were heir to a throne. The Senator, busy with his approaching entrance into local politics, had already introduced him to the leaders, who formed a rather mixed circle of intelligence and power. He had met its kind before on the frontier, where the common denominator in politics was manhood, not blue blood, previous good character, wealth, nor the stamp of Harvard. A member held his place by virtue of courage, popularity, and ability. Arthur made no inquiries, but took everything as it came. All was novelty, all surprise, and to his decorous and orderly disposition, all ferment. The clan seemed to him to be rushing onward like a torrent night and day, from the dance to the ward-meeting, from business to church, interested and yet careless. The Senator informed him with pride that his début would take place at the banquet on St. Patrick's Day, when he should make a speech.

71

"Do you think you can do it, me boy?" said the Senator. "If you think you can, why you can."

"I know I can," said the reckless Dillon, who had never made a speech in his life.

"An' lemme give you a subject," said Judy. They were all together in the sitting-room, where the Senator had surprised them in a game of cards.

"Give a bastin' to Mare Livingstone," said Judy seriously. "I read in the *Sun* how he won't inspect the parade on St. Patrick's Day, nor let the green flag fly on the city hall. There must be an Orange dhrop in his blood, for no dacint Yankee 'ud have anny hathred for the blessed green. Sure two years ago Mare Jones dressed himself up in a lovely green uniform, like an Irish prince, an' lukked at the parade from a platform. It brought the tears to me eyes, he lukked so lovely. They ought to have kep' him Mare for the rest of his life. An' for Mare Livingstone, may never a blade o' grass or a green leaf grow on his grave."

The Senator beamed with secret pleasure, while the others began to talk together with a bitterness beyond Arthur's comprehension.

"He ought to have kept his feelings to himself," said quiet Anne. "If he didn't like the green, there was no need of insultin' us."

"And that wasn't the worst," Louis hotly added. "He gave a talk to the papers the next day, and told how many Irish paupers were in the poorhouse, and said how there must be an end to favoring the Irish."

"I saw that too," said Judy, "an' I sez to meself, sez I, he's wan o' the snakes St. Pathrick dhruv out of Ireland."

"No need for surprise," Mona remarked, studying her cards, "for the man has only one thought: to keep the Irish in the gutter. Do you suppose I would have been a teacher to-day if he could have kept me out of it, with all his pretended friendship for papa."

"If you baste the Mayor like this now, there won't be much left for me to do at the banquet," said Arthur with a laugh for their fierceness.

"Ay, there it is," said Judy. "Yez young Americans have no love for the green, except for the fun yez get out of it; barrin' dacint Louis here, who read the history of Ireland whin he was tin years old, an' niver got over it. Oh, yez may laugh away! Ye are all for the red, white, an' blue, till the Mare belts yez wid the red, white, an' blue, for he says he does everythin' in honor o' thim colors, though I don't see how it honors thim to insult the green. He may be a Livingshtone in name, but he's a dead wan for me."

The Senator grew more cheerful as this talk grew warmer, and then, seeing Arthur's wonderment, he made an explanation.

"Livingstone is a good fellow, but he's not a politician, Artie. He thinks he can ru—manage the affairs of this vil—metropolis without the Irish and especially without the Catholics. Oh, he's death on them, except as boot-blacks, cooks, and ditch-diggers. He'd let them ru—manage all the saloons. He's as mad—as indignant as a hornet that he could not boo—get rid of them entirely during his term of office, and he had to speak out his feelings or bu—die. And he has put his foot in it artistically. He has challenged the Irish and their friends, and he goes out of office forever next fall. No party wants a man that lets go of his mouth at critical moments. It might be a neat thing for you to touch him up in your speech at the banquet."

The Senator spoke with unctuousness and delight, and Arthur saw that the politicians rejoiced at the loquacity and bad temper of the Honorable Quincy Livingstone, whom the Endicotts included among their distant relatives.

"I'll take your subject, Judy," said he.

"Then rade up the histhory of Ireland," replied the old lady flattered.

Close observation of the present proved more interesting and amusing than the study of the past. Quincy Livingstone's strictures on the exiles of Erin stirred them to the depths, and his refusal to float the green flag from the city hall brought a blossoming of green ribbon on St. Patrick's Day which only Spring could surpass in her decorations of the hills. The merchants blessed the sour spirit which had provoked this display to the benefit of their treasuries. The hard streets seemed to be sprouting as the crowds moved about, and even the steps and corridors of the mayor's office glistened with the proscribed color. The cathedral on Mott Street was the center of attraction, and a regiment which had done duty in the late war the center of interest. Arthur wondered at the enthusiasm of the crowd as the veterans carrying their torn battle-flags marched down the street and under the arched entrance of the church to take their places for the solemn Mass. All eyes grew moist, and sobs burst forth at sight of them.

"If they were only marching for Ireland!" one man cried hoarsely.

"They'll do it yet," said another more hopeful.

Within the cathedral a multitude sat in order, reverently quiet, but charged with emotion. With burning eyes they watched the soldiers in front and the priests in the sanctuary, and some beat their breasts in pain, or writhed with sudden stress of feeling. Arthur felt thrilled by the power of an emotion but vaguely understood. These exiles were living over in this moment the scenes which had attended their expulsion from home and country, as he often repeated the horrid scenes of his own tragedy. Under the reverence and decorum due to the temple hearts were bursting with passion and grief. In a little while resignation would bring them relief and peace.

It was like enchantment for Arthur Dillon. He knew the vested priest for his faithful friend; but on the altar, in his mystic robes, uplifted, holding the reverent gaze of these thousands, in an atmosphere clouded by incense and vocal with pathetic harmonies, the priest seemed as far away as heaven; he knew in his strength and his weakness the boy beside him, but this enwrapped attitude, this eloquent, still, unconscious face, which spoke of thoughts and feelings familiar only to the eye of God, seemed to lift Louis into another sphere; he knew the people kneeling about, the headlong, improvident, roystering crowd, but knew them not in this outpouring of deeper emotions than spring from the daily chase for bread and pleasure.

A single incident fixed this scene in his mind and heart forever. Just in front of him sat a young woman with her father, whom she covertly watched with some anxiety. He was a man of big frame and wasted body, too nervous to remain quiet a moment, and deeply moved by the pageant, for he twisted his hands and beat his breast as if in anguish. Once she touched his arm caressingly. And the face which he turned towards her was stained with the unwiped tears; but when he stood up at the close of the Mass to see the regiment march down the grand aisle, his pale face showed so bitter an agony that Arthur recalled with horror his own sufferings. The young woman clung to her father until the last soldier had passed, and the man had sunk into his seat with a half-uttered groan. No one noticed them, and Arthur as he left with the ladies saw her patting the father's hand and whispering to him softly.

Outside the cathedral a joyous uproar attended the beginning of that parade which the Mayor had declined to review. As his party was to enjoy it at some point of Fifth Avenue he did not tarry to witness the surprising scenes about the church, but with Louis took a car uptown. Everywhere they heard hearty denunciations of the Mayor. At one street, their car being detained by the passing of a single division of the parade, the passengers crowded about the front door and the driver, and an anxious traveler asked the cause of the delay, and the probable length of it. The driver looked at him curiously.

"About five minutes," he said. "Don't you know who's paradin' to-day?"

"No."

"See the green plumes an' ribbons?"

"I do," vacantly.

"Know what day o' the month it is?"

"March seventeenth, of course."

"Live near New York?"

"About twenty miles out."

"Gee whiz!" exclaimed the driver with a gasp. "I've bin a-drivin' o' this car for twenty years, an' I never met anythin' quite so innercent. Well, it's St. Patrick's Day, an' them's the wild Irish."

The traveler seemed but little enlightened. An emphatic man in black, with a mouth so wide that its opening suggested the wonderful, seized the hand of the innocent and shook it cordially.

"I'm glad to meet one uncontaminated American citizen in this city," he said. "I hope there are millions like you in the land."

The uncontaminated looked puzzled, and might have spoken but for a violent interruption. A man had entered the car with an orange ribbon in his buttonhole.

"You'll have to take that off," said the conductor in alarm, pointing to the ribbon, "or leave the car."

"I won't do either," said the man.

"And I stand by you in that refusal," said the emphatic gentleman. "It's an outrage that we must submit to the domination of foreigners."

"It's the order of the company," said the conductor. "First thing we know a wild Irishman comes along, he goes for that orange ribbon, there's a fight, the women are frightened, and perhaps the car is smashed."

"An' besides," said the deliberate driver as he tied up his reins and took off his gloves, "it's a darn sight easier an' cheaper for us to put you off than to keep an Irishman from tryin' to murder you."

The uncontaminated citizen and two ladies fled to the street, while the driver and the conductor stood over the offending passenger.

"Goin' to take off the ribbon?" asked the conductor.

"You will be guilty of a cowardly surrender of principle if you do," said the emphatic gentleman.

"May I suggest," said Arthur blandly, "that you wear it in his stead?"

"I am not interested either way," returned the emphatic one, with a snap of the terrible jaws, "but maintain that for the sake of principle——"

A long speech was cut off at that moment by a war-cry from a simple lad who had just entered the car, spied the ribbon, and launched himself like a catapult upon the Orange champion. A lively scramble followed, but the scene speedily resolved itself into its proper elements. The procession had passed, the car moved on its way, and the passengers through the rear door saw the simple lad grinding the ribbon in the dust with triumphant heel, while its late wearer flew toward the horizon pursued by an imaginary mob. Louis sat down and glared at the emphatic man.

"Who is he?" said Arthur with interest, drawing his breath with joy over the delights of this day.

"He's a child-stealer," said Louis with distinctness. "He kidnaps Catholic children and finds them Protestant homes where their faith is stolen from them. He's the most hated man in the city."

The man accepted this scornful description of himself in silence. Except for the emphasis which nature had given to his features, he was a presentable person. Flying side-whiskers made his mouth appear grotesquely wide, and the play of strong feelings had produced vicious wrinkles on his spare face. He appeared to be a man of energy, vivacity and vulgarity, reminding one of a dinner of pork and cabbage. He was soon forgotten in the excitement of a delightful day, whose glories came to a brilliant end in that banquet which introduced the nephew of Senator Dillon into political life.

Standing before the guests, he found himself no longer that silent and disdainful Horace Endicott, who on such an occasion would have cooly stuttered and stammered through fifty sentences of dull congratulation and platitude. Feeling aroused him, illumined him, on the instant, almost without wish of his own, at the contrast between two pictures which traced themselves on his imagination as he rose in his place: the wrecked man who had fled from Sonia Westfield, what would he have been to-night but for the friendly hands outstretched to save him? Behold him in honor, in health, in hope, sure of love and some kind of happiness, standing before the people who had rescued him. The thousand impressions of the past six months sparkled into life; the sublime, pathetic, and amusing scenes of that day rose up like stars in his fancy; and against his lips, like water against a dam, rushed vigorous sentences from the great deeps opened in his soul by grief and change, and then leaped over in a beautiful, glittering flood. He wondered vaguely at his vehemence and fluency, at the silence in the hall, that these great people should listen to him at all. They heard him with astonishment, the leaders with interest, the Senator with tears; and Monsignor looked once towards the gallery where Anne Dillon sat literally frozen with terror and pride.

The long and sincere applause which followed the speech warned him that he had impressed a rather callous crowd of notables, and an exaltation seized him. The guests lost no time in congratulating him, and every tongue wagged in his favor.

"You have the gift of eloquence," said Sullivan.

"It will be a pleasure to hear you again," said Vandervelt, the literary and social light of the Tammany circle.

"You have cleared your own road," Birmingham the financier remarked, and he stayed long to praise the young orator.

"There's nothin' too good for you after to-night," cried the Senator brokenly. "I simply can't—cannot talk about it."

"Your uncle," said Doyle Grahame, the young journalist who was bent on marrying Mona Everard, "as usual closes the delicate sparring of his peers with a knockdown blow; there's nothing too good for you."

"It's embarrassing."

"I wish I had your embarrassment. Shall I translate the praises of these great men for you? Sullivan meant, I must have the use of your eloquence; the lion Vandervelt, when you speak in my favor; Birmingham, please stump for me when I run for office; and the Senator, I will make you governor. You may use your uncle; the others hope to use you."

"I am willing to be of service," said Arthur severely.

"A good-nature thrown away, unless you are asked to serve. They have all congratulated you on your speech. Let me congratulate you on your uncle. They marvel at your eloquence; I, at your luck. Give me such an uncle rather than the gift of poesy. Do not neglect oratory, but cultivate thy uncle, boy."

Arthur laughed, Monsignor came up then, and heaped him with praise.

"Were you blessed with fluency in—your earlier years?" he said.

"Therein lies the surprise, and the joke. I never had an accomplishment except for making an uproar in a crowd. It seems ridiculous to show signs of the orator now, without desire, ambition, study, or preparation."

"Your California experiences," said the priest casually, "may have something to do with it. But let me warn you," and he looked about to make sure no one heard, "that early distinction in your case may attract the attention you wish to escape."

"I feel that it will help me," Arthur answered. "Who that knew Horace Endicott would look for him in a popular Tammany orator? The mantle of an Irish Cicero would disguise even a Livingstone."

The surprise and pleasure of the leaders were cold beside the wild delight of the Dillon clan when the news went around that Arthur had overshadowed the great speakers of the banquet. His speech was read in every gathering, its sarcastic description of the offensive Livingstone filled the Celts with joy, and threw Anne and Judy into an ecstasy.

"Faith, Mare Livingstone'll see green on St. Patrick's Day for the rest of his life," said Judy. "It' ud be a proper punishment if the bread he ate, an' everythin' he touched on that day, shud turn greener than ould Ireland, the land he insulted."

"There's curse enough on him," Anne replied sharply, ever careful to take Arthur's side, as she thought, "and I won't have you spoiling Arthur's luck be cursing any wan. I'm too glad to have an orator in the family. I can now put my orator against Mary Everard's priest, and be as proud as she is."

"The pride was born in ye," said Judy. "You won't have to earn it. Indade, ye'll have a new flirt to yer tail, an' a new toss to yer head, every day from now to his next speech."

"Why shouldn't I? I'm his mother," with emphasis.

CHAPTER IX.

THE VILLA AT CONEY ISLAND.

The awkwardness of his relations with Anne Dillon wore away speedily, until he began to think as well as speak of her as his mother; for she proved with time to be a humorous and delightful mother. Her love for rich colors and gay scenes, her ability to play gracefully the awkward part which he had chosen for her, her affectionate and discreet reserve, her delicate tact and fine wit, and her half-humorous determination to invade society, showed her as a woman of parts. He indulged her fancies, in particular her dream of entering the charmed circle of New York society. How this success should be won, and what was the circle, he did not know, nor care. The pleasure for him lay in her bliss as she exhausted one pleasure after another, and ever sought for higher things: Micksheen at the cat show attended by the liveried mulatto; the opera and the dog show, with bonnets and costumes to match the occasion; then her own carriage, used so discreetly as not to lose the respect of the parish; and finally the renting of the third pew from the front in the middle aisle of the cathedral, a step forward in the social world. How he had enjoyed these events in her upward progress! As a closing event for the first year of his new life, he suggested a villa by the sea for the summer, with Mona and Louis as guests for the season, with as many others as pleased her convenience. The light which broke over her face at this suggestion came not from within, but direct from heaven!

She sent him modestly to a country of the Philistines known as Coney Island, where he found the common herd enjoying a dish called chowder amid much spontaneity and dirt, and mingling their uproarious bathing with foaming beer; a picture framed in white sand and sounding sea, more than pleasant to the jaded taste of an Endicott. The roar of the surf drowned the mean uproar of discordant man. The details of life there were too cheap to be looked at closely; but at a distance the surface had sufficient color and movement. He found an exception to this judgment. La Belle Colette danced with artistic power, though in surroundings unsuited to her skill. He called it genius. In an open pavilion, whose roughness the white sand and the white-green surf helped to condone, on a tawdry stage, she appeared, a slight, pale, winsome beauty, clad in green and white gauze, looking like a sprite of the near-by sea. The witchery of her dancing showed rare art, which was lost altogether on the simple crowd. She danced carelessly, as if mocking the rustics, and made her exit without applause.

"Where did you get your artiste, August?" he said to a waiter.

"You saw how well she dances, hey? Poor Colette! The best creature in the world ... opens more wine than five, and gives too much away. But for the drink she might dance at the opera."

Arthur went often to see her dance, with pity for the talent thrown away, and brought his mother under protest from that cautious lady, who would have nothing to do with so common a place. The villa stood in respectable, even aristocratic, quiet at the far end of the island, and Anne regarded it almost with reverence, moving about as if in a temple. He found, however, that she had made it a stage for a continuous drama, in which she played the leading part, and the Dillon clan with all its ramifications played minor characters and the audience. Her motives and her methods he could not fathom and did not try; the house filled rapidly, that was enough; the round of dinners, suppers, receptions, dances, and whatnots had the regularity of the tides. Everybody came down from Judy's remotest cousin up to His Grace the archbishop. Even Edith Conyngham, apparently too timid to leave the shadow of Sister Magdalen, stole into a back room with Judy, and haunted the beach for a few days. For Judy's sake he turned aside to entertain her, and with the perversity which seems to follow certain actions he told her the pathetic incident of the dancer. Why he should have chosen this poor nun to hear this tale, embellished as if to torture her, he could never make out. Often in after years, when events had given the story significance, he sought for his own motives in vain. It might have been the gray hair, the rusty dress, the depressed manner, so painful a contrast to the sea-green sprite, all youth, and grace, and beauty, which provoked him.

"I shall pray for the poor thing," said rusty Edith, fingering her beads, and then she made to grasp his hand, which he thrust into his pockets.

"Not a second time," he told Louis. "I'd rather get the claw of a boiled lobster."

The young men did not like Miss Conyngham, but Louis pitied her sad state.

The leading characters on Anne's stage, at least the persons whom she permitted occasionally to fill its center, were the anxious lovers Mona and Doyle Grahame. He was a poet to his finger-tips, dark-haired, ruddy, manly, with clear wit, and the tenderest and bravest of dark eyes; and she, red-tressed, lovely, candid, simple, loved him with her whole heart while submitting to the decree of a sour father who forbade the banns. Friends like Anne gave them the opportunity to woo, and the Dillon clan stood as one to blind the father as to what was going on. The sight of this beauty and faith and love feeding on mutual confidence beside the sunlit surf and the moonlight waters gave Arthur profound sadness, steeped his heart in bitterness. Such scenes had been the prelude to his tragedy. Despair looked out of his eyes and frightened Louis.

"Why should you mind it so, after a year?" the lad pleaded.

"Time was when I minded nothing. I thought love and friendship, goodness and happiness, grew on every bush, and that

When we were far from the lips that we loved,
We had but to make love to the lips that were near.

I am wiser now."

"Away with that look," Louis protested. "You have love in plenty with us, and you must not let yourself go like that. It's frightful."

"It's gone," Arthur answered rousing himself. "The feeling will never go farther than a look. She was not worth it—but the sight of these two—I suppose Adam must have grieved looking back at paradise."

"They have their troubles also," Louis said to distract his mind. "Father is unkind and harsh with Irish patriots, and because Grahame went through the mill, conspiracy, arrest, jail, prison, escape, and all the rest of it, he won't hear of marriage for Mona with him. Of course he'll have to come down in time. Grahame is the best fellow, and clever too."

One day seemed much the same as another to Arthur, but his mother's calendar had the dates marked in various colors, according to the rank of her visitors. The visit of the archbishop shone in figures of gold, but the day and hour which saw Lord Constantine cross her threshold and sit at her table stood out on the calendar in letters of flame. The Ledwiths who brought him were of little account, except as the friends of His Lordship. Anne informed the household the day before of the honor which heaven was sending them, and gave minute instructions as to the etiquette to be observed; and if Arthur wished to laugh the blissful light in her face forbade. The rules of etiquette did not include the Ledwiths, who could put up with ordinary politeness and be grateful.

"I can see from the expression of Mona," Arthur observed to the other gentlemen, "that the etiquette of to-morrow puts us out of her sight. And who is Lord Constantine? I ought to know, so I did not dare ask."

"A young English noble, son and heir of a Marquis," said Grahame with mock solemnity, "who is devoted to the cause of bringing London and Washington closer together in brotherly love and financial, that is rogues' sympathy—no, roguish sympathy—that's better. He would like an alliance between England and us. Therefore he cultivates the Irish. And he'd marry Honora Ledwith to-morrow if she'd have him. That's part of the scheme."

"And who are the Ledwiths?" said Arthur incautiously, but no one noticed the slip at the moment.

"People with ideas, strange weird ideas," Louis made answer. "Oh, perfectly sane, of course, but so devoted to each other, and the cause of Ireland, that they can get along with none, and few can get along with them. That's why Pop thinks so much of 'em. They are forever running about the world, deep in conspiracies for freedom, and so on, but they never get anywhere to stay. Outside of that they're the loveliest souls the sun ever shone on, and I adore Honora."

"And if Mona takes to His Lordship," said Grahame, "I'll worship Miss Ledwith."

"Very confusing," Arthur muttered. "English noble,—alliance between two countries—cultivates Irish—wants to marry Irish girl—conspirators and all that—why, there's no head or tail to the thing."

"Well, you keep your eye on Honora Ledwith and me, and you'll get the key. She's the sun of the system. And, by the way, don't you remember old Ledwith, the red-hot lecturer on the woes of Ireland? Didn't you play on her doorstep in Madison street, and treat her to Washington pie?"

When the party arrived next day Arthur saw a handsome, vigorous, blond young man, hearty in his manner, and hesitating in his speech, whom he forgot directly in his surprise over the Ledwiths; for he recognized in them the father and daughter whom he had observed in so passionate a scene in the cathedral on St. Patrick's Day. He had their history by heart, the father being a journalist and the daughter a singer; they had traveled half the world; and while every one loved them none favored their roseate schemes for the freedom of Ireland. Perhaps this had made them peculiar. At the first glance one would have detected oddity as well as distinction in them. Tall, lean, vivacious, Owen Ledwith moved about restlessly, talked much, and with considerable temper. The daughter sat placid and watchful, quite used to playing audience to his entertainments; though her eyes never seemed to look at him, Arthur saw that she missed none of his movements, never failed to catch his words and to smile her approval. The whiteness of her face was like cream, and her dark blue eyes were pencilled by lashes so black that at the first glance they seemed of a lighter shade. Impressed to a degree by what at that instant could not be put into words, he named her in his own mind the White Lady. No trace of disdain spoiled her lofty manner, yet he thought she looked at people as if they were minor instruments in her own scheme. She made herself at home like one accustomed to quick changes of scene. A woman of that sort travels round the globe with a satchel, and dresses for the play with a ribbon and a comb, never finding the horizon too large for personal comfort. Clearly she was beloved in the Dillon circle, for they made much of her; but of course that day not even the master of the house was a good second to Lord Constantine. Anne moved about like herself in a dream. She was heavenly, and Arthur enjoyed it, offering incense to His Lordship, and provoking him into very English utterances. The young man's fault was that he rode his hobby too hard.

"It's a shame, doncheknow," he cried as soon as he could decently get at his favorite theme, "that the English-speaking peoples should be so hopelessly divided just now — —"

"Hold on, Lord Conny," interrupted Grahame, "you're talking Greek to Dillon. Arthur, m'lud has a theory that the English-speaking peoples should do something together, doncheknow, and the devil of it is to get 'em together, doncheknow."

They all laughed save Anne, who looked awful at this scandalous mimicry of a personage, until His Lordship laughed too.

"You are only a journalist," said he gayly, "and talk like your journal. As I was saying, we are divided at home, and here it is much worse. The Irish here hate us worse than their brethren at home hate us, doncheknow—thank you, Miss Ledwith, I really will not use that word again—and all the races settled with you seem to dislike one another extremely. In Canada it's no better, and sometimes I would despair altogether, only a beginning must be made sometime; and I am really doing very well among the Irish."

He looked towards Honora who smiled and turned again to Arthur with those gracious eyes.

"I knew you would not forget it," she said. "The Washington pie in itself would keep it in your mind. How I loved that pie, and every one who gave me some. Your coming home must have been very wonderful to your dear mother."

"More wonderful than I could make you understand," murmured Arthur. "Do you know the old house is still in Madison street, where we played and ate the pie?"

Louis put his head between them slyly and whispered:

"I can run over to the baker's if you wish and get a chunk of that identical pie, if you're so in love with it, and we'll have the whole scene over again."

No persuasion could induce the party to remain over night at the villa, because of important engagements in the city touching the alliance and the freedom of Erin; and the same tremendous interests would take them far away the next morning to be absent for months; but the winter would find them in the city and, when they would be fairly settled, Arthur was bid to come and dine with them often. On the last boat the White Lady sailed away with her lord and father, and Anne watched the boat out of sight, sighing like one who has been ravished to the third heaven, and finds it a distressing job to get a grip on earth again.

Arthur noticed that his mother dressed particularly well for the visits of the politicians, and entertained them sumptuously. Was she planning for his career? Delicious thought! But no, the web was weaving for the Senator. When the last knot was tied, she threw it over his head in perfect style. He complimented her on her latest costume. She swung about the room with mock airs and graces to display it more perfectly, and the men applauded. Good fortune had brought her back a likeness of her former beauty, angles and wrinkles had vanished, there was luster in her hair, and her melting eyes shone clear blue, a trifle faded. In her old age the coquette of twenty years back was returning with a charm which caught brother and son.

"I shall wear one like it at your inauguration, Senator," said she brightly.

"For President? Thank you. But the dress reminds me, Anne," the Senator added with feeling, "of what you were twenty years ago: the sweetest and prettiest girl in the city."

"Oh, you always have the golden word," said she, "and thank you. But you'll not be elected president, only mayor of our own city."

"It might come—in time," the Senator thought.

"And now is the time," cried she so emphatically that he jumped. "Vandervelt told me that no man could be elected unless you said the word. Why shouldn't you say it for yourself? He told me in the same breath he'd like to see you in the place afore any friend he had, because you were a man o' your word, and no wan could lose be your election."

"Did he say all that?"

"Every word, and twice as much," she declared with eagerness. "Now think it over with all your clever brains, Senator dear, and lift up the Dillon name to the first place in the city. Oh, I'd give me life to see that glory."

"And to win it," Arthur added under his breath.

The Senator was impressed, and Arthur had a feeling akin to awe. Who can follow the way of the world? The thread of destiny for the great city up the bay lay between the fingers of this sweet, ambitious house-mother, and of the popular gladiator. Even though she should lead the Senator by the nose to humiliation, the scene was wonderfully picturesque, and her thought daring. He did not know enough history to be aware that this same scene had happened several hundred times in past centuries; but he went out to take another look at the house which sheltered a woman of pluck and genius. The secret of the villa was known. Anne had used it to help in the selection of the next Mayor. He laughed from the depths of his being as he walked along the shore.

The Everard children returned home early in September to enjoy the preparations for the entrance of Louis into the seminary. The time had arrived for him to take up the special studies of the priesthood, and this meant his separation from the home circle forever. He would come and go for years perhaps, but alas! only as a visitor. The soul of Arthur was knit with the lad's as Jonathan with David. He had never known a youth so gracious and so strange, whose heart was like a sanctuary where

Fair gleams the snowy altar-cloth,
   The silver vessels sparkle clean,
The shrill bell rings, the censer swings,
   And solemn chants resound between.

It was with him as with Sir Galahad.

But all my heart is drawn above.
   My knees are bowed in crypt and shrine
I never felt the kiss of love,
   Nor maiden's hand in mine.

Parting with him was a calamity.

"How can you let him go?" he said to Mary Everard, busy with the preparations.

"I am a happy woman that God calls my boy to His service," she answered cheerfully. "The children go anyway ... it's nature. I left father and mother for my own home. How good it is to think he is going to the sanctuary. I know that he is going forever ... he is mine no more ... he will come back often, but he is mine no more. I am heart-broken ... I am keeping a gay face while he is here, for the child must not be worried with our grief ... time enough for that when he is gone ... and he is so happy. My heart is leaving me to go with him. Twenty years since he was born, and in all that time not a moment's pain on his account ... all his life has been ours ... as if he were the father of the family. What shall I be for the rest of my life, listening for his step and his voice, and never a sight or sound of him for months at a time. God give me strength to bear it. If I live to see him on the altar, I shall thank God and die...."

Twenty years she had served him, yet here came the inevitable end, as if such love had never been.

"Oh, you people of faith! I believe you never suffer, nor know what suffering is!"

"Not your kind of suffering, surely, or we would die. Our hope is always with us, and fortunately does not depend on our moods for its power."

89

Mona teased him into good humor. That was a great moment when in presence of the family the lad put on the dress of the seminary, Arthur's gift. Feeling like a prince who clothes his favorite knight in his new armor, Arthur helped him to don the black cassock, tied the ribbons of the surplice, and fixed the three-cornered cap properly on the brown, curly head. A pallor spread over the mother's face. Mona talked much to keep back her tears, and the father declared it a shame to make a priest of so fine a fellow, since there were too many priests in the world for its good. The boy walked about as proud as a young soldier dressed for his first parade. The Trumps, enraptured at the sight, clapped their hands with joy.

"Why, he's a priest," cried Constance, with a twist of her pretty mouth. "Louis is a priest."

"No, Baby," corrected Marguerite, the little mother, "but he is going to be one sometime."

The wonderful garments enchanted them, they feared to touch him, and protested when he swung them high and kissed them on the return flight. The boy's departure for the seminary stirred the region of Cherry Hill. The old neighbors came and went in a steady procession for two days to take their leave of him, to bless his parents, and to wish them the joy of seeing him one day at the altar as a priest of God. They bowed to him with that reverence which belonged to Monsignor, only more familiar and loquacious, and each brought his gift of respect or affection. Even the Senator and the Boss appeared to say a parting word.

"I wish you luck, Louis," the Senator said in his resonant voice, and with the speaker's chair before his eyes, "and I know you'll get it, because you have deserved it, sir. I've seen you grow up, and I've always been proud to know you, and I want to know you as long as I live. If ever you should need a hand like mine in the ga ... I mean, if ever my assistance is of any use to you, you know where to call."

"You have a hard road to travel," the genial Sullivan said at the close of his visit, "but your training has prepared you for it, and we all hope you will walk it honorably to the end. Remember we all take an interest in you, and what happens to you for good or ill will be felt in this parish."

Then the moment of parting came, and Arthur thought less of his own grief than of the revelation it contained for him. Was this the feeling which prompted the tears of his mother, and the tender, speechless embrace of his dear father in the far-off days when he set out for school? Was this the grief which made the parting moment terrible? Then he had thought it nothing that for months of the year they should be without his beloved presence! He shivered at the last embraces of Mary and Mona, at the tears of the children; he saw behind the father's mask of calmness; he wondered no more at himself as he stood looking after the train which bore the boy away. The city seemed as vacant all at once as if turned into a desert. The room in the attic, with its bed, its desk, and its altar, suddenly became a terrible place, like a body from which the soul has fled. Every feature of it gave him pain, and he hurried back with Mona to the frivolity of Anne in her villa by the sea.

CHAPTER X.

THE HUMORS OF ELECTION.

When the villa closed the Senator was hopelessly enmeshed in the golden net which had been so skilfully and genially woven by Anne during the summer. He believed himself to be the coming man, all his natural shrewdness and rich experience going for naught before the witchery of his sister's imagination. In her mind the climax of the drama was a Dillon at the top of the heap in the City Hall. Alas, the very first orders of the chief to his secretary swept away the fine-spun dreams of the Dillons, as the broom brushes into obscure dirt the wondrous cobweb. The Hon. John Sullivan spoke in short sentences, used each man according to that man's nature, stood above and ahead of his cleverest lieutenants, had few prejudices, and these noble, and was truly a hero on the battle-ground of social forces, where no artillery roars, no uniforms glare, and no trumpets sound for the poets. The time having come for action he gave Arthur his orders on the supposition that he understood the political situation, which he did in some degree, but not seriously. The Endicotts looked upon elections as the concern of the rabble, and this Endicott thought it perhaps an occasion for uproarious fun. His orders partly sobered him.

"Go to your uncle," said Sullivan, "and tell him he's not in the race. I don't know where he got that bee in his bonnet. Then arrange with Everard to call on Livingstone. Do what you can to straighten the Mayor out. He ought to be the candidate."

This dealing with men inspired him. Hitherto he had been playing with children in the garden of life; now he stood with the fighters in the terrible arena. And his first task was to extinguish the roseate dreams of Anne and her gladiator, to destroy that exquisite fabric woven of moonlit seas, enchanting dinners, and Parisian millinery. Never! Let the chief commit that sacrilege! He would not say the word whose utterance might wound the hearts that loved him. The Senator and Anne should have a clear field. High time for the very respectable citizens of the metropolis to secure a novelty for mayor, to get a taste of Roman liberty, when a distinguished member of the arena could wear the purple if he had the mind.

Birmingham forced him to change his attitude. The man of money was both good-hearted and large-minded, and had departed from the ways of commerce to seek distinction in politics. Stolid, without enthusiasm or dash, he could be stubbornly great in defence of principle. Success and a few millions had not changed his early theories of life. Pride in his race, delight in his religion, devotion to his party, increased in him as he rose to honor and fame. Arthur Dillon felt still more the seriousness of the position when this man came to ask his aid in securing the nomination.

"There never was a time in the history of the city," said Birmingham, "when a Catholic had such a chance to become mayor as now. Protestants would not have him, if he were a saint. But prejudice has abated, and confidence in us has increased since the war. Sullivan can have the position if he wants it. So can many others. All of them can afford to wait, while I cannot. I am not a politician, only a candidate. At any moment, by the merest accident, I may become one of the impossibles. I am anxious, therefore, to secure the nomination this year. I would like to get your influence. Where the balance is often turned by the weight of a hair one cannot be too alert."

"Do you think I have influence?" said Arthur humbly.

"You are the secretary," Birmingham answered, surprised.

"I shall have to use it in behalf of my uncle then."

"And if your uncle should not run?"

"I should be happy to give you my support."

Birmingham looked as blank as one before whom a door opens unexpectedly.

"You understand," continued Arthur, "that I have been absent too long to grasp the situation clearly. I think my uncle aspires...."

"A very worthy man," murmured Birmingham.

"You seem to think he has not much of a chance...."

"I know something of Sullivan's mind," Birmingham ventured, "and you know it still better. The exploits of the Senator in his youth — really it would be well for him not to expose himself to public ridicule...."

"I had not thought of that," said Arthur, when the other paused delicately. "You are quite right. He should not expose himself. As no other has done me the honor to ask my help, I am free to help you."

"You are more than kind. This nomination means election, and election means the opening of a fine career for me. Beyond lie the governorship, the senate, and perhaps higher things. To us these high offices have been closed as firmly as if they were in Sweden. I want the honor of breaking down the barriers."

"It is time. I hope you will get the honor," said Arthur gravely. He felt sadly about the Senator, and the shining ambition of his mother. How could he shatter their dreams? Yet in very pity the task had to be done, and when next he heard them vaporing on the glory of the future, he said casually:

"I know what your enemies will say if you come into contrast with Livingstone."

"I've heard it often enough," answered the Senator gayly. "If I'd listened to them I'd be still in the ring."

Then a suspicion overcame him, and he cried out bitterly:

"Do you say the same, Artie?"

"Rot. There isn't another like you in the whole world, uncle. If my vote could do it you'd go into the White House to-morrow. If you're in earnest in this business of the nomination, then I'm with you to the last ditch. Now when you become mayor of the first city in the land" —Oh, the smile which flashed on the faces of Anne and the Senator at this phrase! —"you become also the target of every journal in the country, of every comic paper, of every cartoonist. All your little faults, your blunders, past and present, are magnified. They sing of you in the music-halls. Oh, there would be no end to it! Ridicule is worse than abuse. It would hurt your friends more than you. You could not escape it, and no one could answer it. Is the prize worth the pain?"

Then he looked out of the window to escape seeing the pain in his mother's face, and the bitterness in the Senator's. He did not illustrate his contention with examples, for with these the Senator and his friends were familiar. A light arose on the poor man's horizon. Looking timidly at Anne, after a moment's pause, he said:

"I never thought of all that. You've put me on the right track, Artie. I thank you."

"What can I do," he whispered to Anne, "since it's plain he wants me to give in—no, to avoid the comic papers?"

"Whatever he wishes must be done," she replied with a gesture of despair.

"The boy is a wonder," thought the Senator. "He has us all under that little California thumb."

"I was a fool to think of the nomination," he said aloud as Arthur turned from the window. "Of course there'd be no end to the ridicule. Didn't the chap on Harper's, when I was elected for the Senate, rig me out as a gladiator, without a stitch on me, actually, Artie, not a stitch—most indecent thing—and show old Cicero in the same picture looking at me like John Everard, with a sneer, and singing to himself: a senator! No, I couldn't stand it. I give up. I've got as high as my kind can go. But there's one thing, if I can't be mayor myself, I can say who's goin' to be."

"Then make it Birmingham, uncle," Arthur suggested. "I would like to see him in that place next to you."

"And Birmingham it is, unless"—he looked at Anne limp with disappointment—"unless I take it into my head to name you for the place."

She gave a little cry of joy and sat up straight.

"Now God bless you for that word, Senator. It'll be a Dillon anyway."

"In that case I make Birmingham second choice," Arthur said seriously, accepting the hint as a happy ending to a rather painful scene.

The second part of the Chief's order proved more entertaining. To visit the Mayor and sound him on the question of his own renomination appeared to Arthur amusing rather than important; because of his own rawness for such a mission, and also because of their relationship. Livingstone was his kinsman. Of course John Everard gave the embassy character, but his reputation reflected on its usefulness. Nature had not yet provided a key to the character of Louis' father. Arthur endured him because Louis loved him, quoted him admiringly, and seemed to understand him most of the time; but he could not understand an Irishman who maintained, as a principle of history, the inferiority of his race to the English, traced its miseries to its silly pride, opposed all schemes of progress until his principle was accepted, and placed the salvation of his people in that moment when they should have admitted the inferiority imposed by nature, and laid aside their wretched conceit. This perverse nature had a sociable, even humorous side, and in a sardonic way loved its own.

"I have often wondered," Arthur said, when they were discussing the details of the mission to Livingstone, "how your tough fiber ever generated beings so tender and beautiful as Mona, and Louis, and the Trumps. And now I'm wondering why Sullivan associates you and me in this business. Is it his plan to sink the Mayor deeper in his own mud?"

"Whatever his plan I'd like to know what he means in sending with me to the noblest official in the city and the land, for that matter, the notorious orator of a cheap banquet."

"I think it means that Quincy must apologize to the Irish, or nominate himself," said Arthur slowly.

A lively emotion touched him when he first entered the room where the Mayor sat stately and gracious. In him the Endicott features were emphatic and beautiful. Tall, ruddy, perfectly dressed, with white hair and moustache shining like silver, and dark blue eyes full of fire, the aristocrat breathed from him like a perfume. His greeting both for Everard and Dillon had a graciousness tinged with contempt; a contempt never yet perceived by Everard, but perceived and promptly answered on Arthur's part with equal scorn.

"Mr. Dillon comes from Sullivan," said Everard, "to ask you, as a condition of renomination, that you take back your remarks on the Irish last winter. You did them good. They are so soaked in flattery, the flattery of budding orators, that your talk wakes them to the truth."

"I take nothing back," said the Mayor in a calm, sweet voice to which feeling gave an edge.

"Then you do not desire the nomination of Tammany Hall?" Arthur said with a placid drawl, which usually exasperated Everard and other people.

"But I do," the Mayor answered quickly, comprehending on the instant the quality of this antagonist, feeling his own insolence in the tone. "I merely decline the conditions."

"Then you must nominate yourself, for the Irish won't vote for you," cried Everard.

"The leaders would like to give you the nomination, Mr. Livingstone. You may have it, if you can find the means to placate offended voters for your behavior and your utterances on St. Patrick's Day."

"Go down on your knees at once, Mayor," sneered Everard.

"I hope Your Honor does not pay too much attention to the opinions of this gentleman," said Arthur with a gesture for his companion. "He's a Crusoe in politics. There's no one else on his island. You have a history, sir, which is often told in the Irish colony here. I have heard it often since my return home——"

"This is the gentleman who spoke of your policy at the Donnybrook banquet," Everard interrupted.

Livingstone made a sign for silence, and took a closer look at Arthur.

"The Irish do not like you, they have no faith in you as a fair man, they say that you are always planning against them, that you are responsible for the deviltries practised upon them through gospel missions, soup kitchens, kidnapping industries, and political intrigues. Whether these things be true, it seems to me that a candidate ought to go far out of his way to destroy such fancies."

"A very good word, fancies! Are you going to make your famous speech over again?" said Everard with the ready sneer.

"Can you deny that what I have spoken is the truth?"

"It is not necessary that he should," Livingstone answered quietly. "I am not interested in what some people say of me. Tell Mr. Sullivan I am ready to accept the nomination, but that I never retract, never desert a position."

This young man nettled and irritated the Mayor. His insolence, the insolence of his own class, was so subtly and politely expressed, that no fault could be found; and, though his inexperience was evident, he handled a ready blade and made no secret of his disdain. Arthur did not know to what point of the compass the short conversation had carried them, but he took a boy's foolish delight in teasing the irritated men.

"It all comes to this: you must nominate yourself," said Everard.

"And divide the party?"

"I am not sure it would divide the party," Livingstone condescended to say, for he was amused at the simple horror of Dillon. "It might unite it under different circumstances."

"That's the remark of a statesman. And it would rid us, Arthur Dillon, of Sullivan and his kind, who should be running a gin-mill in Hester street."

"If he didn't have a finer experience in politics, and a bigger brain for managing men than any three in the city," retorted Arthur icily. "He is too wise to bring the prejudices of race and creed into city politics. If Your Honor runs on an independent ticket, the Irish will vote against you to a man. One would think that far-seeing men, interested in the city and careful of the future, would hesitate to make dangerous rivalries of this sort. Is there not enough bigotry now?"

"Not that I know," said the Mayor with a pretence of indifference. "We are all eager to keep the races in good humor, but at the same time to prevent the ascendancy of a particular race, except the native. It is the Irish to-day. It will be the Germans to-morrow. Once checked thoroughly, there will be no trouble in the future."

The interview ended with these words. By that time Arthur had gone beyond his political depth, and was glad to make his adieu to the great man. He retained one honest conclusion from the interview.

"Birmingham can thank this pig-headed gentleman," said he to Everard, "for making him mayor of New York."

John snorted his contempt of the statement and its abettors. The report of Arthur disquieted the Chief and his counselors, who assembled to hear and discuss it.

"It's regrettable," was Sullivan's opinion. "Livingstone makes a fine figure in a campaign. He has an attractive name. His independence is popular, and does no harm. He hasn't the interests of the party at heart though. The question now is, can we persuade the Irish to overlook his peculiarities about the green and St. Patrick's Day?"

"A more pertinent question," Vandervelt said after a respectful silence, "would be as to the next available man. I favor Birmingham."

"And I," echoed the Senator.

Arthur listened to the amicable discussion that followed with thoughts not for the candidate, but for the three men who thus determined the history of the city for the next two years. The triumvirs! Cloudy scenes of half-forgotten history rose before him, strange names uttered themselves. Mark Antony and young Octavius and weak Lepidus! He felt suddenly the seriousness of life, and wonder at the ways of men; for he had never stood so near the little gods that harness society to their policies, never till now had he seen with his own eyes how the world is steered. The upshot of endless talk and trickery was the nomination of Birmingham, and the placing of an independent ticket in the field with the Mayor at its head.

"Now for the fun," said Grahame. "It's going to be a big fight. If you want to see the working out of principles keep close to me while the fight is on, and I'll explain things."

The explanation was intricate and long. What did not matter he forgot, but the picturesque things, which touched his own life afterwards very closely, he kept in mind. Trotting about with the journalist they encountered one day a cleric of distinguished appearance.

"Take a good look at him. He's the man that steers Livingstone."

"I thought it was John Everard."

"John doesn't even steer himself," said Grahame savagely. "But take a view of the bishop."

Arthur saw a face whose fine features were shaded by melancholy, tinged with jaundice, gloomy in expression; the mouth drooped at the corners, and the eyes were heavy; one could hardly picture that face lighted by humor or fancy.

"We refuse to discuss certain things in political circles here," Grahame continued. "One of them is the muddle made of politics every little while by dragging in religion. The bishop, Bishop Bradford is his name, never loses a chance to make a mud pie. The independent ticket is his pie this year. He secured Livingstone to bake it, for he's no baker himself. He believes in God, but still more does he believe that the Catholics of this city should be kept in the backyard of society. If they eat his pie, their only ambition will be to live in an American backyard. No word of this ever finds its way into the journals, but it is the secret element in New York politics."

"I thought everything got into the newspapers," Arthur complained. "Blamed if I can get hold of the thing."

"You're right, everything goes into the sewers, but not in a formal way. What's the reason for the independent ticket? Printed: revolt against a domineering boss. Private: to shake the Irish in politics. Do you see? Now, here is a campaign going on. It began last week. It ends in November. But the other campaign has neither beginning nor end. I'll give you object-lessons. There's where the fun comes in."

The first object-lesson brought Arthur to the gospel-hall managed by a gentleman whom he had not seen or thought of since the pleasant celebration of St. Patrick's day. Rev. Mr. McMeeter, evangelist of the expansive countenance, was warming up his gathering of sinners that night with a twofold theme: hell for sinners, and the same, embroidered intensely, for Rome.

"He handles it as Laocoon did the serpents," whispered Grahame.

In a very clerical costume, on a small platform, the earnest man writhed, twisted, and sweated, with every muscle in strain, his face working in convulsions, his lungs beating heaven with sound. He outdid the Trojan hero in the leaps across the platform, the sinuous gestures, the rendings of the enemy; until that moment when he drew the bars of hell for the unrepentant, and flung Rome into the abyss. This effective performance, inartistic and almost grotesque, never fell to the level of the ridiculous, for native power was strong in the man. The peroration raised Livingstone to the skies, chained Sullivan in the lowest depths of the Inferno, and introduced as a terrible example a brand just rescued from the burning.

"Study her, observe her," said Grahame. "These brands have had curious burnings."

She spoke with ease, a little woman in widow's weeds, coquettishly displaying silken brown hair under the ruching of a demure bonnet. Taking her own account—"Which some reporter wrote for her no

101

doubt," Grahame commented—she had been a sinner, a slave of Rome, a castaway bound hand and foot to degrading superstition, until rescued by the noblest of men and led by spirit into the great work of rescuing others from the grinding slavery of the Church of Rome. Very tenderly she appealed to the audience to help her. The prayers of the saints were about to be answered. God had raised up a leader who would strike the shackles off the limbs of the children. The leader, of course, was Mayor Livingstone.

"You see how the spirit works," said Grahame.

Then came an interruption. The Brand introduced a girl of twelve as an illustration of her work of rescue among the dreadful hirelings of Rome. A feeble and ragged woman in the audience rose and cried out that the child was her lost Ellen. The little girl made a leap from the platform but was caught dexterously by the Brand and flung behind the scenes. A stout woman shook her fist in the Brand's face and called her out of her name; and also gave the evangelist a slap in the stomach which taught him a new kind of convulsion. His aids fell upon the stout woman, the tough men of the audience fell upon the aids, the mother of Ellen began shrieking, and some respectable people ran to the door to call the police. A single policeman entered cooly, and laid about him with his stick so as to hit the evangelists with frequency. For a few minutes all things turned to dust, confusion, and bad language. The policeman restored order, dismissed Ellen with her mother, calmed the stout woman, and cautioned the host. The Brand had watched the scene calmly and probably enjoyed it. When Arthur left with Grahame Mr. McMeeter had just begun an address which described the policeman as a satellite, a janizary, and a pretorian of Rome.

"They're doing a very neat job for Livingstone," said Grahame. "Maybe there are fifty such places about the town. Little Ellen was lucky to see her mother again. Most of these stolen children are shipped off to the west, and turned into very good Protestants, while their mothers grieve to death."

"Livingstone ought to be above such work."

"He is. He has nothing in common with a kidnapper like McMeeter. He just accepts what is thrown at him. McMeeter throws his support at him. Only high-class methods attract a man like Livingstone. Sister Claire, the Escaped Nun, is one of his methods. We'll go and see her too. She lectures at Chickering Hall to-night ... comes on about half after nine—tells all about her escape from a prison in a convent ... how she was enslaved ... How sin thrives in convents ... and appeals for help for other nuns not yet escaped ... with reference to the coming election and the great deliverer, Livingstone ... makes a pile of money."

"You seem envious," Arthur hinted.

"Who wouldn't? I can't make a superfluous cent being virtuous, and Sister Claire clears thousands by lying about her neighbors."

They took a seat among the reporters, in front of a decorous, severe, even godly audience, who awaited the coming of the Escaped Nun with religious interest. Amid a profound stillness, she came upon the stage from a rear door, ushered in by an impressive clergyman; and walked forward, a startling figure, to the speaker's place, where she stood with the dignity and modesty of her profession, and a self-possession all her own.

"Stunning," Grahame whispered. "Costume incorrect, but dramatic."

Her dress and veil were of pale yellow, some woolen stuff, the coif and gamp were of white linen, and a red cross marked the entire front of her dress, the arms of the cross resting on her bosom. Arthur stared. Her face of a sickly pallor had deep circles under the eyes, but seemed plump enough for her years. For a moment she stood quietly, with drooping head and uplifted eyes, her hands clasped, a picture of beauty. After a gasp and a pause the audience broke into warm applause long continued. In a sweet and sonorous voice she made her speech, and told her story. It sounded like the *Lady of the Lake* at times. Grahame yawned—he had heard it so often. Arthur gathered that she had somewhere suffered the tortures of the Inquisition, that innocent girls were enjoying the same experience in the convents of the country, that they were deserted both of God and man, and that she alone had taken up their cause. She was a devoted Catholic, and could never change her faith; if she appealed to her audience, it was only to interest them in behalf of her suffering sisters.

"That's the artistic touch," Grahame whispered again. "But it won't pay. Her revelations must get more salaciousness after election."

Arthur hardly heard him. Where had he seen and heard this woman before? Though he could not recall a feature of her face, form, dress, manner, yet he had the puzzling sense of having met her long ago, that her personality was not unfamiliar. Still her features baffled the sense. He studied her in vain. When her lecture ended, with drooping head and clasped hands, she modestly withdrew amid fervid acclamations.

Strange and bewildering were the currents of intrigue that made up a campaign in the great city; not to mention the hidden forces whose current no human could discern. Arthur went about exercising his talent for oratory in behalf of Birmingham, and found consolation in the sincere applause of humble men, and of boys subdued by the charm of his manner. He learned that the true orator expresses not only his own convictions and emotions, but also the unspoken thoughts, the mute feelings, the cloudy convictions of the simple multitude. He is their interpreter to themselves. The thought gave him reverence for that power which had lain long dormant in him until sorrow waked its noble harmonies. The ferment in the city astonished him. The very boys fought in the vacant lots, and reveled in the strategy of crooked streets and blind alleys. Kindly women, suddenly reminded that the Irish were a race of slaves, banged their doors, and flirted their skirts in scorn. Workmen lost their job here and there, mates fought at the workbench, the bully found his excuse to beat the weak, all in the name of Livingstone. The small business men, whose profits came from both sides, did severe penance for their sins of sanded sugar and deficient weight. The police found their nerves overstrained.

To him the entire drama of the campaign had the interest of an impossible romance. It was a struggle between a poor people, cast out by one nation, fighting for a footing on new soil, and a successful few, who had forgotten the sufferings, the similar struggle of their fathers. He rejoiced when Birmingham won. He had not a single regret for the defeat of Livingstone, though it hurt him that a bad cause should have found its leader in his kinsman.

CHAPTER XI.

AN ENDICOTT HEIR.

Meanwhile what of the world and the woman he had left behind? A year had passed, his new personality had begun to fit, and no word or sign direct from the Endicott circle had reached him. Time seemed to have created a profound silence between him and them. Indirectly, however, through the journals, he caught fleeting glimpses of that rage which had filled Sonia with hatred and despair. A description of his person appeared as an advertisement, with a reward of five thousand dollars for information that would lead to the discovery of his whereabouts, or to a certainty of his death. At another time the journals which printed both reward and notice, had a carefully worded plea from his Aunt Lois for letter or visit to soothe the anxieties of her last days. He shook over this reminder of her faithful love until he analyzed the circumstances which had probably led to this burst of publicity. Early in July a letter had informed Sonia of his visit to Wisconsin; two months later a second letter described, in one word, her character, and in six her sentence: adulteress, you shall never see me again. A week's work by her lawyers would have laid bare the fact that the Endicott estate had vanished, and that her own small income was her sole possession.

A careful study of his motives would have revealed in part his plans, and a detective had probably spent a month in a vain pursuit. The detective's report must have startled even the lawyers. All clues led to nothing. Sonia had no money to throw away, nor would she dare to appeal too strongly to Aunt Lois and Horace Endicott's friends, who might learn too much, if she were too candid. The two who loved him were not yet really worried by his disappearance, since they had his significant letter. In time their confidence would give place to anxiety, and heaven and earth would be moved to uncover his hiding-place. This loving notice was a trap set by Sonia. On the road which led from Mulberry Street to Cambridge, from the home of Anne Dillon to the home of Lois Endicott, Sonia's detective lay in wait for the returning steps of the lost husband, and Sonia's eyes devoured the shadows, her ears drank in every sound. He laughed, he grew warm with the feeling of triumph. She would watch and listen in vain. The judgment-seat of God was the appointment he had made for her.

He began now to wonder at the completeness of his own disappearance. His former self seemed utterly beyond the reach of men. The detectives had not only failed to find him, they had not even fallen upon his track by accident. How singular that an Irish colony in the metropolis should be so far in fact and sympathy from the aristocracy. Sonia and her detectives would have thought of Greenland and the Eskimos, Ashanti, Alaska, the court of China, as possible refuges, but never of Cherry Street and the children of Erin, who were farther off from the Endicotts and the Livingstones than the head-hunters of Borneo. Had her detectives by any chance met him on the road, prepared for any disguise, how dumb and deaf and sightless would they become when his position as the nephew of Senator Dillon, the secretary of Sullivan, the orator of Tammany Hall, and the pride of Cherry Hill, shone upon them.

This triumph he would have enjoyed the more could he have seen the effect which the gradual change in his personality had produced on Monsignor O'Donnell, for whom the Endicott episode proved the most curious experience of his career. Its interest was discounted by the responsibility imposed upon him. His only comfort lay in the thought that at any moment he could wash his hands of the affair, before annoying or dangerous consequences began to threaten. He suffered from constant misgivings. The drama of a change in personality went on daily under his eyes, and almost frightened him by its climaxes, which were more distinct to him than to Endicott. First, the pale, worn, savage, and blood-haunted boy who came to him in his first agony; then the melancholy, bearded, yet serene invalid who lay in Anne Dillon's house and was welcomed as her son; next, the young citizen of the Irish colony, known as a wealthy and lucky Californian, bidding for honors as the nephew of Senator Dillon; and last the surprising orator, the idol of the Irish people, their devoted friend, who spared neither labor nor money in serving them.

The awesome things in this process were the fading away of the Endicott and the growing distinctness of the Dillon. At first the old personality lay concealed under the new as under a mask; but something like absorption by degrees obliterated the outlines of Endicott and developed the Dillon. Daily he noticed the new features which sprang into sight between sunrise and sunrise. It was not only the fashion of dress, of body, and of speech, which mimics may adopt; but also a change of countenance, a turn of mind which remained permanent, change of gesture, a deeper color of skin, greater decision in movement; in fact, so many and so minute mutations that he could not recall one-tenth the number. Endicott for instance had possessed an eloquent, lustrous, round eye, with an expression delightfully indolent; in Dillon the roundness and indolence gave way to a malicious wrinkle at the outside corners, which gave his glance a touch of bitterness. Endicott had been gracefully slow in his movement; Dillon was nervous and alert. A fascination of terror held Monsignor as Arthur Dillon grew like his namesake more and more. Out of what depths had this new personality been conjured up? What would be the end of it? He said to himself that a single incident, the death of Sonia, would be enough to destroy on the instant this Dillon and resurrect the Endicott. Still he was not sure, and the longer this terrible process continued the less likely a change back to the normal.

Morbid introspection had become a part of the young man's pain. The study of the changes in himself proved more pleasant than painful. His mind swung between bitter depression, and warm, natural joy. His moments of deepest joy were coincident with an interesting condition of mind. On certain days he completely forgot the Endicott and became the Dillon almost perfectly. Then he no longer acted a part, but was absorbed in it. Most of the time he was Endicott playing the rôle of Dillon, without effort and with much pleasure, indeed, but still an actor. When memory and grief fled from him together, as on St. Patrick's Day, his new personality dominated each instant of consciousness, and banished thought of the old. Then a new spirit rose in him; not merely a feeling of relief from pain, but a positive influence which led him to do surprising and audacious things, like the speech at the banquet. It was a divine forgetfulness, which he prayed might be continuous. He loved to think that some years of his life would see the new personality in full possession of him, while the old would be but a feeble memory, a mere dream of an impossible past. Wonderful, if the little things of the day, small but innumerable, should wipe out in the end an entire youth that took twenty years in building. What is the past after all but a vague horizon made emphatic by the peaks of memory? What is the future but a bare plain with no emphasis at all? Man lives only in the present, like the God whose spirit breathes in him.

Sonia was bent on his not forgetting, however. His heart died within him when he read in the journals the prominent announcement of the birth of a son to the lost Horace Endicott, whose woful fate still troubled the short memory of editors. A son! He crushed the paper in his anguish and fell again into the old depression. Oh, how thoroughly had God punished the hidden crimes of this lost woman! A child would have saved her, and in her hatred of him she had ... he always refused to utter to himself the thought which here rose before his mind. His head bent in agony. This child was not his, perhaps not even hers. She had invented it as a trap for him. Were it really his little one, his flesh and blood, how eagerly he would have thrown off his present life and flown to its rescue from such a mother!

Sonia did not hope for such a result. It was her fraudulent mortgage on the future and its possibilities. The child would be heir to his property; would have the sympathy and inherit the possessions of his Aunt Lois; would lull the suspicions concerning its mother, and conciliate the gossips; and might win him back from hiding, if only to expose the fraud and take shame from the Endicotts. What a clever and daring criminal was this woman! With a cleverness always at fault because of her rare unscrupulousness. Even wickedness has its delicacy, its modesty, its propriety, which a criminal respects in proportion to his genius for crime. Sonia offended all in her daring, and lost at every turn. This trap would catch her own feet. A child! A son! He shuddered at the thought, and thanked God that he had escaped a new dishonor. His blood would never mingle with the puddle in Sonia's veins.

He would not permit her to work this iniquity, and to check her he must risk final success in his plan of disappearance by violating the first principle of the art: that there be no further connection with the past. The detectives were watching the path by which he would return, counting perhaps upon his rage over this fraudulent heir. He must give them their opportunity, if he would destroy Sonia's schemes against Aunt Lois, but felt sure that they would be unprepared to seize it, even if they dreamed it at hand. He had a plan which might accomplish his object without endangering his position; and one night he slipped away from the city on a train for Boston, got off at a lonely station, and plunged into the darkness without a word for a sleepy station-master.

At dawn after two hours' walk he passed the pond which had once seemed to him the door of escape. Poor old friend! Its gray face lay under the morning sky like the face of a dead saint, luminous in its outlines, as if the glory of heaven shone through; still, oh, so still, and deep as if it mirrored immensity. Little complaining murmurs, like the whimperings of a sleepy child, rose up from the reeds, sweeter than any songs. He paused an instant to compare the *then* and *now*, but fled with a groan as the old sorrow, the old madness, suddenly seized him with the powerful grip of that horrid time. In fact, every step of the way to Martha's house was torture. He saw that for him there were other dangers than Sonia and her detectives, in leaving the refuge which God had provided for him. Oh, never could he be too grateful for the blessing, never could he love enough the holy man who had suggested it, never could he repay the dear souls whose love had made it beautiful. They rose up before him as he hurried down the road, the lovable, humorous, rollicking, faulty clan; and he would not have exchanged them for the glories of a court, for the joys of Arcady.

The sun and he found Martha busy with household duties. She did not know him and he said not a word to enlighten her; he was a messenger from a friend who asked of her a service, the carrying of a letter to a certain woman in Boston; and no one should see her deliver the letter, or learn her name, or know her coming and going; for her friend, in hiding, and pursued, must not be discovered. Then she knew that he came from Horace, and shed tears that he lived well and happy, but could not believe, when he had made himself known, that this was the same man of a year before. They spent a happy day together in perfecting the details of her visit to Aunt Lois, which had to be accomplished with great care and secrecy. There was to be no correspondence between them. In two weeks he would come again to hear a report of her success or failure. If she were not at home, he would come two weeks later. She could tell Aunt Lois whatever the old lady desired to hear about him, and assure her that nothing would induce him ever to return to his former life. The letter said as much. When night came they went off over the hills together to the nearest railway station, where he left her to find her way to the city, while he went on to a different station and took a late train to New York. By these methods he felt hopeful that his violation of the rules of disappearing would have no evil results for him, beyond that momentary return of the old anguish which had frightened him more than Sonia's detectives.

In four weeks old Martha returned from her mission, and told this story as they sat in the pleasant kitchen near a cheery fire.

"I rented a room in the neighborhood of your Aunt Lois' house, and settled myself to wait for the most natural opportunity to meet her. It was long in coming, for she had been sick; but when she got better I saw her going out to ride, and a little later she took to walking in the park with her maid. There she often sat, and chatted with passing children, or with old women like herself, poor old things trying to get life from the air. The maid is a spy. She noted every soul about, and had an extra glance for me when your aunt spoke to me, after I had waited three weeks for a word. I told her my story, as I told it to you. She was interested, and I must go to her house to take lunch with her. I refused. I was not used to such invitations, but I would call on her at other times. And the maid listened the more. She was never out of hearing, nor out of sight, until Aunt Lois would get into a rage, and bid her take a walk. It was then I handed her the letter under my shawl. The maid's eyes could not see through the shawl. I told her what you bid me: that you would never return again, no more than if you were dead, that she must burn the letter so that none would know a letter had been received and burned, and that she would understand many things when she had read it; most particular that she was surrounded by spies, and that she must go right on as if nothing had happened, and deceive as she had been deceived.

"I met her only twice after that. I told her my plan to deceive the maid. I was a shrewd beggar studying to get money out of her, with a story about going to my son in Washington. She bid the maid secretly find out if I was worthy, and I saw the maid in private, and begged her to report of me favorably, and she might have half the money, and then I would go away. And the maid was deceived, for she brought me fifty dollars from your aunt, and kept thirty. She would not give even the twenty until I had promised to go away without complaint. So I went away, and stayed with a friend in Worcester. Since I came home I have not seen or heard of any stranger in this neighborhood. So that it is likely I have not been suspected or followed. And the letter was burned. And at the first fair chance your Aunt will go to Europe, taking with her her two dearest relatives. She called them Sonia Endicott and her child Horace, and she would keep them with her while she lived. At the last she sent you her love, though she could not understand some of the things you were doing, but that was your own business. And she never shed a tear, but kept smiling, and her smile was terrible."

He could believe that. Sonia might as well have lived in the glare of Vesuvius as in the enlightened smile of Aunt Lois. The schemer was now in her own toils, and only at the death of the brave old woman would she know her failure. Oh, how sweet and great is even human justice!

"If I do not see you again, Martha," said Arthur as he kissed the dear old mother farewell, "remember that I am happy, and that you made me so."

THE GREEN AGAINST THE RED.

CHAPTER XII.

THE HATE OF HANNIBAL.

Owen Ledwith had a theory concerning the invasion of Ireland, which he began to expound that winter. Since few know much more about the military art than the firing of a shotgun, he won the scorn of all except his daughter and Arthur Dillon. In order to demonstrate his theory Ledwith was willing to desert journalism, to fit out a small ship, and to sail into an Irish harbor from New York and back, without asking leave from any government; if only the money were supplied by the patriots to buy the ship and pay the sailors. His theory held that a fleet of many ships might sail unquestioned from the unused harbors of the American coast, and land one hundred thousand armed men in Ireland, where a blow might be struck such as never had been yet in the good cause. Military critics denied the possibility of such an invasion. He would have liked to perform the feat with a single ship, to convince them.

"I have a suspicion," he said one night to his daughter, "that this young Dillon would give me five thousand dollars for the asking. He is a Fenian now."

"Is it possible?" Honora cried in astonishment.

"Well, I don't see any reason for wonder, Nora. He has been listening to me for three months, vaporing over the wrongs of Ireland; he's of Celtic blood; he has been an adventurer in California; he has the money, it would seem. Why, the wonder would be if he did not do what all the young fellows are doing."

"I have not quite made up my mind about him yet, father," the young woman said thoughtfully.

"He's all man," said the father.

"True, but a man who is playing a part."

He laid down his pipe in his surprise, but she smiled assuringly.

"Well, it's fine acting, if you call it so, my love. In a little over a year he has made himself the pride of Cherry Hill. Your great friend," — this with a sniff—"Monsignor O'Donnell, is his sponsor. He speaks like the orator born and with sincerity, though he knows little of politics. But he has ideas. Then did you ever meet a merrier lad? Such a singer and dancer, such a favorite among boys and girls! He seems to be as lovable as his uncle the Senator, and the proof of it is that all confide in him. However, I have faith in your instincts, Nora. What do they say?"

"He looks at us all like a spectator sitting in front of a stage. Of course I have heard the people talk about him. He is a popular idol, except to his mother who seems to be afraid of him. He has moods of sadness, gloom, and Miss Conyngham told me she would wager he left a wife in California. While all like him, each one has a curious thing to tell about him. They all say it is the sickness which he had on coming home, and that the queer things are leaving him. The impression he gives me is that of one acting a part. I must say it is fading every day, but it hinders me from feeling quite satisfied about him."

"Well, one thing is in his favor: he listens to me," said Ledwith. "He is one of the few men to whom I am not a crazy dreamer, crazy with love of Erin and hate of her shameless foe."

"And I love him for that, father," she said tenderly. "There is no acting in his regard and esteem for you, nothing insincere in his liking for us, even if we cannot quite understand it. For we *are* queer, Daddy," putting her arms about him. "Much love for our old home and much thinking how to help it, and more despair and worry, have shut us off from the normal life, until we have forgotten the qualities which make people liked. Poor Daddy!"

"Better that than doing nothing," he said sadly. "To struggle and fight once in a while mean living; to sit still would be to die."

Arthur was ushered in just then by the servant, and took his place comfortably before the fire. One could see the regard which they felt for him; on the part of Ledwith it was almost affection. Deeply and sincerely he returned their kindly feeling.

He had a host of reasons for his regard. Their position seemed as strange to the humdrum world as his own. They were looked on as queer people, who lived outside the ruts for the sake of an enslaved nation. The idea of losing three meals a day and a fixed home for a hopeless cause tickled the humor of the practical. Their devotion to an idea hardly surpassed their devotion to each other. He mourned for her isolation, she mourned over his failures to free his native land.

"I have almost given the cause up," he said once to Arthur, "because I feel my helplessness. I cannot agree with the leaders nor they with me. But if I gave up she would worry herself to death over my loss of hope. I keep on, half on her account, half in the hope of striking the real thing at the end."

"It seems to be also the breath of her life," said Arthur.

"No, it is not," the father replied. "Have you not heard her talk of your friend, Louis Everard? How she dwells on his calling, and the happiness of it! My poor child, her whole heart yearns for the cloister. She loves all such things. I have urged her to follow her inclinations, though I know it would be the stroke of death for me, but she will not leave me until I die."

"You must not take us too seriously," she had once said, "in this matter of Irish liberties. My father is hopelessly out of the current, for his health is only fair, and he has quarreled with his leaders. I have given up hope of achieving anything. But if he gives up he dies. So, I encourage him and keep marching on, in spite of the bitterest disappointments. Perhaps something may come of it in the end."

"Not a doubt of it," said Arthur, uttering a great thought. "Every tear, every thought, every heart-throb, every drop of sweat and blood, expended for human liberty, must be gathered up by God and laid away in the treasury of heaven. The despots of time shall pay the interest of that fund here or there."

A woman whose ideals embraced the freedom of an oppressed people, devotion to her father, and love for the things of God, would naturally have a strong title to the respect of Arthur Dillon; and she was, besides, a beautiful woman, who spoke great things in a voice so sweetly responsive to her emotions that father and friend listened as to music. The Ledwiths had a comfortable income, when they set to work, earned by his clever pen and her exquisite voice. The young man missed none of her public appearances, though he kept the fact to himself. She was on those occasions the White Lady in earnest. Her art had warmth indeed, but the coldness and aloofness of exalted purity put her beyond the zone of desire; a snowy peak, distinct to the eye, but inaccessible. When they were done with greetings Arthur brought up a specific subject.

"It has gone about that I have become a Fenian," he said, "and I have been called on to explain to many what chance the movement has of succeeding. There was nothing in the initiation which gave me that information."

"You can say: none," Ledwith answered bitterly. "And if you quote me as your authority there will be many new members in the brotherhood."

"Then why keep up the movement, if nothing is to come of it?"

"The fighting must go on," Ledwith replied, "from generation to generation in spite of failure. The Fenian movement will fail like all its predecessors. The only reason for its continuance is that its successor may succeed. Step by step! Few nations are as lucky as this to win in the first fight. Our country is the unluckiest of all. Her battle has been on seven hundred years."

"But I think there must be more consolation in the fight than your words imply;" Arthur declared. "There must be a chance, a hope of winning."

"The hope has never died but the chance does not yet exist, and there is no chance for the Fenians," Ledwith answered with emphasis. "The consolation lies for most of us in keeping up the fight. It is a joy to let our enemy, England, know, and to make her feel, that we hate her still, and that our hate keeps pace with her advancing greatness. It is pleasant to prove to her, even by an abortive rising, that all her crimes, rogueries, and diplomacies against us have been vain to quench our hate. We have been scattered over the world, but our hate has been intensified. It is joy to see her foam at the mouth like a wild beast, then whine to the world over the ingratitude of the Irish; to hear the representatives of her tax-payers howl in Parliament at the expense of putting down regular rebellions; to see the landlords flying out of the country they have ravaged, and the Orangemen white with the fear of slaughter. Then these movements are an education. The children are trained to a knowledge of the position, to hatred of the English power, and their generation takes up the fight where the preceding left it."

"Hate is a terrible thing," said the young man. "Is England so hateful then?"

Honora urged him by looks to change the subject, for her father knew no bounds in speaking of his country's enemy, but he would not lift his eyes to her face. He wished to hear Owen Ledwith express his feelings with full vent on the dearest question to his heart. The man warmed up as he spoke, fire in his eyes, his cheeks, his words, and gestures.

"She is a fiend from hell," he replied, hissing the words quietly. Deep emotion brought exterior calm to Ledwith. "But that is only a feeling of mine. Let us deal with the facts. Like the fabled vampire England hangs upon the throat of Ireland, battening on her blood. Populous England, vanishing Ireland! What is the meaning of it? One people remains at home by the millions, the other flies to other lands by the millions. Because the hell-witch is good to her own. For them the trade of the world, the opening of mines, the building of factories, the use of every natural power, the coddling of every artificial power. They go abroad only to conquer and tax the foreigner for the benefit of those at home. Their harbors are filled with ships, and their treasury with the gold of the world. For our people, there is only permission to work the soil, for the benefit of absentee landlords, or encouragement to depart to America. No mines, no factories, no commerce, no harbors, no ships, in a word no future. So the Irish do not stay at home. The laws of England accomplished this destruction of trade, of art, of education, oh, say it at once, of life. Damnable laws, fashioned by the horrid greed of a rich people, that could not bear to see a poor people grow comfortable. They called over to their departments of trade, of war, of art, to court, camp, and studio, our geniuses, gave them fame, and dubbed them Englishmen; the castaways, the Irish in America and elsewhere are known as 'the mere Irish.'"

"It is very bitter," said Arthur, seeing the unshed tears in Honora's eyes.

"I wonder how we bear it," Ledwith continued. "We have not the American spirit, you may be sure. I can fancy the colonists of a hundred years back meeting an Irish situation; the men who faced the Indian risings, and, worse, the subduing of the wilderness. For them it would have been equal rights and privileges and chances, or the bottom of the sea for one of the countries. But we are poetic and religious, and murderous only when a Cromwell or a Castlereagh opens hell for us. However, the past is nothing; it is the present which galls us. The gilding of the gold and the painting of the lily are symbols of our present sufferings. After stripping and roasting us at home, this England, this hell-witch sends abroad into all countries her lies and slanders about us. Her spies, her professors, her gospellers, her agents, her sympathizers everywhere, can tell you by the yard of our natural inferiority to the Chinese. Was it not an American bishop who protested in behalf of the Chinese of San Francisco that they were more desirable immigrants than the sodden Irish? God! this clean, patient, laborious race, whose chastity is notorious, whose Christianity has withstood the desertion of Christ——"

Honora gave a half scream at the blasphemy, but at once controlled herself.

"I take that back, child—it was only madness," Ledwith said. "You see, Dillon, how scarred my soul is with this sorrow. But the bishop and the Chinese! Not a word against that unfortunate people, whose miseries are greater even than ours, and spring from the same sources. At least *they* are not lied about, and a bishop, forsooth! can compare them, pagans in thought and act and habit though they be, with the most moral and religious people in the world, to his own shame. It is the English lie working. The Irish are inferior, and of a low, groveling, filthy nature; they are buried both in ignorance and superstition; their ignorance can be seen in their hatred of British rule, and their refusal to accept the British religion; wherever they go in the wide world, they reduce the average of decency and intelligence and virtue; for twenty years these lies have been sung in the ears of the nations, until only the enemies of England have a welcome for us. Behold our position in this country. Just tolerated. No place open to us except that of cleaning the sewers. Every soul of us compelled to fight, as Birmingham did the other day, for a career, and to fight against men like Livingstone, who should be our friends. And in the hearts of the common people a hatred for us, a disgust, even a horror, not inspired by the leprous Chinese. We have earned all this hatred and scorn and opposition from England, because in fighting with her we have observed the laws of humanity, when we should have wiped her people off the face of the earth as Saul smote Agag and his corrupt people, as Cromwell treated us. Do you wonder that I hate this England far more than I hate sin, or the devil, or any monstrous creature which feeds upon man."

"I do not wonder," said Arthur. "With you there is always an increasing hatred of England?"

"Until death," cried Ledwith, leaping from his seat, as if the fire of hate tortured him, and striding about the room. "To fight every minute against this monster, to fight in every fashion, to irritate her, to destroy a grain of her influence, in a single mind, in a little community, to expose her pretense, her sham virtues, her splendid hypocrisy, these are the breath of my life. That hate will never perish until— —"

He paused as if in painful thought, and passed his hand over his forehead.

"Until the wrongs of centuries have been avenged," said Arthur. Ledwith sat down with a scornful laugh.

"That's a sentence from the orations of our patriotic orators," he sneered. "What have we to do with the past? It is dead. The oppressed and injured are dead. God has settled their cause long ago. It would be a pretty and consoling sight to look at the present difference between the English Dives and the Irish Lazarus! The vengeance of God is a terrible thing. No! my hate is of the present. It will not die until we have shaken the hold of this vampire, until we have humiliated and disgraced it, and finally destroyed it. I don't speak of retaliation. The sufferings of the innocent and oppressed are not atoned for by the sufferings of other innocents and other oppressed. The people are blameless. The leaders, the accursed aristocracy of blood, of place, of money, these make the corporate vampire, which battens upon the weak and ignorant poor; only in England they give them a trifle more, flatter them with skill, while the Irish are kicked out like beggars."

He looked at Dillon with haggard eyes. Honora sat like a statue, as if waiting for the storm to pass.

"I have not sworn an oath like Hannibal," he said, "because God cannot be called as a witness to hate. But the great foe of Rome never observed his oath more faithfully than I shall that compact which I have made with myself and the powers of my nature: to turn all my strength and time and capacity into the channel of hate against England. Oh, how poor are words and looks and acts to express that fire which rages in the weakest and saddest of men."

He sank back with a gesture of weariness, and found Honora's hand resting on his tenderly.

"The other fire you have not mentioned, Daddy," she said wistfully, "the fire of a love which has done more for Erin than the fire of hate. For love is more than hate, Daddy."

"Ay, indeed," he admitted. "Much as I hate England, what is it to my love for her victim? Love is more than hate. One destroys, the other builds."

Ledwith, quite exhausted by emotion, became silent. The maid entered with a letter, which Honora opened, read silently, and handed to her father without comment. His face flushed with pleasure.

"Doyle Grahame writes me," he explained to Arthur, "that a friend, who wishes to remain unknown, has contributed five thousand dollars to testing my theory of an invasion of Ireland. That makes the expedition a certainty—for May."

"Then let me volunteer the first for this enterprise," said Arthur blithely.

"And me the second," cried Honora with enthusiasm.

"Accepted both," said Ledwith, with a proud smile, new life stealing into his veins.

Not for a moment did he suspect the identity of his benefactor, until Monsignor, worried over the risk for Arthur came to protest some days later. The priest had no faith in the military enterprise of the Fenians, and, if he smiled at Arthur's interest in conspiracy, saw no good reasons why he should waste his money and expose his life and liberty in a feeble and useless undertaking. His protest both to Arthur and others was vigorous.

"If you have had anything to do with making young Dillon a Fenian," he said, "and bringing him into this scheme of invasion, Owen, I would like you to undo the business, and persuade him to stay at home."

"Which I shall not do, you may be sure, Monsignor," replied the patriot politely. "I want such men. The enemy we fight sacrifices the flower of English youth to maintain its despotism; why should we shrink from sacrifice?"

"I do not speak of sacrifice," said Monsignor. "One man is the same as another. But there are grave reasons which demand the presence of this young man in America, and graver reasons why he should not spend his money incautiously."

"Well, he has not spent any money yet, so far as I know," Ledwith said.

The priest hesitated a moment, while the other looked at him curiously.

"You are not aware, then, that he has provided the money for your enterprise?" Honora uttered a cry, and Ledwith sprang from his chair in delighted surprise.

"Do you tell me that?" he shouted. "Honora, Honora, we have found the right man at last! Oh, I felt a hundred times that this young fellow was destined to work immense good for me and mine. God bless him forever and ever."

"Amen," said Honora, rejoicing in her father's joy.

"You know my opinion on these matters, Owen," said Monsignor.

"Ay, indeed, and of all the priests for that matter. Had we no religion the question of Irish freedom would have been settled long ago. Better for us had we been pagans or savages. Religion teaches us only how to suffer and be slaves."

"And what has patriotism done for you?" Monsignor replied without irritation.

"Little enough, to be sure."

"Now, since I have told you how necessary it is that Dillon should remain in America, and that his money should not be expended——"

"Monsignor," Ledwith broke in impatiently, "let me say at once you are asking what you shall not get. I swear to you that if the faith which you preach depended on getting this young fellow to take back his money and to desert this enterprise, that faith would die. I want men, and I shall take the widow's only son, the father of the family, the last hope of a broken heart. I want money, and I shall take the crust from the mouth of the starving, the pennies from the poor-box, the last cent of the poor, the vessels of the altar, anything and everything, for my cause. How many times has our struggle gone down in blood and shame because we let our foolish hearts, with their humanity, their faith, their sense of honor, their ridiculous pride, rule us. I want this man and his money. I did not seek them, and I shall not play tricks to keep them. But now that they are mine, no man shall take them from me."

Honora made peace between them, for these were stubborn men, unwilling to make compromises. Monsignor could give only general reasons. Ledwith thought God had answered his prayers at last. They parted with equal determination.

What a welcome Arthur Dillon received from the Ledwiths on his next visit! The two innocents had been explaining their ideas for years, and traveling the earth to put them into action; and in all that time had not met a single soul with confidence enough to invest a dollar in them. They had spent their spare ducats in attempting what required a bank to maintain. They had endured the ridicule of the hard-hearted and the silent pity of the friends who believed them foolish dreamers. And behold a man of money appears to endow their enterprise, and to show his faith in it by shipping as a common member of the expedition. Was there ever such luck? They thanked him brokenly, and looked at him with eyes so full of tenderness and admiration and confidence, that Arthur swore to himself he would hereafter go about the earth, hunting up just such tender creatures, and providing the money to make their beautiful, heroic, and foolish dreams come true. He began to feel the truth of a philosopher's saying: the dreams of the innocent are the last reasoning of sages.

"And to this joy is added another," said Ledwith, when he could speak steadily. "General Sheridan has promised to lead a Fenian army the moment the Irish government can show it in the field."

"What does that mean?" said Arthur.

"What does it mean that an Irish army on Irish soil should have for its leader a brilliant general like Sheridan?" cried Ledwith. A new emotion overpowered him. His eyes filled with tears. "It means victory for a forlorn cause. Napoleon himself never led more devoted troops than will follow that hero to battle. Washington never received such love and veneration as he will from the poor Irish, sick with longing for a true leader. Oh, God grant the day may come, and that we may see it, when that man will lead us to victory."

His eyes flashed fire. He saw that far-off future, the war with its glories, the final triumph, the crowning of Sheridan with everlasting fame. And then without warning he suddenly fell over into a chair. Arthur lifted up his head in a fright, and saw a pallid face and lusterless eyes. Honora bathed his temples, with the coolness and patience of habit.

"It is nothing, nothing," he said feebly after a moment. "Only the foolishness of it all ... I can forget like a boy ... the thing will never come to pass ... never, never, never! There stands the hero, splendid with success, rich in experience, eager, willing, a demigod whom the Irish could worship ... his word would destroy faction, wipe out treason, weed out fools, hold the clans in solid union ... if we could give him an army, back him with a government, provide him with money! We shall never have the army ... nothing. Treason breeding faction, faction inviting treason ... there's our story. O, God, ruling in heaven, but not on earth, why do you torture us so? To give us such a man, and leave us without the opportunity or the means of using him!"

He burst into violent, silent weeping. Dillon felt the stab of that hopeless grief, which for the moment revived his own, although he could not quite understand it. Ledwith dashed away the tears after a little and spoke calmly.

"You see how I can yield to dreams like a foolish child. I felt for a little as if the thing had come to pass, and gave in to the fascination. This is the awaking. All the joy and sorrow of my life have come mostly from dreams."

CHAPTER XIII.

ANNE DILLON'S FELICITY.

Monsignor was not discouraged by his failure to detach Arthur from the romantic expedition to the Irish coast. With a view to save him from an adventure so hurtful to his welfare, he went to see Anne Dillon. Her home, no longer on Mulberry Street, but on the confines of Washington Square, in a modest enough dwelling, enjoyed that exclusiveness which is like the atmosphere of a great painting. One feels by instinct that the master hand has been here. Although aware that good fortune had wrought a marked change in Anne, Monsignor was utterly taken aback by a transformation as remarkable in its way as the metamorphosis of Horace Endicott.

Judy Haskell admitted him, and with a reverence showed him into the parlor; the same Judy Haskell as of yore, ornamented with a lace cap, a collar, deep cuffs, and an apron; through which her homeliness shone as defiantly as the face of a rough mountain through the fog. She had been instructed in the delicate art of receiving visitors with whom her intimacy had formerly been marked; but for Monsignor she made an exception, and the glint in her eye, the smile just born in the corner of her emphatic mouth, warned him that she knew of the astonishment which his good breeding concealed.

"We're mountin' the laddher o' glory," she said, after the usual questions. "Luk at me in me ould age, dhressed out like a Frinch sportin' maid. If there was a baby in the house ye'd see me, Father Phil, galivantin' behind a baby-carriage up an' down the Square. Faith, she does it well, the climbin', if we don't get dizzy whin we're halfway up, an' come to earth afore all the neighbors, flatter nor pancakes."

"Tut, tut," said Monsignor, "are you not as good as the best, with the blood of the Montgomerys and the Haskells in your veins? Are you to make strange with all this magnificence, as if you were Indians seeing it for the first time?"

"That's what I've been sayin' to meself since it began," she replied.

"Since what began?"

"Why, the changin' from Mulberry Sthreet Irish to Washington Square Yankees," Judy said with a shade of asperity. "It began wid the dog-show an' the opera. Oh, but I thought I'd die wid laughin', whin I had to shtan' at the doors o' wan place or the other, waitin' on Micksheen, or listenin' to the craziest music that ever was played or sung. After that kem politics, an' nothin' wud do her but she'd bate ould Livingstone for Mare all by herself. Thin it was Vandervelt for imbassador to England, an' she gev the Senator an' the Boss no pace till they tuk it up. An' now it's the Countess o' Skibbereen mornin', noon, an' night. I'm sick o' that ould woman. But she owns the soul of Anne Dillon."

"Well, her son can afford it," said Monsignor affably. "Why shouldn't she enjoy herself in her own way?"

"Thrue for you, Father Phil; I ought to call you Morrisania, but the ould names are always the shweetest. He has the money, and he knows how to spind it, an' if he didn't she'd show him. Oh, but he's the fine b'y! Did ye ever see annywan grow more an' more like his father, pace to his ashes. Whin he first kem it wasn't so plain, but now it seems to me he's the very spit o' Pat Dillon. The turn of his head is very like him."

At this point in a chat, which interested Monsignor deeply, a soft voice floated down from the upper distance, calling, "Judy! Judy!" in a delicate and perfect French accent.

"D'ye hear that, Father Phil?" whispered Judy with a grin. "It's nothin' now but Frinch an' a Frinch masther. Wait till yez hear me at it."

She hastened to the hall and cried out, "Oui, oui, Madame," with a murmured aside to the priest, "It's all I know."

"Venez en haut, Judy," said the voice.

"Oui, oui, Madame," answered Judy. "That manes come up, Father Phil," and Judy walked off upright, with folded arms, swinging her garments, actions belied by the broad grin on her face, and the sarcastic motion of her lips, which kept forming the French words with great scorn.

A few minutes afterward Anne glided into the room. The Montgomery girls had all been famous for their beauty in the earlier history of Cherry Hill, and Anne had been the belle of her time. He remembered her thirty years back, on the day of her marriage, when he served as altar-boy at her wedding; and recalled a sweet-faced girl, with light brown silken hair, languorous blue eyes, rose-pink skin, the loveliest mouth, the most provoking chin. Time and sorrow had dealt harshly with her, and changed her, as the fairies might, into a thin-faced, gray-haired, severe woman, whose dim eyes were hidden by glasses. She had retained only her grace and dignity of manner. He recalled all this, and drew his breath; for before him stood Anne Montgomery, as she had stood before him at the altar; allowing that thirty years had artistically removed the youthful brilliance of youth, but left all else untouched. The brown hair waved above her forehead, from her plump face most of the wrinkles had disappeared, her eyes gleamed with the old time radiance, spectacles had been banished, a subdued color tinted her smiling face.

"Your son is not the only one to astound me," said Monsignor. "Anne, you have brought back your youth again. What a magician is prosperity."

"It's the light-heartedness, Monsignor. To have as much money as one can use wisely and well, to be done with scrimpin' forever, gives wan a new heart, or a new soul. I feel as I felt the day I was married."

She might have added some information as to the share which modiste and beautifier might claim in her rejuvenation, but Monsignor, very strict and happily ignorant of the details of the toilet, as an ecclesiastic should be, was lost in admiration of her. It took him ten minutes to come to the object of his visit.

"He has long been ahead of you," she said, referring to Arthur. "I asked him for leave to visit Ireland, and he gave it on two conditions: that I would take Louis and Mona wid me, and refuse to interfere with this Fenian business, no matter who asked me. I was so pleased that I promised, and of course I can't go back on me word."

"This is a very clever young man," said Monsignor, admiring Anne's skill in extinguishing her beautiful brogue, which, however, broke out sweetly at times.

"Did you ever see the like of him?" she exclaimed. "I'm afraid of him. He begins to look like himself and like his father ... glory be to God ... just from looking at the pictures of the two and thinkin' about them. He's good and generous, but I have never got over being afeared of him. It was only when he went back on his uncle ... on Senator Dillon ... that I plucked up courage to face him. I had the Senator all ready to take the place which Mr. Birmingham has to-day, when Arthur called him off."

"He never could have been elected, Anne."

"I never could see why. The people that said that didn't think Mr. Vandervelt could be made ambassador to England, at least this time. But he kem so near it that Quincy Livingstone complimented me on my interest for Mr. Vandervelt. And just the same, Dan Dillon would have won had he run for the office. It was with him a case of not wantin' to be de trop."

"Your French is très propos, Anne," said Monsignor with a laugh.

"If you want to hear an opinion of it," said the clever woman, laughing, too, "go and hear the complaints of Mary and Sister Magdalen. Mais je suis capable de parler Français tout de même."

"And are you still afraid of Arthur? Wouldn't you venture on a little protest against his exposing himself to needless danger?"

"I can do that, certainement, but no more. I love him, he's so fine a boy, and I wish I could make free wid him; but he terrifies me when I think of everything and look at him. More than wanst have I seen Arthur Dillon looking out at me from his eyes; and sometimes I feel that Pat is in the room with me when he is around. As I said, I got courage to face him, and he was grieved that I had to. For he went right into the contest over Vandervelt, and worked beautifully for the Countess of Skibbereen. I'm to dine with her at the Vandervelts' next week, the farewell dinner."

Her tones had a velvet tenderness in uttering this last sentence. She had touched one of the peaks of her ambition.

"I shall meet you there," said Monsignor, taking a pinch of snuff. "Anne, you're a wonderful woman. How have all these wonders come about?"

"It would take a head like your own to tell," she answered, with a meaning look at her handsome afternoon costume. "But I know some of the points of the game. I met Mr. Vandervelt at a reception, and told him he should not miss his chance to be ambassador, even if Livingstone lost the election and wanted to go to England himself. Then he whispered to me the loveliest whisper. Says he, 'Mrs. Dillon, they think it will be a good way to get rid of Mr. Livingstone if he's defeated,' says he; 'but if he wins I'll never get the high place, says he, 'for Tammany will be of no account for years.'"

Anne smiled to herself with simple delight over that whispered confidence of a Vandervelt, and Monsignor sat admiring this dawning cleverness. He noticed for the first time that her taste in dress was striking and perfect, as far as he could judge.

"'Then' says I, 'Mr. Vandervelt,' says I, 'there's only wan thing to be done, wan thing to be done,' says I. 'Arthur and the Senator and Doyle Grahame and Monsignor must tell Mr. Sullivan along wid Mr. Birmingham that you should go to England this year. 'Oh,' said he, 'if you can get such influence to work, nothing will stop me but the ill-will of the President.' 'And even there,' said I, 'it will be paving the way for the next time, if you make a good showing this time.' 'You see very far and well,' said he. That settled it. I've been dinin' and lunching with the Vandervelts ever since. You know yourself, Monsignor, how I started every notable man in town to tell Mr. Sullivan that Vandervelt must go to England. We failed, but it was the President did it; but he gave Mr. Vandervelt his choice of any other first-class mission. Then next, along came the old Countess of Skibbereen, and she was on the hands of the Vandervelts with her scheme of getting knitting-machines for the poor people of Galway. She wasn't getting on a bit, for she was old and queer in her ways, and the Vandervelts were worried over it. Then I said: 'why not get up a concert, and have Honora sing and let Tammany take up one end and society the other, and send home the Countess with ten thousand dollars?' My dear, they jumped at it, and the Countess jumped at me. Will you ever forget it, Monsignor dear, the night that Honora sang as the Genius of Erin? If that girl could only get over her craziness for Ireland and her father—but that's not what I was talking about. Well, the Countess has her ten thousand dollars, and says I'm the best-dressed woman in New York. So, that's the way I come to dine with the Vandervelts at the farewell dinner to the Countess, and when it comes off New York will be ringing with the name of Mrs. Montgomery Dillon."

"Is that the present name?" said Monsignor. "Anne, if you go to Ireland you'll return with a title. Your son should be proud of you."

"I'll give him better reason before I'm done, Monsignor."

The prelate rose to go, then hesitated a moment.

"Do you think there is anything?—do you think there could be anything with regard to Honora Ledwith?"

She stopped him with a gesture.

"I have watched all that. Not a thing could happen. Her thoughts are in heaven, poor child, and his are busy with some woman that bothered him long ago, and may have a claim on him. No wan told me, but my seein' and hearing are sharp as ever."

"Good-by, Mrs. Montgomery Dillon," he said, bowing at the door.

"Au plaisir, Monseigneur," she replied with a curtsey, and Judy opened the outer door, face and mien like an Egyptian statue of the twelfth dynasty.

Anne Dillon watched him go with a sigh of deep contentment. How often she had dreamed of men as distinguished leaving her presence and her house in this fashion; and the dream had come true. All her life she had dreamed of the elegance and importance, which had come to her through her strange son, partly through her own ambition and ability. She now believed that if one only dreams hard enough fortune will bring dreams true. As the life which is past fades, for all its reality, into the mist-substance of dreams, why should not the reverse action occur? Had she been without the rich-colored visions which illuminated her idle hours, opportunity might have found her a spiritless creature, content to take a salary from her son and to lay it by for the miserable days of old age. Out upon such tameness! She had found life in her dreams, and the two highest expressions of that life were Mrs. Montgomery Dillon and the Dowager Countess of Skibbereen.

As a pagan priestess might have arrayed herself for appearance in the sanctuary, she clothed herself in purple and gold on the evening of the farewell dinner.

Arthur escorted his mother and Honora to the Vandervelt residence.

As the trio made their bows, the aspirant for diplomatic honors rejoiced that his gratitude for real favors reflected itself in objects so distinguished. He was a grateful man, this Vandervelt, and broad-minded, willing to gild the steps by which he mounted, and to honor the humblest who honored him: an aristocrat in the American sense of the term, believing that those who wished should be encouraged to climb as high as natural capacity and opportunity permitted. The party sat down slightly bored, they had gone through it so often; but for Anne Dillon each moment and each circumstance shone with celestial beauty. She floated in the ether. The mellow lights, the glitter of silver and glass, the perfume of flowers, the soft voices, all sights and sounds, made up a harmony which lifted her body from the ground as on wings, more like a dream than her richest dreams. For conversation, some one started Lord Constantine on his hobby, and said Arthur was a Fenian, bent on destroying the hobby forever. In the discussion the Countess appealed to Anne.

"We are a fighting race," said she, with admirable caution picking her steps through a long paragraph. "There's—there are times when no one can hold us. This is such a time. A few months back the Fenian trouble could have been settled in one week. Now it will take a year."

"But how?" said Vandervelt. "If you had the making of the scheme, I'm sure it would be a success."

"In this way," she answered, bowing and smiling to his sincere compliment, "by making all the Irish Fenians, that is, those in Ireland, policemen."

The gentlemen laughed with one accord.

"Mr. Sullivan manages his troublesome people that way," she observed triumphantly.

"You are a student of the leader," said Vandervelt.

"Everybody should study him, if they want to win," said Anne.

"And that's wisdom," cried Lord Constantine.

The conversation turned on opera, and the hostess wondered why Honora did not study for the operatic stage. Then they all urged her to think of the scheme.

"I hope," said Anne gently, "that she will never try to spoil her voice with opera. The great singers give me the chills, and the creeps, and the shivers, the most terrible feeling, which I never had since the day Monsignor preached his first sermon, and broke down."

"Oh, you dear creature," cried the Countess, "what a long memory you have."

Monsignor had to explain his first sermon. So it went on throughout the dinner. The haze of perfect happiness gathered about Anne, and her speech became inspired. A crown of glory descended upon her head when the Dowager, hearing of her summer visit to Ireland with Mona and Louis in her care, exacted a solemn promise from her that the party should spend one month with her at Castle Moyna, her dower home.

"That lovely boy and girl," said the Countess, "will find the place pleasant, and will make it pleasant for me; where usually I can induce not even my son's children to come, they find it so dull."

It did not matter much to Anne what happened thereafter. The farewells, the compliments, the joy of walking down to the coach on the arm of Vandervelt, were as dust to this invitation of the Dowager Countess of Skibbereen. The glory of the dinner faded away. She looked down on the Vandervelts from the heights of Castle Moyna. She lost all at once her fear of her son. From that moment the earth became as a rose-colored flame. She almost ignored the adulation of Cherry Hill, and the astonished reverence of her friends over her success. Her success was told in awesome whispers in the church as she walked to the third pew of the middle aisle. A series of legends grew about it, over which the experienced gossips disputed in vain; her own description of the dinner was carried to the four quarters of the world by Sister Magdalen, Miss Conyngham, Senator Dillon, and Judy; the skeptical and envious pretended to doubt even the paragraph in the journals. At last they were struck dumb with the rest when it was announced that on Saturday last Mrs. Montgomery Dillon, Miss Mona Everard, and Mr. Louis Everard had sailed on the City of London for a tour of Europe, the first month of which would be spent at Castle Moyna, Ireland, as guests of the Dowager Countess of Skibbereen!

CHAPTER XIV.

ABOARD THE "ARROW."

One month later sailed another ship. In the depth of night the *Arrow* slipped her anchor, and stole away from the suspicious eyes of harbor officials into the Atlantic; a stout vessel, sailed with discretion, her trick being to avoid no encounters on the high seas and to seek none. Love and hope steered her course. Her bowsprit pointed, like the lance of a knight, at the power of England. Her north star was the freedom of a nation. War had nothing to do with her, however, though her mission was warlike: to prove that one hundred similar vessels might sail from various parts to the Irish coast, and land an army and its supplies without serious interference from the enemy. The crew was a select body of men, whose souls ever sought the danger of hopeless missions, as others seek a holiday. In spite of fine weather and bracing seas, the cloud of a lonely fate hung over the ship. Arthur alone was enthusiastic. Ledwith, feverish over slight success, because it roused the dormant appetite for complete success, and Honora, fed upon disappointment, feared that this expedition would prove ashen bread as usual; but the improvement in her father's health kept her cheerful. Doyle Grahame, always in high spirits, devoted his leisure to writing the book which was to bring him fame and much money. He described its motive and aim to his companions.

"It calls a halt," he said "on the senseless haste of Christians to take up such pagans as Matthew Arnold, and raises a warning cry against surrender to the pagan spirit which is abroad."

"And do you think that the critics will read it and be overcome?" asked Arthur.

"It will convince the critics, not that they are pagans, but that I am. They will review it, therefore, just to annoy me."

"You reason just like a critic, from anywhere to nowhere."

"The book will make a stir, nevertheless," and Doyle showed his confidence.

"It's to be a loud protest, and will tangle the supple legs of Henry Ward Beecher and other semi-pagans like a lasso."

"How about the legs of the publishers?"

"That's their lookout. I have nothing against them, and I hope at the close of the sale they will have nothing against me."

"When, where, with what title, binding and so forth?"

"Speak not overmuch to thy dentist," said Grahame slyly. "Already he knoweth too many of thy mouth's secrets."

The young men kept the little company alive with their pranks and their badinage. Grahame discovered in the Captain a rare personality, who had seen the globe in its entirety, particularly the underside, as a detective and secret service agent for various governments. He was a tall, slender man, rather like a New England deacon than a daring adventurer, with a refined face, a handsome beard, and a speaking, languid gray eye. He spent the first week in strict devotion to his duties, and in close observation of his passengers. In the second week Grahame had him telling stories after dinner for the sole purpose of diverting the sad and anxious thoughts of Honora, although Arthur hardly gave her time to think by the multiplied services which he rendered her. There came an afternoon of storm, followed by a nasty night, which kept all the passengers in the cabin; and after tea there, a demand was made upon Captain Richard Curran for the best and longest story in his repertory. The men lit pipes and cigars, and Honora brought her crotcheting. The rolling and tossing of the ship, the beating of the rain, and the roar of the wind, gave them a sense of comfort. The ship, in her element, proudly and smoothly rode the rough waves, showing her strength like a racer.

"Let us have a choice, Captain," said Grahame, as the officer settled himself in his chair. "You detectives always set forth your successes. Give us now a story of complete failure, something that remains a mystery till now."

"Mystery is the word," said Honora. "This is a night of mystery. But a story without an end to it — —"

"Like the history of Ireland," said Ledwith dryly.

"Is the very one to keep us thinking and talking for a month," said Grahame. "Captain, if you will oblige us, a story of failure and of mystery."

"Such a one is fresh in my mind, for I fled from my ill-success to take charge of this expedition," said the Captain, whose voice was singularly pleasant. "The detective grows stale sometimes, as singers and musicians do, makes a failure of his simplest work, and has to go off and sharpen his wits at another trade. I am in that condition. For twenty months I sought the track of a man, who disappeared as if the air absorbed him where he last breathed. I did not find him. The search gave me a touch of monomania. For two months I have not been able to rest upon meeting a new face until satisfied its owner was not — let us say, Tom Jones."

"Are you satisfied, then," said Arthur, "that we are all right?"

"He was not an Irishman, but a Puritan," replied the Captain, "and would not be found in a place like this. I admit I studied your faces an hour or so, and asked about you among the men, but under protest. I have given up the pursuit of Tom Jones, and I wish he would give up the pursuit of me. I had to quiet my mind with some inquiries."

"Was there any money awaiting Tom? If so, I might be induced to be discovered," Grahame said anxiously.

"You are all hopeless, Mr. Grahame. I have known you and Mr. Ledwith long enough, and Mr. Dillon has his place secure in New York — —"

"With a weak spot in my history," said Arthur. "I was off in California, playing bad boy for ten years."

The Captain waved his hand as admitting Dillon's right to his personality.

"In October nearly two years ago the case of Tom Jones was placed in my care with orders to report at once to Mrs. Tom. The problem of finding a lost man is in itself very simple, if he is simply lost or in hiding. You follow his track from the place where he was last seen to his new abode. But around this simple fact of disappearance are often grouped the interests of many persons, which make a tangle worse than a poor fisherman's line. A proper detective will make no start in his search until the line is as straight and taut as if a black bass were sporting at the other end of it."

All the men exchanged delighted glances at this simile.

"I could spin this story for three hours straight talking of the characters who tangled me at the start. But I did not budge until I had unraveled them every one. Mrs. Jones declared there was no reason for the disappearance of Tom; his aunt Quincy said her flightiness had driven him to it; and Cousin Jack, Mrs. Tom's adviser, thought it just a freak after much dissipation, for Tom had been acting queerly for months before he did the vanishing act. The three were talking either from spleen or the wish to hide the truth. When there was no trace of Tom after a month of ordinary searching much of the truth came out, and I discovered the rest. Plain speech with Mrs. Tom brought her to the half-truth. She was told that her husband would never be found if the detective had to work in the dark. She was a clever woman, and very much worried, for reasons, over her husband's disappearance. It was something to have her declare that he had suspected her fidelity, but chiefly out of spleen, because she had discovered his infidelity. A little sifting of many statements, which took a long time, for I was on the case nearly two years, as I said, revealed Mrs. Tom as a remarkable woman. In viciousness she must have been something of a monster, though she was beautiful enough to have posed for an angel. Her corruption was of the marrow. She breathed crime and bred it. But her blade was too keen. She wounded herself too often. Grit and ferocity were her strong points. We meet such women occasionally. When she learned that I knew as much about her as need be, she threw off hypocrisy, and made me an offer of ten thousand dollars to find her husband."

"I felt sure then of the money. Disappearance, for a living man, if clever people are looking for him, is impossible nowadays. I can admit the case of a man being secretly killed or self-buried, say, for instance, his wandering into a swamp and there perishing: these cases of disappearance are common. But if he is alive he can be found."

"Why are you so sure of that?" said Arthur.

"Because no man can escape from his past, which is more a part of him than his heart or his liver," said Curran. "That past is the pathway which leads to him. If you have it, it's only a matter of time when you will have him."

"Yet you failed to find Tom Jones."

"For the time, yes," said the Captain with an eloquent smile. "Then, I had an antagonist of the noblest quality. Tom Jones was a bud of the Mayflower stock. All his set agreed that he was an exceptional man: a clean, honest, upright chap, the son of a soldier and a peerless mother, apparently an every-day lad, but really as fine a piece of manhood as the world turns out. Anyhow, I came to that conclusion about him when I had studied him through the documents. What luck threw him between the foul jaws of his wife I can't say. She was a——"

The detective coughed before uttering the word, and looked at the men as he changed the form of his sentence.

"She was a cruel creature. He adored her, and she hated him, and when he was gone slandered him with a laugh, and defiled his honest name."

"Oh," cried Honora with a gasp of pain, "can there be such women now? I have read of them in history, but I always felt they were far off——"

"I hope they are not many," said the Captain politely, "but in my profession I have met them. Here was a case where the best of men was the victim of an Agrippina."

"Poor, dear lad," sighed she, "and of course he fled from her in horror."

"He was a wonder, Miss Ledwith. Think what he did. Such a man is more than a match for such a woman. He discovered her unfaithfulness months before he disappeared. Then he sold all his property, turning all he owned into money, and transferred it beyond any reach but his own, leaving his wife just what she brought him—an income from her parents of fifteen hundred a year: a mere drop to a woman whom he had dowered with a share in one hundred thousand. Though I could not follow the tracks of his feet, I saw the traces of his thoughts as he executed his scheme of vengeance. He discovered her villainy, he would have no scandal, he was disgusted with life, so he dropped out of it with the prize for which she had married him, and left her like a famished wolf in the desert. It would have satisfied him to have seen her rage and dismay, but he was not one of the kind that enjoys torture."

"I watched Mrs. Tom for months, and felt she was the nearest thing to a demon I had ever met. Well, I worked hard to find Tom. We tried many tricks to lure him from his hiding-place, if it were near by, and we followed many a false trail into foreign lands. The result was dreadful to me. We found nothing. When a child was born to him, and the fact advertised, and still he did not appear, or give the faintest sign, I surrendered. It would be tedious to describe for you how I followed the sales of his property, how I examined his last traces, how I pursued all clues, how I wore myself out with study. At the last I gave out altogether and cut the whole business. I was beginning to have Tom on the brain. He came to live on my nerves, and to haunt my dreams, and to raise ghosts for me. He is gone two years, and Mrs. Tom is in Europe with her baby and Tom's aunt Quincy. When I get over my present trouble, and get back a clear brain, I shall take up the search. I shall find him yet. I'd like to show some of the documents, but the matter is still confidential, and I must keep quiet, though I don't suppose you know any of the parties. When I find him I shall finish the story for you."

"You will never find him," said Honora with emphasis. "That fearful woman shattered his very soul. I know the sort of a man he was. He will never go back. If he can bear to live, it will be because in his obscurity God gave him new faith and hope in human nature, and in the woman's part of it."

"I shall find him," said the detective.

"You won't," said Grahame. "I'll wager he has been so close to you all this time, that you cannot recognize him. That man is living within your horizon, if he's living at all. Probably he has aided you in your search. You wouldn't be the first detective fooled in that game."

The Captain made no reply, but went off to see how his ship was bearing the storm. The little company fell silent, perhaps depressed by the sounds of tempest without and the thought of the poor soul whose departure from life had been so strange. Arthur sat thinking of many things. He remembered the teaching that to God the past, present, and future are as one living present. Here was an illustration: the old past and the new present side by side to-night in the person of this detective. What a giant hand was that which could touch him, and fail to seize only because the fingers did not know their natural prey. No doubt that the past is more a part of a man than his heart, for here was every nerve of his body tingling to turn traitor to his will. Horace Endicott, so long stilled that he thought him dead, rose from his sleep at the bidding of the detective, and fought to betray Arthur Dillon. The blush, the trembling of the hands, the tension of the muscles, the misty eye, the pallor of the cheek, the tremulous lip, the writhing tongue, seemed to put themselves at the service of Endicott, and to fight for the chance to betray the secret to Curran. He sat motionless, fighting, fighting; until after a little he felt a delightful consciousness of the strength of Dillon, as of a rampart which the Endicott could not overclimb. Then his spirits rose, and he listened without dread to the story. How pitiful! What a fate for that splendid boy, the son of a brave soldier and a peerless mother! A human being allied with a beast! Oh, tender heart of Honora that sighed for him so pitifully! Oh, true spirit that recognized how impossible for Horace Endicott ever to return! Down, out of sight forever, husband of Agrippina! The furies lie in wait for thee, wretched husband of their daughter! Have shame enough to keep in thy grave until thou goest to meet Sonia at the judgment seat!

Captain Curran was not at all flattered by the deep interest which Arthur took for the next two days in the case of Tom Jones; but the young man nettled him by his emphatic assertions that the detective had adopted a wrong theory as to the mysterious disappearance. They went over the question of motives and of methods. The shrewd objections of Dillon gave him favor in Curran's eyes. Before long the secret documents in the Captain's possession were laid before him under obligations of secrecy. He saw various photographs of Endicott, and wondered at the blindness of man; for here side by side were the man sought and his portrait, yet the detective could not see the truth. Was it possible that the exterior man had changed so thoroughly to match the inner personality which had grown up in him? He was conscious of such a change. The mirror which reflected Arthur Dillon displayed a figure in no way related to the portrait.

"It seems to me," said Arthur, after a study of the photograph, "that I would be able to reach that man, no matter what his disguise."

"Disguises are mere veils," said Curran, "which the trained eye of the detective can pierce easily. But the great difficulty lies in a natural disguise, in the case where the man's appearance changes without artificial aids. Here are two photographs which will illustrate my meaning. Look at this."

Arthur saw a young and well-dressed fellow who might have been a student of good birth and training.

"Now look at this," said the Captain, "and discover that they picture one and the same individual, with a difference in age of two years."

The second portrait was a vigorous, rudely-dressed, bearded adventurer, as much like the first as Dillon was like Grahame. Knowing that the portraits stood for the same youth, Arthur could trace a resemblance in the separate features, but in the ensemble there was no likeness.

"The young fellow went from college to Africa," said Curran, "where he explored the wilderness for two years. This photograph was taken on his return from an expedition. His father and mother, his relatives and friends, saw that picture without recognizing him. When told who it was, they were wholly astonished, and after a second study still failed to recognize their friend. What are you going to do in a case of that kind? You or Grahame or Ledwith might be Tom Jones, and how could I pierce such perfect and natural disguises."

"Let me see," said Arthur, as he stood with Endicott's photograph in his hand and studied the detective, "if I can see this young man in you."

Having compared the features of the portrait and of the detective, he had to admit the absence of a likeness. Handing the photograph to the Captain he said,

"You do the same for me."

"There is more likelihood in your case," said Curran, "for your age is nearer that of Tom Jones, and youth has resemblances of color and feature."

He studied the photograph and compared it with the grave face before him.

"I have done this before," said Curran, "with the same result. You are ten years older than Tom Jones, and you are as clearly Arthur Dillon as he was Tom Jones."

The young man and the Captain sighed together.

"Oh, I brought in others, clever and experienced," said Curran, "to try what a fresh mind could do to help me, but in vain."

"There must have been something hard about Tom Jones," said Arthur, "when he was able to stay away and make no sign after his child was born."

The Captain burst into a mocking laugh, which escaped him before he could repress the inclination.

"He may never have heard of it, and if he did his wife's reputation— —"

"I see," said Arthur Dillon smiling, convinced that Captain Curran knew more of Sonia Westfield than he cared to tell. At the detective's request the matter was dropped as one that did him harm; but he complimented Arthur on the shrewdness of his suggestions, which indeed had given him new views without changing his former opinions.

CHAPTER XV.

THE INVASION OF IRELAND.

One lovely morning the good ship sailed into the harbor of
Foreskillen, an obscure fishing port on the lonely coast of Donegal.
The *Arrow* had been in sight of land all the day before. A hush had
fallen on the spirits of the adventurers. The two innocents, Honora
and her father, had sat on deck with eyes fixed on the land of their
love, scarcely able to speak, and unwilling to eat, in spite of Arthur's
coaxing. Half the night they sat there, mostly silent, talking
reverently, every one touched and afraid to disturb them; after a
short sleep they were on deck again to see the ship enter the harbor
in the gray dawn. The sun was still behind the brown hills. Arthur
saw a silver bay, a mournful shore with a few houses huddled
miserably in the distance, and bare hills without verdure or life. It
was an indifferent part of the earth to him; but revealed in the hearts
of Owen Ledwith and his daughter, no jewel of the mines could have
shone more resplendent. He did not understand the love called
patriotism, any more than the love of a parent for his child. These
affections have to be experienced to be known. He loved his country
and was ready to die for it; but to have bled for it, to have writhed
under tortures for it, to have groaned in unison with its mortal
anguish, to have passed through the fire of death and yet lived for it,
these were not his glories.

In the cool, sad morning the father and daughter stood glorified in
his eyes, for if they loved each other much, they loved this strange
land more. The white lady, whiter now than lilies, stood with her
arm about her father, her eyes shining; and he, poor man, trembled
in an ague of love and pity and despair and triumph, with a rapt,
grief-stricken face, his shoulders heaving to the repressed sob, as if
nature would there make an end of him under this torrent of delight
and pain. Arthur writhed in secret humiliation. To love like this was
of the gods, and he had never loved anything so but Agrippina. As
the ship glided to her anchorage the crew stood about the deck in
absolute silence, every man's heart in his face, the watch at its post,
the others leaning on the bulwarks. Like statues they gazed on the

shore. It seemed a phantom ship, blown from ghostly shores by the strength of hatred against the enemy, and love for the land of Eire; for no hope shone in their eyes, or in the eyes of Ledwith and his daughter, only triumph at their own light success. What a pity, thought Dillon, that at this hour of time men should have reason to look so at the power of England. He knew there were millions of them scattered over the earth, studying in just hate to shake the English grip on stolen lands, to pay back the robberies of years in English blood.

The ship came to anchor amid profound silence, save for the orders of the Captain and the movements of the men. Ledwith was speaking to himself more than to Honora, a lament in the Irish fashion over the loved and lost, in a way to break the heart. The tears rolled down Honora's cheek, for the agony was beginning.

"Land of love ... land of despair ... without a friend except among thy own children ... here am I back again with just a grain of hope ... I love thee, I love thee, I love thee! Let them neglect thee ... die every moment under the knife ... live in rags ... in scorn ... and hatred too ... they have spared thee nothing ... I love thee ... I am faithful ... God strike me that day when I forget thee! Here is the first gift I have ever given thee besides my heart and my daughter ... a ship ... no freight but hope ... no guns alas! for thy torturers ... they are still free to tear thee, these wolves, and to lie about thee to the whole world ... blood and lies are their feast ... and how sweet are thy shores ... after all ... because thou art everlasting! Thy children are gone, but they shall come back ... the dead are dead, but the living are in many lands, and they will return ... perhaps soon ... I am the messenger ... helpless as ever, but I bring thee news ... good news ... my beautiful Ireland! Poorer than ever I return ... I shall never see thee free——"

He was working himself into a fever of grief when Honora spoke to him.

"You are forgetting, father, that this is the moment to thank Mr. Dillon in the name of our country——"

"I forget everything when I am here," said Ledwith, breaking into cheerful smiles, and seizing Arthur's hand. "I would be ashamed to say 'thank you,' Arthur, for what you have done. Let this dear land herself welcome you to her shores. Never a foot stepped on them worthier of respect and love than you."

They went ashore in silence, having determined on their course the night previous. They must learn first what had happened since their departure from New York, where there had been rumors of a rising, which Ledwith distrusted. It was too soon for the Fenians to rise; but as the movement had gotten partly beyond the control of the leaders, anything might have happened. If the country was still undisturbed, they might enjoy a ride through wild Donegal; if otherwise, it was safer, having accomplished the purpose of the trip, to sail back to the West. The miserable village at the head of the bay showed a few dwellers when they landed on the beach, but little could be learned from them, save directions to a distant cotter who owned an ass and a cart, and always kept information and mountain dew for travelers and the gentry. The young men visited the cotter, and returned with the cart and the news. The rising was said to have begun, but farther east and south, and the cotter had seen soldiers and police and squads of men hurrying over the country; but so remote was the storm that the whole party agreed a ride over the bare hills threatened no danger.

They mounted the cart in high spirits, now that emotion had subsided. All matters had been arranged with Captain Curran, who was not to expect them earlier than the next day at evening, and had his instructions for all contingencies. They set out for a village to the north, expressly to avoid encounters possible southward. The morning was glorious. Arthur wondered at the miles of uninhabited land stretching away on either side of the road, at the lack of population in a territory so small. He had heard of these things before, but the sight of them proved stranger than the hearing. Perhaps they had gone five miles on the road to Cruarig, when Grahame, driving, pulled up the donkey with suddenness, and cried out in horror. Eight men had suddenly come in sight on the road, armed with muskets, and as suddenly fled up the nearest timbered hill and disappeared.

"I'll wager something," said Grahame, "that these men are being pursued by the police, or—which would be worse for us—by soldiers. There is nothing to do but retreat in good order, and send out a scout to make sure of the ground. We ought to have done that the very first thing."

No one gainsaid him, but Arthur thought that they might go on a bit further cautiously, and if nothing suspicious occurred reach the town. Dubiously Grahame whipped up the donkey, and drove with eyes alert past the wooded hill, which on its north side dropped into a little glen watered by the sweetest singing brook. They paused to look at the brook and the glen. The road stretched away above and below like a ribbon. A body of soldiers suddenly brightened the north end of the ribbon two miles off.

"Now by all the evil gods," said Grahame, "but we have dropped into the very midst of the insurrection."

He was about to turn the donkey, when Honora cried out in alarm and pointed back over the road which they had just traveled. Another scarlet troop was moving upon them from that direction. Without a word Grahame turned the cart into the glen, and drove as far as the limits would permit within the shade. They alighted.

"This is our only chance," he said. "The eight men with muskets are rebels whom the troops have cornered. There may be a large force in the vicinity, ready to give the soldiers of Her Majesty a stiff battle. The soldiers will be looking for rebels and not for harmless tourists, and we may escape comfortably by keeping quiet until the two divisions marching towards each other have met and had an explanation. If we are discovered, I shall do the talking, and explain our embarrassment at meeting so many armed men first, and then so many soldiers. We are in for it, I know."

No one seemed to mind particularly. Honora stole an anxious glance at her father, while she pulled a little bunch of shamrock and handed it to Arthur. He felt like saying it would yet be stained by his blood in defense of her country, but knew at the same moment how foolish and weak the words would sound in her ears. He offered himself as a scout to examine the top of the hill, and discover if the rebels were there, and was permitted to go under cautions from Grahame, to return within fifteen minutes. He returned promptly full of enthusiasm. The eight men were holding the top of the hill, almost over their heads, and would have it out with the two hundred soldiers from the town. They had expected a body of one hundred insurgents at this point, but the party had not turned up. Eager to have a brush with the enemy, they intended to hold the hill as long as possible, and then scatter in different directions, sure that pursuit could not catch them.

"The thing for them to do is to save us," said Grahame. "Let them move on to another hill northward, and while they fight the soldiers we may be able to slip back to the ship."

The suggestion came too late. The troops were in full sight. Their scouts had met in front of the glen, evidently acting upon information received earlier, and seemed disappointed at finding no trace of a body of insurgents large enough to match their own battalion. The boys on the top of the hill put an end to speculations as to the next move by firing a volley into them. A great scattering followed, and the bid for a fight was cheerfully answered by the officer in command of the troops. Having joined his companies, examined the position and made sure that its defenders were few and badly armed, he ordered a charge. In five minutes the troops were in possession of the hilltop, and the insurgents had fled; but on the hillside lay a score of men wounded and dead. The rebels were good marksmen, and fleet-footed. The scouts beat the bushes and scoured the wood in vain. The report to the commanding officer was the wounding of two men, who were just then dying in a little glen close by, and the discovery of a party of tourists in the glen, who had evidently turned aside to escape the trouble, and were now ministering to the dying rebels.

Captain Sydenham went up to investigate. Before he arrived the little drama of death had passed, and the two insurgents lay side by side at the margin of the brook like brothers asleep. When the insurgents fled from their position, the two wounded ones dropped into the glen in the hope of escaping notice for the time; but they were far spent when they fell headlong among the party in hiding below. Grahame and Ledwith picked them up and laid them near the brook, Honora pillowed their heads with coats, Arthur brought water to bathe their hands and faces, grimy with dust of travel and sweat of death; for an examination of the wounds showed Ledwith that they were speedily mortal. He dipped his handkerchief in the flowing blood of each, and placed it reverently in his breast. There was nothing to do but bathe the faces and moisten the lips of the dying and unconscious men. They were young, one rugged and hard, the other delicate in shape and color; the same grace of youth belonged to both, and showed all the more beautifully at this moment through the heavy veil of death.

Arthur gazed at them with eager curiosity, and at the red blood bubbling from their wounds. For their country they were dying, as his father had died, on the field of battle. This blood, of which he had so often read, was the price which man pays for liberty, which redeems the slave; richer than molten gold, than sun and stars, priceless. Oh, sweet and glorious, unutterably sweet to die like this for men!

"Do you recognize him?" said Ledwith to Grahame, pointing to the elder of the two. Grahame bent forward, startled that he should know either unfortunate.

"It is young Devin, the poet," cried Ledwith with a burst of tears. Honora moaned, and Grahame threw up his hands in despair.

"We must give the best to our mother," said Ledwith, "but I would prefer blood so rich to be scattered over a larger soil."

He took the poet's hand in his own, and stroked it gently; Honora wiped the face of the other; Grahame on his knees said the prayers he remembered for sinners and passing souls; secretly Arthur put in his pocket a rag stained with death-sweat and life-blood. Almost in silence, without painful struggle, the boys died. Devin opened his eyes one moment on the clear blue sky and made an effort to sing. He chanted a single phrase, which summed up his life and its ideals: "Mother, always the best for Ireland." Then his eyes closed and his heart stopped. The little party remained silent, until Honora, looking at the still faces, so young and tender, thought of the mothers sitting

149

in her place, and began to weep aloud. At this moment Captain Sydenham marched up the glen with clinking spur. He stopped at a distance and took off his hat with the courtesy of a gentleman and the sympathy of a soldier. Grahame went forward to meet him, and made his explanations.

"It is perfectly clear," said the Captain, "that you are tourists and free from all suspicion. However, it will be necessary for you to accompany me to the town and make your declarations to the magistrate as well. As you were going there anyhow it will be no hardship, and I shall be glad to make matters as pleasant as possible for the young lady."

Grahame thanked him, and introduced him to the party. He bowed very low over the hand which Honora gave him.

"A rather unfortunate scene for you to witness," he said.

Yet she had borne it like one accustomed to scenes of horror. Her training in Ledwith's school bred calmness, and above all silence, amid anxiety, disappointment and calamity.

"I was glad to be here," she replied, the tears still coursing down her face, "to take their mother's place."

"Two beautiful boys," said the Captain, looking into the dead faces. "Killing men is a bad business anywhere, but when we have to kill our own, and such as these, it is so much worse."

Ledwith flashed the officer a look of gratitude.

"I shall have the bodies carried to the town along with our own dead, and let the authorities take care of them. And now if you will have the goodness to take your places, I shall do myself the pleasure of riding with you as far as the magistrate's."

Honora knelt and kissed the pale cheeks of the dead boys, and then accepted Captain Sydenham's arm in the march out of the glen. The men followed sadly. Ledwith looked wild for a while. The tears pressed against Arthur's eyes. What honor gilded these dead heroes!

The procession moved along the road splendidly, the soldiers in front and the cart in the rear, while a detail still farther off carried the wounded and dead. Captain Sydenham devoted himself to Honora, which gave Grahame the chance to talk matters over with Ledwith on the other side of the car.

"Did you ever dream in all your rainbow dreams," said Grahame, "of marching thus into Cruarig with escort of Her Majesty? It's damfunny. But the question now is, what are we to do with the magistrate? Any sort of an inquiry will prove that we are more than suspicious characters. If they run across the ship we shall go to jail. If they discover you and me, death or Botany Bay will be our destination."

"It is simply a case of luck," Ledwith replied. "Scheming won't save us. If Lord Constantine were in London now— —"

"Great God!" cried Grahame in a whisper, "there's the luck. Say no more. I'll work that fine name as it was never worked before."

He called out to Captain Sydenham to come around to his side of the car for a moment.

"I am afraid," he said, "that we have fallen upon evil conditions, and that, before we get through with the magistrates, delays will be many and vexatious. I feel that we shall need some of our English friends of last winter in New York. Do you know Lord Constantine?"

"Are you friends of Lord Leverett?" cried the Captain. "Well, then, that settles it. A telegram from him will smooth the magistrate to the silkiness of oil. But I do not apprehend any annoyance. I shall be happy to explain the circumstances, and you can get away to Dublin, or any port where you hope to meet your ship."

The Captain went back to Honora, and talked Lord Constantine until they arrived in the town and proceeded to the home of the magistrate. Unfortunately there was little cordiality between Captain Sydenham and Folsom, the civil ruler of the district; and because the gallant Captain made little of the episode therefore Folsom must make much of it.

"I can easily believe in the circumstances which threw tourists into so unpleasant a situation," said Folsom, "but at the same time I am compelled to observe all the formalities. Of course the young lady is free. Messrs. Dillon and Grahame may settle themselves comfortably in the town, on their word not to depart without permission. Mr. Ledwith has a name which my memory connects with treasonable doings and sayings. He must remain for a few hours at least in the jail."

"This is not at all pleasant," said Captain Sydenham pugnaciously. "I could have let these friends of my friends go without troubling you about them. I wished to make it easier for them to travel to Dublin by bringing them before you, and here is my reward."

"I wish you had, Captain," said the magistrate. "But now you've done it, neither is free to do more than follow the routine. We have enough real work without annoying honest travelers. However, it's only a matter of a few hours."

"Then you had better telegraph to Lord Constantine," said Sydenham to Grahame.

Folsom started at the name and looked at the party with a puzzled frown. Grahame wrote on a sheet of paper the legend: "A telegram from you to the authorities here will get Honora and her party out of much trouble."

"Is it as warm as that?" said the Captain with a smile, as he read the lines and handed the paper to Folsom with a broad grin.

"I'm in for it now," groaned Folsom to himself as he read. "Wish I'd let the Captain alone and tended to strict business."

While the wires were humming between Dublin and Cruarig, Captain Sydenham spent his spare time in atoning for his blunders against the comfort of the party. Ledwith having been put in jail most honorably, the Captain led the others to the inn and located them sumptuously. He arranged for lunch, at which he was to join them, and then left them to their ease while he transacted his own affairs.

"One of the men you read about," said Grahame, as the three looked at one another dolorously. "Sorry I didn't confide in him from the start. Now it's a dead certainty that your father stays in jail, Honora, and I may be with him."

"I really can't see any reason for such despair," said Arthur.

"Of course not," replied Grahame. "But even Lord Constantine could not save Owen Ledwith from prison in times like these, if the authorities learn his identity."

"What is to be done?" inquired Honora.

"You will stay with your father of course?" Honora nodded.

"I'm going to make a run for it at the first opportunity," said Grahame. "I can be of no use here, and we must get back the ship safe and sound. Arthur, if they hold Ledwith you will have the honor of working for his freedom. Owen is an American citizen. He ought to have all the rights and privileges of a British subject in his trial, if it comes to that. He won't get them unless the American minister to the court of St. James insists upon it. Said minister, being a doughhead, will not insist. He will even help to punish him. It will be your business to go up to London and make Livingstone do his duty if you have to choke him black in the face. If the American minister interferes in this case Lord Constantine will be a power. If the said minister hangs back, or says, hang the idiot, my Lord will not amount to a hill of beans."

"If it comes to a trial," said Arthur, "won't Ledwith get the same chance as any other lawbreaker?"

Honora and Grahame looked at each other as much as to say: "Poor innocent!"

"When there's a rising on, my dear boy, there is no trial for Irishmen. Arrest means condemnation, and all that follows is only form. Go ahead now and do your best."

Before lunch the telegrams had done their best and worst. The party was free to go as they came with the exception of Ledwith. They had a merry lunch, enlivened by a telegram from Lord Constantine, and by Folsom's discomfiture. Then Grahame drove away to the ship, Arthur set out for Dublin, and Honora was left alone with her dread and her sorrows, which Captain Sydenham swore would be the shortest of her life.

CHAPTER XVI.

CASTLE MOYNA.

The Dillon party took possession of Castle Moyna, its mistress, and Captain Sydenham, who had a fondness for Americans. Mona Everard owned any human being who looked at her the second time, as the oriole catches the eye with its color and then the heart with its song; and Louis had the same magnetism in a lesser degree. Life at the castle was not of the liveliest, but with the Captain's aid it became as rapid as the neighboring gentry could have desired. Anne cared little, so that her children had their triumph. Wrapped in her dreams of amethyst, the exquisiteness of this new world kept her in ecstasy. Its smallest details seemed priceless. She performed each function as if it were the last of her life. While rebuffs were not lacking, she parried them easily, and even the refusal of the parish priest to accept her aid in his bazaar did not diminish the delight of her happy situation. She knew the meaning of his refusal: she, an upstart, having got within the gates of Castle Moyna by some servility, when her proper place was a *shebeen* in Cruarig, offered him charity from a low motive. She felt a rebuke from a priest as a courtier a blow from his king; but keeping her temper, she made many excuses for him in her own mind, without losing the firm will to teach him better manners in her own reverent way. The Countess heard of it, and made a sharp complaint to Captain Sydenham. The old dowager had a short temper, and a deep gratitude for Anne's remarkable services in New York. Nor did she care to see her guests slighted.

"Father Roslyn has treated her shabbily. She suggested a booth at his bazaar, offered to fit it up herself and to bring the gentry to buy. She was snubbed: 'neither your money nor your company.' You must set that right, Sydenham," said she.

"He shall weep tears of brine for it," answered the Captain cheerfully.

"Tell him," said the Dowager, "the whole story, if your priest can appreciate it, which I doubt. A Cavan peasant, who can teach the fine ladies of Dublin how to dress and how to behave; whose people are half the brains of New York; the prize-fighter turned senator, the Boss of Tammany, the son with a gold mine. Above all, don't forget to tell how she may name the next ambassador to England."

They laughed in sheer delight at her accomplishments and her triumphs.

"Gad, but she's the finest woman," the Captain declared. "At first I thought it was acting, deuced fine acting. But it's only her nature finding expression. What d'ye think she's planning now? An audience with the Pope, begad, special, to present an American flag and a thousand pounds. And she laid out Lady Cruikshank yesterday, stone cold. Said her ladyship: 'Quite a compliment to Ireland, Mrs. Dillon, that you kept the Cavan brogue so well.' Said Mrs. Dillon: 'It was all I ever got from Ireland, and a brogue in New York is always a recommendation to mercy from the court; then abroad it marks one off from the common English and their common Irish imitators.' Did she know of Lady Cruikshank's effort to file off the Dublin brogue?"

"Likely. She seems to know the right thing at the right minute."

Evidently Anne's footing among the nobility was fairly secure in spite of difficulties. There were difficulties below stairs also, and Judy Haskell had the task of solving them, which she did with a success quite equal to Anne's. She made no delay in seizing the position of arbiter in the servants' hall, not only of questions touching the Dillons, and their present relations with the Irish nobility, but also on such vital topics as the rising, the Fenians, the comparative rank of the Irish at home and those in America, and the standing of the domestics in Castle Moyna from the point of experience and travel. Inwardly Judy had a profound respect for domestics in the service of a countess, and looked to find them as far above herself as a countess is above the rest of the world. She would have behaved humbly among the servants of Castle Moyna, had not their airs betrayed them for an inferior grade.

"These Americans," said the butler with his nose in the air.

"As if ye knew anythin' about Americans," said Judy promptly. "Have ye ever thraveled beyant Donegal, me good little man?"

"It wasn't necessary, me good woman."

"Faith, it's yerself 'ud be blowin' about it if ye had. An' d'ye think people that thraveled five thousan' miles to spind a few dollars on yer miserable country wud luk at the likes o' ye? Keep yer criticisms on these Americans in yer own buzzum. It's not becomin' that an ould gossoon shud make remarks on Mrs. Dillon, the finest lady in New York, an' the best dhressed at this minnit in all Ireland. Whin ye've thraveled as much as I have ye can have me permission to talk on what ye have seen."

"The impidence o' some people," said the cook with a loud and scornful laugh.

"If ye laughed that way in New York," said Judy, "ye'd be sint to the Island for breaking the public peace. A laugh like that manes no increase o' wages."

"The Irish in New York are allowed to live there I belave," said a pert housemaid with a simper.

"Oh, yes, ma'am, an' they are also allowed to sind home the rint o' their houses to kape the poor Irish from starvin', an' to help the lords an' ladies of yer fine castles to kape the likes o' yees in a job."

"'Twas always a wondher to me," said the cook to the housemaid, as if no other was present, "how these American bigbugs wid their inilligant ways ever got as far as the front door o' the Countess."

"I can tell ye how Mrs. Dillon got in so far that her fut is on the neck of all o' yez this minnit," said Judy. "If she crooked her finger at ye this hour, ye'd take yer pack on yer back an' fut it over to yer father's shanty, wid no more chance for another place than if ye wor in Timbuctoo. The Countess o' Skibbereen kem over to New York to hould a concert, an' to raise money for the cooks an' housemaids an' butlers that were out of places in Donegal. Well, she cudn't get a singer, nor she couldn't get a hall, nor she cudn't sell a ticket, till Mrs. Dillon gathered around her the Boss of Tammany Hall, an' Senator Dillon, an' Mayor Birmingham, an' Mayor Livingstone, an' says to thim, 'let the Countess o' Skibbereen have a concert an' let Tammany Hall buy every ticket she has for sale, an' do yeez turn out the town to make the concert a success.' An' thin she got the greatest singer in the world, Honora Ledwith, that ye cudn't buy to sing in Ireland for all the little money there's in it, to do the singin', an' so the Countess med enough money to buy shirts for the whole of Ireland. But not a door wud have opened to her if Mrs. Dillon hadn't opened them all be wan word. That's why Castle Moyna is open to her to the back door. For me I wondher she shtays in the poor little place, whin the palace o' the American ambassador in London expects her."

The audience, awed at Judy's assurance, was urged by pride to laugh haughtily at this last statement.

"An' why wudn't his palace be open to her," Judy continued with equal scorn. "He's afraid of her. She kem widin an ace o' spoilin' his chances o' goin' to London an' bowin' to the Queen. An, bedad, he's not sure of his futtin' while she's in it, for she has her mind on the place for Mr. Vandervelt, the finest man in New York wid a family that goes back to the first Dutchman that ever was, a little fellow that sat fishin' in the say the day St. Pathrick sailed for Ireland. Now Mr. Livingstone sez to Mrs. Dillon whin he was leavin' for London, 'Come over,' sez he, 'an' shtay at me palace as long as I'm in it.' She's goin' there whin she laves here, but I don't see why she shtays in this miserable place, whin she cud be among her aquils, runnin' in an out to visit the Queen like wan o' thimselves."

By degrees, as Judy's influence invaded the audience, alarm spread among them for their own interests. They had not been over polite to the Americans, since it was not their habit to treat any but the nobility with more than surface respect. New York most of them hoped to visit and dwell within some day. What if they had offended the most influential of the great ladies of the western city! Judy saw their fear and guessed its motive.

"Me last word to the whole o' yez is, get down an yer knees to Mrs. Dillon afore she l'aves, if she'll let yez. I hear that some o' ye think of immigratin' to New York. Are yez fit for that great city? What are yer wages here? Mebbe a pound a month. In our city the girls get four pounds for doin' next to nothin'. An' to see the dhress an' the shtyle o' thim fine girls! Why, yez cudn't tell them from their own misthresses. What wud yez be doin' in New York, wid yer clothes thrun on yez be a pitchfork, an' lukkin' as if they were made in the ark? But if ye wor as smart as the lady that waits on the Queen, not wan fut will ye set in New York if Mrs. Dillon says no. Yez may go to Hartford or Newark, or some other little place, an' yez'll be mighty lucky if ye're not sint sthraight on to quarantine wid the smallpox patients an' the Turks."

The cook gave a gasp, and Judy saw that she had won the day. One more struggle, however, remained before her triumph was complete. The housekeeper and the butler formed an alliance against her, and refused to be awed by the stories of Mrs. Dillon's power and greatness; but as became their station their opposition was not expressed in mere language. They did not condescend to bandy words with inferiors. The butler fought his battle with Judy by simply tilting his nose toward the sky on meeting her. Judy thereupon tilted her nose in the same fashion, so that the servants' hall was convulsed at the sight, and the butler had to surrender or lose his dignity. The housekeeper carried on the battle by an attempt to stare Judy out of countenance with a formidable eye; and the greatest staring-match on the part of rival servants in Castle Moyna took place between the representative of the Skibbereens and the maid of New York. The former may have thought her eye as good as that of the basilisk, but found the eye of Miss Haskell much harder.

The housekeeper one day met Judy descending the back stairs. She fixed her eyes upon her with the clear design of transfixing and paralyzing this brazen American. Judy folded her arms and turned her glance upon her foe. The nearest onlookers held their breaths. Overcome by the calm majesty of Judy's iron glance, which pressed against her face like a spear, the housekeeper smiled scornfully and began to ascend the stairs with scornful air. Judy stood on the last step and turned her neck round and her eyes upward until she resembled the Gorgon. She had the advantage of the housekeeper, who in mounting the stairs had to watch her steps; but in any event the latter was foredoomed to defeat. The eyes that had not blinked before Anne Dillon, or the Senator, or Mayor Livingstone, or John Everard, or the Countess of Skibbereen, or the great Sullivan, and had modestly held their own under the charming glance of the Monsignor, were not to be dazzled by the fiercest glance of a mere Donegal housekeeper. The contempt in Judy's eyes proved too much for the poor creature, and at the top of the stairs, with a hysterical shriek, she burst into tears and fled humbled.

"I knew you'd do it," said Jerry the third butler. "It's not in thim wake craythurs to take the luk from you, Miss Haskell."

"Ye're the wan dacint boy in the place," said Judy, remembering many attentions from the shrewd lad. "An' as soon as iver ye come to New York, an' shtay long enough to become an American, I'll get ye a place on the polls."

From that day the position of the Dillon party became something celestial as far as the servants were concerned, while Judy, as arbiter in the servants' hall, settled all questions of history, science, politics, dress, and gossip, by judgments from which there was no present appeal. All these details floated to the ears of Captain Sydenham, who was a favorite with Judy and shared her confidence; and the Captain saw to it that the gossip of Castle Moyna also floated into the parish residence daily. Some of it was so alarming that Father Roslyn questioned his friend Captain Sydenham, who dropped in for a quiet smoke now and then.

"Who are these people, these Americans, do you know, Captain? I mean those just now stopping with the Countess of Skibbereen?"

"That reminds me," replied the Captain. "Didn't you tell me Father William was going to America this winter on a collecting tour? Well, if you get him the interest of Mrs. Dillon his tour is assured of success before he begins it."

A horrible fear smote the heart of the priest, nor did he see the peculiar smile on the Captain's face. Had he made the dreadful mistake of losing a grand opportunity for his brother, soon to undertake a laborious mission?

"Why do you think so?" he inquired.

"You would have to be in New York to understand it," replied the Captain. "But the Countess of Skibbereen is not a patch in this county compared to what Mrs. Dillon is in New York!"

"Oh, dear me! Do you tell me!"

"Her people are all in politics, and in the church, and in business. Her son is a—well, he owns a gold mine, I think, and he is in politics, too. In fact, it seems pretty clear that if you want anything in New York Mrs. Dillon is the woman to get it, as the Countess found it. And if you are not wanted in New York by Mrs. Dillon, then you must go west as far as Chicago."

"Oh, how unfortunate! I am afraid, Captain, that I have made a blunder. Mrs. Dillon came to me—most kindly of course—and made an offer to take care of a booth at the bazaar, and I refused her. You know my feeling against giving these Americans any foothold amongst us——"

"Don't tell that to Father William, or he will never forgive you," said the Captain. "But Mrs. Dillon is forgiving as well as generous. Do the handsome thing by her. Go up to the castle and explain matters, and she will forget your——"

"Oh, call it foolishness at once," said the priest. "I'm afraid I'm too late, but for the sake of charity I'll do what you say."

A velvety welcome Anne gave him. Before all others she loved the priest, and but that she had to teach Father Roslyn a lesson he would have seen her falling at his feet for his blessing. In some fashion he made explanation and apology.

"Father dear, don't mention it. Really, it is my place to make explanations and not yours. I was hurt, of course, that you refused the little I can give you, but I knew other places would be the richer by it, and charity is good everywhere."

"A very just thought, madam. It would give us all great pleasure if you could renew your suggestion to take a booth at the bazaar. We are all very fond of Americans here—that is, when we understand them——"

"Only that I'm going up to London, father dear, I'd be only too happy. It was not the booth I was thinking of, you see, but the bringing of all the nobility to spend a few pounds with you."

"Oh, my dear, you could never have done it," cried he in astonishment; "they are all Protestants, and very dark."

"We do it in America, and why not here? I used to get more money from Protestant friends than from me own. When I told them of my scheme here they all promised to come for the enjoyment of it. Now, I'm so sorry I have to go to London. I must present my letters to the ambassador before he leaves town, and then we are in a hurry to get to Rome before the end of August. Cardinal Simeoni has promised us already a private audience with the Pope. Now, father dear, if there is anything I can do for you in Rome—of course the booth must go up at the bazaar just the same, only the nobility will not be there—but at Rome, now, if you wanted anything."

"My dear Mrs. Dillon you overwhelm me. There is nothing I want for myself, but my brother, Father William——"

"Oh, to be sure, your brother," cried Anne, when the priest paused in confusion; "let him call on us in Rome, and I will take him to the private audience."

"Oh, thank you, thank you, my dear madam, but my brother is not going to Rome. It is to America I refer. His bishop has selected him from among many eminent priests of the diocese to make a collecting tour in America this winter. And I feel sure that if a lady of your rank took an interest in him, it would save him much labor, and, what I fear is unavoidable, hardship."

Anne rose up delighted and came toward Father Roslyn with a smile. She placed her hand lightly on his shoulder.

"Father dear, whisper."

He bent forward. There was not a soul within hearing distance, but Anne loved a dramatic effect.

"He need never leave New York. I'll see that Father William has the *entrée* into the diocese, and I'll take care of him until he leaves for home."

She tapped him on the shoulder with her jeweled finger, and gave him a most expressive look of assurance.

"Oh, how you overwhelm me," cried Father Roslyn. "I thank you a hundred times, but I won't accept so kind an offer unless you promise me that you will preside at a booth in the bazaar."

Of course she promised, much as the delay might embarrass the American minister in London, and the Cardinal who awaited with impatience her arrival in Rome.

The bazaar became a splendid legend in the parish of Cruarig; how its glory was of heaven; how Mrs. Dillon seemed to hover over it like an angel or a queen; how Father Roslyn could hardly keep out of her booth long enough to praise the others; how the nobility flocked about it every night of three, and ate wonderful dishes at fancy prices, and were dressed like princes; and how Judy Haskell ruled the establishment with a rod of iron from two to ten each day, devoting her leisure to the explanation and description of the booths once presided over by her mistress in the great city over seas. All these incidents and others as great passed out of mind before the happenings which shadowed the last days at Castle Moyna with anxiety and dread.

The Dowager gave a fête in honor of her guests one afternoon, and all the county came. As a rule the gentry sneered at the American guests of the Countess, and found half their enjoyment at a garden fête in making fun of the hostess and her friends in a harmless way. There might not have been so much ridicule on this occasion for two reasons: the children were liked, and their guardian was dreaded. Anne had met and vanquished her critics in the lists of wit and polite insolence. Then a few other Americans, discovered by Captain Sydenham, were present, and bore half the brunt of public attention.

The Dillons met their countrymen for a moment and forgot them, even forgot the beautiful woman whose appearance held the eyes of the guests a long time. Captain Sydenham was interesting them in a pathetic story of battle and death which had just happened only a few miles away. When the two boys were dead beside the stream in the glen, and the tourists had met their fate before the magistrate in Cruarig, he closed the story by saying,

"And now down in the hotel is the loveliest Irish girl you ever saw, waiting with the most patient grief for the help which will release her father from jail. Am I not right, Mrs. Endicott?"

The beautiful American looked up with a smile.

"Yes, indeed," she replied in a clear, rich voice. "It is long since I met a woman that impressed me more than this lonely creature. The Captain was kind enough to take me to see her, that I might comfort her a little. But she seemed to need little comfort. Very self-possessed you know. Used to that sort of thing."

"The others got scot free, no thanks to old Folsom," said the Captain, "and one went off to their yacht and the other intended to start for Dublin to interest the secretary. The Countess should interest herself in her. Egad, don't you know, it's worth the trouble to take an interest in such a girl as Honora Ledwith."

"Honora Ledwith," said the Dowager at a little distance. "What do you know of my lovely Honora?"

Already in the course of the story a suspicion had been shaping itself in Anne's mind. The ship must have arrived, it was time to hear from Arthur and his party; the story warned her that a similar fate might have overtaken her friends. Then she braced herself for the shock which came with Honora's name; and at the same moment, as in a dream, she saw Arthur swinging up the lawn towards her group; whereupon she gave a faint shriek, and rose up with a face so pale that all stretched out hands to her assistance; but Arthur was before them, as she tottered to him, and caught her in his arms. After a moment of silence, Mona and Louis ran to his side, Captain Sydenham said some words, and then the little group marched off the lawn to the house, leaving the Captain to explain matters, and to wonder at the stupidity which had made him overlook the similarity in names.

"Why, don't you know," said he to Mrs. Endicott, "her son was one of the party of tourists that Folsom sent to jail, and I never once connected the names. Absurd and stupid on my part."

"Charming young man," said the lady, as she excused herself and went off. Up in one of the rooms of Castle Moyna, when the excitement was over and the explanations briefly made, Mona at the window described to Arthur the people of distinction, as they made their adieus to their hostess and expressed sympathy with the sudden and very proper indisposition of Mrs. Dillon. He could not help thinking how small the world is, what a puzzle is the human heart, how weird is the life of man.

"There she is now," cried Mona, pointing to Mrs. Endicott and an old lady, who were bidding adieu to the Countess of Skibbereen. "A perfectly lovely face, a striking figure—oh, why should Captain Sydenham say our Honora was the loveliest girl he ever saw?—and he saw them together you know——"

"Saw whom together?" said Arthur.

"Why, Mrs. Endicott called on Honora at the hotel, you know."

"Oh!"

He leaned out of the window and took a long look at her with scarcely an extra beat of the heart, except for the triumph of having met her face to face and remained unknown. His longest look was for Aunt Lois, who loved him, and was now helping to avenge him. Strange, strange, strange!

"Well?" cried Mona eagerly.

"The old lady is a very sweet-looking woman," he answered. "On the whole I think Captain Sydenham was right."

CHAPTER XVII.

THE AMBASSADOR.

After the happy reunion at Castle Moyna there followed a council of war. Captain Sydenham treasonably presided, and Honora sat enthroned amid the silent homage of her friends, who had but one thought, to lift the sorrow from her heart, and banish the pallor of anxiety from her lovely face. Her violet eyes burned with fever. The Captain drew his breath when he looked at her.

"And she sings as she looks," whispered the Countess noting his gasp.

"It's a bad time to do anything for Mr. Ledwith," the Captain said to the little assembly. "The Fenian movement has turned out a complete failure here in Ireland, and abroad too. As its stronghold was the United States, you can see that the power of the American Minister will be much diminished. It is very important to approach him in the right way, and count every inch of the road that leads to him. We must not make any mistakes, ye know, if only for Miss Ledwith's sake."

His reward was a melting glance from the wonderful eyes.

"I know the Minister well, and I feel sure he will help for the asking," said Anne.

"Glad you're so hopeful, mother, but some of us are not," Arthur interjected.

"Then if you fail with His Excellency, Artie," she replied composedly, "I shall go to see him myself."

Captain and Dowager exchanged glances of admiration.

"Now, there are peculiarities in our trials here, trials of rebels I mean ... I haven't time to explain them ..." Arthur grinned ... "but they make imperative a certain way of acting, d'ye see? If I were in Mr. Dillon's place I should try to get one of two things from the

American Minister: either that the Minister notify Her Majesty's government that he will have his representative at the trial of Ledwith; or, if the trial is begun ... they are very summary at times ... that the same gentleman inform the government that he will insist on all the forms being observed."

"What effect would these notifications have?" Arthur asked.

"Gad, most wonderful," replied the Captain. "If the Minister got in his warning before the trial began, there wouldn't be any trial; and if later, the trial would end in acquittal."

Every one looked impressed, so much so that the Captain had to explain.

"I don't know how to explain it to strangers—we all know it here, doncheknow—but in these cases the different governments always have some kind of an understanding. Ledwith is an American citizen, for example; he is arrested as an insurgent, no one is interested in him, the government is in a hurry, a few witnesses heard him talk against the government, and off he goes to jail. It's a troublesome time, d'ye see? But suppose the other case. A powerful friend interests the American Minister. That official notifies the proper officials that he is going to watch the trial. This means that the Minister is satisfied of the man's innocence. Government isn't going to waste time so, when there are hundreds to be tried and deported. So he goes free. Same thing if the Minister comes in while the trial is going on, and threatens to review all the testimony, the procedure, the character of the witnesses. He simply knocks the bottom out of the case, and the prisoner goes free."

"I see your points," said Arthur, smiling. "I appreciate them. Just the same, we must have every one working on the case, and if I should fail the others must be ready to play their parts."

"Command us all," said the Captain with spirit. "You have Lord Constantine in London. He's a host. But remember we are in the midst of the trouble, and home influence won't be a snap of my finger compared with the word of the Minister."

"Then the Minister's our man," said Anne with decision. "If Arthur fails with him, then every soul of us must move on London like an Irish army, and win or die. So, my dear Honora, take the puckers out of your face, and keep your heart light. I know a way to make Quincy Livingstone dance to any music I play."

The smiles came back to Honora's face, hearts grew lighter, and Arthur started for London, with little confidence in the good-will of Livingstone, but more in his own ability to force the gentleman to do his duty. He ran up against a dead wall in his mission, however, for the question of interference on behalf of American citizens in English jails had been settled months before in a conference between Livingstone and the Premier, although feeling was cold and almost hostile between the two governments. Lord Constantine described the position with the accuracy of a theorist in despair.

"There's just a chance of doing something for Ledwith," he said dolorously.

"By your looks a pretty poor one, I think," Arthur commented.

"Oh, it's got to be done, doncheknow," he said irritably. "But that da—that fool, Livingstone, is spoiling the stew with his rot. And I've been watching this pot boil for five years at least."

"What's wrong with our representative?" affecting innocence.

"What's right with him would be the proper question," growled his lordship.

"In Ledwith's case the wrong is that he's gone and given assurances to the government. He will not interfere with their disposition of Fenian prisoners, when these prisoners are American citizen. In other words, he has given the government a free hand. He will not be inclined to show Ledwith any favor."

"A free hand," repeated Arthur, fishing for information. "And what is a free hand?"

"Well, he could hamper the government very much when it is trying an American citizen for crimes committed on British soil. Such a prisoner must get all the privileges of a native. He must be tried fairly, as he would be at home, say."

"Well, surely that strong instinct of fair play, that sense of justice so peculiarly British, of which we have all heard in the school-books, would— —"

"Drop it," said Lord Constantine fiercely. "In war there's nothing but the brute left. The Fenians—may the plague take them ... will be hung, shipped to Botany Bay, and left to rot in the home prisons, without respect to law, privilege, decency. Rebels must be wiped out, doncheknow. I don't mind that. They've done me enough harm ... put back the alliance ten years at least ... and left me howling in the wilderness. Livingstone will let every Fenian of American citizenship be tried like his British mates ... that is, they will get no trial at all, except inform. They will not benefit by their American ties."

"Why should he neglect them like that?"

"He has theories, of course. I heard him spout them at some beastly reception somewhere. Too many Irish in America—too strong—too popish—must be kept down—alliance between England and the United States to keep them down— —"

"I remember he was one of your alliance men," provokingly.

"Alas, yes," mourned his lordship. "The Fenians threatened to make mince-meat of it, but they're done up and knocked down. Now, this Livingstone proposes a new form of mincing, worse than the Fenians a thousand times, begad."

"Begad," murmured Arthur. "Surely you're getting excited."

"The alliance is now to be argued on the plea of defense against popish aggressions, Arthur. This is the unkind cut. Before, we had to reunite the Irish and the English. Now, we must soothe the prejudices of bigots besides. Oh, but you should see the programme of His Excellency for the alliance in his mind. You'll feel it when you get back home. A regular programme, doncheknow. The first number has the boards now: general indignation of the hired press at the criminal recklessness of the Irish in rebelling against our benign rule. When that chorus is ended, there comes a solo by an escaped nun. Did you ever hear of Sister Claire Thingamy — — "

"Saw her—know her—at a distance. What is she to sing?"

"A book—confessions and all that thing—revelations of the horrors of papist life. It's to be printed by thousands and scattered over the world. After that Fritters, our home historian at Oxford, is to travel in your county and lecture to the cream of society on the beauty of British rule over the Irish. He is to affect the classes. The nun and the press are to affect the masses. Between them what becomes of the alliance? Am I not patient? My pan demanded harmonious and brotherly feelings among all parties. Isn't that what an alliance must depend on? But Livingstone takes the other tack. To bring about his scheme we shall all be at each other's throats. Talk of the Kilkenny cats and Donnybrook fair, begad!"

"I don't wonder you feel so badly," Arthur said, laughing. "But see here: we're not afraid of Livingstone. We've knocked him out before, and we can do it again. It will be interesting to go back home, and help to undo that programme. If you can manage him here, rely on Grahame and me and a few others in New York, to take the starch out of him at home. What's all this to do with Ledwith?"

"Nothing," said his lordship with an apology. "But my own trouble seems bigger than his. We'll get him out, of course. Go and see Livingstone, and talk to him on the uppish plan. Demand the rights and privileges of the British subject for our man. You won't get any satisfaction, but a stiff talk will pave the way for my share in the scheme. You take the American ground, and I come in on the British ground. We ought to make him ashamed between us, doncheknow."

Arthur had doubts of that, but no doubt at all that Lord Constantine owned the finest heart that ever beat in a man. He felt very cheerful at the thought of shaking up the Minister. Half hopeful of success, curious to test the strings which move an American Minister at the court of St. James, anxious about Honora and Owen, he presented himself at Livingstone's residence by appointment, and received a gracious welcome. Unknown to themselves, the two men had an attraction for each other. Fate opposed them strangely. This hour Arthur Dillon stood forth as the knight of a despised and desperate race, in a bloody turmoil at home, fighting for a little space on American soil, hopeful but spent with the labor of upholding its ideals; and Livingstone represented a triumphant faction in both countries, which, having long made life bitter and bloody for the Irish, still kept before them the choice of final destruction or the acceptance of the Puritan gods. To Arthur the struggle so far seemed but a clever game whose excitement kept sorrow from eating out his heart. He saw the irony rather than the tragedy of the contest. It tickled him immensely just now that Puritan faced Puritan; the new striking at the old for decency's sake; a Protestant fighting a Protestant in behalf of the religious ideals of Papists. He had an advantage over his kinsman beyond the latter's ken; since to him the humor of the situation seemed more vital than the tragedy, a mistake quite easy to youth. Arthur stated Ledwith's case beautifully, and asked him to notify the British officials that the American Minister would send his representative to watch the trial.

"Impossible," said Livingstone. "I am content with the ordinary course for all these cases."

"We are not," replied Arthur as decisively, "and we call upon our government to protect its citizens against the packed juries and other injustices of these Irish trials."

"And what good would my interference do?" said Livingstone. Arthur grinned.

"Your Excellency, such a notification would open the doors of the jail to Ledwith to-morrow. There would be no trial."

"My instructions from the President are precise in this matter. We are satisfied that American citizens will get as fair a trial as Englishmen themselves. There will be no interference until I am satisfied that things are not going properly."

"Can you tell me, then, how I am to satisfy you in Ledwith's case?" said the young man good-naturedly.

"I don't think you or any one else can, Mr. Dillon. I know Ledwith, a conspirator from his youth. He is found in Ireland in a time of insurrection. That's quite enough."

"You forget that I have given you my word he was not concerned with the insurrection, and did not know it was so imminent; that he went to Ireland with his daughter on a business matter."

"All which can be shown at the trial, and will secure his acquittal."

"Neither I nor his daughter will ever be called as witnesses. Instead, a pack of ready informers will swear to anything necessary to hurry him off to life imprisonment."

"That is your opinion."

"Do you know who sent me here, your Excellency, with the request for your aid?"

Livingstone stared his interrogation.

"An English officer with whom you are acquainted, friendly to Ledwith for some one else's sake. In plain words, he gave me to understand that there is no hope for Ledwith unless you interfere. If he goes to trial, he hangs or goes to Botany Bay."

"You are pessimistic," mocked Livingstone. "It is the fault of the Irish that they have no faith in any government, because they cannot establish one of their own."

"Outside of New York," corrected Arthur, with delightful malice.

"Amendment accepted."

"Would you be able to interfere in behalf of my friend while the trial was on, say, just before the summing up, when the informers had sworn to one thing, and the witnesses for the defense to another, if they are not shut out altogether?"

"Impossible. I might as well interfere now."

"Then on the score of sentiment. Ledwith is failing into age. Even a brief term in prison may kill him."

"He took the risk in returning to Ireland at this time. I would be willing to aid him on that score, but it would open the door to a thousand others, and we are unwilling to embarrass the English government at a trying moment."

"Were they so considerate when our moments were trying and they could embarrass us?"

"That is an Irish argument."

"What they said of your Excellency in New York was true, I am inclined to believe: that you accepted the English mission to be of use to the English in the present insurrection."

"Well," said the Minister, laughing in spite of himself at the audacity of Arthur, "you will admit that I have a right to pay back the Irish for my defeat at the polls."

"You are our representative and defender," replied Arthur gravely, "and yet you leave us no alternative but to appeal to the English themselves."

Livingstone began to look bored, because irritation scorched him and had to be concealed. Arthur rose.

"We are to understand, then, the friends of Ledwith, that you will do nothing beyond what is absolutely required by the law, and after all formalities are complied with?" he said.

"Precisely."

"We shall have to depend on his English friends, then. It will look queer to see Englishmen take up your duty where you deserted it."

The Minister waved his hand to signify that he had enough of that topic, but the provoking quality of Arthur's smile, for he did not seem chagrined, reminded him of a question.

"Who are the people interested in Ledwith, may I ask?"

"All your old friends of New York," said Arthur, "Birmingham, Sullivan, and so on."

"Of course. And the English friends who are to take up my duties where I desert them?"

"You must know some of them," and Arthur grinned again, so that the Minister slightly winced. "Captain Sydenham, commanding in Donegal——"

"I met him in New York one winter—younger brother to Lord Groton."

"The Dowager Countess of Skibbereen."

"Very fine woman. Ledwith is in luck."

"And Lord Constantine of Essex."

"I see you know the value of a climax, Mr. Dillon. Well, good-night. I hope the friends of Mr. Ledwith will be able to do everything for him."

It irritated him that Arthur carried off the honors of the occasion, for the young man's smiling face betrayed his belief that the mention of these noble names, and the fact that their owners were working for Ledwith, would sorely trouble the pillow of Livingstone that night. The contrast between the generosity of kindly Englishmen and his own harshness was too violent. He foresaw that to any determined attempt on the part of Ledwith's English friends he must surrender as gracefully as might be; and the problem was to make that surrender harmless. He had solved it by the time Anne Dillon reached London, and had composed that music sure to make the Minister dance whether he would or no. In taking charge of the case Anne briefly expressed her opinion of her son's methods.

"You did the best you could, Arthur," she said sweetly.

He could not but laugh and admire. Her instincts for the game were far surer than his own, and her methods infallible. She made the road easy for Livingstone, but he had to walk it briskly. How could the poor man help himself? She hurled at him an army of nobles, headed by the Countess and Lord Constantine; she brought him letters from his friends at home; there was a dinner at the hotel, the

Dowager being the hostess; and he was almost awed by the second generation of Anne's audacious race: Mona, red-lipped, jewel-eyed, sweeter than wild honey; Louis, whose lovely nature and high purpose shone in his face; and Arthur, sad-eyed, impudent, cynical, who seemed ready to shake dice with the devil, and had no fear of mortals because he had no respect for them. These outcasts of a few years back were able now to seize the threads of intrigue, and shake up two governments with a single pull! He mourned while he described what he had done for them. There would be no trial for Ledwith. He would be released at once and sent home at government expense. It was a great favor, a very great favor. Even Arthur thanked him, though he had difficulty in suppressing the grin which stole to his face whenever he looked at his kinsman. The Minister saw the grin peeping from his eyes, but forgave him.

Arthur had the joy of bringing the good news down to Donegal. Anne bade him farewell with a sly smile of triumph. Admirable woman! she floated above them all in the celestial airs. But she was gracious to her son. The poor boy had been so long in California that he did not know how to go about things. She urged him to join them in Rome for the visit to the Pope, and sent her love to Honora and a bit of advice to Owen. When Arthur arrived in Cruarig, whither a telegram had preceded him, he was surprised to find Honora Ledwith in no way relieved of anxiety.

"You have nothing to do but pack your trunk and get away," he said. "There is to be no trial, you know. Your father will go straight to the steamer, and the government will pay his expenses. It ought to pay more for the outrage."

She thanked him, but did not seem to be comforted. She made no comment, and he went off to get an explanation from Captain Sydenham.

"I meant to have written you about it," said the Captain, "but hoped that it would have come out all right without writing. Ledwith maintains, and I think he's quite right, that he must be permitted to go free without conditions, or be tried as a Fenian conspirator. The case is simple: an American citizen traveling in Ireland is arrested on a charge of complicity in the present rebellion; the government must prove its case in a public trial, or, unable to do that, must release him as an innocent man; but it does neither, for it leads him from jail to the steamer as a suspect, ordering him out of the country. Ledwith demands either a trial or the freedom of an innocent man. He will not help the government out of the hole in which accident, his Excellency the Minister, and your admirable mother have placed it. Of course it's hard on that adorable Miss Ledwith, and it may kill Ledwith himself, if not the two of them. Did you ever in your life see such a daughter and such a father?"

"Well, all we can do is to make the trial as warm as possible for the government," said Arthur. "Counsel, witnesses, publicity, telegrams to the Minister, cablegrams to our Secretary of State, and all the rest of it."

"Of no use," said the Captain moodily. "You have no idea of an Irish court and an Irish judge in times of revolt. I didn't till I came here. If Ledwith stands trial, nothing can save him from some kind of a sentence."

"Then for his daughter's sake I must persuade him to get away."

"Hope you can. All's fair in war, you know, but Ledwith is the worst kind of patriot, a visionary one, exalted, as the French say."

Ledwith thanked Arthur warmly when he called upon him in jail, and made his explanation as the Captain had outlined it.

"Don't think me a fool," he said. "I'm eager to get away. I have no relish for English prison life. But I am not going to promote Livingstone's trickery. I am an American citizen. I have had no part, direct or indirect, in this futile insurrection. I can prove it in a fair trial. It must be either trial or honorable release to do as any American citizen would do under the circumstances. If I go to prison I shall rely on my friends to expose Livingstone, and to warm up the officials at home who connive with him."

Nor would he be moved from this position, and the trial came off with a speed more than creditable when justice deals with pirates, but otherwise scandalous.

It ended in a morning, in spite of counsel, quibbles, and other ornamental obstacles, with a sentence of twenty years at hard labor in an English prison. To this prison Ledwith went the next day at noon. There had not been much time for work, but Arthur had played his part to his own satisfaction; the Irish and American journals buzzed with the items which he provided, and the denunciations of the American Minister were vivid, biting, and widespread; yet how puerile it all seemed before the brief, half contemptuous sentence of the hired judge, who thus roughly shoved another irritating patriot out of the way. The farewell to Ledwith was not without hope. Arthur had declared his purpose to go straight to New York and set every influence to work that could reach the President. Honora was to live near the prison, support herself by her singing, and use her great friends to secure a mitigation of his sentence, and access to him at intervals.

"I am going in joy," he said to her and Arthur. "Death is the lightest suffering of the true patriot. Nora and I long ago offered our lives for Ireland. Perhaps they are the only useful things we could offer, for we haven't done much. Poor old country! I wish our record of service had some brighter spots in it."

"At the expense of my modesty," said Arthur, "can't I mention myself as one of the brighter spots? But for you I would never have raised a finger for my mother's land. Now, I am enlisted, not only in the cause of Erin, but pledged to do what I can for any race that withers like yours under the rule of the slave-master. And that means my money, my time and thought and labor, and my life."

"It is the right spirit," said Ledwith, trembling. "I knew it was in you. Not only for Ireland, but for the enslaved and outraged everywhere. God be thanked, if we poor creatures have stirred this spirit in you, lighted the flame—it's enough."

"I have sworn it," cried Arthur, betrayed by his secret rage into eloquence. "I did not dream the world was so full of injustice. I could not understand the divine sorrow which tore your hearts for the wronged everywhere. I saw you suffer. I saw later what caused your suffering, and I felt ashamed that I had been so long idle and blind.

Now I have sworn to myself that my life and my wealth shall be at the service of the enslaved forever."

They went their different ways, the father to prison, Honora to the prison village, and Arthur with all speed to New York, burning with hatred of Livingstone. The great man had simply tricked them, had studied the matter over with his English friends, and had found a way to satisfy the friends of Ledwith and the government at the same time. Well, it was a long lane that had no turning, and Arthur swore that he would find the turning which would undo Quincy Livingstone.

AN ESCAPED NUN.

CHAPTER XVIII.

JUDY VISITS THE POPE.

He used the leisure of the voyage to review recent events, and to measure his own progress. For the first time since his calamity he had lost sight of himself in this poetic enterprise of Ledwith's, successful beyond all expectation. In this life of intrigue against the injustice of power, this endless struggle to shake the grip of the master on the slave, he found an intoxication. Though many plans had come to nothing, and the prison had swallowed a thousand victims, the game was worth the danger and the failure. In the Fenian uprising the proud rulers had lost sleep and comfort, and the world had raised its languid eyes for a moment to study events in Ireland. Even the slave can stir the selfish to interest by a determined blow at his masters. In his former existence very far had been from him this glorious career, though honors lay in wait for an Endicott who took to statecraft. Shallow Horace, sprung from statesman, had found public life a bore. This feeling had saved him perhaps from the fate of Livingstone, who in his snail-shell could see no other America than a monstrous reproduction of Plymouth colony.

He had learned at last that his dear country was made for the human race. God had guided the little ones of the nations, wretched but hardy, to the land, the only land on earth, where dreams so often come true. Like the waves they surged upon the American shore. With ax and shovel and plow, with sweat of labor and pain, they fought the wilderness and bought a foothold in the new commonwealth. What great luck that his exit from the old life should prove to be his entrance into the very heart of a simple multitude flying from the greed and stupidity of the decadent aristocracy of Europe! What fitness that he, child of a race which had triumphantly fought injustice, poverty, Indian, and wilderness, should now be leader for a people who had fled from injustice at home only to begin a new struggle with plotters like Livingstone, foolish representative of the caste-system of the old world.

Sonia Westfield, by strange fatality, was aboard with her child and Aunt Lois. Her presence, when first they came face to face, startled him; not the event, but the littleness of the great earth; that his hatred and her crime could not keep them farther apart. The Endicott in him rose up for a moment at the sight of her, and to his horror even sighed for her: this Endicott, who for a twelvemonth had been so submerged under the new personality that Dillon had hardly thought of him. He sighed for her! Her beauty still pinched him, and the memory of the first enchantment had not faded from the mind of the poor ghost. It mouthed in anger at the master who had destroyed it, who mocked at it now bitterly: you are the husband of Sonia Westfield, and the father of her fraudulent child; go to them as you desire. But the phantom fled humiliated, while Dillon remained horror-shaken by that passing fancy of the Endicott to take up the dream of youth again. Could he by any fatality descend to this shame? Her presence did not arouse his anger or his dread, hardly his curiosity. He kept out of her way as much as possible, yet more than once they met; but only at the last did the vague inquiry in her face indicate that memory had impressions of him.

Often he studied her from afar, when she sat deep in thought with her lovely eyes ... how he had loved them ... melting, damnable, false eyes fixed on the sea. He wondered how she bore her misery, of which not a sign showed on the velvet face. Did she rage at the depths of that sea which in an instant had engulfed her fool-husband and his fortune? The same sea now mocked her, laughed at her rage, bearing on its bosom the mystery which she struggled to steal from time. No one could punish this creature like herself. She bore her executioner about with her, Aunt Lois, evidently returning home to die. That death would complete the ruin of Sonia, and over the grave she would learn once for all how well her iniquity had been known, how the lost husband had risen from his darkness to accuse her, how little her latest crime would avail her. What a dull fool Horace Endicott had been over a woman suspected of her own world! Her beauty would have kept him a fool forever, had she been less beastly in her pleasures. And this Endicott, down in the depths, sighed for her still!

But Arthur Dillon saw her in another light, as an unclean beast from sin's wilderness, in the light that shone from Honora Ledwith. Messalina cowered under the halo of Beatrice! When that light shone full upon her, Sonia looked to his eye like a painted Phryne surprised by the daylight. Her corruption showed through her beauty. Honora! Incomparable woman! dear lady of whiteness! pure heart that shut out earthly love, while God was to be served, or men suffered, or her country bled, or her father lived! The thought of her purified him. He had not truly known his dear mother till now; when he knew her in Honora, in old Martha, in charming Mona, in Mary Everard, in clever Anne Dillon. These women would bless his life hereafter. They refreshed him in mind and heart. It began to dawn upon him that his place in life was fixed, that he would never go back even though he might do so with honor, his shame remaining unknown. It was mere justice that the wretched past should be in a grave, doomed never to see the light of resurrection.

His mother and her party shared the journey with him. The delay of Ledwith's trial had enabled them to make the short tour on the Continent, and catch his steamer. Anne was utterly vexed with him that Ledwith had not escaped the prison. Her plain irritation gave Judy deep content.

"She needs something to pull her down," was her comment to Arthur, "or she'll fly off the earth with the lightness of her head. My, my, but the airs of her since she laid out the ambassador, an' talked to the Pope! She can hardly spake at all now wid the grandher! Whin Father Phil ... I never can call him Mounsinnyory ... an', be the way, for years wasn't I callin' him Morrisania be mistake, an' the dear man never corrected me wanst ... but I learned the difference over in Rome ... where was I?... whin Father Phil kem back from Rome he gev us a grand lecther on what he saw, an' he talked for two hours like an angel. But Anne Dillon can on'y shut her eyes, an' dhrop her head whin ye ask her a single question about it. Faith, I dinno if she'll ever get over it. Isn't that quare now?"

"Very," Arthur answered, "but give her time. So you saw the Pope?"

"Faith, I did, an' it surprised me a gra'dale to find out that he was a dago, God forgi' me for sayin' as much. I was tould be wan o' the Mounsinnyory that he was pure Italian. 'No,' sez I, 'the Pope may be Rooshin or German, though I don't belave he's aither, but he's not Italian. If he wor, he'd have the blessed sinse to hide it, for fear the Irish 'ud lave the Church whin they found it out.'"

"What blood do you think there's in him?" said Arthur.

"He looked so lovely sittin' there whin we wint in that me sivin sinses left me, an' I cudn't rightly mek up me mind afterwards. Thin I was so taken up wid Mrs. Dillon," and Judy laughed softly, "that I was bothered. But I know the Pope's not a dago, anny more than he's a naygur. I put him down in me own mind as a Roman, no more an' no less."

"That's a safe guess," said Arthur; "and you still have the choice of his being a Sicilian, a Venetian, or a Neapolitan."

"Unless," said the old lady cautiously, "he comes of the same stock as Our Lord Himself."

"Which would make him a Jew," Arthur smoothly remarked.

"God forgive ye, Artie! G'long wid ye! If Our Lord was a Jew he was the first an' last an' on'y wan of his kind."

"And that's true too. And how did you come to see the Pope so easy, and it in the summer time?"

The expressive grin covered Judy's face as with comic sunshine.

"I dunno," she answered. "If Anne Dillon made up her mind to be Impress of France, I dunno annythin' nor anny wan that cud hould her back; an' perhaps the on'y thing that kep' her from tryin' to be Impress was that the Frinch had an Impress already. I know they had, because I heard her ladyship lamentin', whin we wor in Paris, that she didn't get a letther of introduction to the Impress from Lady Skibbereen. She had anny number of letthers to the Pope. I suppose that's how we all got in, for I wint too, an' the three of us looked like sisters of mercy, dhressed in black wid veils on our heads. Whin we dhruv up to the palace, her ladyship gev a screech. 'Mother of heaven,' says she, 'but I forgot me permit, an' we can't get in to see his Holiness.' We sarched all her pockets, but found on'y the square bit o' paper, a milliner's bill, that she tuk for the permit be mistake. 'Well, this'll have to do,' says she. Says I, 'Wud ye insult the Pope be shakin' a milliner's bill in his face as ye go in the dure?' She never answered me, but walked in an' presented her bill to a Mounsinnyory — — "

"What's that?" Arthur asked. "I was never in Rome."

"Somethin' like the man that takes the tickets at the theayter, ou'y he's a priest, an' looks like a bishop, but he cuts more capers than ten bishops in wan. He never opened the paper — faith, if he had, there'd be the fine surprise — so we wint in. I knew the Pope the minnit I set eyes on him, the heavenly man. Oh, but I'd like to be as sure o' savin' me soul as that darlin' saint. His eyes looked as if they saw heaven every night an' mornin'. We dhropped on our knees, while the talkin' was goin' on, an' if I wasn't so frikened at bein' near heaven itself, I'd a died listenin' to her ladyship tellin' the Pope in French — in French, d'ye mind? — how much she thought of him an' how much she was goin' to spind on him while she was in Rome. 'God forgive ye, Anne Dillon,' says I to meself, 'but ye might betther spind yer money an' never let an.' She med quite free wid him, an' he talked back like a father, an' blessed us twinty times. I dinno how I wint in or how I kem out. I was like a top, spinnin' an' spinnin'. Things went round all the way home, so that I didn't dar say a word for fear herself might think I had been drinkin'. So that's how we saw the Pope. Ye can see now the terrible determination of Anne Dillon, though she was the weeniest wan o' the family."

In the early morning the steamer entered the lower bay, picking up Doyle Grahame from a tug which had wandered about for hours, not in search of news, but on the scent for beautiful Mona. He routed out the Dillon party in short order.

"What's up?" Arthur asked sleepily. "Are you here as a reporter — — "

"As a lover," Grahame corrected, with heaving chest and flashing eyes. "The crowd that will gather to receive you on the dock may have many dignitaries, but I am the only lover. That's why I am here. If I stayed with the crowd, Everard, who hates me almost, would have taken pains to shut me out from even a plain how-de-do with my goddess."

"I see. It's rather early for a goddess, but no doubt she will oblige. You mentioned a crowd on the dock to receive us. What crowd?"

"Your mother," said Doyle, "is a wonderful woman. I have often speculated on the absence of a like ability in her son."

"Nature is kind. Wait till I'm as old as she is," said the son.

"The crowd awaits her to do her honor. The common travelers *will land* this morning, glad to set foot on solid ground again. Mrs. Montgomery Dillon and her party are the only personages that *will arrive from Europe*. The crowd gathers to meet, not the passengers who merely land, but the personages who arrive from Europe."

"Nice distinction. And who is the crowd?"

"Monsignor O'Donnell — —"

"A very old and dear friend — —"

"Who hopes to build his cathedral with her help. The Senator — —"

"Representing the Dillon clan."

"Who did not dare absent himself, and hopes for more inspiration like that which took him out of the ring and made him a great man. Vandervelt."

"Well, he, of course, is purely disinterested."

"Didn't she inform him of her triumph over Livingstone in London? And isn't he to be the next ambassador, and more power to him?"

"And John Everard of course."

"To greet his daughter, and to prevent your humble servant from kissing the same," and he sighed with pleasure and triumph. "Where is she? Shall I have long to wait? Is she changed?"

"Ask her brother," with a nod for the upper berth where Louis slept serenely.

"And of course you have news?"

"Loads of it. I have arranged for a breakfast and a talk after the arrival is finished. There'll be more to eat than the steak."

The steamer swung to the pier some hours later, and Arthur walked ashore to the music of a band which played decorously the popular strains for a popular hero returning crowned with glory. His mother arrived as became the late guest of the Irish nobility. Grahame handed Mona into her father's arms with an exasperating gesture, and then plunged into his note-book, as if he did not care. The surprised passengers wondered what hidden greatness had traveled with them across the sea. On the deck Sonia watched the scene with dull interest, for some one had murmured something about a notorious Fenian getting back home to his kind. Arthur saw her get into a cab with her party a few minutes later and drive away. A sadness fell upon him, the bitterness which follows the fading of our human dreams before the strong light of day.

CHAPTER XIX.

LA BELLE COLETTE.

After the situation had been discussed over the breakfast for ten minutes Arthur understood the mournful expression of the Senator, whose gaiety lapsed at intervals when bitterness got the better of him.

"The boys—the whole town is raving about you, Artie," said he with pride, "over the way you managed that affair of Ledwith's. There'll be nothing too good for you this year, if you work all the points of the game—if you follow good advice, I mean. You've got Livingstone in a corner. When this cruel war is over, and it is over for the Fenians—they've had enough, God knows—it ought to be commencing for the Honorable Quincy Livingstone."

"You make too much of it, Senator," Grahame responded. "We know what's back of these attacks on you and others. It's this way, Arthur: the Senator and I have been working hard for the American citizens in English jails, Fenians of course, and the Livingstone crowd have hit back at us hard. The Senator, as the biggest man in sight, got hit hardest."

"What they say of me is true, though. That's what hurts."

"Except that they leave out the man whom every one admires for his good sense, generous heart, and great success," Arthur said to console him.

"Of course one doesn't like to have the sins of his youth advertised for two civilizations," Grahame continued. "One must consider the source of this abuse however. They are clever men who write against us, but to know them is not to admire them. Bitterkin of the *Post* has his brain, stomach, and heart stowed away in a single sack under his liver, which is very torpid, and his stomach is always sour. His blood is three parts water from the Boyne, his food is English, his clothes are a very bad fit, and his whiskers are so hard they dull the scissors. He loves America when he can forget that Irish and other foreign

186

vermin inhabit it, otherwise he detests it. He loves England until he remembers that he can't live in it. The other fellow, Smallish, writes beautiful English, and lives on the old clothes of the nobility. Now who would mourn over the diatribes of such cats?"

The Senator had to laugh at the description despite his sadness.

"This is only one symptom of the trouble that's brewing. There's no use in hiding the fact that things are looking bad. Since the Fenian scheme went to pieces, the rats have left their holes. The Irish are demoralized everywhere, fighting themselves as usual after a collapse, and their enemies are quoting them against one another. Here in New York the hired bravos of the press are in the pay of the Livingstone crowd, or of the British secret service. What can you expect?"

"How long will it last? What is doing against it?" said Arthur.

"Ask me easier questions. Anyway, I'm only consoling the Senator for the hard knocks he's getting for the sake of old Ireland. Cheer up, Senator."

"Even when Fritters made his bow," said the mournful Senator, "they made game of me," and the tears rose to his eyes. Arthur felt a secret rage at this grief.

"You heard of Fritters?" and Arthur nodded. "He arrived, and the Columbia College crowd started him off with a grand banquet. He's an Oxford historian with a new recipe for cooking history. The Columbia professor who stood sponsor for him at the banquet told the world that Fritters would show how English government worked among the Irish, and how impossible is the Anglo-Saxon idea among peoples in whom barbarism does not die with the appearance and advance of civilization. He touched up the elegant parades and genial shindys of St. Patrick's Day as 'inexplicable dumb shows and noise,'—see Hamlet's address to the players—and hoped the banks of our glorious Hudson would never witness the bloody rows peculiar to the banks of the immortal Boyne. Then he dragged in the Senator."

"What's his little game?" Arthur asked.

"Scientific ridicule ... the press plays to the galleries, and Fritters to the boxes ... it's a part of the general scheme ... I tell you there's going to be fun galore this winter ... and the man in London is at the root of the deviltry."

"What's to be done?"

"If we only knew," the Senator groaned. "If we could only get them under our fists, in a fair and square tussle!"

"I think the hinge of the Livingstone plan is Sister Claire, the escaped nun," Grahame said thoughtfully. "She's the star of the combination, appeals to the true blue church-member with descriptions of the horrors of convents. Her book is out, and you'll find a copy waiting for you at home. Dime novels are prayer-books beside it. French novels are virtuous compared with it. It is raising an awful row. On the strength of it McMeeter has begun an enterprise for the relief of imprisoned nuns—to rescue them—house them for a time, and see them safely married. Sister Claire is to be matron of the house of escaped nuns. No one doubts her experience. Now isn't that McMeeter all over? But see the book, the *Confessions of an Escaped Nun.*"

"You think she's the hinge of the great scheme?"

"She has the public eye and ear," said Grahame, thinking out his own theory as he talked. "Her book is the book of the hour ... reviewed by the press ... the theme of pulpits ... the text of speeches galore ... common workmen thump one another over it at the bench. Now all the others, Bradford, Fritters, the Columbia professors, Bitterkin and his followers, seem to play second to her book. They keep away from her society, yet her strongest backing is from them. You know what I mean. It has occurred to me that if we got her history ... it must be pretty savory ... and printed it ... traced her connection with the Livingstone crowd ... it would be quite a black eye for the Honorable Quincy."

"By George, but you've struck it," cried Arthur waking up to the situation. "If she's the hinge, she's the party to strike at. Tell me, what became of Curran?"

"Lucky thought," shouted Grahame. "He's in town yet. The very man for us."

"I'm going to have it out with Livingstone," said Arthur, with a clear vision of an English prison and the patient woman who watched its walls from a window in the town. "In fact, I *must* have it out with Livingstone. He's good game, and I'd like to bring him back from England in a bag. Perhaps Sister Claire may be able to provide the bag."

"Hands on it," said Grahame, and they touched palms over the table, while the Senator broke into smiles. He had unlimited faith in his nephew.

"Lord Conny gave me an outline of Livingstone's program before I left. He's worried over the effect it's going to have on his alliance scheme, and he cursed the Minister sincerely. He'll help us. Let's begin with Sister Claire in the hope of bagging the whole crowd. Let Curran hunt up her history. Above all let him get evidence that Livingstone provides the money for her enterprise."

Having come to a conclusion on this important matter, they dropped into more personal topics.

"Strangely enough," said Grahame cheerfully, "my own destiny is mixed up with this whole business. The bulwark of Livingstone in one quarter is John Everard. I am wooing, in the hope of winning, my future father-in-law."

"He's very dead," the Senator thought.

"The art of wooing a father-in-law!—what an art!" murmured Grahame. "The mother-in-law is easy. She wishes her daughter married. Papa doesn't. At least in this case, with a girl like Mona."

"Has Everard anything against you?"

"A whole litany of crimes."

"What's wrong with Everard?"

"He was born the night of the first big wind, and he has had it in for the whole world ever since. He's perverse. Nothing but another big wind will turn him round."

Seeing Arthur puzzled over these allusions, Grahame explained.

"Think of such a man having children like the twins, little lumps of sweetness ... like Louis ... heavens! if I live to be the father of such a boy, life will be complete ... like my Mona ... oh!"

He stalked about the room throwing himself into poses of ecstasy and adoration before an imaginary goddess to the delight of the Senator.

"I've been there myself," Arthur commented unmoved. "To the question: how do you hope to woo and win Everard?"

"First, by my book. It's the story of just such a fool as he: a chap who wears the American flag in bed and waves it at his meals, as a nightgown and a napkin; then, he is a religious man of the kind that finds no religion to his liking, and would start one of his own if he thought it would pay; finally, he is a purist in politics, believes in blue glass, drinks ten glasses of filtered water a day, which makes him as blue as the glass, wears paper collars, and won't let his son be a monk because there are too many in the world. Now, Everard will laugh himself weak over this character. He's so perverse that he will never see himself in the mirror which I have provided."

"Rather risky, I should think."

"But that's not all," Grahame went on, "since you are kind enough to listen. I'm going to wave the American flag, eat it, sing it, for the next year, myself. Attend: the descendants of the Pilgrim Fathers are going to sit on what is left of Plymouth Rock next spring, and make speeches and read poems, and eat banquets. I am to be invited to sing, to read the poem. Vandervelt is to see to that. Think of it, a wild Irishman, an exile, a conspirator against the British Crown, a subject of the Pope, reading or singing the praises of the pilgrims, the grim pilgrims. Turn in your grave, Cotton Mather, as my melodious verses harrow your ears."

"Will that impress John Everard?"

"Or give him a fatal fit. The book and the poem ought to do the business. He can't resist. 'Never was Everard in this humor wooed, never was Everard in this humor won.' Oh, that Shakespeare had known an Everard, and embalmed him like a fly in the everlasting amber of his verse. But should these things fail, I have another matter. While Everard rips up Church and priest and doctrine at his pleasure, he has one devotion which none may take liberties with. He swears by the nuns. He is foaming at the mouth over the injury and insult offered them by the *Confessions* of Sister Claire. We expose this clever woman. Picture me, then, the despised suitor, after having pleased him by my book, and astounded him with my poem, and mesmerized him with the exposure of Claire, standing before him with silent lips but eyes speaking: I want your daughter. Can even this perverse man deny me? Don't you think I have a chance?"

"Not with Everard," said the Senator solemnly. "He's simply coke."

"You should write a book, Doyle, on the art of wooing a father-in-law, and explain what you have left out here: how to get away with the dog."

"Before marriage," said the ready wit, "the girl looks after the dog; after marriage the dog can be trained to bite the father-in-law."

Arthur found the *Confessions of an Escaped Nun* interesting reading from many points of view, and spent the next three days analyzing the book of the hour. His sympathy for convent life equaled his understanding of it. He had come to understand and like Sister Mary Magdalene, in spite of a prejudice against her costume; but the motive and spirit of the life she led were as yet beyond him. Nevertheless, he could see how earnestly the *Confessions* lied about what it pretended to expose. The smell of the indecent and venal informer exhaled from the pages. The vital feature, however, lay in the revelation of Sister Claire's character, between the lines. Beneath the vulgarity and obscenity, poorly veiled in a mock-modest verbiage, pulsated a burning sensuality reaching the horror of mania. A well-set trap would have easy work in catching the feet of a woman related to the nymphs. Small wonder that the Livingstone party kept her afar off from their perfumed and reputable society while she did her nasty work. The book must have been oil to that conflagration raging among the Irish. The abuse of the press, the criticism of their friends, the reproaches of their own, the hostility of the government, the rage and grief at the failure of their hopes, the plans to annoy and cripple them, scorched indeed their sensitive natures; but the book of the Escaped Nun, defiling their holy ones so shamelessly, ate like acid into their hearts. Louis came in, when he had completed his analysis of the volume, and begun to think up a plan of action. The lad fingered the book gingerly, and said timidly:

"I'm going to see ... I have an appointment with this terrible woman for to-morrow afternoon. In fact, I saw her this morning. I went to her office with Sister Mary Magdalen."

"Of course the good Sister has a scheme to convert the poor thing!" Arthur said lightly, concealing his delight and surprise under a pretense of indifference.

"Well, yes," and the lad laughed and blushed. "And she may succeed too. The greater the sin the deeper the repentance. The unfortunate woman — —"

"Who is making a fortune on her book by the way — —"

"— —received us very kindly. Sister Magdalen had been corresponding with her. She wept in admitting that her fall seemed beyond hope. She felt so tangled in her own sins that she knew no way to get out of them. Really, she *was* so sincere. When we were leaving she begged me to call again, and as I have to return to the seminary Monday I named to-morrow afternoon."

"You may then have the honor of converting her."

"It would be an honor," Louis replied stoutly.

"Try it," said Arthur after thinking the matter over. "I know what force *your* arguments will have with her. And if you don't object I'll stay ... by the way, where is her office?"

"In a quiet business building on Bleecker Street, near Broadway."

"If you don't mind I'll stay outside in the hall, and rush in to act as altar-boy, when she agrees to 'vert."

"I'm going for all your ridicule, Arthur."

"No objection, but keep a cool head, and bear in mind that I am in the hall outside."

He suspected the motive of Sister Claire, both in making this appointment, and in playing at conversion with Sister Magdalen. Perhaps it might prove the right sort of trap for her cunning feet. He doubted the propriety of exposing Louis to the fangs of the beast, and for a moment he thought to warn him of the danger. But he had no right to interfere in Sister Magdalen's affair, and if a beginning had to be made this adventure could be used effectively. He forgot the affair within the hour, in the business of hunting up Curran.

He had a double reason for seeking the detective. Besides the task of ferreting out the record of Sister Claire, he wished to get news of the Endicotts. Aunt Lois had slipped out of life two days after her return from Europe. The one heart that loved him truly beat for him no more. By this time her vengeance must have fallen, and Sonia, learning the full extent of her punishment, must now be writhing under a second humiliation and disappointment. He did not care to see her anguish, but he did care to hear of the new effort that would undoubtedly be made to find the lost husband. Curran would know. He met him that afternoon on the street near his own house.

"Yes, I'm back in the old business," he said proudly; "the trip home so freshened me that I feel like myself again. Besides, I have my own home, here it is, and my wife lives with me. Perhaps you have heard of her, La Belle Colette."

"And seen her too ... a beautiful and artistic dancer."

"You must come in now and meet her. She is a trifle wild, you know, and once she took to drink; but she's a fine girl, a real good fellow, and worth twenty like me. Come right in, and we'll talk business later."

La Belle Colette! The dancer at a cheap seaside resort! The wild creature who drank and did things! This shrewd, hard fellow, who faced death as others faced a wind, was deeply in love and happy in her companionship. What standard of womanhood and wifehood remained to such men? However, his wonder ceased when he had bowed to La Belle Colette in her own parlor, heard her sweet voice, and looked into the most entrancing eyes ever owned by a woman, soft, fiery, tender, glad, candid eyes. He recalled the dancer, leaping like a flame about the stage. In the plainer home garments he recognized the grace, quickness, and gaiety of the artist. Her charm won him at once, the spell which her rare kind have ever been able to cast about the hearts of men. He understood why the flinty detective should be in love with his wife at times, but not why he should continue in that state. She served them with wine and cigars, rolled a cigarette for herself, chatted with the ease and chumminess of a good fellow, and treated Arthur with tenderness.

"Richard has told me so much of you," she explained.

"I have so admired your exquisite art," he replied, "that we are already friends."

"Que vous êtes bien gentil," she murmured, and her tone would have caressed the wrinkles out of the heart of old age.

"Yes, I'm back at the old game," said Curran, when they got away from pleasantry. "I'm chasing after Tom Jones. It's more desperate than ever. His old aunt died some days back, and left Tom's wife a dollar, and Tom's son another dollar."

"I can fancy her," said Colette with a laugh, "repeating to herself that magic phrase, two dollars, for hours and hours. Hereafter she will get weak at sight of the figure two, and things that go in twos, like married people, she will hate."

"How easy to see that you are French, Colette," said Arthur, as a compliment. She threw him a kiss from her pretty fingers, and gave a sidelong look at Curran.

"There's a devil in her," Arthur thought.

"The will was very correct and very sound," resumed the detective. "No hope in a contest if they thought of such a thing among the West ... the Jones'. The heirs took pity on her, and gave her a lump for consolation. She took it and cursed them for their kindness. Her rage was something to see. She is going to use that lump, somewhere about twenty-five thousand, I think, to find her accursed Tom. How do I know? That's part of the prize for me if I catch up with Tom Jones within three years. And I draw a salary and expenses all the time. You should have seen Mrs. Tom the day I went to see her. Colette," with a smile for his wife, "your worst trouble with a manager was a summer breeze to it. You're a white-winged angel in your tempers compared with Mrs. Tom Jones. Her language concerning the aunt and the vanished nephew was wonderful. I tried to remember it, and I couldn't."

"I can see her, I can feel with her," cried La Belle Colette, jumping to her feet, and rushing through a pantomime of fiendish rage, which made the men laugh to exhaustion. As she sat down she said with emphasis, "She must find him, and through you. I shall help, and so will our friend Dillon. It's an outrage for any man to leave a woman in such a scrape ... for a mere trifle."

"She has her consolations," said the detective; "but the devil in her is not good-natured like the devil in you, Colette. She wants to get hold of Tom and cut him in little bits for what he has made her suffer."

"Did you get out any plans?" said Arthur.

"One. Look for him between here and Boston. That's my wife's idea. Tom Jones was not clever, but she says ... Say it yourself, my dear."

"Rage and disappointment, or any other strong feeling," said the woman sharply, with strong puffs at her cigarette, "turns a fool into a wise man for a minute. It would be just like this fool to have a brilliant interval while he dreamed of murdering his clever wife. Then he hit upon a scheme to cheat the detectives. It's easy, if you know how stupid they are, except Dick. Tom Jones is here, on his own soil. He was not going to run away with a million and try to spend it in the desert of Sahara. He's here, or in Boston, enjoying the sight of his wife stewing in poverty. It would be just like the sneak to do her that turn."

She looked wickedly at Arthur. What a face! Thin, broad, yet finely proportioned, with short, flaxen locks framing it, delicate eyebrows marking the brow and emphasizing the beautiful eyes. A woman to be feared, an evil spirit in some of her moods.

"You tried the same plan," Arthur began— —

"But he had no partner to sharpen his wits," she interrupted. Arthur bowed.

"That makes all the difference in the world," he said sincerely. "Let me hope that you will give your husband some hints in a case which I am going to give him."

He described the career of Sister Claire briefly, and expressed the wish to learn as much as possible of her earlier history. The Currans laughed.

"I had that job before," said the detective. "If the Jones case were only half a hundred times harder I might be happy. Her past is unknown except that she has been put out of many convents. I never looked up her birthplace or her relatives. Her name is Kate Kerrigan along with ten other names. She drinks a little, and just now holds a fine stake in New York ... There's the whole of it."

"Not much to build upon, if one wished to worry Claire, or other people."

"Depend upon it," Colette broke in, "that Kate Kerrigan has a pretty history behind her. I'll bet she was an actress once. I've seen her stage poses ... then her name, catchy ... and the way she rolls her eyes and looks at that congregation of elders, and deacons and female saints, when she sets them shivering over the nastiness that's coming."

Curran glanced at her with a look of inquiry. She sat on the window-sill like a bird, watching the street without, half listening to the men within. Arthur made a close study of the weird creature, sure that a strain of madness ran in her blood. Her looks and acts had the grace of a wild nature, which purrs, and kills, and purrs again. Quiet and dreamy this hour, in her dances she seemed half mad with vitality.

"Tell him what you learned about her," said Curran, and then to Arthur, "She can do a little work herself, and likes it."

"To hunt a poor soul down, never!" she cried. "But when a mean thing is hiding what every one has a right to know, I like to tear the truth out of her ... like your case of Tom Jones. Sister Claire is downright mean. Maybe she can't help it. But I know the nuns, and they're God's own children. She knows it too, but, just for the sake of money, she's lying night and day against them, and against her own conscience. There's a devil in her. I could do a thing like that for deviltry, and I could pull a load of money out of her backers, not for the money, but for deviltry too, to skin a miser like McMeeter, and a dandy like Bradford. And she's just skinning them, to the last cent."

She took a fit of laughing, then, over the embarrassment of Sister Claire's chief supporters.

"Here's what I know about her," she went on. "The museum fakirs are worshiping her as a wonderful success. They seem to feel by instinct that she's one of themselves, but a genius. They have a lot of fairy stories about her, but here's the truth: Bishop Bradford and Erastus McMeeter are her backers. The Bishop plays high society for her, and the bawler looks after the mob. She gets fifty per cent. of everything, and they take all the risks. Her book, I know you read it, chock-full of lies, thrilling lies, for the brothers and the sisters who can't read French novels in public—well, she owns the whole thing and gets all the receipts except a beggar's ten per cent., thrown to the publishers ... and they're the crack publishers of the town, the Hoppertons ... but all the same they dassent let their names go on the title-page ... they had that much shame ... so old Johnson, whom nobody knows, is printer and publisher. The book is selling like peanuts. There's more than one way of selling your soul to the devil."

After this surprising remark, uttered without a smile, she looked out of the window sadly, while Curran chuckled with delight.

"It takes the woman to measure the woman," he said. Arthur was delighted at this information.

"I wish you would learn some more about her, Mrs. Curran."

She mimicked the formal name in dumb show.

"Well, La Belle Colette, then," he said laughing. She came over to him and sat on the arm of his chair, her beautiful eyes fixed on his with an expression well understood by both the men.

"You are going to hunt that dreadful creature down," said she. "I won't help you. What do you know about her motives? She may have good reason for playing the part ... she may have suffered?"

"One must protect his own," replied Arthur grimly.

"What are we all but wolves that eat one another?—lambs by day, wolves in the night. We all play our part——"

"All the world's a stage, of course——"

"Even you are playing a part," with sudden violence. "I have studied you, young man, since you came in. Lemme read your palm, and tell you."

She held his hand long, then tossed it aside with petulance, parted his hair and peered into his face, passed her hands lightly over his head for the prominences, dashed unexpected tears from her eyes, and then said with decision:

"There are two of you in there," tapping his chest. "I can't tell why, but I can read, or feel one man, and outside I see another."

"Your instinct is correct," said Arthur seriously. "I have long been aware of the same fact, peculiar and painful. But for a long time the outside man has had the advantage. Now with regard to this Sister Claire, not to change the subject too suddenly——"

Colette deserted his chair, and went to her husband. She had lost interest in the matter and would not open her lips again. The men discussed the search for Endicott, and the inquiry into the history of

Sister Claire, while the dancer grew drowsy after the fashion of a child, her eyes became misty, her red lips pouted, her voice drawled faint and complaining music in whispers, and Curran looked often and long at her while he talked. Arthur went away debating with himself. His mind had developed the habit of reminiscence. Colette reminded him of a face, which he had seen ... no, not a face but a voice ... or was it a manner?... or was it her look, which seemed intimate, as of earlier acquaintance?... what was it? It eluded him however. He felt happy and satisfied, now that he had set Curran on the track of the unclean beast.

CHAPTER XX.

THE ESCAPED NUN.

Sister Claire sat in her office the next afternoon awaiting Louis as the gorged spider awaits the fly, with desire indeed, but without anxiety. Her office consisted of three rooms, opening into one another within, each connected by doors with the hall without. A solemn youth kept guard in the antechamber, a bilious lad whose feverish imagination enshrined Sister Claire and McMeeter on the same altar, and fed its fires on the promises of the worthy pair some day to send him on a mission as glorious as their own. The furnishings had the severe simplicity of the convent. The brilliant costume of the woman riveted the eye by the very dulness of her surroundings. At close view her beauty seemed more spiritual than in her public appearances. The heavy eyebrows were a blemish indeed, but like a beauty-spot emphasized the melting eyes and the peachy skin.

The creamy habit of the nun and the white coif about her head left only her oval face and her lovely hands visible; but what a revelation were these of loveliness and grace! One glance at her tender face and the little hands would have scattered to the winds the slanders of Colette. Success had thrilled but not coarsened the escaped nun. As Grahame had surmised, she was now the hinge of Livingstone's scheme. The success of her book and the popularity of her lectures, together with her discreet behavior, had given her immense influence with her supporters and with the leaders. Their money poured into her lap. She did not need it while her book sold and her lectures were crowded.

The office saw come and go the most distinguished visitors. Even the English historian did not begin to compare with her in glory, and so far his lectures had not been well attended. Thinking of many things with deep pride, she remembered that adversity had divided the leisure of her table with prosperity. Hence, she could not help wondering how long this fine success would last. Her peculiar fate demanded an end to it sometime. As if in answer to her question, the solemn youth in the antechamber knocked at her door, and announced with decorum Mr. Richard Curran.

"I have made the inquiries you wanted," Curran said, as he took a chair at her bidding. "Young Everard is a special pet of Dillon. This boy is the apple of his eye. And Everard, the father, is an ardent supporter of Livingstone. I think you had better drop this affair, if you would escape a tangle—a nasty tangle."

"If the boy is willing, where's the tangle, Mr. Curran?" she answered placidly.

"Well, you know more about the thing than I can tell you," he said, as if worried. "You know them all. But I can't help warning you against this Dillon. If you lay your hand on anything of his, I'm of opinion that this country will not be big enough for you and him at the same time."

"I shall get him also, and that'll put an end to his enmity. He's a fine fellow. He's on my track, but you'll see how enchantment will put him off it. Now, don't grumble. I'll be as tender and sweet with the boy as a siren. You will come in only when I feel that the spell doesn't work. Rely on me to do the prudent thing."

That he did not rely on her his expression showed clearly.

"You have made a great hit in this city, Sister Claire," he began——

"And you think I am about to ruin my chances of a fortune?" she interrupted. "Well, I am willing to take the risk, and you have nothing to say about it. You know your part. Go into the next room, and wait for your cue. I'll bet any sum that you'll never get the cue. If you do, be sure to make a quick entrance."

He looked long at her and sighed, but made no pretense to move. She rose, and pointed to the third room of the suite. Sheepishly, moodily, in silent protest, he obeyed the gesture and went out humbly. Before that look the brave detective surrendered like a slave to his chains. The door had hardly closed behind him, when the office-boy solemnly announced Louis, and at a sign from Sister Claire ushered in the friend of Arthur Dillon. She received him with downcast eyes, standing at a little distance. With a whispered welcome and a drooping head, she pointed to a seat. Louis sat down nervous and overawed, wishing that he had never undertaken this impossible and depressing task. Who was he to be dealing with such a character as this dubious and disreputable woman?

"I feared you would not come," she began in a very low tone. "I feared you would misunderstand ... what can one like you understand of sin and misery?... but thank Heaven for your courage ... I may yet owe to you my salvation!"

"I was afraid," said the lad frankly, gladdened by her cunning words. "I don't know of what ... but I suppose it was distrust of myself. If I can be of any service to you how glad I shall be!"

"Oh, you can, you can," she murmured, turning her beautiful eyes on him. Her voice failed her, and she had to struggle with her sobs.

"What do you think I can do for you?" he asked, to relieve the suspense.

"I shall tell you that later," she replied, and almost burst out laughing. "It will be simple and easy for you, but no one else can satisfy me. We are alone. I must tell you my story, that you may be the better able to understand the service which I shall ask of you. It is a short story, but terrible ... especially to one like you ... promise me that you will not shrink, that you will not despise me — —"

"I have no right to despise you," said Louis, catching his breath.

She bowed her head to hide a smile, and appeared to be irresolute for a moment. Then with sudden, and even violent, resolve, she drew a chair to his side, and began the history of her wretched career. Her position was such, that to see her face he had to turn his head; but her delicate hands rested on the arm of his chair, clasped now, and again twisted with anguish, and then stretched out with upward palms appealing for pity, or drooping in despair. She could see his profile, and watch the growing uneasiness, the shame of innocence brought face to face with dirt unspeakable, the mortal terror of a pure boy in the presence of Phryne. With this sport Sister Claire had been long familiar.

Her caressing voice and deep sorrow stripped the tale of half its vileness. At times her voice fell to a breath. Then she bent towards him humbly, and a perfume swept over him like a breeze from the tropics. The tale turned him to stone. Sister Claire undoubtedly drew upon her imagination and her reading for the facts, since it rarely falls to the lot of one woman to sound all the depths of depravity. Louis had little nonsense in his character. At first his horror urged him to fly from the place, but whenever the tale aroused this feeling in him, the cunning creature broke forth into a strain of penitence so sweet and touching that he had not the heart to desert her. At the last she fell upon her knees and buried her face in his lap, crying out:

"If you do not hate me now ... after all this ... then take pity on me."

Arthur sauntered into the hall outside the office of Sister Claire about half-past four. He had forgotten the momentous interview which bid so fair to end in the conversion of the escaped nun; also his declaration to be within hailing distance in case of necessity. In a lucky moment, however, the thought of Sister Mary Magdalen and her rainbow enterprise, so foolish, so incredible, came to his mind, and sent him in haste to the rescue of his friend. Had Louis kept his engagement and received the vows and the confession of the audacious tool of Livingstone? No sound came from the office. It would hardly do for him to make inquiry.

He observed that Sister Claire's office formed a suite of three rooms. The door of the first looked like the main entrance. It had the appearance of use, and within he heard the cough of the solemn office-boy. A faint murmur came from the second room. This must be the private sanctum of the spider; this murmur might be the spider's enchantment over the fly. What should the third room be? The trap? He turned the knob and entered swiftly and silently, much to the detective's surprise and his own.

"I had no idea that door was unlocked," said Curran helplessly.

"Nor I. Who's within? My friend, young Everard?"

"Don't know. She shoved me in here to wait until some visitor departed. Then we are to consider a proposition I made her," said the calm detective.

"So you have made a beginning? That's good. Don't stir. Perhaps it is as well that you are here. Let me discover who is in here with the good sister."

"I can go to the first room, the front office, and inquire," said Curran.

"Never mind."

He could hear no words, only the low tones of the woman speaking; until of a sudden the strong, manly voice of Louis, but subdued by emotion, husky and uncertain, rose in answer to her passionate outburst.

"He's inside ... my young man ... hopes to convert her," Arthur whispered to Curran, and they laughed together in silence. "Now I have my own suspicion as to her motive in luring the boy here. If he goes as he came, why I'm wrong perhaps. If there's a rumpus, I may have her little feet in the right sort of a trap, and so save you labor, and the rest of us money. If anything happens, Curran, leave the situation to me. I'm anxious for a close acquaintance with Sister Claire."

Curran sat as comfortably, to the eye, as if in his own house entertaining his friend Dillon. The latter occasionally made the very natural reflection that this brave and skilful man lay in the trap of just such a creature as Sister Claire. Suddenly there came a burst of sound from the next room, exclamations, the hurrying of feet, the crash of a chair, and the trying of the doors. A frenzied hand shook the knob of the door at which Arthur was looking with a satisfied smile.

"Locked in?" he said to Curran, who nodded in a dazed way.

Then some kind of a struggle began on the other side of that door. Arthur stood there like a cat ready to pounce on the foolish mouse, and the detective glared at him like a surly dog eager to rend him, but afraid. They could hear smothered calls for help in a woman's voice.

"If she knew how near the cat is," Arthur remarked patiently.

At last the key clicked in the lock, the door half opened, and as Arthur pushed it inwards Sister Claire flung herself away from it, and gasped feebly for help. She was hanging like a tiger to Louis, who in a gentle way tried to shake her hands and arms from his neck. The young fellow's face bore the frightful look of a terrified child struggling for life against hopeless odds—mingled despair and pain. Arthur remained quietly in the entrance, and the detective glared over his shoulder warningly at Claire. At sight of the man who stood there, she would have shrieked in her horror and fright, but that sound died away in her throat. She loosened her grip, and stood staring a moment, then swiftly and meaningly began to arrange her disordered clothing. Louis made a dash for the door, seeing only a way of escape and not recognizing his friend. Arthur shook him.

"Ah, you will go converting before your time," he said gayly.

"Oh, Arthur, thank God— —" the lad stammered.

"Seize him," Claire began to shriek, very cautiously however. "Hold him, gentlemen. Get the police. He is an emissary of the papists— —"

"Let me go," Louis cried in anguish.

"Steady all round," Arthur answered with a laugh. "Sister Claire, if you want the police raise your voice. One harlot more on the Island will not matter. Louis, get your nerve, man. Did I not tell you I would be in the hall? Go home, and leave me to deal with this perfect lady. Look after him," he flung at Curran, and closed the door on them, quite happy at the result of Sister Magdalen's scheme of conversion.

He did not see the gesture from Curran which warned Sister Claire to make terms in a hurry with this dangerous young man. The fury stood at the far end of the office, burning with rage and uncertainty.

Having fallen into her own trap, she knew not what to do. The situation had found its master. Arthur Dillon evidently took great pleasure in this climax of her making. He looked at her for a moment as one might at a wild animal of a new species. The room had been darkened so that one could not see distinctly. He knew that trick too. Her beauty improved upon acquaintance. For the second time her face reminded him that they had met before, and he considered the point for an instant. What did it matter just then? She had fallen into his hands, and must be disposed of. Pointing to a chair he sat down affably, his manner making his thought quite plain. She remained standing.

"You may be very tired before our little talk is concluded — —"

"Am I to receive your insults as well as your agent's?" she interrupted.

"Now, now, Sister Claire, this will never do. You have been acting" ... he looked at his watch ... "since four o'clock. The play is over. We are in real life again. Talk sense. Since Everard failed to convert you, and you to convert Everard, try the arts of Cleopatra on me. Or, let me convince you that you have made a blunder — —"

"I do not wish to listen you," she snapped. "I will not be insulted a second time."

"Who could insult the author of the *Confessions*? You are beyond insult, Claire. I have read your book with the deepest interest. I have read you between every line, which cannot be said of most of your readers. I am not going to waste any words on you. I am going to give you an alternative, which will do duty until I find rope enough to hang you as high as Jack Sheppard. You know what you are, and so do I. The friends of this young man who fell so nicely into your claws will be anxious to keep his adventure with you very quiet."

A light leaped into her eyes. She had feared that outside, in the hall, this man might have his hirelings ready to do her mischief, that some dreadful plot had come to a head which meant her ruin. Light began to dawn upon her. He laughed at her thoughts.

"One does not care to make public an adventure with such a woman as you," said he affably. "A young man like that too. It would be fatal for him. Therefore, you are to say nothing about it. You are not eager to talk about your failure ... Cleopatra blushes for your failure ... but a heedless tongue and a bitter feeling often get the better of sense. If you remain silent, so shall I."

"Very generous," she answered calmly, coming back to her natural coolness and audacity. "As you have all to lose, and I have all to gain by a description of the trap set for me by your unclean emissary, your proposition won't go. I shall place the matter before my friends, and before the public, when I find it agreeable."

"When!" he mocked. "You know by this time that you are playing a losing game, Claire. If you don't know it, then you are not smart enough for the game. Apart from that, remember one thing: when you speak I shall whisper the truth to the excitable people whom your dirty book is harrying now."

"I am not afraid of whispers, quite used to them in fact," she drawled, as if mimicking him.

"I see you are not smart enough for the game," and the remark startled her. "You can see no possible results from that whisper. Did you ever hear of Jezebel and her fate? Oh, you recall how the dogs worried her bones, do you? So far your evil work has been confined to glittering generalities. To-day you took a new tack. Now you must answer to me. Let it once become known that you tried to defile the innocent, to work harm to one of mine, and you may suffer the fate of the unclean things to which you belong by nature. The mob kills without delicacy. It will tear you as the dogs tore the painted Jezebel."

"You are threatening me," she stammered with a show of pride.

"No. That would be a waste of time. I am warning you. You have still the form of a woman, therefore I give you a chance. You are at the end of your rope. Stretch it further, and it may become the noose to hang you. You have defiled with your touch one whom I love. He kept his innocence, so I let it pass. But a rat like you must be destroyed. Very soon too. We are not going to stand your abominations, even if men like Livingstone and Bradford encourage you. I am giving you a chance. What do you say? Have I your promise to be silent?"

"You have," she replied brokenly.

He looked at her surprised. The mask of her brazen audacity remained, but some feeling had overpowered her, and she began to weep like any woman in silent humiliation. He left her without a word, knowing enough of her sex to respect this inexplicable grief, and to wait for a more favorable time to improve his acquaintance. "Sonia's mate," he said to himself as he reached the street. The phrase never left him from that day, and became a prophecy of woe afterwards. He writhed as he saw how nearly the honor and happiness of Louis had fallen into the hands of this wretch. Protected by the great, she could fling her dirt upon the clean, and go unpunished. Sonia's mate! He had punished one creature of her kind, and with God's help he would yet lash the backs of Sister Claire and her supporters.

CHAPTER XXI.

AN ANXIOUS NIGHT.

Curran caught up with him as he turned into Broadway. He had waited to learn if Arthur had any instructions, as he was now to return to Sister Claire's office and explain as he might the astounding appearance of Dillon at a critical moment.

"She's a ripe one," Arthur said, smiling at thought of her collapse, but the next moment he frowned. "She's a devil, Curran, a handsome devil, and we must deal with her accordingly—stamp her out like a snake. Did you notice her?"

"No doubt she's a bad one," Curran answered thickly, but Arthur's bitter words gave him a shiver, and he seemed to choke in his utterance.

"Make any explanation you like, Curran. She will accuse you of letting me in perhaps. It looks like a trap, doesn't it? By the way, what became of the boy?"

"He seemed pretty well broken up," the detective answered, "and sent me off as soon as he learned that I had him in charge. I told him that you had the whole business nicely in hand, and not to worry. He muttered something about going home. Anyway, he would have no more of me, and he went off quite steady, but looking rather queer, I thought."

Arthur, with sudden anxiety, recalled that pitiful, hopeless look of the terrified child in Louis' face. Perhaps he had been too dazed to understand how completely Arthur had rescued him in the nick of time. To the lad's inexperience this cheap attempt of Claire to overcome his innocence by a modified badger game might have the aspect of a tragedy. Moreover, he remained ignorant of the farce into which it had been turned.

"I am sorry you left him," he said, thoughtfully weighing the circumstances. "This creature threatened him, of course, with publicity, an attack on her honor by a papist emissary. He doesn't know how little she would dare such adventure now. He may run away in his fright, thinking that his shame may be printed in the papers, and that the police may be watching for him. Public disgrace means ruin for him, for, as you know, he is studying to be a priest."

"I didn't know," Curran answered stupidly, a greenish pallor spreading over his face. "That kind of work won't bring her much luck."

"It occurs to me now that he was too frightened to understand what my appearance meant, and what your words meant," Arthur resumed. "He may feel an added shame that we know about it. I must find him. Do you go at once to Sister Claire and settle your business with her. Then ride over to the Everards, and tell the lad, if he be there, that I wish to see him at once. If he has not yet got back, leave word with his mother ... keep a straight face while you talk with her ... to send him over to me as soon as he gets home. And tell her that if I meet him before he does get home, that I shall keep him with me all night. Do you see the point? If he has gone off in his fright, we have sixteen hours to find him. No one must know of his trouble, in that house at least, until he is safe. Do you think we can get on his trail right away, Curran?"

"We must," Curran said harshly, "we must. Has he any money?"

"Not enough to carry him far."

"Then ten hours' search ought to capture him."

"Report then to me at my residence within an hour. I have hopes that this search will not be needed, that you will find him at home. But be quicker than ever you were in your life, Curran. I'd go over to Cherry Street myself, but my inquiries would frighten the Everards. There must be no scandal."

Strange that he had not foreseen this possibility. For him the escapade with the escaped nun would have been a joke, and he had not thought how differently Louis must have regarded it. If the lad had really fled, and his friends must learn of it, Sister Claire's share in the matter would have to remain a profound secret. With all their great love for this boy, his clan would rather have seen him borne to the grave than living under the shadow of scandal in connection with this vicious woman. Her perfidy would add disgrace to grief, and deepen their woe beyond time's power to heal.

For with this people the prejudice against impurity was so nobly unreasonable that mere suspicion became equal to crime. This feeling intensified itself in regard to the priesthood. The innocence of Louis would not save him from lifelong reproach should his recent adventure finds its way into the sneering journals. Within the hour Curran, more anxious than Arthur himself, brought word that the lad had not yet reached home. His people were not worried, and promised to send him with speed to Arthur.

"Begin your search then," said Arthur, "and report here every hour. I have an idea he may have gone to see an aunt of his, and I'll go there to find out. What is your plan?"

"He has no money, and he'll want to go as far as he can, and where he won't be easily got at. He'll ship on an Indiaman. I'll set a few men to look after the outgoing ships as a beginning."

"Secrecy above all things, understand," was the last admonition.

Darkness had come on, and the clocks struck the hour of seven as Arthur set out for a visit to Sister Mary Magdalen. Possibly Louis had sought her to tell the story of failure and shame, the sad result of her foolish enterprise; and she had kept him to console him, to put him in shape before his return home, so that none might mark the traces of his frightful emotion. Alas, the good nun had not seen him since their visit to Claire's office in Bleecker Street the day before. He concealed from her the situation.

"How in the name of Heaven," said he, "did you conceive this scheme of converting this woman?"

"She has a soul to be saved, and it's quite saveable," answered the nun tartly. "The more hopeless from man's view, the more likely from God's. I have a taste for hopeless enterprises."

"I wish you had left Louis out of this one," Arthur thought. "But to deal with a wretch like her, so notorious, so fallen," he said aloud, "you must have risked too much. Suppose, after you had entered her office, she had sent for a reporter to see you there, to see you leaving after kissing her, to hear a pretty story of an embassy from the archbishop to coax her back to religion; and the next morning a long account of this attempt on her resolution should appear in the papers? What would your superiors say?"

"That could happen," she admitted with a shiver, "but I had her word that my visit was to be kept a secret."

"Her word!" and he raised his hands.

"Oh, I assure you the affair was arranged beforehand to the smallest detail," she declared. "Of course no one can trust a woman like that absolutely. But, as you see, in this case everything went off smoothly."

"I see indeed," said Arthur too worried to smile.

"I arranged the meeting through Miss Conyngham," the nun continued, "a very clever person for such work. I knew the danger of the enterprise, but the woman has a soul, and I thought if some one had the courage to take her by the hand and lead her out of her wicked life, she might do penance, and even become a saint. She received Miss Conyngham quite nicely indeed; and also my message that a helping hand was ready for her at any moment. She was afraid too of a trap; but at the last she begged to see me, and I went, with the consent of my superior."

"And how did you come to mix Louis up in the thing?"

"He happened to drop in as I was going, and I took him along. He was very much edified, we all were."

"And he has been more edified since," observed Arthur, but the good nun missed the sarcasm.

"She made open confession before the three of us," warming up at the memory of that scene. "With tears in her eyes she described her fall, her present remorse, her despair of the future, and her hope in us. Most remarkable scene I ever witnessed. I arranged for her to call at this convent whenever she could to plan for her return. She may be here any time. Oh, yes, I forgot. The most touching moment of all came at the last. When we were leaving she took Louis' hand, pressed it to her heart, kissed it with respect, and cried out: 'You happy soul, oh, keep the grace of God in your heart, hold to your high vocation through any torment: to lose it, to destroy it, as I destroyed mine, is to open wide the soul to devils.' Wasn't that beautiful now? Then she asked him in the name of God to call on her the next day, and he promised. He may be here to-night to tell me about it."

"You say three. Was Edith Conyngham the third?"

"Oh, no, only a sister of our community."

He burst out laughing at the thought of the fox acting so cleverly before the three geese. Claire must have laughed herself into a fit when they had gone. He had now to put the Sister on her guard at the expense of her self-esteem. He tried to do so gently and considerately, fearing hysterics.

"You put the boy in the grasp of the devil, I fear," he said. "Convert Sister Claire! You would better have turned your prayers on Satan! She got him alone this afternoon in her office, as you permitted, and made him a proposition, which she had in her mind from the minute she first saw him. I arrived in time to give her a shock, and to rescue him. Now we are looking for him to tell him he need not fear Sister Claire's threats to publish how he made an attack upon her virtue."

"I do not quite understand," gasped Sister Magdalen stupefied. What Arthur thought considerate others might have named differently. Exasperation at the downright folly of the scheme, and its threatened results, may have actuated him. His explanation satisfied the nun, and her fine nerve resisted hysterics and tears.

"It is horrible," she said at the last word. "But we acted honestly, and God will not desert us. You will find Louis before morning, and I shall spend the night in prayer until you have found him ... for him and you ... and for that poor wretch, that dreadful woman, more to be pitied than any one."

His confidence did not encourage him. Hour by hour the messengers of Curran appeared with the one hopeless phrase: no news. He walked about the park until midnight, and then posted himself in the basement with cigar and journal to while away the long hours. Sinister thoughts troubled him, and painful fancies. He could see the poor lad hiding in the slums, or at the mercy of wretches as vile as Claire; wandering about the city, perhaps, in anguish over his ruined life, horrified at what his friends must read in the morning papers, planning helplessly to escape from a danger which did not exist, except in his own mind. Oh, no doubt Curran would find him! Why, he *must* find him!

Across the sea in London, Minister Livingstone slept, full fed with the flatteries of a day, dreaming of the pleasures and honors sure to come with the morning. Down in the prison town lived Honora, with her eyes dulled from watching the jail and her heart sore with longing. For Owen the prison, for Louis the pavement, for Honora and himself the sleepless hours of the aching heart; but for the responsible Minister and his responsible tool sweet sleep, gilded comfort, overwhelming honors. Such things could be only because men of his sort were craven idiots. What a wretched twist in all things human! Why not, if nothing else could be done, go and set fire to Claire's office, the bishop's house, and the Livingstone mansion?

However, joy came at the end of the night, for the messenger brought word that the lad had been found, sound as a bell, having just shipped as a common sailor on an Indiaman. Since Curran could not persuade him to leave his ship, the detective had remained on the vessel to await Arthur's arrival. A cab took him down to the wharf, and a man led him along the dock to the gang-plank, thence across the deck to a space near the forecastle, where Curran sat with Louis in the starlight.

"Then it's all true ... what he has been telling me?" Louis cried as he leaped to his feet and took the hearty grasp of his friend.

"As true as gospel," said Arthur, using Judy's phrase. "Let's get out of this without delay. We can talk about it at home. Curran, do you settle with the captain."

They hurried away to the cab in silence. Before entering Arthur wrung the hand of the detective warmly.

"It would take more than I own to pay you for this night's work, Curran. I want you to know how I feel about it, and when the time comes ask your own reward."

"What you have just said is half of it," the man answered in a strange tone. "When the time comes I shall not be bashful."

"It would have been the greatest blunder of your life," Arthur said, as they drove homeward, "if you had succeeded in getting away. It cannot be denied, Louis, that from five o'clock this afternoon till now you made a fool of yourself. Don't reply. Don't worry about it. Just think of this gold-plate fact: no one knows anything about it. You are supposed to be sleeping sweetly at my house. I settled Claire beautifully. And Sister Magdalen, too. By the way, I must send her word by the cabby ... better let her do penance on her knees till sunrise ... she's praying for you ... but the suspense might kill her ... no, I'll send word. As I was saying, everything is as it was at four o'clock this afternoon."

He chattered for the lad's benefit, noting that at times Louis shivered as with ague, and that his hands were cold. He has tasted calamity, Arthur thought with resignation, and life will never be quite the same thing again. In the comfortable room the marks of suffering became painfully evident. Even joy failed to rouse his old self. Pale, wrinkled like age, shrunken, almost lean, he presented a woful spectacle. Arthur mixed a warm punch for him, and spread a substantial lunch.

"The sauce for this feast," said he, "is not appetite, but this fact: that your troubles are over. Now eat."

Louis made a pretense of eating, and later, under the influence of the punch, found a little appetite. By degrees his mind became clearer as his body rested, the wrinkles began to disappear, his body seemed to fill out while the comfort of the situation invaded him. Arthur, puffing his cigar and describing his interview with Claire, looked so stanch and solid, so sure of himself, so at ease with his neighbors, that one could scarcely fail to catch his happy complaint.

"She has begun her descent into hell," he said placidly, "but since you are with us still, I shall give her plenty of time to make it. What I am surprised at is that you did not understand what my entrance meant. She understood it. She thought Curran was due as her witness of the assault. What surprises me still more is that you so completely forgot my advice: no matter what the trouble and the shame, come straight to me. Here was a grand chance to try it."

"I never thought of this kind of trouble," said Louis dully. "Anyway, I got such a fright that I understood nothing rightly up to midnight. The terrible feeling of public disgrace eat into me. I saw and heard people crying over me as at a funeral, you know that hopeless crying. The road ahead looked to be full of black clouds. I wanted to die. Then I wanted to get away. When I found a ship they took me for a half-drunk sailor, and hustled me into the forecastle in lively shape. When Curran found me and hauled me out of the bunk, I had been asleep enjoying the awfullest dreams. I took him for a trickster, who wanted to get me ashore and jail me. I feel better. I think I can sleep now."

"Experience maybe has given you a better grip on the meaning of that wise advice which I repeat now: no matter what the trouble, come to me."

"I shall come," said the lad with a show of spirit that delighted Arthur. "Even if you should see me hanged the next day."

"That's a fine sentiment to sleep on, so we'll go to bed. However, remind yourself that a little good sense when you resume business ... by the way, it's morning ... no super-sensitiveness, no grieving, for you were straight all through ... go right on as if nothing had happened ... and in fact nothing has happened yet ... I can see that you understand."

They went to bed, and slept comfortably until noon. After breakfast Louis looked passably well, yet miserable enough to make explanations necessary for his alarmed parents. Arthur undertook the disagreeable office, which seemed to him delightful by comparison with that other story of a runaway son *en route* in fancied disgrace for India. All's well that ends well. Mary Everard wept with grief, joy, and gratitude, and took her jewel to her arms without complaint or question. The crotchety father was disposed to have it out with either the knaves or the fools in the game, did not Arthur reduce him to quiet by his little indictment.

"There is only one to quarrel with about this sad affair, John Everard," said he smoothly, "and that only one is your friend and well wisher, Quincy Livingstone. I want you to remember that, when we set out to take his scalp. It's a judgment on you that you are the first to suffer directly by this man's plotting. You needn't talk back. The boy is going to be ill, and you'll need all your epithets for your chief and yourself before you see comfort again."

Recalling his son's appearance the father remained silent. Arthur's prevision came true. The physician ordered Louis to bed for an indefinite time, having found him suffering from shock, and threatened with some form of fever. The danger did not daunt his mother. Whatever of suffering yet remained, her boy would endure it in the shelter of her arms.

"If he died this night," she said to Arthur, "I would still thank God that sent him back to die among his own; and after God, you, son dear, who have been more than a brother to him."

Thus the items in his account with kinsman Livingstone kept mounting daily.

CHAPTER XXII.

THE END OF A MELODRAMA.

Louis kept his bed for some weeks, and suffered a slow convalescence. Private grief must give way to public necessity. In this case the private grief developed a public necessity. Arthur took pains to tell his story to the leaders. It gave point to the general onslaught now being made on the Irish by the hired journals, the escaped nun, and, as some named him, the escaped historian. A plan was formulated to deal with all three. Grahame entered the lists against Bitterkin and Smallish, Vandervelt denounced the *Confessions* and its author at a banquet *vis-à-vis* with Bradford, and Monsignor pursued the escaped historian by lecturing in the same cities, and often on the same platform. Arthur held to Sister Claire as his specialty, as the hinge of the Livingstone scheme, a very rotten hinge on which to depend. Nevertheless, she kept her footing for months after her interview with him.

Curran had laid bare her life and exposed her present methods nicely; but neither afforded a grip which might shake her, except inasmuch as it gave him an unexpected clue to the Claire labyrinth. Her history showed that she had often played two parts in the same drama. Without doubt a similar trick served her now, not only to indulge her riotous passions, but to glean advantages from her enemies and useful criticism from her friends. He cast about among his casual acquaintance for characters that Claire might play. Edith Conyngham? Not impossible! The Brand who held forth at the gospel hall? Here was a find indeed! Comparing the impressions left upon him by these women, as a result he gave Curran the commission to watch and study the daily living of Edith Conyngham. Even this man's nerve shook at a stroke so luckily apt.

"I don't know much about the ways of escaped nuns," said Arthur, "but I am going to study them. I'll wager you find Claire behind the rusty garments of this obscure, muddy, slimy little woman. They have the same appetite anyway."

This choice bit of news, carried at once to the escaped nun, sounded in Sister Claire's ear like the crack of doom, and she stared at Curran, standing humbly in her office, with distorted face.

"Is this the result of your clever story-telling, Dick Curran?" she gasped.

"It's the result of your affair with young Everard," he replied sadly. "That was a mistake altogether. It waked up Arthur Dillon."

"The mistake was to wake that man," she said sourly. "I fear him. There's something hiding in him, something terrible, that looks out of his eyes like a ghost in hell. The dogs ... Jezebel ... that was his threat ... ugh!"

"He has waked up the whole crowd against you and frightened your friends. If ever he tells the Clan-na-Gael about young Everard, your life won't be worth a pin."

"With you to defend me?" ironically.

"I could only die with you ... against that crowd."

"And you would," she said with conviction, tears in her eyes. "My one friend."

His cheeks flushed and his eyes sparkled at the fervent praise of his fidelity.

"Well, it's all up with me," changing to a mood of gaiety. "The Escaped Nun must escape once more. They will all turn their coldest shoulders to me, absolutely frightened by this Irish crowd, to which we belong after all, Dick. I'm not sorry they can stand up for themselves, are you? So, there's nothing to do but take up the play, and begin work on it in dead earnest."

"It's a bad time," Curran ventured, as she took a manuscript from a desk. "But you know how to manage such things, you are so clever," he hastened to add, catching a fiery glance from her eye. "Only you must go with caution."

"It's a fine play," she said, turning the pages of the manuscript. "Dick, you are little short of a genius. If I had not liked the real play so well, playing to the big world this rôle of escaped nun, I would have taken it up long ago. The little stage of the theater is nothing to the grand stage of the world, where a whole nation applauds; and men like the Bishop take it for the real thing, this impersonation of mine. But since I am shut out ... and my curse on this Arthur Dillon ... no, no, I take that back ... he's a fine fellow, working according to his nature ... since he will shut me out I must take to the imitation stage. Ah, but the part is fine! First act: the convent garden, the novice reading her love in the flowers, the hateful old mother superior choking her to get her lover's note from her, the reading of the note, and the dragging of the novice to her prison cell, down in the depths of the earth. How that will draw the tears from the old maids of Methodism all over the country!"

She burst into hearty laughter.

"Second act: the dungeon, the tortures, old superior again, and the hateful hag who is in love with the hero and would like to wreak her jealousy on me, poor thing, all tears and determination. I loathe the two women. I denounce the creed which invents such tortures. I lie down to die in the dungeon while the music moans and the deacons and their families in the audience groan. Don't you think, Dicky dear, I can do the dying act to perfection?"

"On the stage perfectly."

"You're a wretch," she shrieked with sudden rage. "You hint at the night I took a colic and howled for the priest, when you know it was only the whisky and the delirium. How dare you!"

"It slipped on me," he said humbly.

"The third act is simply beautiful: chapel of the convent, a fat priest at the altar, all the nuns gathered about to hear the charges against me, I am brought in bound, pale, starved, but determined; the trial, the sentence, the curse ... oh, that scene is sublime, I can see Booth in it ... pity we can't have him ... then the inrush of my lover, the terror, the shrieks, the confusion, as I am carried off the stage with the curtain going down. At last the serene fourth act: another garden, the villains all punished, my lover's arms about me, and we two reading the flowers as the curtain descends. Well," with a sigh of pleasure, "if that doesn't take among the Methodists and the general public out West and down South, what will?"

"I can see the fire with which you will act it," said Curran eagerly. "You are a born actress. Who but you could play so many parts at once?"

"And yet," she answered dreamily, giving an expressive kick with unconscious grace, "this is what I like best. If it could be introduced into the last act ... but of course the audiences wouldn't tolerate it, dancing. Well," waking up suddenly to business, "are you all ready for the *grand coup*—press, manager, all details?"

"Ready long ago."

"Here then is the program, Dicky dear. To-morrow I seek the seclusion of the convent at Park Square—isn't *seclusion* good? To-night letters go out to all my friends, warning them of my utter loneliness, and dread of impending abduction. In two or three days you get a notice in the papers about these letters, and secure interviews with the Bishop if possible, with McMeeter anyway ... oh, he'll begin to howl as soon as he gets his letter. Whenever you think the public interest, or excitement, is at its height, then you bring your little ladder to the convent, and wait outside for a racket which will wake the neighborhood. In the midst of it, as the people are gathering, up with the ladder, and down with me in your triumphant arms. Pity we can't have a calcium light for that scene. If there should be any failure ... of course there can't be ... then a note of warning will reach me, with any instructions you may wish to give me ... to the old address of course."

Both laughed heartily at this allusion.

"It has been great fun," she said, "fooling them all right and left. That Dillon is suspicious though ... fine fellow ... I like him. Dicky, ... you're not jealous. What a wonder you are, dear old faithful Dicky, my playwright, manager, lover, detective, everything to me. Well, run along to your work. We strike for fortune this time—for fortune and for fame. You will not see me again until you carry me down the ladder from the convent window. What a lark! And there's money in it for you and me."

He dared not discourage her, being too completely her slave, like wax in her hands; and he believed, too, that her scheme of advertising the drama of *The Escaped Nun* would lead to splendid and profitable notoriety. A real escape, from a city convent, before the very eyes of respectable citizens, would ring through the country like an alarm, and set the entire Protestant community in motion. While he feared, he was also dazzled by the brilliancy of the scheme.

It began very well. The journals one morning announced the disappearance of Sister Claire, and described the alarm of her friends at her failure to return. Thereupon McMeeter raised his wonderful voice over the letter sent him on the eve of her flight, and printed the pathetic epistle along with his denunciation of the cowardice which had given her over to her enemies. Later Bishop Bradford, expressing his sympathy in a speech to the Dorcas' Society, referred to the walling up of escaped nuns during the dark ages. A little tide of paragraphs flowed from the papers, plaintively murmuring the one sad strain: the dear sister could not be far distant; she might be in the city, deep in a convent dungeon; she had belonged to the community of the Good Shepherd, whose convent stood in Morris Street, large enough, sufficiently barred with iron to suggest dungeons; the escaped one had often expressed her dread of abduction; the convents ought to be examined suddenly and secretly; and so on without end.

"What is the meaning of it?" said Monsignor. "I thought you had extinguished her, Arthur."

"Another scheme of course. I was too merciful with her, I imagine. All this noise seems to have one aim: to direct attention to these convents. Now if she were hidden in any of them, and a committee should visit that convent and find her forcibly detained, as she would call it; or if she could sound a fire alarm and make a spectacular escape at two in the morning, before the whole world, what could be said about it?"

"Isn't it rather late in history for such things?" said Monsignor.

"A good trick is as good to-day as a thousand years ago. I can picture you explaining to the American citizen, amid the howls of McMeeter and the purring speeches of the Bishop, how Sister Claire came to be in the convent from which her friends rescued her."

"It would be awkward enough I admit. You think, then, that she ... but what could be her motive?"

"Notoriety, and the sympathy of the people. I would like to trip her up in this scheme, and hurl her once for all into the hell which she seems anxious to prepare for other people. You Catholics are altogether too easy with the Claires and the McMeeters. Hence the tears of the Everards."

"We are so used to it," said the priest in apology. "It would be foolish, however, not to heed your warning. Go to the convents of the city from me, and put them on their guard. Let them dismiss all strangers and keep out newcomers until the danger appears to be over."

The most careful search failed to reveal a trace of Sister Claire's hiding-place among the various communities, who were thrown into a fever of dread by the warning. The journals kept up their crescendo of inquiry and information. One must look for that snake, Arthur thought, not with the eyes, but through inspiration. She hid neither in the clouds nor in Arizona, but in the grass at their feet. Seeking for inspiration, he went over the ground a second time with Sister Magdalen, who had lost flesh over the shame of her dealings with Claire, the Everard troubles, and the dread of what was still to come. She burned to atone for her holy indiscretions. The Park Square convent, however, held no strangers. In the home attached to it were many poor women, but all of them known. Edith Conyngham the obscure, the mute, the humble, was just then occupying a room in the place, making a retreat of ten days in charge of Sister Magdalen. At this fact Arthur was seized by his inspiration.

"She must give up her retreat and leave the place," he said quietly, though his pulse was bounding. "Make no objection. It's only a case of being too careful. Leave the whole matter to me. Say nothing to her about it. To-night the good creature will have slipped away without noise, and she can finish her retreat later. It's absurd, but better be absurd than sorry."

And Sister Magdalen, thinking of the long penance she must undergo for her folly, made only a polite objection. He wrote out a note at once in a disguised hand, giving it no signature:

"The game is up. You cannot get out of the convent too quick or too soon. At ten o'clock a cab will be at the southwest corner of Park Square. Take it and drive to the office. Before ten I shall be with you. Don't delay an instant. State prison is in sight. Dillon is on your track."

"At eight o'clock this evening where will Miss Conyngham be, Sister?"

"In her room," said the nun, unhappy over the treatment intended for her client, "preparing her meditation for the morning. She has a great love for meditation on the profound mysteries of religion."

"Glad to know it," he said dryly. "Well, slip this note under her door, make no noise, let no one see you, give her no hint of your presence. Then go to bed and pray for us poor sinners out in the wicked world."

One must do a crazy thing now and then, under cover of the proprieties, if only to test one's sanity. Edith and Claire, as he had suggested to Curran, might be the same person. What if Claire appeared tall, portly, resonant, youthful, abounding in life, while Edith seemed mute, old, thin, feeble? The art of the actor can work miracles in personal appearance. A dual life provided perfect security in carrying out Claire's plans, and it matched the daring of the Escaped Nun to live as Edith in the very hearts of the people she sought to destroy. Good sense opposed his theory of course, but he made out a satisfactory argument for himself. How often had Sister Claire puzzled him by her resemblance to some one whom he could not force out of the shadows of memory! Even now, with the key of the mystery in his hands, he could see no likeness between them. Yet no doubt remained in his mind that a dual life would explain and expose Sister Claire.

That night he sat on the seat of a cab in proper costume, at the southwest corner of Park Square. The convent, diagonally opposite, was dark and silent at nine o'clock; and far in the rear, facing the side street, stood the home of the indigent, whose door would open for the exit of a clever actress at ten o'clock, or, well closed, reproach him for his stupidity. The great front of the convent, dominating the Square, would have been a fine stage for the scene contemplated by Sister Claire, and he laughed at the spectacle of the escaped one leaping from a window into her lover's arms, or sliding down a rope amid the cheers of the mob and the shrieks of the disgraced poor souls within. Then he gritted his teeth at the thought of Louis, and Mary his mother, and Mona his sister. His breath came short. Claire was a woman, but some women are not dishonored by the fate of Jezebel.

Shortly after ten o'clock a small, well-wrapped figure turned the remote corner of the Home, came out to the Square, saw the cab, and coming forward with confidence opened the door and stepped in. As Arthur drove off the blood surged to his head and his heart in a way that made his ears sing. It seemed impossible that the absurd should turn out wisdom at the first jump. As he drove along he wondered over the capacities of art. No two individuals could have been more unlike in essentials than Edith Conyngham and Sister Claire. Now it would appear that high-heeled shoes, padded clothes, heavy eyebrows, paint, a loud and confident voice, a bold manner, and her beautiful costume had made Sister Claire; while shoes without heels, rusty clothes, a gray wig, a weak voice, and timid manner, had given form to Edith Conyngham.

A soul is betrayed by its sins. The common feature of the two characters was the sensuality which, neither in the nun nor in her double, would be repressed or disguised. Looking back, Arthur could see some points of resemblance which might have betrayed the wretch to a clever detective. Well, he would settle all accounts with her presently, and he debated only one point, the flinging of her to the dogs. In twenty minutes they reached the office of the Escaped

Nun. He opened the door of the cab and she stepped out nervously, but walked with decision into the building, for which she had the keys.

"Anything more, mum?" he said respectfully.

"Come right in, and light up for me," she said ungraciously, in a towering rage. He found his way to the gas jets and flooded the office with the light from four. She pulled down the curtains, and flung aside her rusty shawl. At the same moment he flung an arm about her, and with his free hand tore the gray wig from her head, and shook free the mass of yellow hair which lay beneath it. Then he flung her limp into the nearest chair, and stood gazing at her, frozen with amaze. She cowered, pale with the sudden fright of the attack. It was not Sister Claire who stood revealed, but the charming and lovely La Belle Colette. The next instant he laughed like a hysterical woman.

"By heavens, but that *was* an inspiration!" he exclaimed. "Don't be frightened, beautiful Colette. I was prepared for a tragedy, but this discovery reveals a farce."

Her terror gave way to stupefaction when she recognized him.

"So it's three instead of two," he went on. "The lovely dancer is also the Escaped Nun and the late Edith Conyngham. And Curran knew it of course, who was our detective. That's bad. But Judy Haskell claims you as a goddaughter. You are Curran's wife. You are Sister Magdalen's poor friend. You are Katharine Kerrigan. You are Sister Claire. You are Messalina. La Belle Colette, you are the very devil."

She recovered from her fright at his laugh, in which some amusement tinkled, and also something terrible. They were in a lonely place, he had made the situation, and she felt miserably helpless.

"You need not blame Curran," she said decisively. "He knew the game, but he has no control over me. I want to go home, and I want to know right away your terms. It's all up with me. I confess. But let me know what you are going to do with me."

"Take you home to your husband," said Arthur. "Come."

They drove to the little apartment where Curran lay peacefully sleeping, and where he received his erratic wife with stupor. The three sat down in the parlor to discuss the situation, which was serious enough, though Arthur now professed to take it lightly. Colette stared at him like a fascinated bird and answered his questions humbly.

"It's all very simple," said she. "I am truly Edith Conyngham, and Judy Haskell is my godmother, and I was in a convent out West. I was expelled for a love caper, and came back to my friends much older in appearance than I had need to be. The Escaped-Nun-racket was a money-maker. What I really am, you see. I am the dancer, La Belle Colette. All the rest is disguise."

Curran asked no questions and accepted the situation composedly.

"She is in your hands," he said.

"I place her in yours for the present," Arthur replied, glowering as he thought of Louis. "Detectives will shadow you both until I come to a decision what to do with you. Any move to escape and you will be nipped. Then the law takes its course. As for you, La Belle Colette, say your prayers. I am still tempted to send you after Jezebel."

"You are a terrible man," she whimpered, as he walked out and left them to their sins.

CHAPTER XXIII.

THE FIRST BLOW.

Mayor Birmingham and Grahame, summoned by messengers, met him in the forever-deserted offices of Sister Claire. He made ready for them by turning on all the lights, setting forth a cheerful bottle and some soda from Claire's hidden ice-box, and lighting a cigar. Delight ran through his blood like fire. At last he had his man on the hip, and the vision of that toss which he meant to give him made his body tingle from the roots of his hair to the points of his toes. However, the case was not for him to deal with alone. Birmingham, the man of weight, prudence, fairness, the true leader, really owned the situation. Grahame, experienced journalist, had the right to manage the publicity department of this delicious scandal. His own task would be to hold Claire in the traces, and drive her round the track, show the world her paces, past the judge's stand. Ah, to see the face of the Minister as he read the story of exposure—her exposure and his own shame!

The two men stared at his comfortable attitude in that strange inn, and fairly gasped at the climax of his story.

"The devil's in you. No one but you would have thought out such a scheme," said Grahame, recalling the audacity, the cleverness, the surprises of his friend's career from the California episode to the invasion of Ireland. "Great heavens! but you have the knack of seizing the hinge of things."

"I think we have Livingstone and his enterprise in the proper sort of hole," Arthur answered. "The question is how to use our advantage?"

The young men turned to Birmingham with deference.

"The most thorough way," said the Mayor, after complimenting Arthur on his astonishing success, "would be to hale Claire before the courts for fraud, and subpœna all our distinguished enemies. That course has some disagreeable consequences, however."

"I think we had better keep out of court," Arthur said quickly.

His companions looked surprised at his hesitation. He did not understand it himself. For Edith Conyngham he felt only disgust, and for Sister Claire an amused contempt; but sparkling Colette, so clever, bright, and amiable, so charmingly conscienceless, so gracefully wicked, inspired him with pity almost. He could not crush the pretty reptile, or thrust her into prison.

"Of course I want publicity," he hastened to add, "the very widest, to reach as far as London, and strike the Minister. How can that be got, and keep away from the courts?"

"An investigating committee is what you are thinking of," said the Mayor. "I can call such a body together at the Fifth Avenue Hotel, our most distinguished citizens. They could receive the confession of this woman, and report to the public on her character."

"That's the plan," Arthur interrupted with joy. "That *must* be carried out. I'll see that Claire appears before that committee and confesses her frauds. But mark this: on that committee you should have the agents of Livingstone: Bradford, Bitterkin ... I owe him one for his meanness to the Senator ... Smallish in particular, and McMeeter for the fun of the thing."

"Wild horses wouldn't drag them to it," Grahame thought.

"I have something better than wild horses, the proofs of their conspiracy, of their league with this woman," and Arthur pointed to the locked drawers of the office. "How will our minister to England like to have his name connected with this scandal openly. Now, if these people refuse to serve, by heavens, I'll take the whole case to court, and give it an exposure as wide as the earth. If they're agreeable, I'll keep away from the courts, and the rougher part of the scandal."

"There's your weapon," said the Mayor, "the alternative of committee or court. I'll see to that part of the business. Do you get the escaped nun ready for her confession, and I'll guarantee the committee, let us say inside of ten days. Your part, Grahame, will be to write up a story for the morning papers, covering dramatically the details of this very remarkable episode."

They sat long discussing the various features of the scheme.

Next morning Curran and Arthur sat down to talk over the terms of surrender in the detective's house. Colette still kept her bed, distracted with grief, and wild with apprehension over the sensational articles in the morning papers. Curran saw little hope for himself and his wife in the stern face of Dillon.

"At the start I would like to hear your explanation," Arthur began coldly. "You were in my employ and in hers."

"In hers only to hinder what evil I could, and to protect her from herself," the detective answered steadily and frankly. "I make no excuse, because there isn't any to make. But if I didn't live up to my contract with you, I can say honestly that I never betrayed your interest. You can guess the helplessness of a man in my fix. I have no influence over Colette. She played her game against my wish and prayer. Most particular did I warn her against annoying you and yours. I was going to break up her designs on young Everard, when you did it yourself. I hope you— —"

In his nervous apprehension for Colette's fate the strong-willed man broke down. He remained silent, struggling for his vanishing self-control.

"I understand, and I excuse you. The position was nasty. I have always trusted you without knowing why exactly," and he reflected a moment on that interesting fact. "You did me unforgettable service in saving Louis Everard."

"How glad I am you remember that service," Curran gasped, like one who grasping at a straw finds it a plank. "I foresaw this moment when I said to you that night, 'I shall not be bashful about reminding you of it and asking a reward at the right time.' I ask it now. For the boy's sake be merciful with her. Don't hand her over to the courts. Deal with her yourself, and I'll help you."

For the boy's sake, for that service so aptly rendered, for the joy it brought and the grief it averted, he could forget justice and crown Colette with diamonds! Curran trembled with eagerness and suspense. He loved her, — this wretch, witch, fiend of a woman!

"The question is, can I deal with her myself? She is intractable."

"You ought to know by this time that she will do anything for you ... and still more when she has to choose between your wish and jail."

"I shall require a good deal of her, not for my own sake, but to undo the evil work — —"

"How I have tried to keep her out of that evil work," Curran cried fiercely. "We are bad enough as it is without playing traitors to our own, and throwing mud on holy things. There can be no luck in it, and she knows it. When one gets as low as she has, it's time for the funeral. Hell is more respectable."

Arthur did not understand this feeling in Curran. The man's degradation seemed so complete to him that not even sacrilege could intensify it; yet clearly the hardened sinner saw some depths below his own which excited his horror and loathing.

"If you think I can deal with her, I shall not invoke the aid of the law."

The detective thanked him in a breaking voice. He had enjoyed a very bad night speculating on the probable course of events. Colette came in shortly, and greeted Arthur as brazenly as usual, but with extreme sadness, which became her well; so sweet, so delicate, so fragile, that he felt pleased to have forgiven her so early in the struggle. He had persecuted her, treated her with violence, and printed her history for the scornful pleasure of the world; he had come to offer her the alternative of public shame or public trial and jail; yet she had a patient smile for him, a dignified submission that touched him. After all, he thought with emotion, she is of the same nature with myself; a poor castaway from conventional life playing one part or another by caprice, for gain or sport or notoriety; only the devil has entered into her, while I have been lucky enough to cast my lot with the exorcists of the race. He almost regretted his duty.

"I have taken possession of your office and papers, Colette," said he with the dignity of the master. "I dismissed the office-boy with his wages, and notified the owner that you would need the rooms no more after the end of the month."

"Thanks," she murmured with downcast eyes.

"I am ready now to lay before you the conditions — —"

"Are you going to send me to jail?"

"I leave that to you," he answered softly. "You must withdraw your book from circulation. You must get an injunction from the courts to restrain the publishers, if they won't stop printing at your request, and you must bring suit against them for your share of the profits. I want them to be exposed. My lawyer is at your service for such work."

"This for the beginning?" she said in despair.

"You must write for me a confession next, describing your career, and the parts which you played in this city; also naming your accomplices, your supporters, and what money they put up for your enterprise."

"You will find all that in my papers."

"Is Mr. Livingstone's name among your papers?"

"He was the ringleader. Of course."

"Finally you must appear before a committee of gentlemen at the Fifth Avenue Hotel, and show how you disguised yourself for the three parts of Edith Conyngham, Sister Claire, and the Brand of the gospel-hall."

She burst out crying then, looking from one man to the other with the tears streaming down her lovely face. Curran squirmed in anguish. Arthur studied her with interest. Who could tell when she was not acting?

"Ah, you wretch! I am bad. Sometimes I can't bear myself. But you are worse, utterly without heart. You think I don't feel my position."

Her sobbing touched him by its pathos and its cleverness.

"You are beyond feeling, but you *must* talk about feeling," was his hard reply. "Probably I shall make you feel before the end of this adventure."

"As if you hadn't done it already," she fairly bawled like a hurt child. "For months I have not left the house without seeing everywhere the dogs that tore Jezebel."

"You might also have seen that poor child whom you nearly drove to death," he retorted, "and the mother whose heart you might have broken."

"Poor child!" she sneered, and burst out laughing while the tears still lingered on her cheek. "He was a milksop, not a man. I thought he was a man, or I never would have offered him pleasure. And you want me to make a show of myself before...."

"Your old friends and well-wishers, McMeeter, Bradford and Co."

"Never, never, never," she screamed, and fell to weeping again. "I'll die first."

"You won't be asked to die, madam. You'll go to jail the minute I leave this house, and stand trial on fifty different charges. I'll keep you in jail for the rest of your life. If by any trick you escape me, I'll deliver you to the dogs."

"Can he do this?" she said scornfully to Curran, who nodded.

"And if I agree to it, what do I get?" turning again to Dillon.

"You can live in peace as La Belle Colette the dancer, practise your profession, and enjoy the embraces of your devoted husband. I let you off lightly. Your private life, your stage name, will be kept from the public, and, by consequence, from the dogs."

233

She shivered at the phrase. Shame was not in her, but fear could grip her heart vigorously. Her nerve did not exclude cowardice. This man she had always feared, perceiving in him not only a strength beyond the common, but a mysterious power not to be analyzed and named. Her flimsy rage would break hopelessly on this rock. Still before surrendering, her crooked nature forced her to the petty arts in which she excelled. Very clearly in this acting appeared the various strokes of character peculiar to Edith, Claire, and the Brand. She wheedled and whined one moment in the husky tones of Sister Magdalen's late favorite; when dignity was required she became the escaped nun; and in her rage she would burst into the melodramatic frenzy dear to the McMeeter audiences; but Colette, the heedless, irresponsible, half-mad butterfly, dominated these various parts, and to this charming personality she returned. Through his own sad experience this spectacle interested him. He subdued her finally by a precise description of consequences.

"You have done the Catholics of this city harm that will last a long time, Colette," said he. "That vile book of yours ... you ought to be hung for it. It will live to do its miserable work when you are in hell howling. I really don't know why I should be merciful to you. Did you ever show mercy to any one? The court would do this for you and for us: the facts, figures, and personages of your career would be dragged into the light of day ... what a background that would be ... not a bad company either ... not a fact would escape ... you would be painted as you are. I'll not tell you what you are, but I know that you would die of your own colors ... you would go to jail, and rot there ... every time you came out I'd have a new charge on which to send you back. Your infamy would be printed by columns in the papers ... and the dogs would be put on your trail ... ah, there's the rub ... if the law let you go free, what a meal you'd make for the people who think you ought to be torn limb from limb, and who would do it with joy. I really do not understand why I offer you an alternative. Perhaps it's for the sake of this man who loves you ... for the great service he did me."

He paused to decide this point, while she gazed like a fascinated bird.

"What I want is this really," he went on. "I want to let the city see just what tools Livingstone, your employer, is willing to do his dirty work with. I want this committee to assemble with pomp and circumstance ... those are the right words ... and to see you, in your very cleverest way, act the parts through which you fooled the wise. I want them to hear you say in that sweetest of voices, how you lied to them to get their dollars ... how you lied about us, your own people, threw mud on us, as Curran says, to get their dollars ... how your life, and your book, and your lectures, are all lies ... invented and printed because the crowd that devoured them were eager to believe us the horrible creatures you described. When you have done that, you can go free. No one will know your husband, or your name, or your profession. I don't see why you hesitate. I don't know why I should offer you this chance. When Birmingham hears your story he will not approve of my action. But if you agree to follow my directions to the letter I'll promise that the law will not seize you."

What could she do but accept his terms, protesting that death was preferable? The risk of losing her just as the committee would be ready to meet, for her fickleness verged on insanity, he had to accept. He trusted in his own watchfulness, and in the fidelity of Curran to keep her in humor. Even now she forgot her disasters in the memory of her success as an impersonator, and entertained the men with scenes from her masquerade as Edith, Claire, and the Brand. From such a creature, so illy balanced, one might expect anything.

However, by judicious coddling and terrorizing, her courage and spirit were kept alive to the very moment when she stood before Birmingham and his committee, heard her confession of imposture read, signed it with perfect sang-froid, and illustrated for the scandalized members her method of impersonation. So had Arthur worked upon her conceit that she took a real pride in displaying her costumes, and in explaining how skilfully she had led three lives in that city. Grim, bitter, sickened with disappointment, yet masked in smiles, part of the committee watched her performance to the end. They felt the completeness of Arthur's triumph. With the little airs and graces peculiar to a stage artiste, Edith put on the dusty costume of Edith Conyngham, and limped feebly across the floor; then the decorous garments of the Brand, and whispered tenderly in

McMeeter's ear; last, the brilliant habit of the escaped nun, the curious eyebrows, the pallid face; curtseying at the close of the performance with her bold eyes on her audience, as if beseeching the merited applause. In the dead silence afterwards, Arthur mercifully led her away.

The journals naturally gave the affair large attention, and the net results were surprisingly fine. The house of cards so lovingly built up by Livingstone and his friends tumbled in a morning never to rise again. All the little plans failed like kites snipped of their tails. Fritters went home, because the public lost interest in his lectures. The book of the escaped nun fell flat and disappeared from the market. McMeeter gave up his scheme of rescuing the inmates of convents and housing them until married. The hired press ignored the Paddies and their island for a whole year. Best of all, suddenly, on the plea of dying among his friends, Ledwith was set free, mainly through the representations of Lord Constantine in London and Arthur in Washington. These rebuffs told upon the Minister severely. He knew from whose strong hand they came, and that the same hand would not soon tire of striking.

CHAPTER XXIV.

ANNE MAKES HISTORY.

In the months that followed Anne Dillon lived as near to perfect felicity as earthly conditions permit. A countess and a lord breathed under her roof, ate at her table, and talked prose and poetry with her as freely as Judy Haskell. The Countess of Skibbereen and Lord Constantine had accompanied the Ledwiths to America, after Owen's liberation from jail, and fallen victims to the wiles of this clever woman. Arthur might look after the insignificant Ledwiths. Anne would have none of them. She belonged henceforth to the nobility. His lordship was bent on utilizing his popularity with the Irish to further the cause of the Anglo-American Alliance. As the friend who had stood by the Fenian prisoners, not only against embittered England, but against indifferent Livingstone, he was welcomed; and if he wanted an alliance, or an heiress, or the freedom of the city, or anything which the Irish could buy for him, he had only to ask in order to receive. Anne sweetly took the responsibility off his shoulders, after he had outlined his plans.

"Leave it all to me," said she. "You shall win the support of all these people without turning your hand over."

"You may be sure she'll do it much better than you will," was the opinion of the Countess, and the young man was of the same mind.

She relied chiefly on Doyle Grahame for one part of her programme, but that effervescent youth had fallen into a state of discouragement which threatened to leave him quite useless. He shook his head to her demand for a column in next morning's *Herald*.

"Same old story ... the Countess and you ... lovely costumes ... visits ... it won't go. The editors are wondering why there's so much of you."

"Hasn't it all been good?"

"Of course, or it would not have been printed. But there must come an end sometime. What's your aim anyway?"

"I want a share in making history," she said slyly.

"Take a share in making mine," he answered morosely, and thereupon she landed him.

"Oh, run away with Mona, if you're thinking of marrying."

"Thinking of it! Talking of it! That's as near as I can get to it," he groaned. "John Everard is going to drive a desperate bargain with me. I wrote a book, I helped to expose Edith Conyngham, I drove Fritters out of the country with my ridicule, I shocked Bradford, and silenced McMeeter; and I have failed to move that wretch. All I got out of my labors was permission to sit beside Mona in her own house with her father present."

"You humor the man too much," Anne said with a laugh. "I can twist John Everard about my finger, only — —"

"There it is," cried Grahame. "Behold it in its naked simplicity! Only! Well, if anything short of the divine can get around, over, under, through, or by his sweet, little 'only,' he's fit to be the next king of Ireland. What have I not done to do away with it? Once I thought, I hoped, that the invitation to read the poem on the landing of the Pilgrim Fathers, coming as a climax to multitudinous services, would surely have fetched him. Now, with the invitation in my pocket, I'm afraid to mention it. What if he should scorn it?"

"He won't if I say the word. Give me the column to-morrow, and any time I want it for a month or two, and I'll guarantee that John Everard will do the right thing by you."

"You can have the column. What do you want it for?"

"The alliance, of course. I'm in the business of making history, as I told you. Don't open your mouth quite so wide, please. There's to be a meeting of the wise in this house, after a dinner, to express favorable opinions about the alliance. Then in a month or two a distinguished peer, member of the British Cabinet, is coming over to sound the great men on the question.... What are you whistling for?"

"You've got a fine thing, Mrs. Dillon," said he. "By Jove, but I'll help you spread this for all it's worth."

"Understand," she said, tapping the table with emphasis, "the alliance must go through as far as we can make it go. Now, do your best. When you go over to see John Everard next, go with a mind to kill him if he doesn't take your offer to marry his daughter. I'll see to it that the poem on the Pilgrims does the trick for you."

"I'd have killed him long ago, if I thought it worth the trouble," he said.

He felt that the crisis had come for him and Mona. That charming girl, in spite of his entreaties, of his threats to go exploring Africa, remained as rigidly faithful to her ideas of duty as her father to his obstinacy. She would not marry without his consent. With all his confidence in Anne's cleverness, how could he expect her to do the impossible? To change the unchangeable? John Everard showed no sign of the influence which had brought Livingstone to his knees, when Grahame and Mona stood before him, and the lover placed in her father's hands the document of honor.

"Really, this is wonderful," said Everard, impressed to the point of violence. "You are to compose and to read the poem on the Pilgrim Fathers?"

"That's the prize," said Grahame severely. He might be squaring off at this man the next moment, and could not carry his honors lightly. "And now that it has come I want my reward. We must be married two weeks before I read that poem, and the whole world must see and admire the source of my inspiration."

He drew his beloved into his arms and kissed her pale cheek.

"Very well. That will be appropriate," the father said placidly, clearing his throat to read the invitation aloud. He read pompously, quite indifferent to the emotion of his children, proud that they were to be prominent figures in a splendid gathering. They, beatified, pale, unstrung by this calm acceptance of what he had opposed bitterly two years, sat down foolishly, and listened to the pompous utterance of pompous phrases in praise of dead heroes and a living poet. Thought and speech failed together. If only some desperado would break in upon him and try to kill him! if the house would take fire, or a riot begin in the street! The old man finished his reading, congratulated the poet, blessed the pair in the old-fashioned style, informed his wife of the date of the wedding, and marched off to bed. After pulling at that door for years it was maddening to have the very frame-work come out as if cemented with butter. What an outrage to come prepared for heroic action, and to find the enemy turned friend! Oh, admirable enchantress was this Anne Dillon!

The enchantress, having brought Grahame into line and finally into good humor, took up the more difficult task of muzzling her stubborn son. To win him to the good cause, she had no hope; sufficient, if he could be won to silence while diplomacy shaped the course of destiny.

"Better let me be on that point," Arthur said when she made her attack. "I'm hostile only when disturbed. Lord Conny owns us for the present. I won't say a word to shake his title. Neither will I lift my eyebrows to help this enterprise."

"If you only will keep quiet," she suggested.

"Well, I'm trying to. I'm set against alliance with England, until we have knocked the devil out of her, begging your pardon for my frankness. I must speak plainly now so that we may not fall out afterwards. But I'll be quiet. I'll not say a word to influence a soul. I'll do just as Ledwith does."

He laughed at the light which suddenly shone in her face.

"That's a fair promise," she said smoothly, and fled before he could add conditions.

Her aim and her methods alike remained hidden from him. He knew only that she was leading them all by the nose to some brilliant climax of her own devising. He was willing to be led. The climax turned out to be a dinner. Anne had long ago discovered the secret influence of a fine dinner on the politics of the world. The halo of a saint pales before the golden nimbus which well-fed guests see radiating from their hostess after dinner. A good man may possess a few robust virtues, but the dinner-giver has them all. Therefore, the manager of the alliance gathered about her table one memorable evening the leaders whose good opinion and hearty support Lord Constantine valued in his task of winning the Irish to neutrality or favor for his enterprise. Arthur recognized the climax only when Lord Constantine, after the champagne had sparkled in the glasses, began to explain his dream to Sullivan.

"What do you think of it?" said he.

"It sounds as harmless as a popgun, and looks like a vision. I don't see any details in your scheme," said the blunt leader graciously.

"We can leave the details to the framers of the alliance," said His Lordship, uneasy at Arthur's laugh. "What we want first is a large, generous feeling in its favor, to encourage the leaders."

"Well, in general," said the Boss, "it is a good thing for all countries to live in harmony. When they speak the same language, it's still better. I have no feeling one way or the other. I left Ireland young, and would hardly have remembered I'm Irish but for Livingstone. What do you think of it, Senator?"

"An alliance with England!" cried he with contempt. "Fancy me walking down to a district meeting with such an auctioneer's tag hanging on my back. Why, I'd be sold out on the spot. Those people haven't forgot how they were thrown down and thrown out of Ireland. No, sir. Leave us out of an alliance."

"That's the popular feeling, I think," Sullivan said to His Lordship.

"I can understand the Senator's feelings," the Englishman replied softly. "But if, before the alliance came to pass, the Irish question should be well settled, how would that affect your attitude, Senator?"

"My attitude," replied the Senator, posing as he reflected that a budding statesman made the inquiry, "would be entirely in your favor."

"Thank you. What more could I ask?" Lord Constantine replied with a fierce look at Arthur. "I say myself, until the Irish get their rights, no alliance."

"Then we are with you cordially. We want to do all we can for a man who has been so fair to our people," the Boss remarked with the flush of good wine in his cheek. "Champagne sentiments," murmured Arthur.

Monsignor, prompted by Anne, came to the rescue of the young nobleman.

"There would be a row, if the matter came up for discussion just now," he said. "Ten years hence may see a change. There's one thing in favor of Irish ... well, call it neutrality. Speaking as a churchman, Catholics have a happier lot in English-speaking lands than in other countries. They have the natural opportunity to develop, they are not hampered in speech and action as in Italy and France."

"How good of you to say so," murmured His Lordship.

"Then again," continued Monsignor, with a sly glance at Arthur, "it seems to me inevitable that the English-speaking peoples must come into closer communion, not merely for their own good, or for selfish aims, but to spread among less fortunate nations their fine political principles. There's the force, the strength, of the whole scheme. Put poor Ireland on her feet, and I vote for an alliance."

"Truly, a Daniel come to judgment," murmured Arthur.

"It's a fine view to take of it," the Boss thought.

"Are you afraid to ask Ledwith for an opinion?" Arthur suggested.

"What's he got to do with it?" Everard snapped, unsoftened by the mellow atmosphere of the feast.

"It is no longer a practical question with me," Owen said cheerfully. "I have always said that if the common people of the British Isles got an understanding of each other, and a better liking for each other, the end of oppression would come very soon. They are kept apart by the artificial hindrances raised by the aristocracy of birth and money. The common people easily fraternize, if they are permitted. See them in this country, living, working, intermarrying, side by side."

"How will that sound among the brethren?" said Arthur disappointed.

His mother flashed him a look of triumph, and Lord Constantine looked foolishly happy.

"As the utterance of a maniac, of course. Have they ever regarded me as sane?" he answered easily.

"And what becomes of your dream?" Arthur persisted.

"I have myself become a dream," he answered sadly. "I am passing into the land of dreams, of shadows. My dream was Ireland; a principle that would bring forth its own flower, fruit, and seed; not a department of an empire. Who knows what is best in this world of change? Some day men may realize the poet's dream:

"The parliament of man, the federation of the world."

Arthur surrendered with bad grace. He had expected from Ledwith the last, grand, fiery denunciation which would have swept the room as a broadside sweeps a deck, and hurled the schemes of his mother and Lord Constantine into the sea. Sad, sad, to see how champagne can undo such a patriot! For that matter the golden wine had undone the entire party. Judy declared to her dying day that the alliance was toasted amid cheers before the close of the banquet; that Lord Constantine in his delight kissed Anne as she left the room; with many other circumstances too improbable to find a place in a veracious history. It is a fact, however, that the great scheme which still agitates the peoples interested, had its success depended on the guests of Anne Dillon, would have been adopted that night. The dinner was a real triumph.

Unfortunately, dinners do not make treaties; and, as Arthur declared, one dinner is good enough until a better is eaten. When the member of the British Cabinet came to sit at Anne's table, if one might say so, the tables were turned. Birmingham instead of Monsignor played the lead; the man whose practical temperament, financial and political influence, could soothe and propitiate his own people and interest the moneyed men in the alliance. It was admitted no scheme of this kind could progress without his aid. He had been reserved for the Cabinet Minister.

No one thought much about the dinner except the hostess, who felt, as she looked down the beautiful table, that her glory had reached its brilliant meridian. A cabinet minister, a lord, a countess, a leading Knickerbocker, the head of Tammany, and a few others who did not matter; what a long distance from the famous cat-show and Mulberry Street! Arthur also looked up the table with satisfaction. If his part in the play had not been dumb show (by his mother's orders), he would have quoted the famous grind of the mills of the gods. The two races, so unequally matched at home, here faced each other on equal ground. Birmingham knew what he had to do.

"I am sure," he said to the cabinet minister, "that in a matter so serious you want absolute sincerity?"

"Absolute, and thank you," replied the great man.

"Then let me begin with myself. Personally I would not lift my littlest finger to help this scheme. I might not go out of my way to hinder it, but I am that far Irish in feeling, not to aid England so finely. For a nation that will soon be without a friend in the world, an alliance with us would be of immense benefit. No man of Irish blood, knowing what his race has endured and still endures from the English, can keep his self-respect and back the scheme."

Arthur was sorry for his lordship, who sat utterly astounded and cast down wofully at this expression of feeling from such a man.

"The main question can be answered in this way," Birmingham continued. "Were I willing to take part in this business, my influence with the Irish and their descendants, whatever it may be, would not be able to bring a corporal's guard into line in its behalf."

Lord Constantine opened his mouth, Everard snorted his contempt, but the great man signaled silence. Birmingham paid no attention.

"In this country the Irish have learned much more than saving money and acquiring power; they have learned the unredeemed blackness of the injustice done them at home, just as I learned it. What would Grahame here, Sullivan, Senator Dillon, or myself have been at this moment had we remained in Ireland? Therefore the Irish in this country are more bitter against the English government than their brethren at home. I am certain that no man can rally even a minority of the Irish to the support of the alliance. I am sure I could not. I am certain the formal proposal of the scheme would rouse them to fiery opposition."

"Remember," Arthur whispered to Everard, raging to speak, "that the Cabinet Minister doesn't care to hear anyone but Birmingham."

"I'm sorry for you, Conny," he whispered to his lordship, "but it's the truth."

"Never enjoyed anything so much," said Grahame *sotto voce*, his eyes on Everard.

"However, let us leave the Irish out of the question," the speaker went on. "Or, better, let us suppose them favorable, and myself able to win them over. What chance has the alliance of success? None."

"Fudge!" cried Everard, unabashed by the beautiful English stare of the C. M.

"The measure is one-sided commercially. This country has nothing to gain from a scheme, which would be a mine to England; therefore the moneyed men will not touch it, will not listen to it. Their time is too valuable. What remains? An appeal to the people on the score of humanity, brotherhood, progress, what you please? My opinion is that the dead weight there could not be moved. The late war and the English share in it are too fresh in the public mind. The outlook to me is utterly against your scheme."

"It might be objected to your view that feeling is too strong an element of it," said the Cabinet Minister.

"Feeling has only to do with my share in the scheme," Birmingham replied. "As an Irishman I would not further it, yet I might be glad to see it succeed. My opinion is concerned with the actual conditions as I see them."

With this remark the formal discussion ended. Mortified at this outcome of his plans, Lord Constantine could not be consoled.

"As long as Livingstone is on your side, Conny," said Arthur, "you are foredoomed."

"I am not so sure," His Lordship answered with some bitterness. "The Chief Justice of the United States is a good friend to have."

A thrill shot through Dillon at this emphasis to a rumor hitherto too light for printing. The present incumbent of the high office mentioned by Lord Constantine lay dying. Livingstone coveted few places, and this would be one. In so exalted a station he would be "enskied and sainted." Even his proud soul would not disdain to step from the throne-room of Windsor to the dais of the Supreme Court of his country. And to strike him in the very moment of his triumph, to snatch away the prize, to close his career like a broken sentence with a dash and a mark of interrogation, to bring him home like any dead game in a bag: here would be magnificent justice!

"Have I found thee, O mine enemy?" Arthur cried in his delight.

CHAPTER XXV.

THE CATHEDRAL.

Ledwith was dying in profound depression, like most brave souls, whose success has been partial, or whose failure has been absolute. This mournful ending to a brave, unselfish life seemed to Arthur pitiful and monstrous. A mere breathing-machine like himself had enjoyed a stimulating vengeance for the failure of one part of his life. Oh, how sweet had been that vengeance! The draught had not yet reached the bottom of the cup! His cause for the moment a ruin, dragged down with Fenianism; his great enemy stronger, more glorious, and more pitiless than when he had first raised his hand against her injustice; now the night had closed in upon Ledwith, not merely the bitter night of sickness and death and failure, but that more savage night of despondency, which steeps all human sorrow in the black, polluted atmosphere of hell. For such a sufferer the heart of Arthur Dillon opened as wide as the gates of heaven. Oh, had he not known what it is to suffer so, without consolation!

He was like a son to Owen Ledwith.

Every plan born in the poetic and fertile brain of the patriot he took oath to carry out; he vowed his whole life to the cause of Ireland; and he consoled Owen for apparent failure by showing him that he had not altogether failed, since a man, young, earnest, determined, and wealthy should take up the great work just where he dropped it. Could any worker ask more of life? A hero should go to his eternity with lofty joy, leaving his noble example to the mean world, a reproach to the despicable among rulers, a star in the night to the warriors of justice.

In Honora her father did not find the greatest comfort. His soul was of the earth and human liberty was his day-star; her soul rose above that great human good to the freedom of heaven. Her heart ached for him, that he should be going out of life with only human consolation. The father stood in awe of an affection, which at the same time humbled and exalted him; she had never loved man or

247

woman like him; he was next to God in that virginal heart, for with all her love of country, the father had the stronger hold on her. Too spiritual for him, her sublime faith did not cheer him. Yet when they looked straight into each other's eyes with the consciousness of what was coming, mutual anguish terribly probed their love. He had no worry for her.

"She has the best of friends," he said to Arthur, "she is capable, and trained to take care of herself handsomely; but these things will not be of any use. She will go to the convent."

"Not if Lord Constantine can hinder it," Arthur said bluntly.

"I would like to see her in so exalted and happy a sphere as Lord Constantine could give her. But I am convinced that the man is not born who can win the love of this child of mine. Sir Galahad might, but not the stuff of which you and I are made."

"I believe you," said Arthur.

Honora herself told him of her future plans, as they sat with the sick man after a trying evening, when for some hours the end seemed near. The hour invited confidences, and like brother and sister at the sick-bed of a beloved parent they exchanged them. When she had finished telling him how she had tried to do her duty to her father, and to her country, and how she had laid aside her idea of the convent for their sake, but would now take up her whole duty to God by entering a sisterhood, he said casually:

"It seems to me these three duties work together; and when you were busiest with your father and your country, then were you most faithful to God."

"Very true," she replied, looking up with surprise. "Obedience is better than sacrifice."

"Take care that you are not deceiving yourself, Honora. Which would cause more pain, to give up your art and your cause, or to give up the convent?"

"To give up the convent," she replied promptly.

"That looks to me like selfishness," he said gently. "There are many nuns in the convents working for the wretched and helping the poor and praying for the oppressed, while only a few women are devoted directly to the cause of freedom. It strikes me that you descend when you retire from a field of larger scope to one which narrows your circle and diminishes your opportunities. I am not criticizing the nun's life, but simply your personal scheme."

"And you think I descend?" she murmured with a little gasp of pain. "Why, how can that be?"

"You are giving up the work, the necessary work, which few women are doing, to take up a work in which many women are engaged," he answered, uncertain of his argument, but quite sure of his intention. "You lose great opportunities to gain small ones, purely personal. That's the way it looks to me."

With wonderful cunning he unfolded his arguments in the next few weeks. He appealed to her love for her father, her wish to see his work continued; he described his own helplessness, very vaguely though, in carrying out schemes with which he was unacquainted, and to which he was vowed; he mourned over the helpless peoples of the world, for whom a new community was needed to fight, as the Knights of St. John fought for Christendom; and he painted with delicate satire that love of ease which leads heroes to desert the greater work for the lesser on the plea of the higher life. Selfishly she sought rest, relief for the taxing labors, anxieties, and journeys of fifteen years, and not the will of God, as she imagined. Was he conscious of his own motives? Did he discover therein any selfishness? Who can say?

He discoursed at the same time to Owen, and in the same fashion. Ledwith felt that his dreams were patch work beside the rainbow visions of this California miner, who had the mines which make the wildest dreams come true sometimes. The wealthy enthusiast might fall, however, into the hands of the professional patriot, who would bleed him to death in behalf of paper schemes. To whom could he confide him? Honora! It had always been Honora with him, who could do nothing without her. He did not wish to hamper her in the last moment, as he had hampered her since she had first planned her own life.

It was even a pleasant thought for him, to think of his faithful child living her beautiful, quiet, convent life, after the fatigues and pilgrimages of years, devoted to his memory, mingling his name with her prayers, innocent of any other love than for him and her Creator. Yes, she must be free as the air after he died. However, the sick are not masters of their emotions. A great dread and a great anguish filled him. Would it be his fate to lose Arthur to Ireland by consideration for others? But he loved her so! How could he bind her in bonds at the very moment of their bitter separation? He would not do it! He would not do it! He fought down his own longing until he woke up in a sweat of terror one night, and called to her loudly, fearing that he would die before he exacted from her the last promise. He must sacrifice all for his country, even the freedom of his child.

"Honora," he cried, "was I ever faithless to Erin? Did I ever hesitate when it was a question of money, or life, or danger, or suffering for her sake?"

"Never, father dear," she said, soothing him like a child.

"I have sinned now, then. For your sake I have sinned. I wished to leave you free when I am gone, although I saw you were still necessary to Eire. Promise me, my child, that you will delay a little after I am gone, before entering the convent; that you will make sure beforehand that Erin has no great need of you ... just a month or a year ... any delay — —"

"As long as you please, father," she said quietly. "Make it five years if you will — —"

"No, no," he interrupted with anguish in his throat. "I shall never demand again from you the sacrifices of the past. What may seem just to you will be enough. I die almost happy in leaving Arthur Dillon to carry on with his talent and his money the schemes of which I only dreamed. But I fear the money patriots will get hold of him and cheat him of his enthusiasm and his money together. If you were by to let him know what was best to be done—that is all I ask of you——"

"A year at least then, father dear! What is time to you and me that we should be stingy of the only thing we ever really possessed."

"And now I lose even that," with a long sigh.

Thus gently and naturally Arthur gained his point.

Monsignor came often, and then oftener when Owen's strength began to fail rapidly. The two friends in Irish politics had little agreement, but in the gloom of approaching death they remembered only their friendship. The priest worked vainly to put Owen into a proper frame of mind before his departure for judgment. He had made his peace with the Church, and received the last rites like a believer, but with the coldness of him who receives necessities from one who has wronged him. He was dying, not like a Christian, but like the pagan patriot who has failed: only the shades awaited him when he fled from the darkness of earthly shame. They sat together one March afternoon facing the window and the declining sun. To the right another window gave them a good view of the beautiful cathedral, whose twin spires, many turrets, and noble walls shone blue and golden in the brilliant light.

"I love to look at it from this elevation," said Monsignor, who had just been discoursing on the work of his life. "In two years, just think, the most beautiful temple in the western continent will be dedicated."

"The money that has gone into it would have struck a great blow for Erin," said Ledwith with a bitter sigh.

"So much of it as escaped the yawning pockets of the numberless patriots," retorted Monsignor dispassionately. "The money would not have been lost in so good a cause, but its present use has done more for your people than a score of the blows which you aim at England."

"Claim everything in sight while you are at it," said Owen. "In God's name what connection has your gorgeous cathedral with any one's freedom?"

"Father dear, you are exciting yourself," Honora broke in, but neither heeded her.

"Christ brought us true freedom," said Monsignor, "and the Church alone teaches, practises, and maintains it."

"A fine example is provided by Ireland, where to a dead certainty freedom was lost because the Church had too unnatural a hold upon the people."

"What was lost on account of the faith will be given back again with compound interest. Political and military movements have done much for Ireland in fifty years; but the only real triumphs, universal, brilliant, enduring, significant, leading surely up to greater things, have been won by the Irish faith, of which that cathedral, shining so gloriously in the sun this afternoon, is both a result and a symbol."

"I believe you will die with that conviction," Ledwith said in wonder.

"I wish you could die with the same, Owen," replied Monsignor tenderly.

They fell silent for a little under the stress of sudden feeling.

"How do men reason themselves into such absurdities?" Owen asked himself.

"You ought to know. You have done it often enough," said the priest tartly.

Then both laughed together, as they always did when the argument became personal.

"Do you know what Livingstone and Bradford and the people whom they represent think of that temple?" said Monsignor impressively.

"Oh, their opinions!" Owen snorted.

"They are significant," replied the priest. "These two leaders would give the price of the building to have kept down or destroyed the spirit which undertook and carried out the scheme. They have said to themselves many times in the last twenty years, while that temple rose slowly but gloriously into being, what sort of a race is this, so despised and ill-treated, so poor and ignorant, that in a brief time on our shores can build the finest temple to God which this country has yet seen? What will the people, to whom we have described this race as sunk in papistical stupidity, debased, unenterprising, think, when they gaze on this absolute proof of our mendacity?"

Ledwith, in silence, took a second look at the shining walls and towers.

"Owen, your generous but short-sighted crowd have fought England briefly and unsuccessfully a few times on the soil of Ireland ... but the children of the faith have fought her with church, and school, and catechism around the globe. Their banner, around which they fought, was not the banner of the Fenians but the banner of Christ. What did you do for the scattered children of the household? Nothing, but collect their moneys. While the great Church followed them everywhere with her priests, centered them about the temple, and made them the bulwark of the faith, the advance-guard, in many lands. Here in America, and in all the colonies of England, in Scotland, even in England itself, wherever the Irish settled, the faith took root and flourished; the faith which means death to the English heresy, and to English power as far as it rests upon the heresy."

"The faith kept the people together, scattered all over the world. It organized them, it trained them, it kept them true to the Christ preached by St. Patrick; it built the fortress of the temple, and the rampart of the school; it kept them a people apart, it kept them civilized, saved them from inevitable apostasy, and founded a force from which you collect your revenues for battle with your enemies; a force which fights England all over the earth night and day, in legislatures, in literature and journalism, in social and commercial life ... why, man, you are a fragment, a mere fragment, you and your warriors, of that great fight which has the world for an audience and the English earths for its stage."

"When did you evolve this new fallacy?" said Ledwith hoarsely.

"You have all been affected with the spirit of the anti-Catholic revolution in Europe, whose cry is that the Church is the enemy of liberty; yours, that it has been no friend to Irish liberty. Take another look at that cathedral. When you are dead, and many others that will live longer, that church will deliver its message to the people who pass: 'I am the child of the Catholic faith and the Irish; the broad shoulders of America waited for a simple, poor, cast-out people, to dig me from the earth and shape me into a thing of beauty, a glory of the new continent; I myself am not new; I am of that race which in Europe speaks in divine language to you pigmies of the giants that lived in ancient days; I am a new bond between the old continent and the new, between the old order and the new; I speak for the faith of the past; I voice the faith of the hour; the hands that raised me are not unskilled and untrained; from what I am judge, ye people, of what stuff my builders are made.' And around the world, in all the capitals, in the great cities, of the English-speaking peoples, temples of lesser worth and beauty, are speaking in the same strain."

Honora anxiously watched her father. A new light shone upon him, a new emotion disturbed him; perhaps that old hardness within was giving way. Ledwith had the poetic temperament, and the philosopher's power of generalization. A hint could open a grand horizon before him, and the cathedral in its solemn beauty was the hint. Of course, he could see it all, blind as he had been before. The Irish revolution worked fitfully, and exploded in a night, its achievement measured by the period of a month; but this temple and its thousand sisters lived on doing their good work in silence, fighting for the truth without noise or conspiracy.

"And this is the glory of the Irish," Monsignor continued, "this is the fact which fills me with pride, American as I am, in the race whose blood I own; they have preserved the faith for the great English-speaking world. Already the new principle peculiar to that faith has begun its work in literature, in art, in education, in social life. Heresy allowed the Christ to be banished from all the departments of human activity, except the home and the temple. Christ is not in the schools of the children, nor in the books we read, nor in the pictures and sculptures of our studios, nor in our architecture, even of the churches, nor in our journalism, any more than in the market-place and in the government. These things are purely pagan, or worthless composites. It looks as if the historian of these times, a century or two hence, will have hard work to fitly describe the Gesta Hibernicorum, when this principle of Christianity will have conquered the American world as it conquered ancient Europe. I tell you, Owen," and he strode to the window with hands outstretched to the great building, "in spite of all the shame and suffering endured for His sake, God has been very good to your people, He is heaping them with honors. As wide as is the power of England, it is no wider than the influence of the Irish faith. Stubborn heresy is doomed to fall before the truth which alone can set men free and keep them so."

Ledwith had begun to tremble, but he said never a word.

"I am prouder to have had a share in the building of that temple," Monsignor continued, "than to have won a campaign against the English. This is a victory, not of one race over another, but of the faith over heresy, truth over untruth. It will be the Christ-like glory of Ireland to give back to England one day the faith which a corrupt king destroyed, for which we have suffered crucifixion. No soul ever loses by climbing the cross with Christ."

Ledwith gave a sudden cry, and raised his hands to heaven, but grew quiet at once.

The priest watched contentedly the spires of his cathedral.

"You have touched heart and reason together," Honora whispered.

Ledwith remained a long time silent, struggling with a new spirit. At last he turned the wide, frank eyes on his friend and victor.

"I am conquered, Monsignor."

"Not wholly yet, Owen."

"I have been a fool, a foolish fool,—not to have seen and understood."

"And your folly is not yet dead. You are dying in sadness and despair almost, when you should go to eternity in triumph."

"I go in triumph! Alas! if I could only be blotted out with my last breath, and leave neither grave nor memory, it would be happiness. Why do you say, 'triumph'?"

"Because you have been true to your country with the fidelity of a saint. That's enough. Besides you leave behind you the son born of your fidelity to carry on your work——"

"God bless that noble son," Owen cried.

"And a daughter whose prayers will mount from the nun's cell, to bless your cause. If you could but go from her resigned!"

"How I wish that I might. I ought to be happy, just for leaving two such heirs, two noble hostages to Ireland. I see my error. Christ is the King, and no man can better His plans for men. I surrender to Him."

"But your submission is only in part. You are not wholly conquered."

"Twice have you said that," Owen complained, raising his heavy eyes in reproach.

"Love of country is not the greatest love."

"No, love of the race, of humanity, is more."

"And the love of God is more than either. With all their beauty, what do these abstract loves bring us? The country we love can give us a grave and a stone. Humanity crucifies its redeemers. Wolsey summed up the matter: 'Had I but served my God with half the zeal with which I served my king, He would not in mine age, have left me naked to mine enemies.'"

He paused to let his words sink into Ledwith's mind.

"Owen, you are leaving the world oppressed by the hate of a lifetime, the hate ingrained in your nature, the fatal gift of persecutor and persecuted from the past."

"And I shall never give that up," Owen declared, sitting up and fixing his hardest look on the priest. "I shall never forget Erin's wrongs, nor Albion's crimes. I shall carry that just and honorable hate beyond the grave. Oh, you priests!"

"I said you were not conquered. You may hate injustice, but not the unjust. You will find no hate in heaven, only justice. The persecutors and their victims have long been dead, and judged. The welcome of the wretched into heaven, the home of justice and love, wiped out all memory of suffering here, as it will for us all. The justice measured out to their tyrants even you would be satisfied with. Can your hate add anything to the joy of the blessed, or the woe of the lost?"

"Nothing," murmured Owen from the pillow, as his eyes looked afar, wondering at that justice so soon to be measured out to him. "You are again right. Oh, but we are feeble ... but we are foolish ... to think it. What is our hate any more than our justice ... both impotent and ridiculous."

There followed a long pause, then, for Monsignor had finished his argument, and only waited to control his own emotion before saying good-by.

"I die content," said Ledwith with a long restful sigh, coming back to earth, after a deep look into divine power and human littleness. "Bring me to-morrow, and often, the Lord of Justice. I never knew till now that in desiring Justice so ardently, it was He I desired. Monsignor, I die content, without hate, and without despair."

If ever a human creature had a foretaste of heaven it was Honora during the few weeks that followed this happy day. The bitterness in the soul of Owen vanished like a dream, and with it went regret, and vain longing, and the madness which at odd moments sprang from these emotions. His martyrdom, so long and ferocious, would end in the glory of a beautiful sunset, the light of heaven in his heart, shining in his face. He lay forever beyond the fire of time and injustice.

Every morning Honora prepared the little altar in the sick-room, and Monsignor brought the Blessed Sacrament. Arthur answered the prayers and gazed with awe upon the glorified face of the father, with something like anger upon the exalted face of the daughter; for the two were gone suddenly beyond him. Every day certain books provided by Monsignor were read to the dying man by the daughter or the son; describing the migration of the Irish all over the English-speaking world, their growth to consequence and power. Owen had to hear the figures of this growth, see and touch the journals printed by the scattered race, and to hear the editorials which spoke their success, their assurance, their convictions, their pride.

Then he laughed so sweetly, so naturally, chuckled so mirthfully that Honora had to weep and thank God for this holy mirthfulness, which sounded like the spontaneous, careless, healthy mirth of a boy. Monsignor came evenings to explain, interpret, put flesh and life into the reading of the day with his vivid and pointed comment. Ledwith walked in wonderland. "The hand of God is surely there," was his one saying. The last day of his pilgrimage he had a long private talk with Arthur. They had indeed become father and son, and their mutual tenderness was deep.

Honora knew from the expression of the two men that a new element had entered into her father's happiness.

"I free you from your promise, my child," said Ledwith, "my most faithful, most tender child. It is the glory of men that the race is never without such children as you. You are free from any bond. It is my wish that you accept your release."

She accepted smiling, to save him from the stress of emotion. Then he wished to see the cathedral in the light of the afternoon sun, and Arthur opened the door of the sick-room. The dying man could see from his pillow the golden spires, and the shining roof, that spoke to him so wonderfully of the triumph of his race in a new land, the triumph which had been built up in the night, unseen, uncared for, unnoticed.

"God alone has the future," he said.

Once he looked at Honora, once more, with burning eyes, that never could look enough on that loved child. With his eyes on the great temple, smiling, he died. They thought he had fallen asleep in his weakness. Honora took his head in her arms, and Arthur Dillon stood beside her and wept.

CHAPTER XXVI.

THE FALL OF LIVINGSTONE.

The ending of Quincy Livingstone's career in England promised to be like the setting of the sun: his glory fading on the hills of Albion only to burn with greater splendor in his native land: Chief Justice of the Supreme Court! He needed the elevation. True, his career at court had been delightful, from the English point of view even brilliant; the nobility had made much of him, if not as much as he had made of the nobility; the members of the government had seriously praised him, far as they stood from Lord Constantine's theory of American friendship. However pleasant these things looked to the Minister, of what account could they be to a mere citizen returning to private life in New York? Could they make up for the failures of the past year at home, the utter destruction of his pet schemes for the restraint of the Irish in the land of the Puritans?

What disasters! The alliance thrust out of consideration by the strong hand of Birmingham; the learned Fritters chased from the platform by cold audiences, and then from the country by relentless ridicule; Sister Claire reduced to the rank of a tolerated criminal, a ticket-of-leave girl; and the whole movement discredited! Fortunately these calamities remained unknown in London.

The new honors, however, would hide the failure and the shame. His elevation was certain. The President had made known his intention, and had asked Minister Livingstone to be ready within a short time to sail for home for final consultation. His departure from the court of St. James would be glorious, and his welcome home significant; afterwards his place would be amongst the stars. He owned the honorable pride that loves power and place, when these are worthy, but does not seek them. From the beginning the Livingstones had no need to run after office. It always sought them, receiving as rich a lustre as it gave in the recognition of their worth. His heart grew warm that fortune had singled him out for the loftiest place in his country's gift. To die chief-justice atoned for life's shortcomings. Life itself was at once steeped in the color and perfume of the rose.

Felicitations poured in from the great. The simplicities of life suddenly put on a new charm, the commonplaces a new emphasis. My Lord Tomnoddy's 'how-de-do' was uttered with feeling, men took a second look at him, the friends of a season felt a warmth about their language, if not about the heart, in telling of his coming dignity. The government people shook off their natural drowsiness to measure the facts, to understand that emotion should have a share in uttering the words of farewell. "Oh, my *dear*, DEAR Livingstone!" cried the Premier as he pressed his hand vigorously at their first meeting after the news had been given out. Society sang after the same fashion. Who could resist the delight of these things?

His family and friends exulted. Lovable and deep-hearted with them, harsh as he might be with opponents, their gladness gave him joy. The news spread among the inner circles with due reserve, since no one forgot the distance between the cup and the lip; but to intimates the appointment was said to be a certainty, and confirmation by the Senate as sure as anything mortal. Of course the Irish would raise a clamor, but no arm among them had length or strength enough to snatch away the prize. Not in many years had Livingstone dipped so deeply into the waters of joy as in the weeks that followed the advice from the President.

Arthur Dillon knew that mere opposition would not affect Livingstone's chances. His position was too strong to be stormed, he learned upon inquiry in Washington. The political world was quiet to drowsiness, and the President so determined in his choice that candidates would not come forward to embarrass his nominee. The public accepted the rumor of the appointment with indifference, which remained undisturbed when a second rumor told of Irish opposition. But for Arthur's determination the selection of a chief-justice would have been as dull as the naming of a consul to Algiers.

"We can make a good fight," was Grahame's conclusion, "but the field belongs to Livingstone."

"Chance is always kind to the unfit," said Arthur, "because the Irish are good-natured."

"I don't see the connection."

"I should have said, because mankind is so. In this case Quincy gets the prize, because the Irish think he will get it."

"You speak like the oracle," said Grahame.

"Well, the fight must be made, a stiff one, to the last cartridge. But it won't be enough, mere opposition. There must be another candidate. We can take Quincy in front; the candidate can take him in the rear. It must not be seen, only said, that the President surrendered to Irish pressure. There's the plan: well-managed opposition, and another candidate. We can see to the first, who will be the other?"

They were discussing that point without fruit when Anne knocked at the door of the study, and entered in some anxiety.

"Is it true, what I heard whispered," said she, "that they will soon be looking for a minister to England, that Livingstone is coming back?"

"True, mother dear," and he rose to seat her comfortably. "But if you can find us a chief-justice the good man will not need to come back. He can remain to help keep patriots in English prisons."

"Why I want to make sure, you know, is that Vandervelt should get the English mission this time without fail. I wouldn't have him miss it for the whole world."

"There's your man," said Grahame.

"Better than the English mission, mother," Arthur said quickly, "would be the chief-justiceship for so good a man as Vandervelt. If you can get him to tell his friends he wants to be chief-justice, I can swear that he will get one place or the other. I know which one he would prefer. No, not the mission. That's for a few years, forgotten honors. The other's for life, lasting honor. Oh, how Vandervelt must sigh for that noble dais, the only throne in the Republic, the throne of American justice. Think, how Livingstone would defile it! The hater and persecutor of a wronged and hounded race, who begrudges us all but the honors of slavery, how could he understand and administer justice, even among his own?"

"What are you raving about, Artie?" she complained. "I'll get Vandervelt to do anything if it's the right thing for him to do; only explain to me what you want done."

He explained so clearly that she was filled with delight. With a quickness which astonished him, she picked up the threads of the intrigue; some had their beginning five years back, and she had not forgotten. Suddenly the root of the affair bared itself to her: this son of hers was doing battle for his own. She had forgotten Livingstone long ago, and therefore had forgiven him. Arthur had remembered. Her fine spirit stirred dubious Grahame.

"Lave Vandervelt to me," she said, for her brogue came back and gently tripped her at times, "and do you young men look after Livingstone. I have no hard feelings against him, but, God forgive me, when I think of Louis Everard, and all that Mary suffered, and Honora, and the shame put upon us by Sister Claire, something like hate burns me. Anyway we're not worth bein' tramped upon, if we let the like of him get so high, when we can hinder it."

"Hurrah for the Irish!" cried Grahame, and the two cheered her as she left the room to prepare for her share of the labor.

The weight of the work lay in the swift and easy formation of an opposition whose strength and temper would be concealed except from the President, and whose action would be impressive, consistent, and dramatic. The press was to know only what it wished to know, without provocation. The main effort should convince the President of the unfitness of one candidate and the fitness of the other. There were to be no public meetings or loud denunciations. What cared the officials for mere cries of rage? Arthur found his task delightful, and he worked like a smith at the forge, heating, hammering, and shaping his engine of war. When ready for action, his mother had won Vandervelt, convinced him that his bid for the greater office would inevitably land him in either place. He had faith in her, and she had prophesied his future glory!

Languidly the journals gave out in due time the advent of another candidate for the chief-justiceship, and also cloudy reports of Irish opposition to Livingstone. No one was interested but John Everard, still faithful to the Livingstone interest in spite of the gibes of Dillon and Grahame. The scheme worked so effectively that Arthur did not care to have any interruptions from this source. The leaders talked to the President singly, in the order of their importance, against his nominee, on the score of party peace. What need to disturb the Irish by naming a man who had always irritated and even insulted them? The representation in the House would surely suffer by his action, because in this way only could the offended people retaliate. They detested Livingstone.

Day after day this testimony fairly rained upon the President, unanimous, consistent, and increasing in dignity with time, each protester seeming more important than he who just went out the door. Inquiries among the indifferent proved that the Irish would give much to see Livingstone lose the honors. And always in the foreground of the picture of protest stood the popular and dignified Vandervelt surrounded by admiring friends!

Everard had the knack of ferreting out obscure movements. When this intrigue was laid bare he found Arthur Dillon at his throat on the morning he had chosen for a visit to the President. To promise the executive support from a strong Irish group in the appointment of Livingstone would have been fatal to the opposition. Hence the look which Arthur bestowed on Everard was as ugly as his determination to put the marplot in a retreat for the insane, if no other plan kept him at home.

"I want to defeat Livingstone," said Arthur, "and I think I have him defeated. You had better stay at home. You are hurting a good cause."

"I am going to destroy that good cause," John boasted gayly. "You thought you had the field to yourself. And you had, only that I discovered your game."

"It's a thing to be proud of," Arthur replied sadly, "this steady support of the man who would have ruined your boy. Keep quiet.

You've got to have the truth rammed down your throat, since you will take it in no other way. This Livingstone has been plotting against your race for twenty years. It may not matter to a disposition as crooked as yours, that he opened the eyes of English government people to the meaning of Irish advance in America, that he is responsible for Fritters, for the alliance, for McMeeter, for the escaped nun, for her vile *Confessions*, for the kidnapping societies here. You are cantankerous enough to forget that he used his position in London to do us harm, and you won't see that he will do as much with the justiceship. Let these things pass. If you were a good Catholic one might excuse your devotion to Livingstone on the score that you were eager to return good for evil. But you're a half-cooked Catholic, John. Let that pass too. Have you no manhood left in you? Are you short on self-respect? This man brought out and backed the woman who sought to ruin your son, to break your wife's heart, to destroy your own happiness. With his permission she slandered the poor nuns with tongue and pen, a vile woman hired to defile the innocent. And for this man you throw dirt on your own, for this man you are going to fight your own that he may get honors which he will shame. Isn't it fair to think that you are going mad, Everard?"

"Don't attempt," said the other in a fury, "to work off your oratory on me. I am going to Washington to expose your intrigues against a gentleman. What! am I to tremble at your frown——?"

"Rot, man! Who asked you to tremble? I saved your boy from Livingstone, and I shall save you from yourself, even if I have to put you in an asylum for the harmless insane. Don't you believe that Livingstone is the patron of Sister Claire? that he is indirectly responsible for that scandal?"

"I never did, and I never shall," with vehemence. "You are one of those that can prove anything——"

"If you were sure of his responsibility, would you go to Washington?"

"Haven't I the evidence of my own senses? Were not all Livingstone's friends on the committee which exposed Sister Claire?"

"Because we insisted on that or a public trial, and they came with sour stomachs," said Arthur, glad that he had begun to discuss the point. "Would you go to Washington if you were sure he backed the woman?"

"Enough, young man. I'm off for the train. Here, Mary, my satchel— —"

Two strong bands were laid on his shoulders, he was pushed back into his chair, and the face which glowered on him after this astonishing violence for the moment stilled his rage and astonishment.

"Would you go to Washington if you were sure Livingstone backed Sister Claire?" came the relentless question.

"No, I wouldn't," he answered vacantly.

"Do you wish to be made sure of it?"

He began to turn purple and to bluster.

"Not a word," said his master, "not a cry. Just answer that question. Do you wish to be made sure of this man's atrocious guilt and your own folly?"

"I want to know what is the meaning of this," Everard sputtered, "this violence? In my own house, in broad day, like a burglar."

"Answer the question."

Alarm began to steal over Everard, who was by no means a brave man. Had Arthur Dillon, always a strange fellow, gone mad? Or was this scene a hint of murder? The desperate societies to which Dillon was said to belong often indulged in violence. It had never occurred to him before that these secret forces must be fighting Livingstone through Dillon. They would never permit him to use his influence at Washington in the Minister's behalf. Dreadful! He must dissemble.

"If you can make me sure, I am willing," he said meekly.

"Read that, then," and Arthur placed his winning card, as he thought, in his hands; the private confession of Sister Claire as to the persons who had assisted her in her outrageous schemes; and the chief, of course, was Livingstone. Everard read it with contempt.

"Legally you know what her testimony is worth," said he.

"You accepted her testimony as to her own frauds, and so did the whole committee."

"We had to accept the evidence of our own senses."

Obstinate to the last was Everard.

"You will not be convinced," said Arthur rudely, "but you can be muzzled. I say again: keep away from Washington, and keep your hands off my enterprise. You have some idea of what happens to men like you for interfering. If I meet you in Washington, or find any trace of your meddling in the matter, here is what I shall do; this whole scandal of the escaped nun shall be reopened, this confession shall be printed, and the story of Louis' adventure, from that notable afternoon at four o'clock until his return, word for word, with portraits of his interesting family, of Sister Claire, all the details, will be given to the journals. Do you understand? Meanwhile, study this problem in psychology: how long will John Everard be able to endure life after I tell the Irish how he helped to enthrone their bitterest enemy?"

He did not wait for an answer, but left the baffled man to wrestle with the situation, which must have worsted him, for his hand did not appear in the game at Washington. Very smoothly the plans of Arthur worked to their climax. The friends of Vandervelt pressed his cause as urgently and politely as might be, and with increasing energy as the embarrassment of the President grew. The inherent weakness of Vandervelt's case appeared to the tireless Dillon more appalling in the last moments than at the beginning: the situation had no logical outcome. It was merely a question whether the President would risk a passing unpopularity.

He felt the absence of Birmingham keenly, the one man who could say to the executive with authority, this appointment would be a blunder. Birmingham being somewhere on the continent, out of reach of appeals for help, his place was honorably filled by the General of the Army, with an influence, however, purely sentimental. Arthur accompanied him for the last interview with the President. Only two days intervened before the invitation would be sent to Livingstone to return home. The great man listened with sympathy to the head of the army making his protest, but would promise nothing; he had fixed an hour however for the settlement of the irritating problem; if they would call the next morning at ten, he would give them his unalterable decision.

Feeling that the decision must be against his hopes, Arthur passed a miserable night prowling with Grahame about the hotel. Had he omitted any point in the fight? Was there any straw afloat which could be of service? Doyle used his gift of poetry to picture for him the return of Livingstone, and his induction into office; the serenity of mind, the sense of virtue and patriotism rewarded, his cold contempt of the defeated opposition and their candidate, the matchless dignity, which would exalt Livingstone to the skies as the Chief-Justice. Their only consolation was the fight itself, which had shaken for a moment the edifice of the Minister's fame.

The details went to London from friends close to the President, and enabled Livingstone to measure the full strength of a young man's hatred. The young man should be attended to after the struggle. There was no reason to lose confidence. While the factions were still worrying, the cablegram came with the request that he sail on Saturday for home, the equivalent of appointment. When reading it at the Savage Club, whither a special messenger had followed him, the heavy mustache and very round spectacles of Birmingham rose up suddenly before him, and they exchanged greetings with the heartiness of exiles from the same land. The Minister remembered that his former rival had no share in the attempt to deprive him of his coming honors, and Birmingham recalled the rumor picked up that day in the city.

"I suppose there's no truth in it," he said.

The Minister handed him the cablegram.

"Within ten days," making a mental calculation, "I should be on my way back to London, with the confirmation of the Senate practically secured."

"When it comes I shall be pleased to offer my congratulations," Birmingham replied, and the remark slightly irritated Livingstone.

Could he have seen what happened during the next few hours his sleep would have lost its sweetness. Birmingham went straight to the telegraph office, and sent a cipher despatch to his man of business, ordering him to see the President that night in Washington, and to declare in his name, with all the earnestness demanded by the situation, that the appointment of Livingstone would mean political death to him and immense embarrassment to his party for years. As it would be three in the morning before a reply would reach London, Birmingham went to bed with a good conscience. Thus, while the two young men babbled all night in the hotel, and thought with dread of the fatal hour next morning, wire, and train, and business man flew into the capital and out of it, carrying one man's word in and another man's glory out, fleet, silent, unrecognized, unhonored, and unknown.

At breakfast Birmingham read the reply from his business man with profound satisfaction. At breakfast the Minister read a second cablegram with a sudden recollection of Birmingham's ominous words the night before. He knew that he would need no congratulations, for the prize had been snatched away forever. The cablegram informed him that he should not sail on Saturday, and that explanations would follow. For a moment his proud heart failed him. Bitterness flowed in on him, so that the food in his mouth became tasteless. What did he care that his enemies had triumphed? Or, that he had been overthrown? The loss of the vision which had crowned his life, and made a hard struggle for what he thought the fit and right less sordid, even beautiful; that was a calamity.

He had indulged it in spite of mental protests against the dangerous folly. The swift imagination, prompted by all that was Livingstone in him, had gone over the many glories of the expected dignity; the departure from beautiful and flattering England, the distinction of the return to his beloved native land, the splendid interval before the glorious day, the crowning honors amid the applause of his own, and the long sweet afternoon of life, when each day would bring its own distinction! He had had his glimpse of Paradise. Oh, never, never would life be the same for him! He began to study the reasons for his ill-success....

At ten o'clock that day the President informed the General of the Army in Mr. Dillon's presence that he had sent the name of Hon. Van Rensselaer Vandervelt to the Senate for the position of Chief-Justice!

THE TEST OF DISAPPEARANCE.

CHAPTER XXVII.

A PROBLEM OF DISAPPEARANCE.

After patient study of the disappearance of Horace Endicott, for five years, Richard Curran decided to give up the problem. All clues had come to nothing. Not the faintest trace of the missing man had been found. His experience knew nothing like it. The money earned in the pursuit would never repay him for the loss of self-confidence and of nerve, due to study and to ill success. But for his wife he would have withdrawn long ago from the search.

"Since you have failed," she said, "take up my theory. You will find that man in Arthur Dillon."

"That's the strongest reason for giving up," he replied. "Once before I felt my mind going from insane eagerness to solve the problem. It would not do to have us both in the asylum at once."

"I made more money in following my instincts, Dick, than you have made in chasing your theories. Instinct warned me years ago that Arthur Dillon is another than what he pretends. It warns me now that he is Horace Endicott. At least before you give up for good, have a shy at my theory."

"Instinct! Theory! It is pure hatred. And the hate of a woman can make her take an ass for Apollo."

"No doubt I hate him. Oh, how I hate that man ... and young Everard...."

"Or any man that escapes you," he filled in with sly malice.

"Be careful, Dick," she screamed at him, and he apologized. "That hate is more to me than my child. It will grow big enough to kill him yet. But apart from hate, Arthur Dillon is not the man he seems. I could swear he is Horace Endicott. Remember all I have told you about his return. He came back from California about the time Endicott disappeared. I was playing Edith Conyngham then with great success, though not to crowded houses."

She laughed heartily at the recollection.

"I remarked to myself even then that Anne Dillon ... she's the choice hypocrite ... did not seem easy in showing the letter which told of his coming back, how sorry he was for his conduct, how happy he would make her with the fortune he had earned."

"All pure inference," said Curran. "Twenty men arrived home in New York about the same time with fortunes from the mines, and some without fortunes from the war."

"Then how do you account for this, smart one? Never a word of his life in California from that day to this. Mind that. No one knows, or seems to know, just where he had been, just how he got his money ... you understand ... all the little bits o' things that are told, and guessed, and leak out in a year. I asked fifty people, I suppose, and all they knew was: California. You'd think Judy Haskell knew, and she told me everything. What had she to tell? that no one dared to ask him about such matters."

"Dillon is a very close man."

"Endicott had to be among that long-tongued Irish crowd. I watched him. He was stupid at first ... stuck to the house ... no one saw him for weeks ... except the few. He listened and watched ... I saw him ... his eyes and his ears ought to be as big as a donkey's from it ... and he said nothing. They made excuses for a thing that everyone saw and talked about. He was ill. I say he wanted to make no mistakes; he was learning his part; there was nothing of the Irish in him, only the sharp Yankee. It made me wonder for weeks what was wrong. He looked as much like the boy that ran away as you do. And then I had no suspicions, mind you. I believed Anne Dillon's boy had come back with a fortune, and I was thinking how I could get a good slice of it."

"And you didn't get a cent," Curran remarked.

"He hated me from the beginning. It takes one that is playing a part to catch another in the same business. After a while he began to bloom. He got more Irish than the Irish. There's no Yankee living, no Englishman, can play the Irishman. He can give a good imitation maybe, d'ye hear? That's what Dillon gave. He did everything that young Dillon used to do before he left home ... a scamp he was too. He danced jigs, flattered the girls, chummed with the ditch-diggers and barkeepers ... and he hated them all, women and men. The Yankees hate the Irish as easy as they breathe. I tell you he had forgotten nothing that he used to do as a boy. And the fools that looked on said, oh, it's easy to see he was sick, for now that he is well we can all recognize our old dare-devil, Arthur."

"He's dare-devil clear enough," commented her husband.

"First point you've scored," she said with contempt. "Horace Endicott was a milksop: to run away when he should have killed the two idiots. Dillon is a devil, as I ought to know. But the funniest thing was his dealings with his mother. She was afraid of him ... as much as I am ... she is till this minute. Haven't I seen her look at him, when she dared to say a sharp thing? And she's a good actress, mind you. It took her years to act as a mother can act with a son."

"Quite natural, I think. He went away a boy, came back a rich man, and was able to boss things, having the cash."

"You think! You! I've seen ten years of your thinking! Well, I thought too. I saw a chance for cash, where I smelled a mystery. Do you know that he isn't a Catholic? Do you know that he's strange to all Catholic ways? that he doesn't know how to hear Mass, to kneel when he enters a pew, to bless himself when he takes the holy water at the door? Do you know that he never goes to communion? And therefore he never goes to confession. Didn't I watch for years, so that I might find out what was wrong with him, and make some money?"

"All that's very plausible," said her husband. "Only, there are many Catholics in this town, and in particular the Californians, that forgot as much as he forgot about their religion, and more."

"But he is not a Catholic," she persisted. "There's an understanding between him and Monsignor O'Donnell. They exchange looks when they meet. He visits the priest when he feels like it, but in public they keep apart. Oh, all round, that Arthur Dillon is the strangest fellow; but he plays his part so well that fools like you, Dick, are tricked."

"You put a case well, Dearie. But it doesn't convince me. However," for he knew her whim must be obeyed, "I don't mind trying again to find Horace Endicott in this Arthur Dillon."

"And of course," with a sneer, "you'll begin with the certainty that there's nothing in the theory. What can the cleverest man discover, when he's sure beforehand that there's nothing to discover?"

"My word, Colette, if I take up the matter, I'll convince you that you're wrong, or myself that you're right. And I'll begin right here this minute. I believe with you that we have found Endicott at last. Then the first question I ask myself is: who helped Horace Endicott to become Arthur Dillon?"

"Monsignor O'Donnell of course," she answered.

"Then Endicott must have known the priest before he disappeared: known him so as to trust him, and to get a great favor from him? Now, Sonia didn't know that fact."

"That fool of a woman knows nothing, never did, never will," she snapped.

"Well, for the sake of peace let us say he was helped by Monsignor, and knew the priest a little before he went away. Monsignor helped him to find his present hiding-place; quite naturally he knew Mrs. Dillon, how her son had gone and never been heard of: and he knew it would be a great thing for her to have a son with an income like Endicott's. The next question is: how many people know at this moment who Dillon really is?"

"Just two, sir. He's a fox ... they're three foxes ... Monsignor, Anne Dillon, and Arthur himself. I know, for I watched 'em all, his uncle, his friends, his old chums ... the fellows he played with before he ran away ... and no one knows but the two that had to know ... sly Anne and smooth Monsignor. They made the money that I wasn't smart enough to get hold of."

"Then the next question is: is it worth while to make inquiries among the Irish, his friends and neighbors, the people that knew the real Dillon?"

"You won't find out any more than I've told you, but you may prove how little reason they have for accepting him as the boy that ran away."

"After that it would be necessary to search California."

"Poor Dick," she interrupted with compassion, smoothing his beard. "You are really losing your old cleverness. Search California! Can't you see yet the wonderful 'cuteness of this man, Endicott? He settled all that before he wrote the letter to Anne Dillon, saying that her son was coming home. He found out the career of Arthur Dillon in California. If he found that runaway he sent him off to Australia with a lump of money, to keep out of sight for twenty years. Did the scamp need much persuading? I reckon not. He had been doing it for nothing ten years. Or, perhaps the boy was dead: then he had only to make the proper connections with his history up to the time of his death. Or he may have disappeared forever, and that made the matter all the simpler for Endicott. Oh, you're not clever, Dick," and she kissed him to sweeten the bitterness of the opinion.

"I'm not convinced," he said cheerfully. "Then tell me what to do."

"I don't know myself. Endicott took his money with him. Where does Arthur Dillon keep his money? How did it get there? Where was it kept before that? How is he spending it just now? Does he talk in his sleep? Are there any mementoes of his past in his private boxes? Could he be surprised into admissions of his real character by some trick, such as bringing him face to face on a sudden with Sonia? Wouldn't that be worth seeing? Just like the end of a drama. You know the marks on Endicott's body, birthmarks and the like ... are they on Dillon's body? The boy that ran away must have had some marks.... Judy Haskell would know ... are they on Endicott's body?"

"You've got the map of the business in that pretty head perfect," said Curran in mock admiration. "But don't you see, my pet, that if this man is as clever as you would have him he has already seen to these things? He has removed the birthmarks and peculiarities of Horace, and adopted those of Arthur? You'll find it a tangled business the deeper you dive into it."

"Well, it's your business to dive deeper than the tangle," she answered crossly. "If I had your practice— —"

"You would leave me miles behind, of course. Here's the way I would reason about this thing: Horace Endicott is now known as Arthur Dillon; he has left no track by which Endicott can be traced to his present locality; but there must be a very poor connection between the Dillon at home and the real Dillon in California, in Australia, or in his grave; if we can trace the real Arthur Dillon then we take away the foundations of his counterfeit. Do you see? I say a trip to California and a clean examination there, after we have done our best here to pick flaws in the position of the gentleman who has been so cruel to my pet. He must get his punishment for that, I swear."

"Ah, there's the rub," she whimpered in her childish way. "I hate him, and I love him. He's the finest fellow in the world. He has the strength of ten. See how he fought the battles of the Irish against his own. One minute I could tear him like a wolf, and now I could let him tear me to pieces. You are fond of him too, Dick."

"I would follow him to the end of the world, through fire and flood and fighting," said the detective with feeling. "He loves Ireland, he loves and pities our poor people, he is spending his money for them. But I could kill him just the same for his cruelty to you. He's a hard man, Colette."

"Now I know what you are trying to do," she said sharply. "You think you can frighten me by telling me what I know already. Well, you can't."

"No, no," he protested, "I was thinking of another thing. We'll come to the danger part later. There is one test of this man that ought to be tried before all others. When I have sounded the people about Arthur Dillon, and am ready for California, Sonia Endicott should be brought here to have a good look at him in secret first; and then, perhaps, in the open, if you thought well of it."

"Why shouldn't I think well of it? But will it do any good, and mayn't it do harm? Sonia has no brains. If you can't see any resemblance between Arthur and the pictures of Horace Endicott, what can Sonia see?"

"The eyes of hate, and the eyes of love," said he sagely.

"Then I'd be afraid to bring them together," she admitted whispering again, and cowering into his arms. "If he suspects I am hunting him down, he will have no pity."

"No doubt of it," he said thoughtfully. "I have always felt the devil in him. Endicott was a fat, gay, lazy sport, that never so much as rode after the hounds. Now Arthur Dillon has had his training in the mines. That explains his dare-devil nature."

"And Horace Endicott was betrayed by the woman he loved," she cried with sudden fierceness. "That turns a man sour quicker than all the mining-camps in the world. That made him lean and terrible like a wolf. That sharpened his teeth, and gave him a taste for woman's blood. That's why he hates me."

"You're wrong again, my pet. He has a liking for you, but you spoil it by laying hands on his own. You saw his looks when he was hunting for young Everard."

"Oh, how he frightens me," and she began to walk the room in a rage. "How I would like to throw off this fear and face him and fight him, as I face you. I'll do it if the terror kills me. I shall not be terrified by any man. You shall hunt him down, Dick Curran. Begin at once. When you are ready send for Sonia. I'll bring them together myself, and take the responsibility. What can he do but kill me?"

Sadness came over the detective as she returned to her seat on his knee.

"He is not the kind, little girl," said he, "that lays hands on a woman or a man outside of fair, free, open fight before the whole world."

"What do you mean?" knowing very well what he meant.

"If he found you on his trail," with cunning deliberation, so that every word beat heart and brain like a hammer, "and if he is really Horace Endicott, he would only have to give your character and your address——"

"To the dogs," she shrieked in a sudden access of horror.

Then she lay very still in his arms, and the man laughed quietly to himself, sure that he had subdued her and driven her crazy scheme into limbo. The wild creature had one dread and by reason of it one master. Never had she been so amenable to discipline as under Dillon's remote and affable authority. Curran had no fear of consequences in studying the secret years of Arthur Dillon's existence. The study might reveal things which a young man preferred to leave in the shadows, but would not deliver up to Sonia her lost Horace; and even if Arthur came to know what they were doing, he could smile at Edith's vagaries.

"What shall we do?" he ventured to say at last.

"Find Horace Endicott in Arthur Dillon," was the unexpected answer, energetic, but sighed rather than spoken. "I fear him, I love him, I hate him, and I'm going to destroy him before he destroys me. Begin to-night."

CHAPTER XXVIII.

A FIRST TEST.

Curran could not study the Endicott problem. His mind had lost edge in the vain process, getting as confused over details as the experimenter in perpetual motion after an hundred failures. In favor of Edith he said to himself that her instincts had always been remarkable, always helpful; and her theory compared well with the twenty upon which he had worked years to no purpose. Since he could not think the matter out, he went straight on in the fashion which fancy had suggested. Taking it for granted that Dillon and Endicott were the same man, he must establish the connection; that is, discover the moment when Horace Endicott passed from his own into the character of Arthur Dillon.

Two persons would know the fact: Anne Dillon and her son. Four others might have knowledge of it; Judy, the Senator, Louis, and Monsignor. A fifth might be added, if the real Arthur Dillon were still living in obscurity, held there by the price paid him for following his own whim. Others would hardly be in the secret. The theory was charming in itself, and only a woman like Edith, whose fancy had always been sportive, would have dreamed it. The detective recalled Arthur's interest in his pursuit of Endicott; then the little scenes on board the *Arrow*; and grew dizzy to think of the man pursued comparing his own photograph with his present likeness, under the eyes of the detective who had grown stale in the chase of him.

He knew of incidents quite as remarkable, which had a decent explanation afterwards, however. He went about among the common people of Cherry Hill, who had known Arthur Dillon from his baptism, had petted him every week until he disappeared, and now adored him in his success. He renewed acquaintance with them, and heaped them with favors. Loitering about in their idling places, he threw out the questions; hints, surmises, which might bring to the surface their faith in Arthur Dillon. He reported the result to Edith.

"Not one of them" said he, "but would go to court and swear a bushel of oaths that Arthur Dillon is the boy who ran away. They have their reasons too; how he dances, and sings, and plays the fiddle, and teases the girls, just as he did when a mere strip of a lad; how the devil was always in him for doing the thing that no one looked for; how he had no fear of even the priest, or of the wildest horse; and sought out terrible things to do and to dare, just as now he shakes up your late backers, bishops, ministers, ambassadors, editors, or plots against England; all as if he earned a living that way."

She sneered at this bias, and bade him search deeper.

It was necessary to approach the Senator on the matter. He secured from him a promise that their talk would remain a secret, not only because the matter touched one very dear to the Senator, but also because publicity might ruin the detective himself. If the Senator did not care to give his word, there would be no talk, but his relative might also be exposed to danger. The Senator was always gracious with Curran.

"Do you know anything about Arthur's history in California?" and his lazy eyes noted every change in the ruddy, handsome face.

"Never asked him but one question about it. He answered that straight, and never spoke since about it. Nothing wrong, I hope?" the Senator answered with alarm.

"Lots, I guess, but I don't know for sure. Here are the circumstances. Think them out for yourself. A crowd of sharp speculators in California mines bought a mine from Arthur Dillon when he was settling up his accounts to come home to his mother. As trouble arose lately about that mine, they had to hunt up Arthur Dillon. They send their agent to New York, he comes to Arthur, and has a talk with him. Then he goes back to his speculators, and declares to them that this Arthur Dillon is not the man who sold the mine. So the company, full of suspicion, offers me the job of looking up the character of Arthur, and what he had been doing these ten years. They say straight out that the real Arthur Dillon has been put out of the way, and that the man who is holding the name and the stakes here in New York is a fraud."

This bit of fiction relieved the Senator's mind.

"A regular cock-and-bull story," said he with indignation. "What's their game? Did you tell them what we think of Artie? Would his own mother mistake him? Or even his uncle? If they're looking for hurt, tell them they're on the right road."

"No, no," said Curran, "these are straight men. But if doubt is cast on a business transaction, they intend to clear it away. It would be just like them to bring suit to establish the identity of Arthur with the Arthur Dillon who sold them the mine. Now, Senator, could you go into court and swear positively that the young man who came back from California five years ago is the nephew who ran away from home at the age of fifteen?"

"Swear it till I turned blue; why, it's foolish, simply foolish. And every man, woman, and child in the district would do the same. Why don't you go and talk with Artie about it?"

"Because the company doesn't wish to make a fuss until they have some ground to walk on," replied Curran easily. "When I tell them how sure the relatives and friends of Arthur are about his identity, they may drop the affair. But now, Senator, just discussing the thing as friends, you know, if you were asked in court why you were so sure Arthur is your nephew, what could you tell the court?"

"If the court asked me how I knew my mother was my mother ——"

"That's well enough, I know. But in this case Arthur was absent ten years, in which time you never saw him, heard of him, or from him."

"Good point," said the Senator musingly. "When Artie came home from California, he was sick, and I went to see him. He was in bed. Say, I'll never forget it, Curran. I saw Pat sick once at the same age ... Pat was his father, d'ye see?... and here was Pat lying before me in the bed. I tell you it shook me. I never thought he'd grow so much like his father, though he has the family features. Know him to be

Pat's son? Why, if he told me himself he was any one else, I wouldn't believe him."

Evidently the Senator knew nothing of Horace Endicott and recognised Arthur Dillon as his brother's son. The detective was not surprised; neither was Edith at the daily report.

"There isn't another like him on earth," she said with the pride of a discoverer. "Keep on until you find his tracks, here or in California."

Curran had an interesting chat with Judy Haskell on a similar theme, but with a different excuse from that which roused the Senator. The old lady knew the detective only as Arthur's friend. He approached her mysteriously, with a story of a gold mine awaiting Arthur in California, as soon as he could prove to the courts that he was really Arthur Dillon. Judy began to laugh. "Prove that he's Arthur Dillon! Faith, an' long I'd wait for a gold mine if I had to prove I was Judy Haskell. How can any one prove themselves to be themselves, Misther Curran? Are the courts goin' crazy?"

The detective explained what evidence a court would accept as proof of personality.

"Well, Arthur can give that aisy enough," said she.

"But he won't touch the thing at all, Mrs. Haskell. He was absent ten years, and maybe he doesn't want that period ripped up in a court. It might appear that he had a wife, you know, or some other disagreeable thing might leak out. When the lawyers get one on the witness stand, they make hares of him."

"Sure enough," said Judy thoughtfully. Had she not suggested this very suspicion to Anne? The young are wild, and even Arthur could have slipped from grace in that interval of his life. Curran hoped that Arthur could prove his identity without exposing the secrets of the past.

"For example," said he smoothly, with an eye for Judy's expression, "could you go to court to-morrow and swear that Arthur is the same lad that ran away from his mother fifteen years ago?"

"I cud swear as manny oaths on that point as there are hairs in yer head," said Judy.

"And what would you say, Mrs. Haskell, if the judge said to you: Now, madam, it's very easy for you to say you know the young man to be the same person as the runaway boy; but how do you know it? what makes you think you know it?"

"I'd say he was purty sassy, indade. Of coorse I'd say that to meself, for ye can't talk to a judge as aisy an' free as to a lawyer. Well, I'd say manny pleasant things. Arthur was gone tin years, but I knew him an' he knew me the minute we set eyes on aich other. Then, agin, I knew him out of his father. He doesn't favor the mother at all, for she's light an' he's dark. There's a dale o' the Dillon in him. Then, agin, how manny things he tould me of the times we had together, an' he even asked me if Teresa Flynn, his sweetheart afore he wint off, was livin' still. Oh, as thrue as ye're sittin' there! Poor thing, she was married. An' he remembered how fond he was o' rice puddin' ice cold. An' he knew Louis Everard the minute he shtud forninst him in the door. But what's the use o' talkin'? I cud tell ye for hours all the things he said an' did to show he was Arthur Dillon."

"Has he any marks on his body that would help to identify him, if he undertook to get the gold mine that belongs to him?"

"Artie had only wan mark on him as a boy ... he was the most spotless child I ever saw ... an' that was a mole on his right shoulder. He tuk it wid him to California, an' he brought it back, for I saw it meself in the same spot while he was sick, an' I called his attintion to it, an' he was much surprised, for he had never thought of it wanst."

"It's my opinion," said Curran solemnly, "that he can prove his identity without exposing his life in the west. I hope to persuade him to it. Maybe the photographs of himself and his father would help. Have you any copies of them?"

"There's jist two. I wudn't dare to take thim out of his room, but if ye care to walk up-stairs, Mr. Curran, an' luk at thim there, ye're welcome. He an' his mother are away the night to a gran' ball."

They entered Arthur's apartments together, and Judy showed the pictures of Arthur Dillon as a boy of fourteen, and of his youthful father; old daguerreotypes, but faithful and clear as a likeness. Judy rattled on for an hour, but the detective had achieved his object. She had no share in the secret.

Arthur Dillon was his father's son, for her. He studied the pictures, and carefully examined the rooms, his admiration provoking Judy into a display of their beauties. With the skill and satisfaction of an artist in man-hunting, he observed how thoroughly the character of the young man displayed itself in the trifles of decoration and furnishing.

The wooden crucifix with the pathetic figure in bronze on the wall over the desk, the holy water stoup at the door, carved figures of the Holy Family, a charming group, on the desk, exquisite etchings of the Christ and the Madonna after the masters, a *prie-dieu* in the inner room with a group of works of devotion: and Edith had declared him no Catholic. Here was the refutation.

"He is a pious man," Curran said.

"And no wan sees it but God and himself. So much the betther, I say," Judy remarked. "Only thim that had sorra knows how to pray, an' he prays like wan that had his fill of it."

The tears came into the man's eyes at the indications of Arthur's love for poor Erin. Hardness was the mark of Curran, and sin had been his lifelong delight; but for his country he had kept a tenderness and devotion that softened and elevated his nature at times. Of little use and less honor to his native land, he felt humbled in this room, whose books, pictures, and ornaments revealed thought and study in behalf of a harried and wretched people, yet the student was not a native of Ireland. It seemed profane to set foot here, to spy upon its holy privacy. He felt glad that its details gave the lie so emphatically to Edith's instincts.

The astonishing thing was the absence of Californian relics and mementoes. Some photographs and water colors, whose names Curran mentally copied for future use, pictured popular scenes on the Pacific slope; but they could be bought at any art store. Surely his life in the mines, with all the luck that had come to him, must have held some great bitterness, that he never spoke of it casually, and banished all remembrances.

That would come up later, but Curran had made up his mind that no secret of Arthur's life should ever see the light because he found it. Not even vengeful Edith, and she had the right to hate her enemy, should wring from him any disagreeable facts in the lad's career. So deeply the detective respected him!

In the place of honor, at the foot of his bed, where his eyes rested on them earliest and latest, hung a group of portraits in oil, in the same frame, of Louis the beloved, from his babyhood to the present time: on the side wall hung a painting of Anne in her first glory as mistress of the new home in Washington Square; opposite, Monsignor smiled down in purple splendor; two miniatures contained the grave, sweet, motherly face of Mary Everard and the auburn hair and lovely face of Mona.

"There are the people he loves," said Curran with emotion.

"Ay, indade," Judy said tenderly, "an' did ever a wild boy like him love his own more? Night an' day his wan thought is of them. The sun rises an' sets for him behind that picther there," pointing to Louis' portraits. "If annythin' had happened to that lovely child last Spring he'd a-choked the life out o' wan woman wid his own two hands. He's aisy enough, God knows, but I'd rather jump into the say than face him when the anger is in him."

"He's a terrible man," said Curran, repeating Edith's phrase.

He examined some manuscript in Arthur's handwriting. How different from the careless scrawl of Horace Endicott this clear, bold, dashing script, which ran full speed across the page, yet turned with ease and leisurely from the margin. What a pity Edith could not see with her own eyes these silent witnesses to the truth. Beyond the study was a music-room, where hung his violin over some scattered music. Horace Endicott hated the practising of the art, much as he loved the opera. It was all very sweet, just what the detective would have looked for, beautiful to see. He could have lingered in the rooms and speculated on that secret and manly life, whose currents were so feebly but shiningly indicated in little things. It occurred to him that copies of the daguerreotypes, Arthur at fourteen and his father at twenty-five, would be of service in the search through California. He spoke of it to Judy.

"Sure that was done years ago," said Judy cautiously. "Anne Dillon wouldn't have it known for the world, ye see, but I know that she sint a thousand o' thim to the polis in California; an' that's the way she kem across the lad. Whin he found his mother shtill mournin' him, he wrote to her that he had made his pile an' was comin' home. Anne has the pride in her, an' she wants all the world to believe he kem home of himself, d'ye see? Now kape that a secret, mind."

"And do you never let on what I've been telling you," said Curran gravely. "It may come to nothing, and it may come to much, but we must be silent."

She had given her word, and Judy's word was like the laws of the Medes and Persians. Curran rejoiced at the incident of the daguerreotypes, which anticipated his proposed search in California. Vainly however did he describe the result of his inquiry for Edith. She would have none of his inferences. He must try to entrap Anne Dillon and the priest, and afterwards he might scrape the surface of California.

CHAPTER XXIX.

THE NERVE OF ANNE.

Curran laid emphasis in his account to his wife on the details of Arthur's rooms, and on the photographs which had helped to discover the lost boy in California. Edith laughed at him.

"Horace Endicott invented that scheme of the photographs," said she. "The dear clever boy! If he had been the detective, not a stupid like you! I saw Arthur Dillon in church many times in four years, and I tell you he is not a Catholic born, no matter what you saw in his rooms. He's playing the part of Arthur Dillon to the last letter. Don't look at me that way, Dick or I'll scratch your face. You want to say that I am crazy over this theory, and that I have an explanation ready for all your objections."

"I have nothing to say, I am just working on your lines, dearie," he replied humbly.

"Just now your game is busy with an affair of the heart. He won't be too watchful, unless, as I think, he's on our tracks all the time. You ought to get at his papers."

"A love affair! Our tracks!" Curran repeated in confusion.

"Do you think you can catch a man like Arthur napping?" she sneered. "Is there a moment in the last four years that he has been asleep? See to it that you are not reported to him every night. But if he is in love with Honora Ledwith, there's a chance that he won't see or care to see what you are doing. She's a lovely girl. A hint of another woman would settle his chances of winning her. I can give her that. I'd like to. A woman of her stamp has no business marrying."

She mused a few minutes over her own statements, while Curran stared. He began to feel that the threads of this game were not all in his hands.

"You must now go to the priest and Anne Dillon," she resumed, "and say to them plump ... take the priest first ... say to them plump before they can hold their faces in shape: do you know Horace Endicott? Then watch the faces, and get what you can out of them."

"That means you will have Arthur down on you next day."

"Sure," catching her breath. "But it is now near the end of the season. When he comes to have it out with me, he will find himself face to face with Sonia. If it's to be a fight, he'll find a tiger. Then we can run away to California, if Sonia says so."

"You are going to bring Sonia down, then?"

"You suggested it. Lemme tell you what you're going to find out to-day. You're going to find out that Monsignor knew Horace Endicott. After that I think it would be all right to bring down Sonia."

Little use to argue with her, or with any woman for that matter, once an idea lodged so deep in her brain. He went to see Monsignor, with the intention of being candid with him: in fact there was no other way of dealing with the priest. In his experience Curran had found no class so difficult to deal with as the clergy. They were used to keeping other people's secrets as well as their own. He did not reveal his plan to Edith, because he feared her criticism, and could not honestly follow her methods. He had not, with all his skill and cunning, her genius for ferreting.

Monsignor, acquainted with him, received him coldly. Edith's instructions were, ask the question plump, watch his face, and then run to Anne Dillon before she can be warned by the Monsignor's messenger. Looking into the calm, well-drilled countenance of the priest, Curran found it impossible to surprise him so uncourteously. Anyway the detective felt sure that there would be no surprise, except at the mere question.

"I would like to ask you a question, Monsignor," said Curran smoothly, "which I have no right to ask perhaps. I am looking for a man who disappeared some time ago, and the parties interested hope that you can give some information. You can tell me if the question is at all impertinent, and I will go. Do you know Horace Endicott?"

There was no change in the priest's expression or manner, no starting, no betrayal of feeling. Keeping his eyes on the detective's face, he repeated the name as one utters a half-forgotten thing.

"Why has that name a familiar sound?" he asked himself.

"You may have read it frequently in the papers at the time Horace Endicott disappeared," Curran suggested.

"Possibly, but I do not read the journals so carefully," Monsignor answered musingly. "Endicott, Endicott ... I have it ... and it brings to my mind the incident of the only railroad wreck in which I have ever had the misfortune to be ... only this time it was good fortune for one poor man."

Very deliberately he told the story of the collision and of his slight acquaintance with the young fellow whose name, as well as he could remember, was Endicott. The detective handed him a photograph of the young man.

"How clearly this picture calls up the whole scene," said Monsignor much pleased. "This is the very boy. Have you a copy of this? Do send me one."

"You can keep that," said Curran, delighted at his progress, astonished that Edith's prophecy should have come true. Naturally the next question would be, have you seen the young man since that time? and Curran would have asked it had not the priest broken in with a request for the story of his disappearance. It was told.

"Of course I shall be delighted to give what information I possess," said Monsignor. "There was no secret about him then ... many others saw him ... of course this must have been some time before he disappeared. But let me ask a question before we go any further. How did you suspect my acquaintance with a man whom I met so casually? The incident had almost faded from my mind. In fact I have never mentioned it to a soul."

"It was a mere guess on the part of those interested in finding him."

"Still the guess must have been prompted by some theory of the search."

"I am almost ashamed to tell it," Curran said uneasily. "The truth is that my employers suspect that Horace Endicott has been hiding for years under the character of Arthur Dillon."

Monsignor looked amazed for a moment and then laughed.

"Interesting for Mr. Dillon and his friends, particularly if this Endicott is wanted for any crime...."

"Oh, no, no," cried the detective. "It is his wife who is seeking him, a perfectly respectable man, you know ... it's a long story. We have chased many a man supposed to be Endicott, and Mr. Dillon is the latest. I don't accept the theory myself. I know Dillon is Dillon, but a detective must sift the theories of his employers. In fact my work up to this moment proves very clearly that of all our wrong chases this is the worst."

"It looks absurd at first sight. I remember the time poor Mrs. Dillon sent out her photographs, scattered a few hundred of them among the police and the miners of California, in the hope of finding her lost son. That was done with my advice. She had her first response, a letter from her son, about the very time that I met young Endicott. For the life of me I cannot understand why anyone should suppose Arthur Dillon...."

He picked up the photograph of Endicott again.

"The two men look as much alike as I look like you. I'm glad you mentioned the connection which Dillon has with the matter. You will kindly leave me out of it until you have made inquiries of Mr. Dillon himself. It would not do, you understand, for a priest in my position to give out any details in a matter which may yet give trouble. I fear that in telling you of my meeting with Endicott I have already overstepped the limits of prudence. However, that was my fault, as you warned me. Thanks for the photograph, a very nice souvenir of a tragedy. Poor young fellow! Better had he perished in the smash-up than to go out of life in so dreary a way."

"If I might venture another — —"

"Pardon, not another word. In any official and public way I am always ready to tell what the law requires, or charity demands."

"You would be willing then to declare that Arthur Dillon — —"

"Is Mrs. Dillon's son? Certainly ... at any time, under proper conditions. Good morning. Don't mention it," and Curran was outside the door before his thoughts took good shape; so lost in wonder over the discovery of Monsignor's acquaintance with Endicott, that he forgot to visit Anne Dillon. Instead he hurried home with the news to Edith, and blushed with shame when she asked if he had called on Anne. She forgave his stupidity in her delight, and put him through his catechism on all that had been said and seen in the interview with Monsignor.

"You are a poor stick," was her comment, and for the first time in years he approved of her opinion. "The priest steered you about and out with his little finger, and the corner of his eye. He did not give you a chance to ask if he had ever seen Horace Endicott since. Monsignor will not lie for any man. He simply refuses to answer on the ground that his position will not permit it. You will never see the priest again on this matter. Arthur Dillon will bid you stand off. Well, you see what my instinct is now! Are you more willing to believe in it when it says: Arthur Dillon is Horace Endicott?"

"Not a bit, sweetheart."

"I won't fight with you, since you are doing as I order. Go to Anne Dillon now. Mind, she's already prepared by this time for your visit. You may run against Arthur instead of her. While you are gone I shall write to Sonia that we have at last found a clue, and ask her to come on at once. Dillon may not give us a week to make our escape after he learns what we have been doing. We must be quick. Go, my dear old stupid, and bear in mind that Anne Dillon is the cunningest cat you've had to do with yet."

She gave an imitation of the lady that was funny to a degree, and sent the detective off laughing, but not at all convinced that there was any significance in his recent discovery. He felt mortified to learn again for the hundredth time how a prejudice takes the edge off intellect. Though certain Edith's theory was wrong, why should he act like a donkey in disproving it? On the contrary his finest skill was required, and methods as safe as if Dillon were sure to turn out Endicott. He sharpened his blade for the coming duel with Anne, whom Monsignor had warned, without doubt. However, Anne had received no warning and she met Curran with her usual reserve. He was smoothly brutal.

"I would like to know if you are acquainted with Mr. Horace Endicott?" said he.

Anne's face remained as blank as the wall, and her manner tranquil. She had never heard the name before, for in the transactions between herself and her son only the name of Arthur Dillon had been mentioned, while of his previous life she knew not a single detail. Curran not disappointed, hastened, after a pause, to explain his own rudeness.

"I never heard the name," said Anne coldly. "Nor do I see by what right you come here and ask questions."

"Pardon my abruptness," said the detective. "I am searching for a young man who disappeared some years ago, and his friends are still hunting for him, still anxious, so that they follow the most absurd clues. I am forced to ask this question of all sorts of people, only to get the answer which you have given. I trust you will pardon me for my presumption for the sake of people who are suffering."

His speech warned her that she had heard her son's name for the first time, that she stood on the verge of exposure; and her heart failed her, she felt that her voice would break if she ventured to speak, her knees give way if she resented this man's manner by leaving the room. Yet the weakness was only for a moment, and when it passed a wild curiosity to hear something of that past which had been a sealed book to her, to know the real personality of Arthur Dillon, burned her like a flame, and steadied her nerves. For two years she had been resenting his secrecy, not understanding his reasons. He was guarding against the very situation of this moment.

"Horace Endicott," she repeated with interest. "There is no one of that name in my little circle, and I have never heard the name before. Who was he? And how did he come to be lost?"

And she rose to indicate that his reply must be brief.

Curran told with eloquence of the disappearance and the long search, and gave a history of Endicott's life in nice detail, pleased with the unaffected interest of this severe but elegant woman. As he spoke his eye took in every mark of feeling, every gesture, every expression. Her self-command, if she knew Horace Endicott, remained perfect; if she knew him not, her manner seemed natural.

"God pity his poor people," was her fervent comment as she took her seat again. "I was angry with you at first, sir," looking at his card, "and of a mind to send you away for what looked like impertinence. But it's I would be only too glad to give you help if I could. I never even heard the young man's name. And it puzzles me, why you should come to me."

"For this reason, Mrs. Dillon," he said with sincere disgust. "The people who are hunting for Horace Endicott think that Arthur Dillon is the man; or to put it in another way, that you were deceived when you welcomed back your son from California. Horace Endicott and not Arthur Dillon returned."

"My God!" cried she, and sat staring at him; then rose up and began to move towards the door backwards, keeping an eye upon him. Her thought showed clear to the detective: she had been entertaining a lunatic. He laughed.

"Don't go," he said. "I know what you imagine, but I'm no lunatic. I don't believe that your son is an impostor. He is a friend of mine, and I know that he is Arthur Dillon. But a man in my business must do as he is ordered by his employers. I am a detective."

For a minute she hesitated with hand outstretched to the bell-rope. Her mind acted with speed; she had nothing to fear, the man was friendly, his purpose had failed, whatever it was, the more he talked the more she would learn, and it might be in her power to avert danger by policy. She went back to her seat, having left it only to act her part. Taking the hint provided by Curran, she pretended belief in his insanity, and passed to indignation at this attempt upon her happiness, her motherhood. This rage became real, when she reflected that the Aladdin palace of her life was really threatened by Curran's employers. To her the prosperity and luxury of the past five years had always been dream-like in its fabric, woven of the mists of morning, a fairy enchantment, which might vanish in an hour and leave poor Cinderella sitting on a pumpkin by the roadside, the sport of enemies, the burden of friends. How near she had been to this public humiliation! What wretches, these people who employed the detective!

"My dear boy was absent ten years," she said, "and I suffered agony all that time. What hearts must some people have to wish to put me through another time like that! Couldn't any wan see that I accepted him as my son? that all the neighbors accepted him? What could a man want to deceive a poor mother so? I had nothing to give him but the love of a mother, and men care little for that, wild boys care nothing for it. He brought me a fortune, and has made my life beautiful ever since he came back. I had nothing to give him. Who is at the bottom of this thing?"

The detective explained the existence and motives of a deserted, poverty-stricken wife and child.

"I knew a woman would be at the bottom of it," she exclaimed viciously, feeling against Sonia a hatred which she knew to be unjust. "Well, isn't she able to recognize her own husband? If I could tell my son after ten years, when he had grown to be a man, can't she tell her own husband after a few years? Could it be that my boy played Horace Endicott in Boston and married that woman, and then came back to me?"

"Oh, my dear Mrs. Dillon," cried the detective in alarm, "do not excite yourself over so trifling a thing. Your son is your son no matter what our theories may be. This Endicott was born and brought up in the vicinity of Boston, and came from a very old family. Your suspicion is baseless. Forget the whole matter I beg of you."

"Have you a picture of the young man?"

He handed her the inevitable photograph reluctantly, quite sure that she would have hysterics before he left, so sincere was her excitement. Anne studied the portrait with keen interest, it may be imagined, astonished to find it so different from Arthur Dillon. Had she blundered as well as the detective? Between this portrait and any of the recent photographs of Arthur there seemed no apparent resemblance in any feature. She had been exciting herself for nothing.

"Wonderful are the ways of men," was her comment. "How any one ..." her brogue had left her ... "could take Arthur Dillon for this man, even supposing he was disguised now, is strange and shameful. What is to be the end of it?"

"Just this, dear madam," said Curran, delighted at her returning calmness. "I shall tell them what you have said, what every one says, and they'll drop the inquiry as they have dropped about one hundred others. If they are persistent, I shall add that you are ready to go into any court in the land and swear positively that you know your own son."

"Into twenty courts," she replied with fervor, and the tears, real tears came into her eyes; then, at sight of Aladdin's palace as firm as ever on its frail foundations, the tears rolled down her cheeks.

"Precisely. And now if you would be kind enough to keep this matter from the ears of Mr. Dillon ... he's a great friend of mine ... I admire him ... I was with him in the little expedition to Ireland, you know ... and it was to save him pain that I came to you first ... if it could be kept quiet — —"

"I want it kept quiet," she said with decision, "but at the same time Arthur must know of these cruel suspicions. Oh, how my heart beats when I think of it! Without him ten years, and then to have strangers plan to take him from me altogether ... forever ... forever ... oh!"

Curran perspired freely at the prospect of violent hysterics. No man could deal more rudely with the weak and helpless with right on his side, or if his plans demanded it. Before a situation like this he felt lost and foolish.

"Certainly he must know in time. I shall tell him myself, as soon as I make my report of the failure of this clue to my employers. I would take it as a very great favor if you would permit me to tell him. It must come very bitter to a mother to tell her son that he is suspected of not being her son. Let me spare you that anguish."

Anne played with him delightfully, knowing that she had him at her mercy, not forgetting however that the sport was with tigers. Persuaded to wait a few days while Curran made his report, in return he promised to inform her of the finding of poor Endicott at the proper moment. The detective bowed himself out, the lady smiled. A fair day's work! She had learned the name and the history of the young man known as Arthur Dillon in a most delightful way. The doubt attached to this conclusion did not disturb her. Wonderful, that Arthur Dillon should look so little like the portrait of Horace Endicott! More wonderful still that she, knowing Arthur was not her son, had come to think of him, to feel towards him, and to act accordingly, as her son! Her rage over this attempt upon the truth and the fact of their relationship grew to proportions.

CHAPTER XXX.

UNDER THE EYES OF HATE.

Edith's inference from the interviews with the Monsignor and Anne did justice to her acuteness. The priest alone knew the true personality of Arthur. From Anne all but the fact of his disappearance had been kept, probably to guard against just such attempts as Curran's. The detective reminded her that her theory stood only because of her method of selection from his investigations. Nine facts opposed and one favored her contention: therefore nine were shelved, leaving one to support the edifice of her instincts or her suspicions. She stuck out her tongue at him.

"It shows how you are failing when nine out of ten facts, gathered in a whole day's work, are worthless. Isn't that one fact, that the priest knew Horace Endicott, worth all your foolish reasonings? Who discovered it? Now, will you coax Sonia Endicott down here to have a look at this Arthur Dillon? Before we start for California?"

He admitted humbly that the lady would not accept his invitation, without stern evidence of a valuable clue. The detectives had given her many a useless journey.

"She'll be at the Everett House to-morrow early in the morning," said Edith proudly. "Want to know why, stupid? I sent her a message that her game had been treed at last ... by me."

He waved his hands in despair.

"Then you'll do the talking, Madam Mischief."

"And you'll never say a word, even when asked. What! would I let you mesmerize her at the start by telling her how little you think of my idea and my plans? She would think as little of them as you do, when you got through. No! I shall tell her, I shall plan for her, I shall lead her to the point of feeling where that long experience with Horace Endicott will become of some use in piercing the disguise of Arthur Dillon. You would convince her she was not to see Horace

Endicott, and of course she would see only Arthur Dillon. I'll convince her she is to see her runaway husband, and then if she doesn't I'll confess defeat."

"There's a good deal in your method," he admitted in a hopeless way.

"We are in for it now," she went on, scorning the compliment. "By this time Arthur Dillon knows, if he did not before, that I am up to mischief. He may fall on us any minute. He will not suffer this interference: not because he cares two cents one way or the other, but because he will not have us frightening his relatives and friends, telling every one that he is two. Keep out of his way so that he shall have to come here, and to send word first that he is coming. I'll arrange a scene for him with his Sonia. It may be sublime, and again it may be a fizzle. One way or the other, if Sonia says so, we'll fly to the west out of his way. The dear, dear boy!"

"He'll *dear* you after that scene!"

"Now, do you make what attempts you may to find out where he keeps his money, he must have piles of it, and search his papers, his safe...."

"He has nothing of the kind ... everything about him is as open as the day ... it's an impertinence to bother him so ... well, he can manage you, I think ... no need for me to interfere or get irritated."

Then she had a tantrum, which galled the soul of Curran, except that it ended as usual in her soft whimpering, her childish murmuring, her sweet complaint against the world, and her falling asleep in his arms. Thus was he regularly conquered and led captive.

They went next day at noon to visit Sonia Endicott at the Everett House, where she had established herself with her little boy and his nurse. Her reception of the Currans, while supercilious in expression, was really sincere. They represented her hope in that long search of five years, which only a vigorous hate had kept going. Marked with the characteristics of the cat, velvety to eye and touch, insolent and elusive in her glance, undisciplined, she could act a part for a time. To Horace Endicott she had played the rôle of a child of

298

light, an elf, a goddess, for which nature had dressed her with golden hair, melting eyes of celestial blue, and exquisite form.

The years had brought out the animal in her. She found it more and more difficult to repress the spite, rage, hatred, against Horace and fate, which consumed her within, and violated the external beauty with unholy touches, wrinkles, grimaces, tricks of sneering, distortions of rage. Her dreams of hatred had only one scene: a tiger in her own form rending the body of the man who had discovered and punished her with a power like omnipotence; rending him but not killing him, leaving his heart to beat and his face unmarked, that he might feel his agony and show it.

"If *you* had sent me the telegram," she remarked to Curran, "I would not have come. But this dear Colette, she is to be my good angel and lead me to success, aren't you, little devil? Ever since she took up the matter I have had my beautiful dreams once more, oh, such thrilling dreams! Like the novels of Eugene Sue, just splendid. Well, why don't you speak?"

He pointed to Edith with a gesture of submission. She was hugging the little boy before the nurse took him away, teasing him into baby talk, kissing him decorously but lavishly, as if she could not get enough of him.

"He's not to speak until asked," she cried.

"And then only say what she thinks," he added.

"La! are you fighting over it already? That's not a good sign."

With a final embrace which brought a howl from young Horace, Edith gave the boy to the nurse and began her story of finding Horace Endicott in the son of Anne Dillon. She acted the story, admirably keeping back the points which would have grated on Sonia's instincts, or rather expectations. The lady, impressed, evidently felt a lack of something when Curran refused his interest and his concurrence to the description.

"What do you wish me to do?" said she.

"To see this Dillon and to study him, as one would a problem. The man's been playing this part, living it indeed, nearly five years. Can any one expect that the first glance will pierce his disguise? He must be watched and studied for days, and if that fetches nothing, then you must meet him suddenly, and say to him tenderly, 'at last, Horace!' If that fetches nothing, then we must go to California, and work until we get the evidence which will force him to acknowledge himself and give up his money. But by that time, if we can make sure it is he, and if we can get his money, then I would recommend one thing! Kill him!"

Sonia's eyes sparkled at the thought of that sweet murder.

"And wait another five years for all this," was her cynical remark.

"If the question is not settled this Fall, then let it go forever," said Edith with energy.

"The scheme is well enough," Sonia said lazily. "Is this Arthur Dillon handsome, a dashing blade?"

"Better," murmured Edith with a smack of her lips, "a virtuous sport, who despises the sex in a way, and can master woman by a look. He is my master. And I hate him! It will be worth your time to see him and meet him."

"And now you," to Curran.

Sonia did not know, nor care why Edith hated Dillon.

"I protest, Sonia. He will put a spell on you, and spoil our chances. Let him talk later when we have succeeded or failed."

"Nonsense, you fool. I must hear both sides, but I declare now that I submit myself to you wholly. What do you say, Curran?"

"Just this, madam: if this man Arthur Dillon is really your husband, then he's too clever to be caught by any power in this world. Any way you choose to take it, you will end as this search has always ended."

"Why do you think him so clever? My Horace was anything but clever ... at least we thought so ... until now."

"Until he has foiled every attempt to find him," said Curran. "Colette has her own ideas, but she has kept back all the details that make or unmake a case. She is so sure of her instincts! No doubt they are good."

"But not everything, hey?" said the lady tenderly. "Ah, a woman's instincts lead her too far sometimes...." they all laughed. "Well, give me the details Colette left out. No winking at each other. I won't raise a hand in this matter until I have heard both sides."

"This Arthur Dillon is Irish, and lives among the Irish in the old-fashioned Irish way, half in the slums, and half in the swell places...."

"*Mon Dieu*, what is this I hear! The Irish! My Horace live among the Irish! That's not the man. He could live anywhere, among the Chinese, the Indians, the niggers, but with that low class of people, never!" and she threw up her hands in despair. "Did I come from Boston to pursue a low Irishman!"

"You see," cried Edith. "Already he has cast his spell on you. He doesn't believe I have found your man, and he won't let you believe it. Can't you see that this Horace went to the very place where you were sure he would not go?"

"You cannot tell him now from an Irishman," continued the detective. "He has an Irish mother, he is a member of Tammany Hall, he is a politician who depends on Irish voters, he joined the Irish revolutionists and went over the sea to fight England, and he's in love with an Irish girl."

"Shocking! Horace never had any taste or any sense, but I know he detested the Irish around Boston. I can't believe it of him. But, as Colette says truly, he would hide himself in the very place where we least think of looking for him."

"Theories have come to nothing," screamed Edith, until the lady placed her hands on her ears. "Skill and training and coolness and all that rot have come to nothing. Because I hate Arthur Dillon I have discovered Horace Endicott. Now I want to see your eyes looking at this man, eyes with hate in them, and with murder in them. They will discover more than all the stupid detectives in the country. See what hate did for Horace Endicott. He hated you, and instead of murdering you he learned to torture you. He hated you, and it made him clever. Oh, hate is a great teacher! This fool of mine loves Arthur Dillon, because he is a patriot and hates England. Hate breeds cleverness, it breeds love, it opens the mind, it will dig out Horace Endicott and his fortune, and enrich us all."

"La, but you are strenuous," said the lady placidly, but impressed. She was a shallow creature in the main, and Curran compared his little wife, eloquent, glowing with feeling, dainty as a flame, to the slower-witted beauty, with plain admiration in his gaze. She deserves to succeed, he thought. Sonia came to a conclusion, languidly.

"We must try the eyes of hate," was her decision.

The pursuit of Arthur proved very interesting. The detective knew his habits of labor and amusement, his public haunts and loitering-places. Sonia saw him first at the opera, modestly occupying a front seat in the balcony.

"Horace would never do that when he could get a box," and she leveled her glass at him.

Edith mentally dubbed her a fool. However, her study of the face and figure and behavior of the man showed care and intelligence. Edith's preparation had helped her. She saw a lean, nervous young man, whose flowing black hair and full beard were streaked with gray. His dark face, hollow in the cheeks and not too well-colored with the glow of health, seemed to get light and vivacity from his melancholy eyes. Seriousness was the characteristic expression. Once he laughed, in the whole evening. Once he looked straight into her face, with so fixed, so intense an expression, so near a gaze, so intimate and penetrating, that she gave a low cry.

"You have recognized him?" Edith whispered mad with joy.

"No, indeed," she answered sadly, "That is not Horace Endicott. Not a feature that I recall, certainly no resemblance. I was startled because I saw just now in his look, ... he looked towards me into the glass ... an expression that seemed familiar ... as if I had seen it before, and it had hurt me then as it hurts me now."

"There's a beginning," said Edith with triumph. "Next time for a nearer look."

"Oh, he could never have changed so," Sonia cried with bitterness of heart.

Curran secured tickets for a ball to be held by a political association in the Cherry Hill district, and placed the ladies in a quiet corner of the gallery of the hall. Arthur Dillon, as a leading spirit in the society, delighted to mingle with the homely, sincere, warm-hearted, and simple people for whom this occasion was a high festival; and nowhere did his sorrow rest so lightly on his soul, nowhere did he feel so keenly the delight of life, or give freer expression to it. Edith kept Sonia at the highest pitch of excitement and interest.

"Remember," she said now, "that he probably knows you are in town, that you are here watching him; but not once will he look this way, nor do a thing other than if you were miles away. My God, to be an actor like that!"

The actor played his part to perfection and to the utter disappointment of the women. The serious face shone now with smiles and color, with the flash of wit and the play of humor. Horace Endicott had been a merry fellow, but a Quaker compared with the butterfly swiftness and gaiety of this young man, who led the grand march, flirted with the damsels and chatted with the dames, danced as often as possible, joked with the men, found partners for the unlucky, and touched the heart of every rollicking moment. The old ladies danced jigs with him, proud to their marrow of the honor, and he allowed himself ... Sonia gasped at the sight ... to execute a wild Irish *pas seul* amid the thunderous applause of the hearty and adoring company.

"That man Horace Endicott!" she exclaimed with contempt. "Bah! But it's interesting, of course."

"What a compliment! what acting! oh, incomparable man!" said Edith, enraged at his success before such an audience. Her husband smiled behind his hand.

"You have a fine imagination, Colette, but I would not give a penny for your instinct," said Sonia.

"My instinct will win just the same, but I fear we shall have to go to California. This man is too clever for commonplace people."

"Arthur Dillon is a fine orator," said Curran mischievously, "and to-morrow night you shall hear him at his best on the sorrows of Ireland."

Sonia laughed heartily and mockingly. Were not these same sorrows, from their constancy and from repetition, become the joke of the world? Curran could have struck her evil face for the laugh.

"Was your husband a speaker?" he asked.

"Horace would not demean himself to talk in public, and he couldn't make a speech to save his life. But to talk on the sorrows of Ireland ... oh, it's too absurd."

"And why not Ireland's sorrows as well as those of America, or any other country?" he replied savagely.

"Oh, I quite forgot that you were Irish ... a thousand pardons," she said with sneering civility. "Of course, I shall be glad to hear his description of the sorrows. An orator! It's very interesting."

The occasion for the display of Arthur's powers was one of the numerous meetings for which the talking Irish are famous all over the world, and in which their clever speakers have received fine training. Even Sonia, impressed by the enthusiasm of the gathering, and its esteem for Dillon, could not withhold her admiration. Alas, it was not her Horace who poured out a volume of musical tone, vigorous English, elegant rhetoric, with the expression, the abandonment, the picturesqueness of a great actor. She shuddered at his descriptions, her heart melted and her eyes moistened at his pathos, she became filled with wonder. It was not Horace! Her husband might have developed powers of eloquence, but would have to be remade to talk in that fashion of any land. This Dillon had terrible passion, and her Horace was only a a handsome fool. She could have loved Dillon.

"So you will have to arrange the little scene where I shall stand before him without warning, and murmur tenderly, 'at last, Horace!' And it must be done without delay," was her command to Edith.

"It can be done perhaps to-morrow night," Edith said in a secret rage, wondering what Arthur Dillon could have seen in Sonia. "But bear in mind why I am doing this scene, with the prospects of a furious time afterwards with Dillon. I want you to see him asleep, just for ten minutes, in the light of a strong lamp. In sleep there is no disguise. When he is dressed for a part and playing it, the sharpest eyes, even the eyes of hate, may not be able to escape the glamour of the disguise. The actor asleep is more like himself. You shall look into his face, and turn it from side to side with your own hands. If you do not catch some feeling from that, strike a resemblance, I shall feel like giving up."

"La, but you are an audacious creature," said Sonia, and the triviality of the remark sent Edith into wild laughter. She would like to have bitten the beauty.

The detective consented to Edith's plans, in his anxiety to bring the farce to an end before the element of danger grew. Up to this point they might appeal to Arthur for mercy. Later the dogs would be upon them. As yet no sign of irritation on Arthur's part had appeared. The day after the oration on the sorrows of Erin he sent a note to Curran announcing his intention to call the same evening. Edith, amazed at her own courage in playing with the fire which in an instant could destroy her, against the warning of her husband, was bent on carrying out the scene.

Dearly she loved the dramatic off the stage, spending thought and time in its arrangement. How delicious the thought of this man and his wife meeting under circumstances so wondrous after five years of separation. Though death reached her the next moment she would see it. The weakness of the plot lay in Sonia's skepticism and Arthur's knowledge that a trap was preparing. He would brush her machinery aside like a cobweb, but that did not affect the chance of his recognition by Sonia.

Dillon had never lost his interest in the dancer and her husband. They attracted him. In their lives ran the same strain of madness, the madness of the furies, as in his own. Their lovable qualities were not few. Occasionally he dropped in to tease Edith over her lack of conscience, or her failures, and to discuss the cause of freedom with the smooth and flinty Curran. Wild humans have the charm of their wilderness. One must not forget their teeth and their claws. This night the two men sat alone. Curran filled the glasses and passed the cigars. Arthur made no comment on the absence of Edith. He might have been aware that the curtains within three feet of his chair, hiding the room beyond, concealed the two women, whose eyes, peering through small glasses fixed in the curtains, studied his face. He might even have guessed that his easy chair had been so placed as to let the light fall upon him while Curran sat in the dim light beyond. The young man gave no sign, spoke freely with Curran on the business of the night, and acted as usual.

"Of course it must be stopped at once," he said. "Very much flattered of course that I should be taken for Horace Endicott ... you gave away Tom Jones' name at last ... but these things, so trifling to you, jar the nerves of women. Then it would never do for me, with my little career in California unexplained, to have stories of a double identity ... is that what you call it?... running around. Of course I know it's that devil Edith, presuming always on good nature ... that's *her* nature ... but if you don't stop it, why I must."

"You'll have to do it, I think," the detective replied maliciously. "I can do only what she orders. I had to satisfy her by running to the priest, and your mother, and the Senator——"

"What! even my poor uncle! Oh, Curran!"

"The whole town, for that matter, Mr. Dillon. It was done in such a way, of course, that none of them suspected anything wrong, and we talked under promise of secrecy. I saw that the thing had to be done to satisfy her and to bring you down on us. Now you're down and the trouble's over as far as I am concerned."

"And Tom Jones was Horace Endicott," Arthur mused, "I knew it of course all along, but I respected your confidence. I had known Endicott."

"You knew Horace Endicott?" said Curran, horrified by a sudden vision of his own stupidity.

"And his lady, a lovely, a superb creature, but just a shade too sharp for her husband, don't you know. He was a fool in love, wasn't he? judging from your story of him. Has she become reconciled to her small income, I wonder? She was not that kind, but when one has to, that's the end of it. *And there are consolations.* How the past month has tired me. I could go to sleep right in the chair, only I want to settle this matter to-night, and I must say a kind word to the little devil——"

His voice faded away, and he slept, quite overpowered by the drug placed in his wine. After perfect silence for a minute, Curran beckoned to the women, who came noiseless into the room, and bent over the sleeping face. In his contempt for them, the detective neither spoke nor left his seat. Harpies brooding over the dead! Even he knew that!

Arthur's face lay in profile, its lines all visible, owing to the strong light, through the disguise of the beard. The melancholy which marks the face of any sleeper, a foreshadow of the eternal sleep, had become on this sleeper's countenance a profound sadness. From his seat Curran could see the pitiful droop of the mouth, the hollowness of the eyes, the shadows under the cheek-bones; marks of a sadness too deep for tears. Sonia took his face in her soft hands and turned the right profile to the light. She looked at the full face, smoothed his hair as if trying to recall an ancient memory.

"The eyes of hate," murmured Edith between tears and rage. She pitied while she hated him, understanding the sorrow that could mark a man's face so deeply, admiring the courage which could wear the mask so well. Sonia was deeply moved in spite of disappointment. At one moment she caught a fleeting glimpse of her Horace, but too elusive to hold and analyze. Something pinched her feelings and the great tears fell from her soft eyes. Emotion merely pinched her. Only in hate could she writhe and foam and exhaust nature. She studied his hands, observed the fingers, with the despairing conviction that this was not the man; too lean and too coarse and too hard; and her rage began to burn against destiny. Oh, to have Horace as helpless under her hands! How she could rend him!

"Do you see any likeness?" whispered Edith.

"None," was the despairing answer.

"Be careful," hissed Curran. "In this sleep words are heard and remembered sometimes."

Edith swore the great oaths which relieved her anger. But what use to curse, to look and curse again? At the last moment Curran signalled them away, and began talking about his surprise that Arthur should have known the lost man.

"Because you might have given me a clue," Arthur heard him saying as he came back from what he thought had been a minute's doze, "and saved me a year's search, not to mention the money I could have made."

"I'll tell you about it some other time," said Arthur with a yawn, as he lit a fresh cigar. "Ask madam to step in here, will you. I must warn her in a wholesome way."

"I think she is entertaining a friend," Curran said, hinting plainly at a surprise.

"Let her bring the friend along," was the careless answer.

The two women entered presently, and Edith made the introduction. The husband and wife stood face to face at last. Her voice failed in her throat from nervousness, so sure was she that the Endicotts had met again! They had the center of the stage, and the interest of the audience, but acted not one whit like the people in a play.

"Delighted," said Arthur in his usual drawling way on these occasions. "I have had the pleasure of meeting Mrs. Endicott before."

"Indeed," cried the lady. "I regret that my memory...."

"At Castle Moyna, a little fête, mother fainted because she saw me running across the lawn ... of course you remember...."

"Why, certainly ... we all felt so sorry for the young singer ... her father...."

"He was in jail and died since, poor man. Then I saw you coming across on the steamer with a dear, sweet, old lady...."

"My husband's aunt," Sonia gasped at the thought of Aunt Lois.

"Oh, but he's letter-perfect," murmured Edith in admiration.

"And you might remember me," said the heartless fellow, "but of course on a wedding-tour no one can expect the parties to remember anything, as the guide for a whole week to your party in California."

"Of course there was a guide," she admitted, very pleasant to meet him again, and so on to the empty end. Edith, stunned by her defeat, sat crushed, for this man no more minded the presence of his wife than did Curran. It was true. Arthur had often thought that a meeting like this in the far-off years would rock his nature as an earthquake rocks the solid plain. Though not surprised at her appearance, for Edith's schemes had all been foreseen, he felt surprise at his own indifference. So utterly had she gone out of his thought, that her sudden appearance, lovely and seductive as of old, gave him no twinge of hate, fear, repugnance, disgust, horror, shame, or pain.

He took no credit to himself for a self-control, which he had not been called upon by any stress of feeling to exercise. He was only Arthur Dillon, encountering a lady with a past; a fact in itself more or less amusing. Once she might have been a danger to be kept out like a pest, or barricaded in quarantine. That time had gone by. His indifference for the moment appalled him, since it showed the hopeless depth of Endicott's grave. After chatting honestly ten minutes, he went away light of heart, without venturing to warn Edith. Another day, he told her, and be good meanwhile.

Curran became thoughtful, and the women irritable after he had gone. Edith felt that her instincts had no longer a value in the market. In this wretched Endicott affair striking disappointment met the most brilliant endeavors. Sonia made ready to return to her hotel. Dolorously the Currans paid her the last courtesies, waiting for the word which would end the famous search for her Horace.

"I have been thinking the matter over," she said sweetly, "and I have thought out a plan, not in your line of course, which I shall see to at once. I think it worth while to look through California for points in the life of this interesting young man, Mr. Dillon."

When the door closed on her, Edith began to shriek in hysterical laughter.

CHAPTER XXXI.

THE HEART OF HONORA.

While Edith urged the search for Endicott, the little world to be horrified by her success enjoyed itself north and south as the season suggested, and the laws of fashion permitted. At the beginning of June, Anne settled herself comfortably for the summer in a roomy farmhouse, overlooking Lake Champlain and that particular island of Valcour, which once witnessed the plucky sea-fight and defeat of dare-devil Arnold. Only Honora accompanied her, but at the close of the month Louis, the deacon, and Mrs. Doyle Grahame joined them; and after that the whole world came at odd times, with quiet to-day and riot to-morrow. Honora, the center of interest, the storm-center, as we call it in these days, turned every eye in her direction with speculative interest. Would she retire to the convent, or find her vocation in the world? She had more than fulfilled her father's wish that she remain in secular life for a year. Almost two years had passed. He could not reproach her from his grave.

One divine morning she came upon the natural stage which had been the scene of a heart-drama more bitter to her than any sorrow. Walking alone in the solemn woods along the lake shore, the path suddenly ended on a rocky terrace, unshaded by trees, and directly over the water. Raspberry bushes made an enclosure there, in the center of which the stumps of two trees held a rough plank to make a seat. A stony beach curved inward from this point, the dark woods rose behind, and the soft waters made music in the hollows of the rock beneath her feet. Delightful with the perfume of the forest, the placid shores of Valcour, sun, and flower, and bird filling eye and ear with beauty, the sight of the spot chilled her heart. Here Lord Constantine had offered her his love and his life the year before. To her it had been a frightful scene, this strong, handsome, clever man, born to the highest things of mind, heart, talent and rank, kneeling before her, pleading with pallid face for her love, ... and all the rest of it! She would have sunk down with shame but for his kindness in accepting the situation, and carrying her through it.

Why his proposal shocked her his lordship could not see at first. He understood before his mournful interview and ended. Honora was of that class, to whom marriage does not present itself as a personal concern. She had the true feminine interest in the marriage of her friends, and had vaguely dreamed of her own march to the altar, an adoring lover, a happy home and household cares. Happy in the love of a charming mother and a high-hearted father, she had devoted her youthful days to them and to music. They stood between her and importunate lovers, whose intentions she had never divined.

With the years came trouble, the death of the mother, the earning of her living by her art, the care of her father, and the work for her native land. Lovers could not pursue this busy woman, occupied with father and native land, and daily necessity. The eternal round of travel, conspiracy, scheming, planning, spending, with its invariable ending of disappointment and weariness of heart, brought forth a longing for the peace of rest, routine, satisfied aspirations; and from a dream the convent became a passion, longed for as the oasis by the traveler in the sands.

Simple and sincere as light, the hollow pretence of the world disgusted her. Her temperament was of that unhappy fiber which sees the end almost as speedily as the beginning; change and death and satiety treading on the heels of the noblest enterprise. For her there seemed no happiness but in the possession of the everlasting, the unchangeable, the divinely beautiful. Out of these feelings and her pious habits rose the longing for the convent, for what seemed to be permanent, fixed, proportioned, without dust and dirt and ragged edges, and wholly devoted to God.

After a little Lord Constantine understood her astonishment, her humiliation, her fright. He had a wretched satisfaction in knowing that no other man would snatch this prize; but oh, how bitter to give her up even to God! The one woman in all time for him, more could be said in her praise still; her like was not outside heaven. How much this splendid lake, with sapphire sky and green shores, lacked of true beauty until she stepped like light into view; then, as for the first time, one saw the green woods glisten, the waters sparkle anew, the sky deepen in richness! One had to know her heart, her nature, so nobly dowered, to see this lighting up of nature's finest work at her coming. She was beautiful, white as milk, with eyes like jewels, framed in lashes of silken black, so dark, so dark!

Honora wept at the sight of his face as he went away. She had seen that despair in her father's face. And she wept to-day as she sat on the rough bench. Had she been to blame? Why had she delayed her entrance into the convent a year beyond the time? Arthur had declared his work could not get on without her for at least an extra half year. She was lingering still? Had present comfort shaken her resolution?

A cry roused her from her mournful thoughts, and she looked up to see Mona rounding the point at the other end of the stony beach, laboring at the heavy oars. Honora smiled and waved her handkerchief. Here was one woman for whom life had no problems, only solid contentment, and perennial interest; and who thought her husband the finest thing in the world. She beached her boat and found her way up to the top of the rock. To look at her no one would dream, Honora certainly did not, that she had any other purpose than breathing the air.

Mrs. Doyle Grahame enjoyed the conviction that marriage settles all difficulties, if one goes about it rightly. She had gone about it rightly, with marvellous results. That charming bear her father had put his neck in her yoke, and now traveled about in her interest as mild as a clam. All men gasped at the sight of his meekness. When John Everard Grahame arrived on this planet, his grandfather fell on his knees before him and his parents, and never afterwards departed from that attitude. Doyle Grahame laid it to his art of winning a father-in-law. Mona found the explanation simply in the marriage, which to her, from the making of the trousseau to the christening of the boy, had been wonderful enough to have changed the face of the earth. The delicate face, a trifle fuller, had increased in dignity. Her hair flamed more glorious than ever. As a young matron she patronized Honora now an old maid.

"You've been crying," said she, with a glance around, "and I don't wonder. This is the place where you broke a good man's heart. It will remain bewitched until you accept some other man in the same spot. How did we know, Miss Cleverly? Do you think Conny was as secret as you? And didn't I witness the whole scene from the point yonder? I couldn't hear the words, but there wasn't any need of it. Heavens, the expression of you two!"

"Mona, do you mean to tell me that every one knew it?"

"Every soul, my dear ostrich with your head in the sand. The hope is that you will not repeat the refusal when the next lover comes along. And if you can arrange to have the scene come off here, as you arranged for the last one ... I have always maintained that the lady with a convent vocation is by nature the foxiest of all women. I don't know why, but she shows it."

The usual fashion of teasing Honora attributed to her qualities opposed to a religious vocation.

"Well, I have made up my mind to fly at once to the convent," she said, "with my foxiness and other evil qualities. If it was my fault that one man proposed to me — —"

"It was your fault, of course. Why do you throw doubt upon it?"

"It will not be my fault that the second man proposes. So, this place may remain accursed forever. Oh, my poor Lord Constantine! After all his kindness to father and me, to be forced to inflict such suffering on him! Why do men care for us poor creatures so much, Mona?"

"Because we care so much for them ..." Honora laughed ... "and because we are necessary to their happiness. You should go round the stations on your knees once a day for the rest of your life, for having rejected Lord Conny. It wasn't mere ingratitude ... that was bad enough; but to throw over a career so splendid, to desert Ireland so outrageously," this was mere pretence ... "to lose all importance in life for the sake of a dream, for the sake of a convent."

"You have a prejudice against convents, Mona."

"No, dear, I believe in convents for those who are made that way. I have noticed, perhaps you have too, that many people who should go to a convent will not, and many people at present in the cloisters ought to have stayed where nature put them first."

"It's pleasant on a day like this for you to feel that you are just where nature intended you to be, isn't it? How did you leave the baby?"

Mona leaped into a rhapsody on the wonderful child, who was just then filling the time of Anne, and at the same time filling the air with howlings, but returned speedily to her purpose.

"Did you say you had fixed the day, Honora?"

"In September, any day before the end of the month."

"You were never made for the convent," with seriousness. "Too fond of the running about in life, and your training is all against it."

"My training!" said Honora.

"All your days you were devoted to one man, weren't you? And to the cause of a nation, weren't you? And to the applause of the crowd, weren't you? Now, my dear, when you find it necessary to make a change in your habits, the changes should be in line with those habits. Otherwise you may get a jolt that you won't forget. In a convent, there will be no man, no Ireland, and no crowd, will there? What you should have done was to marry Lord Conny, and to keep right on doing what you had done before, only with more success. Now when the next man comes along, do not let the grand opportunity go."

"I'll risk the jolt," Honora replied. "But this next man about whom you have been hinting since you came up here? Is this the man?"

She pointed to the path leading into the woods. Louis came towards them in a hurry, having promised them a trip to the rocks of Valcour. The young deacon was in fighting trim after a month on the farm, the pallor of hard study and confinement had fled, and the merry prospect ahead made his life an enchantment. Only his own could see the slight but ineffaceable mark of his experience with Sister Claire.

"Take care," whispered Mona. "He is not the man, but the man's agent."

Louis bounced into the raspberry enclosure and flung himself at their feet.

"Tell me," said Honora mischievously. "Is there any man in love with me, and planning to steal away my convent from me? Tell me true, Louis."

The deacon sat up and cast an indignant look on his sister.

"Shake not thy gory locks at me," she began cooly....

"There it is," he burst out. "Do you know, Honora, I think marriage turns certain kinds of people, the redheads in particular, quite daft. This one is never done talking about her husband, her baby, her experience, her theory, her friends who are about to marry, or who want to marry, or who can't marry. She can't see two persons together without patching up a union for them...."

"Everybody should get married," said Mona serenely, "except priests and nuns. Mona is not a nun, therefore she should get married."

"The reasoning is all right," replied the deacon, "but it doesn't apply here. Don't you worry, Honora. There's no man about here that will worry you, and even if there was, hold fast to that which is given thee...."

"Don't quote Scripture, Reverend Sir," cried Mona angrily.

"The besotted world is not worth the pother this foolish young married woman makes over it."

The foolish young woman received a warning from her brother when Mona went into the woods to gather an armful of wild blossoms for the boat.

"Don't you know," said he with the positiveness of a young theologian, "that Arthur will probably never marry? Has he looked at a girl in that way since he came back from California? He's giddy enough, I know, but one that studies him can see he has no intention of marrying. Now why do you trouble this poor girl, after her scene with the Englishman, with hints of Arthur? I tell you he will never marry."

"You may know more about him than I do," his sister placidly answered, "but I have seen him looking at Honora for the last five years, and working for her, and thinking about her. His look changed recently. Perhaps you know why. There's something in the air. I can feel it. You can't. None of you celibates can. And you can't see beyond your books in matters of love and marriage. That's quite right. We can manage such things better. And if Arthur makes up his mind to win her, I'm bound she shall have him."

"We can manage! I'm bound!" he mimicked. "Well, remember that I warned you. It isn't so much that your fingers may be burned ... that's what you need, you married minx. You may do harm to those two. They seem to be at peace. Let 'em alone."

"What was the baby doing when you left the house?" said she for answer.

"Tearing the nurse's hair out in handfuls," said the proud uncle, as he plunged into a list of the doings of the wonderful child, who fitted into any conversation as neatly as a preposition.

Mona, grew sad at heart. Her brother evidently knew of some obstacle to this union, something in Arthur's past life which made his marriage with any woman impossible. She recalled his silence about the California episode, his indifference to women, his lack of enthusiasm as to marriage.

They rowed away over the lake, with the boat half buried in wild bushes, sprinkled with dandelion flowers and the tender blossoms of the apple trees. Honora was happy, at peace. She put the scene with Lord Constantine away from her, and forgot the light words of Mona.

Whoever the suitor might be, Arthur did not appear to her as a lover. So careful had he been in his behavior, that Louis would have as much place in her thought as Arthur, who had never discouraged her hope of the convent, except by pleading for Ireland. The delay in keeping her own resolution had been pleasant. Now that the date was fixed, the grateful enclosure of the cloister seemed to shut her in from all this dust and clamor of men, from the noisome sights and sounds of world-living, from the endless coming and going and running about, concerning trifles, from the injustice and meanness and hopeless crimes of men.

In the shade of the altar, in the restful gloom of Calvary, she could look up with untired eyes to the calm glow of the celestial life, unchanging, orderly, beautiful with its satisfied aspiration, and rich in perfect love and holy companionship. Such a longing came over her to walk into this perfect peace that moment! Mona well knew this mood, and Louis in triumph signalled his sister to look. Her eyes, turned to the rocky shore of Valcour, saw far beyond. On her perfect face lay a shadow, the shadow of her longing, and from her lips came now and then the perfume of a sigh.

In silence these two watched her, Louis recognizing the borderland of holy ecstasy, Mona hopeful that the vision was only a mirage. The boat floated close to the perpendicular rocks and reflected itself in the deep waters; far away the farmhouse lay against the green woods; to the north rose the highest point of the bluff, dark with pines; farther on was the sweep of the curved shore, and still farther the red walls of the town. Never boat carried freight so beautiful as this which bore along the island the young mother, the young deacon, and deep-hearted Honora, who was blessing God.

CHAPTER XXXII.

THE PAULINE PRIVILEGE.

For a week at the end of July Arthur had been in the city closing up the Curran episode. On his return every one felt that change of marked and mysterious kind had touched him. His face shone with joy. The brooding shadow, acquired in his exile, had disappeared. Light played about his face, emanated from it, as from moonlit water, a phosphorescence of the daylight. His mother studied him with anxiety, without which she had not been since the surprising visit of Curran. The old shadow seemed to have fled forever.

One night on the lake, as Louis and he floated lazily towards the island, he told the story. After enjoying a moonlight swim at the foot of the bluff, they were preparing to row over to Valcour when Honora's glorious voice rang out from the farmhouse on the hill above, singing to Mona's accompaniment. The two sat in delight. A full moon stood in the sky, and radiance silvered the bosom of the lake, the mystic shores, the far-off horizon. This singer was the voice of the night, whose mystic beauty and voiceless feeling surged into the woman's song like waters escaping through a ravine. Dillon was utterly oppressed by happiness. When the song had ceased, he stretched out his arms towards her.

"Dearest and best of women! By God's grace I shall soon call you mine!"

Louis took up the oars and pulled with energy in the direction of Valcour. "Is that the meaning of the look on your face since your return?" said he.

"That's the meaning. I saw you all watching me in surprise. My mother told me of it in her anxiety. If my face matched my feelings the moon there would look sickly besides its brightness. I have been in jail for five years, and to-day I am free."

"And how about that other woman ...?"

"Dead as far as I am concerned, the poor wretch! Yesterday I could curse her. I pity her to-day. She has gone her way and I go mine. Monsignor has declared me free. Isn't that enough?"

"That's enough," cried Louis, dropping the oars in his excitement. "But is it enough to give you Honora? I'm so glad you think of her that way. Mona told her only yesterday that some lover was pursuing her, not mentioning your name. I assured her on the contrary that the road to the convent would have no obstacles. And I rebuked Mona for her interference."

"You were right, and she was right," said Arthur sadly. "I never dared to show her my love, because I was not free. But now I shall declare it. What did she think of Mona's remarks?"

"She took them lightly. I am afraid that your freedom comes at a poor time, Arthur; that you may be too late. I have had many talks with her. Her heart is set on the convent, she has fixed the date for September, and she does not seem to have love in her mind at all."

"Love begets love. How could she think of love when I never gave any sign, except what sharp-eyed Mona saw. You can conceal nothing from a woman. Wait until I have wooed her ... but apart from all that you must hear how I came to be free ... oh, my God, I can hardly believe it even now after three days ... I have been so happy that the old anguish which tore my soul years ago seemed easier to bear than this exquisite pain. I must get used to it. Listen now to the story of my escape, and row gently while you listen so as to miss not a word."

Arthur did not tell his chum more than half of the tale, chiefly because Louis was never to know the story of Horace Endicott. He had gone to New York at the invitation of Livingstone. This surprising incident began a series of surprises. The Currans had returned from California, and made their report to Sonia; and to Livingstone of all men the wife of Horace Endicott had gone for advice in so delicate an affair as forcing Arthur Dillon to prove and defend his identity. After two or three interviews with Livingstone Arthur carried his report to Monsignor.

"All this looks to me," said the priest, "as if the time for a return to your own proper personality had come. You know how I have feared the consequences of this scheme. The more I look into it, the more terrible it seems."

"And why should I give up now of all times? when I am a success?" cried the young fellow. "Do I fear Livingstone and the lawyers? Curran and his wife have done their best, and failed. Will the lawyers do any better?"

"It is not that," said the priest. "But you will always be annoyed in this way. The sharks and blackmailers will get after you later...."

"No, no, no, Monsignor. This effort of the Currans and Mrs. Endicott will be the last. I won't permit it. There will be no result from Livingstone's interference. He can go as far as interviews with me, but not one step beyond. And I can guarantee that no one will ever take up the case after him."

"You are not reasonable," urged the priest. "The very fact that these people suspect you to be Horace Endicott is enough; it proves that you have been discovered."

"I am only the twentieth whom they pursued for Horace," he laughed. "Curran knows I am not Endicott. He has proved to the satisfaction of Livingstone that I am Arthur Dillon. But the two women are pertinacious, and urge the men on. Since these are well paid for their trouble, why should they not keep on?"

"They are not the only pertinacious ones," the priest replied.

"You may claim a little of the virtue yourself," Arthur slyly remarked. "You have urged me to betray myself into the hands of enemies once a month for the last five years."

"In this case would it not be better to get an advantage by declaring yourself, before Livingstone can bring suit against you?"

"There will be no suit," he answered positively. "I hold the winning cards in this game. There is no advantage in my returning to a life which for me holds nothing but horror. Do you not see, Monsignor, that the same reasons which sent me out of it hold good to keep me out of it?"

"Very true," said Monsignor reluctantly, as he viewed the situation.

"And new reasons, not to be controverted, have sprung up around Arthur Dillon. For Horace Endicott there is nothing in that old life but public disgrace. Do you know that I hate that fat fool, that wretched cuckold who had not sense enough to discover what the uninterested knew about that woman? I would not wear his name, nor go back to his circle, if the man and woman were dead, and the secret buried forever."

"He was young and innocent," said the priest with a pitiful glance at Arthur.

"And selfish and sensual too. I despise him. He would never have been more than an empty-headed pleasure-seeker. With that wife he could have become anything you please. The best thing he did was his flight into everlasting obscurity, and that he owed to the simple, upright, strong-hearted woman who nourished him in his despair. Monsignor," and he laid his firm hand on the knee of the priest and looked at him with terrible eyes, "I would choose death rather than go back to what I was. I shall never go back. I get hot with shame when I think of the part an Endicott played as Sonia Westfield's fool."

"And the reason not to be controverted?"

"In what a position my departure would leave my mother. Have you thought of that? After all her kindness, her real affection, as if I had been her own son. She thinks now that I am her son, and I feel that she is my mother. And what would induce me to expose her to the public gaze as the chief victim, or the chief plotter in a fraud? If it had to be done, I would wait in any event until my mother was dead. But beyond all these minor reasons is one that overshadows everything. I am Arthur Dillon. That other man is not only dead, he is as unreal to me as the hero of any book I read in my boyhood. It was hard to give up the old personality; to give up what I am now would be impossible. I am what I seem. I feel, think, speak, dream

Arthur Dillon. The roots would bleed if I were to transplant myself. I found my career among your people, and the meaning of life. There is no other career for me. These are the people I love. I will never raise between them and me so odious a barrier as the story of my disappearance would be. They could never take to Horace Endicott. Oh, I have given the matter a moment's thought, Monsignor. The more I dwell on it, the worse it seems."

He considered the point for a moment, and then whispered with joyous triumph, "I have succeeded beyond my own expectations. I have disappeared even from myself. An enemy cannot find me, not even my own confession would reveal me. The people who love me would swear to a man that I am Arthur Dillon, and that only insanity could explain my own confession. At the very least they would raise such a doubt in the mind of a judge that he would insist on clean proofs from both sides. But there's the clear fact. I have escaped from myself, disappeared from the sight of Arthur Dillon. Before long I can safely testify to a dream I had of having once been a wretch named Horace Endicott. But I have a doubt even now that I was such a man."

"My God, but it's weird," said Monsignor with emotion, as he rose to walk the room. "I have the same notion myself at times."

"It's a matter to be left undisturbed, or some one will go crazy over it," Arthur said seriously.

"And you are happy, really happy? The sight of this woman did not revive in you any regret...."

"I am happy, Monsignor, beyond belief," with a contented sigh. "It would be too much to expect perfect happiness. Yet that is within my reach. If I were only free to marry Honora Ledwith."

"I heard of that too," said the priest meditatively. "Has she any regard for you?"

"As a brother. How could I have asked any other love? And I am rich in that. Since there is no divorce for Catholics, I could not let her see the love which burned in me. I had no hope."

"And she goes into the convent, I believe. You must not stand in God's way."

"I have not, though I delayed her going because I could not bear to part from her. Willingly I have resigned her to God, because I know that in His goodness, had I been free, He would have given her to me."

Monsignor paused as if struck by the thought and looked at him for a moment.

"It is the right spirit," was his brief comment.

He loved this strange, incomprehensible man, who had stood for five years between his adopted people and their enemies in many a fight, who had sought battle in their behalf and heaped them with favors. His eyes saw the depth of that resignation which gave to God the one jewel that would have atoned for the horrid sufferings of the past. If he were free! He thought of old Lear moaning over dead Cordelia.

>   She lives!
>   If it be so,
>   It is a chance which does redeem all sorrows
>   That ever I have felt.

"It is the right spirit," he repeated as he considered the matter. "One must not stand in the way of a soul, or in the way of God. Yet were you free, where would be the advantage? She is for the convent, and has never thought of you in the way of love."

"Love begets love, father dear. I could light the flame in her heart, for I am dear to her as a brother, as her father's son."

"Then her dream of the convent, which she has cherished so many years, cannot be more than a dream, if she resigned it for you."

"I cannot argue with you," he said hopelessly, "and it's a sad subject. There is only the will of God to be done."

"And if you were free," went on Monsignor smiling, "and tried and failed to light love in her heart, you would suffer still more."

"A little more or less would not matter. I would be happy still to give her to God."

"I see, I see," shaking his sage head. "To God! As long as it is not to another and luckier fellow, the resignation is perfect."

Arthur broke into a laugh, and the priest said casually:

"I think that by the law of the Church you are a free man."

Arthur leaped to his feet with a face like death.

"In the name of God!" he cried.

Monsignor pushed him back into his chair.

"That's my opinion. Just listen, will you. Then take your case to a doctor of the law. There is a kind of divorce in the Church known as the Pauline Privilege. Let me state the items, and do you examine if you can claim the privilege. Horatius, an infidel, that is, unbaptized, deserts his wife legally and properly, because of her crimes; later he becomes a Catholic; meeting a noble Catholic lady, Honoria, he desires to marry her; question, is he free to contract this marriage? The answer of the doctors of the law is in the affirmative, with the following conditions: that the first wife be an infidel, that is, unbaptized; that to live with her is impossible; that she has been notified of his intention to break the marriage. The two latter conditions are fulfilled in your case the moment the first wife secures the divorce which enables her to marry her paramour. Horatius is then free to marry Honoria, or any other Catholic lady, but not a heretic or a pagan. This is called the Pauline Privilege because it is described in the Epistle of St. Paul to the Corinthians. My opinion is that you are free."

The man, unable to speak, or move, felt his hope grow strong and violent out of the priest's words.

"Mind, it's only my opinion," said Monsignor, to moderate his transports.

"You must go to Dr. Bender, the theologian, to get a purely legal decision. I fear that I am only adding to your misery. What if he should decide against you? What if she should decide against you?"

"Neither will happen," with painful effort. Sudden joy overcame him with that anguish of the past, and this was overwhelming, wonderful.

"The essence of love is sacrifice," said Monsignor, talking to give him time for composure. "Not your good only, but the happiness of her you love must control your heart and will; and above all there must be submission to God. When He calls, the child must leave the parent, the lover his mistress, all ties must be broken."

"I felt from the beginning that this would come to pass," said Arthur weakly. "Oh, I made my sacrifice long ago. The facts were all against me, of course. Easy to make the sacrifice which had to be made. I can make another sacrifice, but isn't it now her turn? Oh, Monsignor, all my joy seems to come through you! From that first moment years ago, when we met, I can date — —"

"All your sorrow," the priest interrupted.

"And all my joy. Well, one cannot speak of these great things, only act. I'm going to the theologian. Before I sleep to-night he must settle that case. I know from your eyes it will be in my favor. I can bear disappointment. I can bear anything now. I am free from that creature, she is without a claim on me in any way, law, fact, religion, sympathy. Oh, my God!"

Monsignor could not hinder the tears that poured from his eyes silently. He clasped Arthur's hand and saw him go as he wept. In his varied life he had never seen so intimately any heart, none so strange and woful in its sorrow and its history, none so pathetic. The man lived entirely on the plane of tragedy, in the ecstasy of pain; a mystery, a problem, a wonder, yet only an average, natural, simple man, that had fought destiny with strange weapons.

This story Arthur whispered to Louis, floating between the moonlit shores of Champlain. He lay in the stern watching the rhythmic rise of the oar-blades, and the flashing of the water-drops falling back like diamonds into the wave. Happiness lay beside him steering the boat, a seraph worked the oars, the land ahead must be paradise. His was a lover's story, clear, yet broken with phrases of love; for was he not speaking to the heart, half his own, that beat with his in unison? The tears flowed down the deacon's cheek, tears of dread and of sympathy. What if Honora refused this gift laid so reverently at her feet? He spoke his dread.

"One must take the chance," said the lover calmly. "She is free too. I would not have her bound. The very air up here will conspire with me to win her. She must learn at once that I want her for my wife. Then let the leaven work."

The boat came back to the landing. The ladies sat on the veranda chatting quietly, watching the moon which rose higher and higher, and threw Valcour into shadow so deep, that it looked like a great serpent asleep on a crystal rock, nailed by a golden spike through its head to the crystal rock beneath. The lighthouse lamp burning steadily at the south point, and its long reflection in the still waters, was the golden nail. A puffing tug passed by with its procession of lumber boats, fanciful with colored lights, resounding with the roaring songs of the boatmen; and the waves recorded their protest against it in long groans on the shore. Arthur drank in the scene without misgiving, bathed in love as in moonlight. This moon would see the consummation of his joy.

CHAPTER XXXIII.

LOVE IS BLIND.

Next morning after breakfast the house began to echo with the singing of the inmates. Mona sang to the baby in an upper room, the Deacon thrummed the piano and hummed to himself in the raucous voice peculiar to most churchmen. Judy in the kitchen meditatively crooned to her maids an ancient lamentation, and out on the lawn, Arthur sang to his mother an amorous ditty in compliment to her youthful appearance. Honora, the song-bird, silent, heard with amusement this sudden lifting up of voices, each unconscious of the other. Arthur's bawling dominated.

"Has the house gone mad?" she inquired from the hallway stairs, so clearly that the singers paused to hear. "What is the meaning of all this uproar of song. Judy in the kitchen, Mona in the nursery, Louis in the parlor, Arthur on the lawn?"

The criminals began to laugh at the coincidence.

"I always sing to baby," Mona screamed in justification.

"I wasn't singing, I never sing," Louis yelled from the parlor.

"Mother drove me to it," Arthur howled through the door.

"I think the singin' was betther nor the shoutin'," Judy observed leaning out of the window to display her quizzical smile.

A new spirit illumined the old farmhouse. Love had entered it, and hope had followed close on his heels; hope that Honora would never get to her beloved convent. They loved her so and him that with all their faith, their love and respect for the convent life, gladly would they have seen her turn away from the holy doors into Arthur's reverential arms. With the exception of Anne. So surely had she become his mother that the thought of giving him up to any woman angered her. She looked coldly on Honora for having inspired him with a foolish passion.

"Come down, celestial goddess," said Arthur gayly, "and join the Deacon and me in a walk over the bluff, through the perfumed woods, down the loud-resounding shore. Put on rubbers, for the dew has no respect for the feet of such divinity."

They went off together in high spirits, and Mona came down to the veranda with the baby in her arms to look after them. Anne grieved at the sight of their intimacy.

"I have half a mind," she said, "to hurry Honora off to her convent, or to bring Sister Magdalen and the Mother Superior up here to strengthen her. If that boy has his way, he'll marry her before Christmas. He has the look of it in his eye."

"And why shouldn't he?" Mona asked. "If she will have him, then she has no business with the convent, and it will be a good opportunity for her to test her vocation."

"And what luck will there be in it for him?" said the mother bitterly. "How would you feel if some hussy cheated Louis out of his priesthood, with blue eyes and golden hair and impudence? If Arthur wants to marry after waiting so long, let him set eyes on women that ask for marriage. He'll never have luck tempting a poor girl from the convent."

"Little ye think o' the luck," said Judy, who had come out to have her morning word with the mistress. "Weren't ye goin' into a convent yerself whin Pat Dillon kem along, an' wid a wink tuk ye to church undher his arm. An' is there a woman in the whole world that's had greater luck than yerself?"

"Oh, I know you are all working for the same thing, all against me," Anne said pettishly.

"Faith we are, and may the angels guide him and her to each other. Can't a blind man see they wor made to be man an' wife? An' I say it, knowin' that the convent is the best place in the world for anny girl. I wish every girl that was born wint there. If they knew what is lyin' in wait for thim whin they take up wid a man, there wouldn't be convents enough to hould all that wud be runnin' to thim. But ye know as well as I do that the girls are not med for the convent, except the blessed few...."

Anne fled from the stream of Judy's eloquence, and the old lady looked expressively at Mona.

"She's afraid she's goin' to lose her Artie. Oh, these Irish mothers! they'd kape a boy till his hairs were gray, an' mek him belave it too, if they cud. I never saw but wan mother crazy to marry her son. That was Biddy Brady, that wint to school wid yer mother, an' poor Micksheen was a born ijit, wid a lip hangin' like a sign, so's ye cud hang an auction notice on it. Sure, the poor boy wudn't lave his mother for Vanus herself, an' the mother batin' him out o' the house every day, an' he bawlin' for fear the women wud get hould of him."

Honora had observed the happy change in Arthur, her knight of service, who had stood between her and danger, and had fought her battles with chivalry; asking no reward, hinting at none, because she had already given him all, a sister's love. What tenderness, what adoration, what service had he lavished on her, unmarred by act, or word, or hint! God would surely reward him for his consideration. Walking through the scented woods she found it easy to tell them of the date fixed for her entrance into the convent. Grand trees were marshalled along the path, supporting a roof of gold and green, where the sun fell strong on the heavy foliage.

"September," said Arthur making a calculation. "Why not wait until October and then shed your colors with the trees. I can see her," he went on humorously, "decorously arranging the black dress so that it will hang well, and not make her a fright altogether before the other women; and getting a right tilt to the black bonnet and enough lace in it to set off her complexion."

"Six months later," said the Deacon taking up the strain, "she will do better than that. Discarding the plain robes of the postulant, she will get herself into the robes of a bride...."

"Oh, sooner than that," said Arthur with a meaning which escaped her.

"No, six months is the period," she corrected seriously.

"In wedding finery she will prance before her delighted friends for a few minutes, and then march out to shed white silk and fleecy tulle. A vengeful nun, whose hair has long been worn away, will then clip with one snip of the scissors her brown locks from her head...."

"Horror!" cried Arthur.

"Sure, straight across the neck, you know, like the women's-rights people. Then the murder of the hair has to be concealed, so they put on a nightcap, and hide that with a veil, and then bring her into the bishop to tell him it's all right, and that she's satisfied."

"And what do they make of the hair?" said Arthur.

"That's one of the things yet to be revealed."

"And after that she is set at chasing the rule, or being chased by the rule for two years. She studies striking examples of observing the rule, and of the contrary. She has a shy at observing it herself, and the contrary. The rule is it when she observes it; she's it when she doesn't. At this point the mother superior comes into the game."

"Where do the frowsy children come in?"

"At meals usually. Honora cuts the bread and her fingers, butters it, and passes it round; the frowsy butter themselves, and Honora; this is an act of mortification, which is intensified when the mistress of novices discovers the butter on her habit."

"Finally the last stage is worse than the first, I suppose. Having acquired the habit she gets into it so deeply...."

"She sheds it once more, Arthur. Then she's tied to the frowsy children forever, and is known as Sister Mary of the Cold Shoulder to the world."

"This is a case of rescue," said Arthur with determination, "I move we rescue her this minute. Help, help!"

The woods echoed with his mocking cries. Honora had not spoken, the smile had died away, and she was plainly offended. Louis observant passed a hint to Arthur, who made the apology.

331

"We shall be there," he said humbly, "with our hearts bleeding because we must surrender you. And who are we that you need care? It is poor Ireland that will mourn for the child that bathed and bound her wounds, that watched by her in the dark night, and kept the lamp of hope and comfort burning, that stirred hearts to pity and service, that woke up Lord Constantine and me, and strangers and enemies like us, to render service; the child whose face and voice and word and song made the meanest listen to a story of injustice; all shut out, concealed, put away where the mother may never see or hear her more."

His voice broke, his eyes filled with tears at the vividness of the vision called up in the heart of the woods; and he walked ahead to conceal his emotion. Honora stopped dead and looked inquiringly at the Deacon, who switched the flowers with downcast eyes.

"What is the meaning of it, Louis?"

He knew not how to make answer, thinking that Arthur should be the first to tell his story.

"Do you think that we can let you go easily?" he said. "If we tease you as we did just now it is to hide what we really suffer. His feeling got the better of him, I think."

The explanation sounded harmless. For an instant a horrid fear that these woods must witness another scene like Lord Constantine's chilled her heart. She comforted Arthur like a sister.

"Do not feel my going too deeply. Change must come. Let us be glad it is not death, or a journey into distant lands with no return. I shall be among you still, and meanwhile God will surely comfort you."

"Oh, if we could walk straight on like this," Arthur answered, "through the blessed, free, scented forest, just as we are, forever! And walking on for years, content with one another, you, Louis, and I, come out at last, as we shall soon come out here on the lake, on the shore of eternity, just as life's sun sets, and the moon of the immortal life rises; and then without change, or the anguish of separation and dying, if we could pass over the waters, and enter the land of eternity, taking our place with God and His children, our friends, that have been there so long!"

"Is not that just what we are to do, not after your fashion, but after the will of God, Arthur? Louis at the altar, I in the convent before the altar, and you in the field of battle fighting for us both. Aaron, Miriam, Moses, here are the three in the woods of Champlain, as once in the desert of Arabia," and she smiled at the young men.

Louis returned the smile, and Arthur gave her a look of adoration, so tender, so bold, that she trembled. The next moment, when the broad space through which they were walking ended in a berry-patch, he plunged among the bushes with eagerness, to gather for her black raspberries in his drinking-cup. Her attempt to discuss her departure amiably had failed.

"I am tired already," said she to Louis helplessly. "I shall go back to the house, and leave you to go on together."

"Don't blame him," the Deacon pleaded, perceiving how useless was concealment. "If you knew how that man has suffered in his life, and how you opened heaven to him ..." she made a gesture of pain ... "remember all his goodness and be gentle with him. He must speak before you go. He will take anything from you, and you alone can teach him patience and submission."

"How long...." she began. He divined what she would have asked.

"Mona has known it more than a year, but no one else, for he gave no sign. I know it only a short time. After all it is not to be wondered at. He has been near you, working with you for years. His life has been lonely somehow, and you seemed to fill it. Do not be hasty with him. Let him come to his avowal and his refusal in his own way. It is all you can do for him. Knowing you so well he probably knows what he has to receive."

Arthur came back with his berries and poured them out on a leaf for her to eat. Seated for a little on a rock, while he lay on the ground at her feet, she ate to please him; but her soul in terror saw only the white face of Lord Constantine, and thought only of the pain in store for this most faithful friend. Oh, to have it out with him that moment! Yet it seemed too cruel. But how go on for a month in dread of what was to come?

She loved him in her own beautiful way. Her tears fell that night as she sat in her room by the window watching the high moon, deep crimson, rising through the mist over the far-off islands. How bitter to leave her beloved even for God, when the leaving brought woe to them! So long she had waited for the hour of freedom, and always a tangle at the supreme moment! How could she be happy and he suffering without the convent gates? This pity was to be the last temptation, her greatest trial. Its great strength did not disarm her. If twenty broke their hearts on that day, she would not give up her loved design. Let God comfort them, since she could not. But the vision of a peaceful entrance into the convent faded. She would have to enter, as she had passed through life, carrying the burden of another's woe, in tears.

She could see that he never lost heart. The days passed delightfully, and somehow his adoration pleased her. Having known him in many lights, there was novelty in seeing him illumined by candid love. How could he keep so high a courage with the end so dark and so near? Honora had no experience of love, romantic love, and she had always smiled at its expression in the novels of the time. If Arthur only knew the task he had set for himself! She loved him truly, but marriage repelled her almost, except in others.

Therefore, having endured the uncertainty of the position a week, she had it out with Arthur. Sitting on the rocks of an ancient quarry, high above the surface of the lake, they watched the waters rough and white from the strong south wind. The household had adjourned that day for lunch to this wild spot, and the members were scattered about, leaving them, as they always did now, by common consent alone.

"Perhaps," she said calmly, "this would be a good time to talk to you, Arthur, as sister to brother ... can't we talk as brother and sister?"

For a change came over his face that sickened her. The next moment he was ready for the struggle.

"I fear not, Honora," said he humbly. "I fear we can never do that again."

"Then you are to stand in my way too?" with bitterness.

"No, but I am not going to stand in my own way," he replied boldly. "Have I ever stood in your way, Honora?"

"You have always helped me. Do not fail me at the last, I beg of you."

"I shall never fail you, nor stand in your way. You are free now as your father wished you to be. You shall go to the convent on the date which you have named. Neither Ireland, nor anything but your heart shall hinder you. You have seen my heart for a week as you never saw it before. Do not let what you saw disturb or detain you. I told your father of it the last day of his life, and he was glad. He said it was like ... he was satisfied. Both he and I were of one mind that you should be free. And you are."

Ideas and words fled from her. The situation of her own making she knew not how to manage. What could be more sensible than his speech?

"Very well, thank you," she said helplessly.

He had perfect control of himself, but his attitude expressed his uneasiness, his face only just concealed his pain. All his life in moments like this, Arthur Dillon would suffer from his earliest sorrow.

"I hope you will all let me go with resignation," she began again.

"I give you to God freely," was his astonishing answer, "but I may tell you it is my hope He will give you back to me. I have nothing, and He is the Lord of all. He has permitted my heart to be turned to ashes, and yet gave it life again through you. I have confidence in Him. To you I am nothing; in the future I shall be only a memory to be prayed for. If we had not God to lift us up, and repay us for our suffering, to what would we come? I could not make my heart clear to you, show you its depths of feeling, frightful depths, I think sometimes, and secure your pity. God alone, the master of hearts, can do that. I have been generous to the last farthing. He will not be outdone by me."

"Oh, my God!" she murmured, looking at him in wonder, for his words sounded insanely to her ear.

"I love you, Honora," he went on, with a flush on his cheek, and so humble that he kept his eyes on the ground. "Go, in spite of that, if God demands it. If you can, knowing that I shall be alone, how much alone no one may know, go nevertheless. Only bear it in mind, that I shall wait for you outside the convent gate. If you cannot remain thinking of me, I shall be ready for you. If not here, then hereafter, as God wills. But you are free, and I love you. Before you go, God's beloved," and he looked at her then with eyes so beautiful that her heart went out to him, "you must let me tell you what I have been. You will pray for me better, when you have learned how far a man can sink into hell, and yet by God's grace reach heaven again."

CHAPTER XXXIV.

A HARPY AT THE FEAST.

Honora now saw that suffering was not to be avoided. Experience had taught her how to economize with it. In the wood one day she watched for minutes two robins hopping about in harmony, feeding, singing now and then low notes of content from a bough, and always together. A third robin made appearance on the scene, and their content vanished. Irritated and uneasy, even angered, they dashed at the intruder, who stood his ground, confident of his strength. For a long time he fought them, leaving only at his own pleasure. Longer still the pair remained unquiet, distressed by the struggle rather than wearied, complaining to each other tenderly.

Behold a picture of her own mind, its order upset by the entrance of a new idea. That life of the mind, which is our true life, had to change its point of view in order to meet and cope with the newcomer. Arthur's love had the fiber of tragedy. She felt rather than knew its nature. For years it had been growing in his strong heart, disciplined by steady buffeting, by her indifference, by his own hard circumstances; no passion of an hour like Romeo's; more like her father's love for Erin.

Former ideas began to shift position, and to struggle against the intruder vainly. Some fought in his favor. The vision of convent peace grew dim. She must take it with tears, and his sorrow would cloud its beauty. Marriage, always so remote from her life, came near, and tried to prove the lightness of its yoke with Arthur as the mate. The passion of her father's life awoke. Dear Erin cried out to her for the help which such a union would bring.

Her fixed resolve to depart for her convent in September kept the process from tangle. Sweet indeed was the thought of how nobly he loved her. She was free. God alone was the arbiter. None would hinder her going, if her heart did not bid her stay for his sake. Her father had needed her. She would never have forgiven herself had she left him to carry his sorrow alone. Perhaps this poor soul needed her more. With delight one moment and shame the next, she saw herself drifting towards him. Nevertheless she did not waver, nor change the date of her departure.

Arthur continued to adore at her shrine as he had done for years, and she studied him with the one thought: how will he bear new sorrow? No man bore the mark of sorrow more terribly when he let himself go, and at times his mask fell off in spite of resolve. As a lover Honora, with all her distaste for marriage, found him more lovable than ever, and had to admit that companionship with her hero would not be irritating. The conspiracy in his favor flourished within and without the citadel. Knowing that he adored her, she liked the adoration. To any goddess the smell of the incense is sweet, the sight of the flowers, the humid eyes, the leaping heart delightful. Yet she put it one side when the day over, and she knelt in her room for prayer. Like a dream the meanings of the day faded, and the vision of her convent cell, its long desired peace and rest, returned with fresher coloring. The men and women of her little world, the passions and interests of the daylight, so faded, that they seemed to belong to another age.

While this comedy went on the farmhouse and its happy life were keenly and bitterly watched by the wretched wife of Curran. It was her luck, like Sonia's, to spoil her own feast in defiling her enemy's banquet. Having been routed at all points and all but sent to Jezebel's fate by Arthur Dillon, she had stolen into this paradise to do what mischief she could. Thus it happened, at the moment most favorable for Arthur's hopes, when Honora inclined towards him out of sisterly love and pity, that the two women met in a favorite haunt of Honora's, in the woods near the lake shore.

To reach it one took a wild path through the woods, over the bluff, and along the foot of the hill, coming out on a small plateau some fifteen feet above the lake. Behind rose a rocky wall, covered with slender pines and cedars; noble trees shaded the plateau, leaving a clearing towards the lake; so that one looked out as from a frame of foliage on the blue waters, the islet of St. Michel, and the wooded cape known as Cumberland Head.

As Honora entered this lovely place, Edith sat on a stone near the edge of the precipice, enjoying the view. She faced the newcomer with unfailing impertinence, and coolly studied the woman whom Arthur Dillon loved. Sickness of heart filled her with rage. The evil beauty of Sonia and herself showed purely animal beside the pale spiritual luster that shone from this noble, sad-hearted maid. Honora bowed distantly and passed on. Edith began to glow with delight of torturing her presently, and would not speak lest her pleasure be hurried. The instinct of the wild beast, to worry the living game, overpowered her. What business had Honora with so much luck? The love of Arthur, fame as a singer, beauty, and a passion for the perfect life? God had endowed herself with three of these gifts. Having dragged them through the mud, she hated the woman who had used them with honor. What delight that in a moment she could torture her with death's anguish!

"I came here in the hope of meeting you, madam," she began suddenly, "if you are Miss Ledwith. I come to warn you."

"I do not need warnings from strangers," Honora replied easily, studying the other for an instant with indifferent eyes, "and if you wished me to see on proper matters you should have called at the house."

"For a scene with the man who ran away from his wife before he deceived me, and then made love to you? I could hardly do that," said she as demure and soft as a purring cat.

Honora's calm look plainly spoke her thought: the creature was mad.

"I am not mad. Miss Ledwith, and your looks will not prevent me warning you. Arthur Dillon is not the man he pretends — —"

"Please go away," Honora interrupted.

"He is not the son of Anne Dillon — —"

"Then I shall go," said Honora, but Edith barred the only way out of the place, her eyes blazing with the insane pleasure of torturing the innocent. Honora turned her back on her and walked down to the edge of the cliff, where she remained until the end.

"I know Arthur Dillon better than you know him," Edith went on, "and I know you better than you think. Once I had the honor of your acquaintance. That doesn't matter. Neither does it matter just who Arthur Dillon is. He's a fraud from cover to cover. His deserted wife is living, poor as well as neglected. The wretched woman has sought him long— —"

"Why don't you put her on the track?" Honora asked, relieved that the lunatic wished only to talk.

"He makes love to you now as he has done for years, and he hopes to marry you soon. I can tell that by his behavior. I warn you that he is not free to marry. His wife lives. If you marry him I shall put her on his track, and give you a honeymoon of scandal. It was enough for him to have wrecked my life and broken my heart. I shall not permit him to repeat that work on any other unfortunate."

"Is that all?"

Edith, wholly astonished at the feeble impression made by her story, saw that her usual form had been lacking. Her scorn for Honora suggested that acting would be wasted on her; that the mere news of the living wife would be sufficient to plunge her into anguish. But here was no delight of pallid face and trembling limbs. Her tale would have gone just as well with the trees.

"I have risked my life to tell you this," said she throwing in the note of pathos. "If Arthur Dillon, or whoever he is, hears of it, he will kill me."

"Don't worry then," and Honora turned about with benign face and manner, quite suited to the need of a crazy patient escaped from her keepers, "I shall never tell him. But please go, for some one is coming. It may be he."

Edith turned about swiftly and saw a form approaching through the trees. She had her choice of two paths a little beyond, and fled by the upper one. Her fear of Arthur had become mortal. As it was she rushed into the arms of Louis, who had seen the fleeing form, and thought to play a joke upon Mona or Honora. He dropped the stranger and made apologies for his rudeness. She curtsied mockingly, and murmured:

"Possibly we have met before."

The blood rose hot to his face as he recognized her, and her face paled as he seized her by the wrist with scant courtesy.

"I scarcely hoped for the honor of meeting you again, Sister Claire. Of course you are here only for mischief, and Arthur Dillon must see you and settle with you. I'll trouble you to come with me."

"You have not improved," she snarled. "You would attack my honor again."

Then she screamed for help once, not the second time, which might have brought Arthur to the scene; but Honora came running to her assistance.

"Ah, this was your prey, wolf?" said Louis coolly. "Honora, has she been lying to you, this fox, Sister Claire, Edith Conyngham, with a string of other names not to be remembered? Didn't you know her?"

Honora recoiled. Edith stood in shame, with the mortified expression of the wild beast, the intelligent fox, trapped by an inferior boy.

"Oh, let her go, Louis," she pleaded.

"Not till she has seen Arthur. The mischief she can do is beyond counting. Arthur knows how to deal with her."

"I insist," said Honora. "Come away, Louis, please, come away."

He flung away her wrist with contempt, and pointed out her path. In a short time she had disappeared.

"And what had she to tell you, may I ask?" said the Deacon. "Like the banshee her appearance brings misfortune to us."

"You have always been my confidant, Louis," she answered after some thought. "Do you know anything about the earlier years of Arthur Dillon?"

341

"Much. Was that her theme?"

"That he was married and his wife still lives."

"He will tell you about that business himself no doubt. I know nothing clear or certain ... some hasty expressions of feeling ... part of a dream ... the declaration that all was well now ... and so on. But I shall tell him. Don't object, I must. The woman is persistent and diabolical in her attempts to injure us. He must know at least that she is in the vicinity. He will guess what she's after without any further hint. But you mustn't credit her, Honora. As you know...."

"Oh, I know," she answered with a smile. "The wretched creature is not to be believed under any circumstances. Poor soul!"

Nevertheless she felt the truth of Edith's story. It mattered little whether Arthur was Anne Dillon's son, he would always be the faithful, strong friend, and benefactor. That he had a wife living, the living witness of the weakness of his career in the mines, shocked her for the moment. The fact carried comfort too. Doubt fled, and the weighing of inclinations, the process kept up by her mind apart from her will, ceased of a sudden. The great pity for Arthur, which had welled up in her heart like a new spring, dried up at its source. For the first time she felt the sin in him, the absence of the ideal. He had tripped and fallen like all his kind in the wild days of youth; and according to his nature had been repeating with her the drama enacted with his first love. She respected his first love. She respected the method of nature, but did not feel forced to admire it.

Her distaste for the intimacy of marriage returned with tenfold strength. One might have become submissive and companionable with a virgin nature; to marry another woman's lover seemed ridiculous. This storm cleared the air beautifully. Her own point of view became plainer, and she saw how far inclination had hurried her. For some hours she had been near to falling in love with Arthur, had been willing to yield to tender persuasion. The woman guilty of such weakness did not seem at this moment to have been Honora Ledwith; only a poor soul, like a little ship in a big wind, borne away by the tempest of emotion.

She had no blame for Arthur. His life was his own concern. Part of it had brought her much happiness. Edith's scandalous story did not shake her confidence in him. Undoubtedly he was free to marry, or he would not have approached her. His freedom from a terrible bond must have been recent, since his manner towards herself had changed only that summer, within the month in fact. The reserve of years had been prompted by hard conditions. In honor he could not woo. Ah, in him ran the fibre of the hero, no matter what might have been his mistakes! He had resisted every natural temptation to show his love. Once more they were brother and sister, children of the dear father whose last moments they had consoled. Who would regret the sorrow which led to such a revealing of hearts?

The vision of her convent rose again to her pleased eye, fresh and beautiful as of old, and dearer because of the passing darkness which had concealed it for a time; the light from the chapel windows falling upon the dark robes in the choir, the voices of the reader, chanter, and singer, and the solemn music of the organ; the procession filing silently from one duty to another, the quiet cell when the day was over, and the gracious intimacy with God night and day. Could her belief and her delight in that holy life have been dim for an instant? Ah, weakness of the heart! The mountain is none the less firm because clouds obscure its lofty form. She had been wrapped in the clouds of feeling, but never once had her determination failed.

CHAPTER XXXV.

SONIA CONSULTS LIVINGSTONE.

Edith's visit, so futile, so unlike her, had been prompted by the hatefulness of her nature. The expedition to California had failed, her effort to prove her instincts true had come to nothing, and Arthur Dillon had at last put his foot down and extinguished her and Sonia together. Free to snarl and spit if they chose, the two cats could never plot seriously against him more. Curran triumphed in the end. Tracking Arthur Dillon through California had all the features of a chase through the clouds after a bird. The scene changed with every step, and the ground just gone over faded like a dream.

They found Dillons, a few named Arthur, some coincidences, several mysteries, and nothing beyond. The police still had the photographs sent out by Anne Dillon, and a record that the man sought for had been found and returned to his mother. The town where the search ended had only a ruined tavern and one inhabitant, who vaguely remembered the close of the incident. Edith surrendered the search in a violent temper, and all but scratched out the eyes of her devoted slave. To Sonia the detective put the net result very sensibly.

"Arthur Dillon did not live in California under his own name," said he, "and things have so changed there in five years that his tracks have been wiped out as if by rain. All that has been done so far proves this man to be just what he appears. We never had a worse case, and never took up a more foolish pursuit. We have proved just one sure thing: that if this man be Horace, then he can't be found. He is too clever to be caught, until he is willing to reveal himself. If you pursue him to the point which might result in his capture, there'll be murder or worse waiting for you at that point. It might be better for you two not to find him."

This suggestion, clever and terrifying, Sonia could not understand as clearly as Curran. She thought the soft nature of Horace quite manageable, and if murder were to be done her knife should do it. Oh, to seize his throat with her beautiful hands, to press and squeeze and dig until the blood gorged his face, and to see him die by inches, gasping! He had lied like a coward! Nothing easier to destroy than such a wretch!

"Don't give up, Sonia," was Edith's comment on the wise words of Curran. "Get a good lawyer, and by some trick drag Dillon and his mother and the priest to court, put them on oath as to who the man is; they won't perjure themselves, I'll wager."

"That is my thought," said Sonia tenderly nursing the idea. "There seems to be nothing more to do. I have thought the matter over very carefully. We are at the end. If this fails I mean to abandon the matter. But for his money I would have let him go as far as he wanted, and I would let this man pass too but for the hope of getting at his money. It is the only way to punish Horace, as he punished me. I feel like you, that the mystery is with this Arthur Dillon. Since I saw you last, he has filled my dreams, and always in the dreams he has been so like Horace that I now see more of a likeness in Arthur Dillon. I have a relative in the city, a very successful lawyer, Quincy Livingstone. I shall consult him. Perhaps it would be well for you to accompany me, Edith. You explain this case so well."

"No, she'll keep out of it, by your leave," the detective answered for her. "Dillon has had patience with this woman, but he will resent interference so annoying."

Edith made a face at him.

"As if I could be bossed by either you or Arthur. Sonia, you have the right stuff in you, clear grit. This trick will land your man."

"You'll find an alligator who will eat the legs off you both before you can run away," said Curran.

"Do you know what I think, Dick Curran?" she snapped at him. "That you have been playing the traitor to us, telling Arthur Dillon all we've been doing. Oh, if I could prove that, you wretch!"

"You have a high opinion of his softness, if you think he would throw away money to learn what any schoolboy might learn by himself. How much did you, with all your cleverness, get out of him in the last five years?"

He laughed joyfully at her wicked face.

"Let me tell you this," he added. "You have been teasing that boy as a monkey might a lion. Now you will set on him the man that he likes least in this world, Livingstone. What a pretty mouthful you will be when he makes up his mind that you've done enough."

Nevertheless the two women called on Livingstone. The great man, no longer great, no longer in the eye of the world, out of politics because the charmed circle had closed, and no more named for high places because his record had made him impossible, had returned to the practice of law. Eminent by his ability, his achievement, and his blood, but only a private citizen, the shadow of his failure lay heavy on his life and showed clearly in his handsome face. That noble position which he had missed, so dear to heart and imagination, haunted his moments of leisure and mocked his dreams. He had borne the disappointment bravely, had lightly called it the luck of politics. Now that the past lay in clear perspective, he recognized his own madness.

He had fought with destiny like a fool, had stood in the path of a people to whom God had given the chance which the rulers of the earth denied them; and this people, through a youth carrying the sling of David, had ruined him. He had no feeling against Birmingham, nor against Arthur Dillon. The torrent, not the men, had destroyed him. Yet he had learned nothing. With a fair chance he would have built another dam the next morning. He was out of the race forever. In the English mission he had touched the highest mark of his success. He mourned in quiet. Life had still enough for him, but oh! the keenness of his regret.

Sonia's story he had heard before, at the beginning of the search, as a member of the Endicott family. The details had never reached him. The cause of Horace Endicott's flight he had forgotten. Edith in her present costume remained unknown, nor did she enlighten him. Her thought as she studied him was of Dillon's luck in his enterprises.

Behold three of his victims. Sonia repeated for the lawyer the story of her husband's disappearance, and of the efforts to find him.

"At last I think that I have found him," was her conclusion, "in the person of a man known in this city as Arthur Dillon."

Livingstone started slightly. However, there must be many Arthur Dillons, the Irish being so numerous, and tasteless in the matter of names. When she described her particular Arthur his astonishment became boundless at the absurdity of the supposition.

"You have fair evidence I suppose that he is Horace Endicott, madam?"

"I am sorry to tell you that I have none, because the statement makes one feel so foolish. On the contrary the search of a clever detective ... he's really clever, isn't he, Edith?... shows that Dillon is just what he appears to be, the son of Mrs. Anne Dillon. The whole town believes he is her son. The people who knew him since he was born declare him to be the very image of his father. Still, I think that he is Horace Endicott. Why I think so, ... Edith, my dear, it is your turn now. Do explain to the lawyer."

Livingstone wondered as the dancer spoke where that beautiful voice and fluent English had become familiar. Sister Claire had passed from his mind with all the minor episodes of his political intrigues. He could not find her place in his memory. Her story won him against his judgment. The case, well put, found strength in the contention that the last move had not been made, since the three most important characters in the play had not been put to the question.

His mind ran over the chief incidents in that remarkable fight which Arthur Dillon had waged in behalf of his people: the interview before the election of Birmingham, ... the intrigues in London, the dexterous maneuvers which had wrecked the campaign against the Irish, had silenced McMeeter, stunned the Bishop, banished Fritters, ruined Sister Claire, tumbled him from his lofty position, and cut off his shining future. How frightful the thought that this wide ruin might have been wrought by an Endicott, one of his own blood!

"A woman's instincts are admirable," he said, politely and gravely, "and they have led you admirably in this case. But in face of three facts, the failure of the detective, the declaration of Mr. Dillon, and your failure to recognize your husband after five years, it would be absurd to persist in the belief that this young man is your husband. Moreover there are intrinsic difficulties, which would tell even if you had made out a good case for the theory. No Endicott would take up intimate connection with the Irish. He would not know enough about them, he could not endure them; his essence would make the scheme, even if it were presented to him by others, impossible. One has only to think of two or three main difficulties to feel and see the utter absurdity of the whole thing,"

"No doubt," replied Sonia sweetly. "Yet I am determined not to miss this last opportunity to find my husband. If it fails I shall get my divorce, and ... bother with the matter no more."

Edith smiled faintly at the suggestive pause, and murmured the intended phrase, "marry Quincy Lenox."

"Very well," said the lawyer. "You have only to begin divorce proceedings here, issue a summons for the real Horace Endicott, and serve the papers on Mr. Arthur Dillon. You must be prepared for many events however. The whole business will be ventilated in the journals. The disappearance will come up again, and be described in the light of this new sensation. Mr. Dillon is eminent among his people, and well known in this city. It will be a year's wonder to have him sued in a divorce case, to have it made known that he is supposed to be Horace Endicott."

"That is unavoidable," Edith prompted, seeing a sudden shrinking on the part of Sonia. "Do not forget, sir, that all Mrs. Endicott wants is the sworn declaration of Arthur Dillon that he is not Horace Endicott, of his mother that he is her son, of Father O'Donnell that he knows nothing of Horace Endicott since his disappearance."

"You would not like the case to come to trial?" said the lawyer to Sonia.

"I must get my divorce," she answered coolly, "whether this is the right man or no."

"Let me tell you what may happen after the summons, or notice, is served on Mr. Dillon," said the lawyer. "The serving can be done so quietly that for some time no others but those concerned need know about it. I shall assume that Mr. Dillon is not Horace Endicott. In that case he can ignore the summons, which is not for him, but for another man. He need never appear. If you insisted on his appearance, you would have to offer some evidence that he is really Horace Endicott. This you cannot do. He could make affidavit that he is not the man. By that time the matter would be public property, and he could strike back at you for the scandal, the annoyance, and the damage done to his good name."

"What I want is to have his declaration under oath that he is not Horace. If he is Horace he will never swear to anything but the truth."

For the first time Sonia showed emotion, tears dropped from her lovely eyes, and the lawyer wondered what folly had lost to her husband so sweet a creature. Evidently she admired one of Horace's good qualities.

"You can get the declaration in that way. To please you, he might at my request make affidavit without publicity and scenes at court."

"I would prefer the court," said Sonia firmly.

"She's afeared the lawyer suspects her virtue," Edith said to herself.

"Let me now assume that Arthur Dillon is really Horace Endicott," continued Livingstone. "He must be a consummate actor to play his part so well and so long. He can play the part in this matter also, by ignoring the summons, and declaring simply that he is not the man. In that case he leaves himself open to punishment, for if he should thereafter be proved to be Horace Endicott, the court could punish him for contempt. Or, he can answer the summons by his lawyer, denying the fact, and stating his readiness to swear that he is not any other than Arthur Dillon. You would then have to prove that he is Horace Endicott, which you cannot do."

"All I want is the declaration under oath," Sonia repeated.

"And you are ready for any ill consequences, the resentment and suit of Mr. Dillon, for instance? Understand, my dear lady, that suit for divorce is not a trifling matter for Mr. Dillon, if he is not Endicott."

"Particularly as he is about to marry a very handsome woman," Edith interjected, heedless of the withering glance from Sonia.

"Ah, indeed!"

"Then I think some way ought to be planned to get Anne Dillon and the priest into court," Edith suggested. "Under oath they might give us some hint of the way to find Horace Endicott. The priest knows something about him."

"I shall be satisfied if Arthur Dillon swears that he is not Horace," Sonia said, "and then I shall get my divorce and wash my hands of the tiresome case. It has cost me too much money and worry."

"Was there any reason alleged for the remarkable disappearance of the young man? I knew his father and mother very well, and admired them. I saw the boy in his schooldays, never afterwards. You have a child, I understand."

Edith lowered her eyes and looked out of the window on the busy street.

"It is for my child's sake that I have kept up the search," Sonia answered with maternal tenderness. "Insanity is supposed to be the cause. Horace acted strangely for three months before his disappearance, he grew quite thin, and was absent most of the time. As it was summer, which I spent at the shore with friends, I hardly noticed his condition. It was only when he had gone, without warning, taking considerable money with him, that I recalled his queer behavior. Since then not a scrap of information, not a trace, nor a hint of him, has ever come back to me. The detectives did their best until this moment. All has failed."

"Very sad," Livingstone said, touched by the hopeless tone. "Well, as you wish it then, I shall bring suit for divorce and alimony against

Horace Endicott, and have the papers served on Arthur Dillon. He can ignore them or make his reply. In either case he must be brought to make affidavit that he is not the man you look for."

"And the others? The priest and Mrs. Dillon?" asked Edith.

"They are of no consequence," was Sonia's opinion.

After settling unimportant details the two women departed. Livingstone found the problem which they had brought to his notice fascinating. He had always marked Arthur Dillon among his associates, as an able and peculiar young man, he had been attracted by him, and had listened to his speeches with more consideration than most young men deserved. His amazing success in dealing with a Livingstone, his audacity and nerve in attacking the policy which he brought to nothing, were more wonderful to the lawyer than to the friends of Dillon, who had not seen the task in its entirety.

And this peculiar fellow was thought to be an Endicott, of his own family, of the English blood, more Irish than the Irish, bitterer towards him than the priests had been. The very impossibility of the thing made it charming. What course of thought, what set of circumstances, could turn the Puritan mind in the Celtic direction? Was there such genius in man to convert one personality into another so neatly that the process remained undiscoverable, not to be detected by the closest observation? He shook off the fascination. These two women believed it, but he knew that no Endicott could ever be converted.

CHAPTER XXXVI.

ARTHUR'S APPEAL.

Suit was promptly begun by Livingstone on behalf of Sonia for a divorce from Horace Endicott. Before the papers had been fully made out, even before the officer had been instructed to serve them on Arthur Dillon, the lawyer received an evening visit from the defendant himself. As a suspicious act he welcomed it; but a single glance at the frank face and easy manner, when one knew the young man's ability, disarmed suspicion. The lawyer studied closely, for the first time with interest, the man who might yet prove to be his kinsman. He saw a form inclined to leanness, a face that might have been handsome but for the sunken cheeks, dark and expressive eyes whose natural beauty faded in the dark circles around them, a fine head with dead black hair, and a handsome beard, streaked with gray. His dress, gentleman-like but of a strange fashion, the lawyer did not recognize as the bachelor costume of Cherry Hill prepared by his own tailor. Nothing of the Endicott in face or manner, nothing tragical, the expression decorous and formal, perhaps a trifle quizzical, as this was their first meeting since the interview in London.

"I have called to enter a protest," Arthur began primly, "against the serving of the papers in the coming Endicott divorce case on your humble servant."

"As the papers are to be served only on Horace Endicott, I fail to see how you have any right or reason to protest," was the suave answer.

"I know all about the matter, sir, for very good reasons. For some months the movements of the two women concerned in this affair have been watched in my interest. Not long after they left you a few days ago, the result of their visit was made known to me. To anticipate the disagreeable consequences of serving the papers on me, I have not waited. I appeal to you not only as the lawyer of Mrs. Endicott, but also as one much to blame for the new persecution which is about to fall upon me."

"I recognize the touch," said Livingstone, unable to resist a smile. "Mr. Dillon must be audacious or nothing."

"I am quite serious," Arthur replied. "You know part of the story, what Mrs. Endicott chose to tell you, but I can enlighten you still more. I appeal to you, as the lady's lawyer, to hinder her from doing mischief; and again I appeal to you as one to blame in part for the threatened annoyances. But for the lady who accompanied Mrs. Endicott, I would not be suspected of relationship with your honored family. But for the discipline which I helped to procure for that lady, she would have left me in peace. But for your encouragement of the lady, I would not have been forced to subject a woman to discipline. You may remember the effective Sister Claire?"

So true was the surprise that Livingstone blushed with sudden violence.

"That woman was the so-called escaped nun?" he exclaimed.

"Now Mrs. Curran, wife of the detective employed by Mrs. Endicott for five years to discover her lost husband. She satisfies her noblest aspirations by dancing in the theaters, ... and a very fine dancer she is. Her leisure is devoted to plotting vengeance on me. She pretends to believe that I am Horace Endicott; perhaps she does believe it. Anyway she knows that persecution will result, and she has persuaded Mrs. Endicott to inaugurate it. I do not know if you were her selection to manage the case."

This time Livingstone did not blush, being prepared for any turn of mood and speech from this singular young man.

"As the matter was described to me," he said, "only a sentimental reason included you in the divorce proceedings. I can understand Mrs. Curran's feelings, and to what they would urge a woman of that character. Still, her statements here were very plausible."

"Undoubtedly. She made her career up to this moment on the plausible. Let me tell you, if it is not too tedious, how she has pursued this theory in the face of all good sense."

The lawyer bowed his permission.

"I am of opinion that the creature is half mad, or subject to fits of insanity. Her husband had talked much of the Endicott case, which was not good for a woman of her peculiarities. By inspiration, insane suggestion, she assumed that I was the man sought for, and built up the theory as you have heard. First, she persuaded her good-natured husband, with whom I am acquainted, to investigate among my acquaintances for the merest suspicion, doubt, of my real personality. A long and minute inquiry, the details of which are in writing in my possession, was made by the detective with one result: that no one doubted me to be what I was born."

Livingstone cast a look at him to see the expression which backed that natural and happy phrase. Arthur Dillon might have borne it.

"She kept at her husband, however, until he had tried to surprise my relatives, my friends, my nurse, and my mother, ... yes, even my confessor, into admissions favorable to her mad dream. My rooms, my papers, my habits, my secrets were turned inside out; Mrs. Endicott was brought on from Boston to study me in my daily life; for days I was watched by the three. In the detective's house I was drugged into a profound sleep, and for ten minutes the two women examined my sleeping face for signs of Horace Endicott. When all these things failed, Sister Claire dragged her unwilling husband to California, where I had spent ten years of my life, and tried hard to find another Arthur Dillon, or to disconnect me with myself. She proved to her own satisfaction that these things could not be done. But there is a devil of perversity in her. She is like a boa constrictor ... I think that's the snake which cannot let go its prey once it has seized it. She can't let go. In desperation she is risking her own safety and happiness to make public her belief that I am Horace Endicott. In spite of the overwhelming proofs against the theory, and in favor of me, she is bent on bringing the case into court."

"Risking her own safety and happiness?" Livingstone repeated.

"If the wild geese among the Irish could locate Sister Claire, who is supposed to have fled the town long ago, her life would be taken. If this suit continues she will have to leave the city forever. Knowing this the devil in her urges her to her own ruin."

"You have kept close track of her," said Livingstone.

"You left me no choice," was the reply, "having sprung the creature on us, and then thrown her off when you found out her character. If she had only turned on her abettors and wracked them I wouldn't have cared."

"You protest then against the serving of these papers on you. Would it not be better to settle forever the last doubts in so peculiar a matter?"

"What have I to do with the doubts of an escaped nun, and of Mrs. Endicott? Must I go to court and stand the odium of a shameful imputation to settle the doubts of a lunatic criminal and a woman whose husband fled from her with his entire fortune?"

"It is regrettable," the lawyer admitted with surprise. "As Mrs. Endicott is perhaps the most deeply interested, I fear that the case must go on."

"I have come to show you that it will not be to the interest of the two women that it should go on. In fact I feel quite certain that you will not serve those papers on me after I have laid a few facts before you."

"I shall be glad to examine them in the interest of my client."

"Having utterly failed to prove me other than I am," Arthur said easily, while the lawyer watched with increasing interest the expressive face, "these women have accepted your suggestion to put me under oath as to my own personality. I would not take affidavit," and his contempt was evident. "I am not going to permit any public or official attempt to cast doubt on my good name. You can understand the feeling. My mother and my friends are not accustomed to the atmosphere of courts, nor of scandal. It would mean severe suffering for them to be dragged into so sensational a trial. The consequences one cannot measure beforehand. The unpleasantness lives after all the parties are dead. Since I can prevent it I am going to do it. As far as I am concerned Mrs. Endicott must be content with a simple denial, or a simple affirmation rather, that I am Arthur Dillon, and therefore not her husband. It is more than she deserves, because there is not a shred of evidence to warrant her making a single move against me. She has not been able to find in me a feature resembling her husband."

"Then, you are prepared to convince Mrs. Endicott that she has more to lose than to gain by bringing you into her divorce suit?"

"Precisely. Here is the point for her to consider: if the papers in this suit are served upon me, then there will be no letting-up afterward. Her affairs, the affairs of this woman Curran, the lives of both to the last detail, will be served up to the court and the public. You know how that can be done. I would rather not have it done, but I proffer Mrs. Endicott the alternative."

"I do not know how strong an argument that would be with Mrs. Endicott," said Livingstone with interest.

"She is too shallow a woman to perceive its strength, unless you, as her lawyer and kinsman, make it plain to her," was the guileless answer. "Mrs. Curran knows nothing of court procedure, but she is clever enough to foresee consequences, and her history before her New York fiasco includes bits of romance from the lives of important people."

Livingstone resisted the inclination to laugh, and then to get angry.

"You think then, that if Mrs. Endicott could be made to see the possibilities of a desperate trial, the possible exposures of her sins and the sins of others, that she would not risk it?"

"She has family pride," said Arthur seriously, "and would not care to expose her own to scorn. I presume you know something about the Endicott disappearance?"

"Nothing more than the fact, and the failure to find the young man?"

"His wife employed the detective Curran to make the search for Endicott, and Curran is a Fenian, as interested as myself in such matters. He was with me in the little enterprise which ended so fatally for Ledwith and ... others." Livingstone was too sore on this subject to smile at the pause and the word. "Curran told me the details after he had left the pursuit of Endicott. They are known now to Mrs. Endicott's family in part. It is understood that she will marry her cousin Quincy Lenox when she gets a divorce. He was devoted to her before her marriage and is faithful still, I am told."

Not a sign of feeling in the utterance of these significant words!

"It is not affection, then, which prompts the actions of my client? She wishes to make sure of the existence or non-existence of her husband before entering upon this other marriage?"

"Of course I can tell you only what the detective and one other told us," Arthur said. "When Horace Endicott disappeared, it is said, he took with him his entire fortune, something over a million, leaving not one cent to his wife. He had converted his property into cash secretly. Her anxiety to find him is very properly to get her lawful share in that property, that is, alimony with her divorce?"

"I see," said Livingstone, and he began to understand the lines and shadows on this young man's face. "A peculiar, and I suppose thorough, revenge."

"If the papers are served on me, you understand, then in one fashion or another Mrs. Endicott shall be brought to court, and Quincy Lenox too, with the detective and his wife, and a few others. It is almost too much that you have been made acquainted with the doubts of these people. I bear with it, but I shall not endure one degree more of publicity. Once it is known that I am thought to be Horace Endicott, then the whole world must know quite as thoroughly that I am Arthur Dillon; and also who these people are that so foolishly pursue me. It cannot but appear to the average crowd that this new form of persecution is no more than an outgrowth of the old."

Then they glared at each other mildly, for the passions of yesterday were still warm. Livingstone's mood had changed, however. He felt speculatively certain that Horace Endicott sat before him, and he knew Sonia to be a guilty woman. As his mind flew over the humiliating events which connected him with Dillon, consolation soothed his wounded heart that he had been overthrown perhaps by one of his own, rather than by the Irish. The unknown element in the contest had given victory to the lucky side. He recalled his sense of this young fellow's superiority to his environment. He tried to fathom Arthur's motive in this visit, but failed. As a matter of fact Arthur was merely testing the thoroughness of his own disappearance. His visit to Livingstone the real Dillon would have made. It would lead the lawyer to believe that Sonia, in giving up her design, had been moved by his advice and not by a quiet, secret conversation with her husband. Livingstone quickly made up his mind that the divorce suit would have to be won by default, but he wished to learn more of this daring and interesting kinsman.

"The decision must remain with Mrs. Endicott," he said after a pause. "I shall tell her, before your name is mixed up with the matter, just what she must expect. If she has anything to fear from a public trial you are undoubtedly the man to bring it out."

"Thank you."

"I might even use persuasion ..."

"It would be a service to the Endicott family," Arthur said earnestly, "for I can swear to you that the truth will come out, the scandal which Horace Endicott fled to avoid and conceal forever."

"Did you know Endicott?"

"Very well indeed. I was his guide in California every time he made a trip to that country."

"I might persuade Mrs. Endicott," said the lawyer with deeper interest, "for the sake of the family name, to surrender her foolish theory. It is quite clear to any one with unbiased judgment that you are not Horace Endicott, even if you are not Arthur Dillon. I knew the young man slightly, and his family very well. I can see myself playing the part which you have presented to us for the past five years, quite as naturally as Horace Endicott would have played it. It was not in Horace's nature, nor in the Endicott nature to turn Irish so completely."

Arthur felt all the bitterness and the interest which this shot implied.

"I had the pleasure of knowing Endicott well, much better than you, sir," he returned warmly, "and while I know he was something of a good-natured butterfly, I can say something for his fairness and courage. If he had known what I know of the Irish, of their treatment by their enemies at home and here, of English hypocrisy and American meanness, of their banishment from the land God gave them and your attempt to drive them out of New York or to keep them in the gutter, he would have taken up their cause as honestly as I have done."

"You are always the orator, Mr. Endi ... Dillon."

"I have feeling, which is rare in the world," said Arthur smiling. "Do you know what this passion for justice has done for me, Mr. Livingstone? It has brought out in me the eloquence which you have praised, and inspired the energy, the deviltry, the trickery, the courage, that were used so finely at your expense.

"I was like Endicott, a wild irresponsible creature, thinking only of my own pleasure. Out of my love for one country which is not mine, out of a study of the wrongs heaped upon the Irish by a civilized people, I have secured the key to the conditions of the time. I have learned to despise and pity the littleness of your party, to recognize the shams of the time everywhere, the utter hypocrisy of those in power.

"I have pledged myself to make war on them as I made war on you; on the power that, mouthing liberty, holds Ireland in slavery; on the powers that, mouthing order and peace, hold down Poland, maintain Turkey, rob and starve India, loot the helpless wherever they may. I was a harmless hypocrite and mostly a fool once. Time and hardship and other things, chiefly Irish and English, have given me a fresh start in the life of thought. You hardly understand this, being thoroughly English in your make-up.

"You love good Protestants, pagans who hate the Pope, all who bow to England, and that part of America which is English. You can blow about their rights and liberties, and denounce their persecutors, if these happen to be French or Dutch or Russian. For a Pole or an Irishman you have no sympathy, and you would deny him any place on the earth but a grave. Liberty is not for him unless he becomes a good English Protestant at the same time. In other words liberty may be the proper sauce for the English goose but not for the Irish gander."

"I suppose it appears that way to you," said Livingstone, who had listened closely, not merely to the sentiments, but to the words, the tone, the idiom. Could Horace Endicott have ever descended to this view of his world, this rawness of thought, sentiment, and expression? So peculiarly Irish, anti-English, rich with the flavor of the Fourth Ward, and nevertheless most interesting.

"I shall not argue the point," he continued. "I judge from your earnestness that you have a well-marked ambition in life, and that you will follow it."

"My present ambition is to see our grand cathedral completed and dedicated as soon as possible, as the loudest word we can speak to you about our future. But I fear I am detaining you. If during the next few days the papers in the divorce case are not served on me, I may feel certain that Mrs. Endicott has given up the idea of including me in the suit?"

"I shall advise her to leave you in peace for the sake of the Endicott name," said Livingstone politely.

Arthur thanked him and departed, while the lawyer spent an hour enjoying his impressions and vainly trying to disentangle the Endicott from the Dillon in this extraordinary man.

CHAPTER XXXVII.

THE END OF MISCHIEF.

Arthur set out for the Curran household, where he was awaited with anxiety. Quite cheerful over his command of the situation, and inclined to laugh at the mixed feelings of Livingstone, he felt only reverence and awe before the human mind as seen in the light of his own experience. His particular mind had once been Horace Endicott's, but now represented the more intense and emotional personality of Arthur Dillon. He was neither Horace, nor the boy who had disappeared; but a new being fashioned after the ideal Arthur Dillon, as Horace Endicott had conceived him. What he had been seemed no more a part of his past, but a memory attached to another man. All his actions proved it.

The test of his disappearance delighted him. He had gone through its various scenes with little emotion, with less than Edith had displayed; far less than Arthur Dillon would have felt and shown. Who can measure the mind? Itself the measure of man's knowledge, the judge in the court of human destiny, how feeble its power over itself! A few years back this mind directed Horace Endicott; to-day it cheerfully served the conscience of Arthur Dillon!

Edith and her husband awaited their executioner. The detective suffered for her rather than himself. From Dillon he had nothing to fear, and for his sake, also for the strange regard he had always kept for Curran's wife, Arthur had been kind when harshness would have done more good. Now the end had come for her and Sonia. As the unexpected usually came from this young man, they had reason to feel apprehension. He took his seat comfortably in the familiar chair, and lit his cigar while chaffing her.

"They who love the danger shall perish in it," he said for a beginning. "You court it, Colette, and not very wisely."

"How, not wisely?" she asked with a pretence of boldness.

"You count on the good will of the people whom you annoy and wrong, and yet you have never any good will to give them in return. You have hated me and pursued me on the strength of my good will for you. It seems never to have occurred to you to do me a good turn for the many I have done for you. You are a bud of incarnate evil, Colette."

How she hated him when he talked in that fashion!

"Well, it's all settled. I have had the last talk with Livingstone, and spoiled your last trick against the comfort of Arthur Dillon. There will be no dragging to court of the Dillon clan. Mr. Livingstone believes with me that the publicity would be too severe for Mrs. Endicott and her family, not to mention the minor revelations connected with yourself. So there's the end of your precious tomfoolery, Colette."

She burst into vehement tears.

"But you weep too soon," he protested. "I have saved you as usual from yourself, but only to inflict my own punishment. Don't weep those crocodile diamonds until you have heard your own sentence. Of course you know that I have followed every step you took in this matter. You are clever enough to have guessed that. You discovered all that was to be discovered, of course. But you are too keen. If this trial had come to pass you would have been on the witness stand, and the dogs would have caught the scent then never to lose it. You would have ruined your husband as well as yourself."

"Why do you let him talk to me so?" she screamed at Curran.

"Because it is for your good," Arthur answered. "But here's briefness. You must leave New York at once, and forever. Get as far from it as you can, and stay there while I am alive. And for consolation in your exile take your child with you, your little boy, whom Mrs. Endicott parades as her little son, the heir of her beloved Horace."

A frightful stillness fell in the room with this terrific declaration. But for pity he could have laughed at the paralysis which seized both the detective and his wife. Edith sat like a statue, white-faced, pouting at him, her hands clasped in her lap.

"Well, are you surprised? You, the clever one? If I am Horace Endicott, as you pretend to believe, do I not know the difference between my own child and another's? I am Arthur Dillon only, and yet I know how you conspired with Mrs. Endicott to provide her with an heir for the Endicott money. You did this in spite of your husband, who has never been able to control you, not even when you chose to commit so grave a crime. Now, it is absolutely necessary for the child's sake that you save him from Mrs. Endicott's neglect, when he is of no further use to her. She loves children, as you know."

"Who are you, anyway?" Curran burst out hoarsely after a while.

"Not half as good a detective as you are, but I happen in this matter to be on the inside," Arthur answered cheerfully. "I knew Horace Endicott much better than his wife or his friends. The poor fellow is dead and gone, and yet he left enough information behind him to trouble the clever people. Are you satisfied, Colette, that this time everything must be done as I have ordered?"

"You have proved yourself Horace Endicott," she gasped in her rage, burning with hate, mortification, shame, fifty tigerish feelings that could not find expression.

"Fie, fie, Colette! You have proved that I am Arthur Dillon. Why go back on your own work? If you had known Horace Endicott as I did, you would not compare the meek and civilized Dillon with the howling demon into which his wife turned him. That fellow would not have sat in your presence ten minutes knowing that you had palmed off your child as his, without taking your throat in his hands for a death squeeze. His wife would not have escaped death from the madman had he ever encountered her. Here are your orders now; it is late and I must not keep you from your beauty sleep; take the child as soon as the Endicott woman sends him to you, and leave New York one hundred miles behind you. If you are found in this city any time after the month of September, you take all the risks. I shall not stand between you and justice again. You are the most ungrateful sinner that I have ever dealt with. Now go and weep for yourself. Don't waste any tears on Mrs. Endicott."

Sobbing like an angry and humiliated child, Edith rushed out of the room. Curran felt excessively foolish. Though partly in league with Arthur, the present situation went beyond him.

"Be hanged if I don't feel like demanding an explanation," he said awkwardly.

"You don't need it," said Arthur as he proceeded to make it. "Can't you see that Horace Endicott is acting through me, and has been from the first, to secure the things I have secured. He is dead as I told you. How he got away, kept himself hid, and all that, you are as good an authority as I. While he was alive you could have found him as easily as I could, but he was beyond search always, though I guess not beyond betrayal. Well, let me congratulate you on getting your little family together again. Don't worry over what has happened to-night. Drop the Endicott case. You can see there's no luck in it for any one."

Certainly there had been no luck in it for the Currans. Arthur went to his club in the best humor, shaking with laughter over the complete crushing of Edith, with whom he felt himself quite even in the contest that had endured so long. Next morning it would be Sonia's turn. Ah, what a despicable thing is man's love, how unstable and profitless! No wonder Honora valued it so lightly. How Horace Endicott had raved over this whited sepulcher five years ago, believed in her, sworn by her virtue and truth! And to-day he regarded her without feeling, neither love nor hate, perfect indifference only marking his mental attitude in her regard. Somehow one liked to feel that love is unchangeable, as with the mother, the father; as with God also, for whom sin does not change relationship with the sinner.

When he stood before her the next day in the hotel parlor, she reminded him in her exquisite beauty of a play seen from the back of the stage; the illusion so successful with the audience is there an exposed sham, without coherence, and without beauty. Her eyes had a scared look. She had to say to herself, if this is Horace then my time has come, if it is Arthur Dillon I have nothing to worry about, before her hate came to her aid and gave her courage. She murmured the usual formula of unexpected pleasure. He bowed, finding no pleasure in this part of his revenge. Arthur Dillon could not have been more considerate of Messalina.

"It is certainly a privilege and an honor," said he, "to be suspected of so charming a relationship with Mrs. Endicott. Nevertheless I have persuaded your lawyer, Mr. Livingstone, that it would be unprofitable and imprudent to bring me into the suit for divorce. He will so advise you I think to-day."

She smiled at the compliment and felt reassured.

"There were some things which I could not tell the lawyer," he went on, "and so I made bold to call on you personally. It is disagreeable, what I must tell you. My only apology is that you yourself have made this visit necessary by bringing my name into the case."

Her smile died away, and her face hardened. She prepared herself for trouble.

"I told your lawyer that if the papers were served on me, and a public and official doubt thrown on my right to the name of Arthur Dillon, I would not let the business drop until the Endicott-Curran-Dillon mystery had been thoroughly ventilated in the courts. He agreed with me that this would expose the Endicott name to scandal."

"We have been perhaps too careful from the beginning about the Endicott name," she said severely. "Which is the reason why no advance has been made in the search for my dear husband."

"That may be true, Mrs. Endicott. You must not forget, however, that you will be a witness, and Mrs. Curran, and her husband, and Mr. Quincy Lenox, and others besides. How do you think these people would stand questioning as to who your little boy, called Horace Endicott, really is?"

She sat prepared for a dangerous surprise, but not for this horror; and the life left her on the spot, for the poor weed was as soft and cowardly as any other product of the swamp. He rang for restoratives and sent for her maid. In ten minutes, somewhat restored, she faced the ordeal, if only to learn what this terrible man knew.

"Who are you?" she asked feebly, the same question asked by Curran in his surprise.

"A friend of Horace Endicott," he answered quietly.

"And what do you know of us?"

"All that Horace knew."

She could not summon courage to put a third question. He came to her aid.

"Perhaps you are not sure about what Horace knew? Shall I tell you? I did not tell your lawyer. I only hinted that the truth would be brought out if my name was dragged into the case against my protest. Shall I tell you what Horace knew?"

With closed eyes she made a sign of acquiescence.

"He knew of your relations with Quincy Lenox. He saw you together on a certain night, when he arrived home after a few days' absence. He also heard your conversation. In this you admitted that out of hatred for your husband you had destroyed his heir before the child was born. He knew your plan of retrieving that blunder by adopting the child of Edith Curran, and palming him off as your own. He knew of your plan to secure the good will of his Aunt Lois for the impostor, and found the means to inform his aunt of the fraud. All that he knew will be brought out at any trial in which my name shall be included. Your lawyer will tell you that it cannot be avoided. Therefore, when your lawyer advises you to get a divorce from your former husband without including me as that husband, yon had better accept that advice."

She opened her eyes and stared at him with insane fright. Who but Horace Endicott could know her crimes? All but the crime which he had named her blunder. Could this passionless stranger, this Irish politician, looking at her as indifferently as the judge on the bench, be Horace? No, surely no! Because that fool, dolt though he was, would never have seen this wretched confession of her crimes, and not slain her the next minute. Into this ambuscade had she been led by the crazy wife of Curran, whose sound advice she herself had thrown aside to follow the instincts of Edith. Recovering her nerve quickly, she began her retreat as well as one might after so disastrous a field.

"It was a mistake to have disturbed you, Mr. Dillon," she said. "You may rest assured that no further attempt will be made on your good name. Since you pretend to such intimacy with my unfortunate husband I would like to ask you...."

"That was the extent of my intimacy, Mrs. Endicott, and I would never have revealed it except to defend myself," he interrupted suavely. "Of course the revelation brings consequences. You must arrange to have your little Horace die properly in some remote country, surround his funeral with all the legal formalities, and so on. That will be easy. Meanwhile you can return the boy to his mother, who is ready to receive him. Then your suit for divorce must continue, and you will win it by default, that is, by the failure of Horace Endicott to defend his side. When these things are done, it would be well for your future happiness to lay aside further meddling with the mystery of your husband's disappearance."

"I have learned a lesson," she said more composedly. "I shall do as you command, because I feel sure it is a command. I have some curiosity however about the life which Horace led after he disappeared. Since you must have known him a little, would it be asking too much from you...."

She lost her courage at sight of his expression. Her voice faded. Oh, shallow as any frog-pond, indecently shallow, to ask such a question of the judge who had just ordered her to execution. His contempt silenced her. With a formal apology for having caused her so much pain, he bowed and withdrew. Some emotion had stirred him during the interview, but he had kept himself well under control. Later he found it was horror, ever to have been linked with a monster; and dread too that in a sudden access of passion he might have done her to death. It seemed natural and righteous to strike and destroy the reptile.

CHAPTER XXXVIII.

A TALE WELL TOLD.

Of these strange and stirring events no one knew but Arthur himself; nor of the swift consequences, the divorce of Sonia from her lost husband, her marriage to Quincy Lenox, the death and burial of her little boy in England, and the establishment of La Belle Colette and her son Horace in Chicago, where the temptation to annoy her enemies disappeared, and the risk to herself was practically removed forever. Thus faded the old life out of Arthur's view, its sin-stained personages frightened off the scene by his well-used knowledge of their crimes. Whatever doubt they held about his real character, self-interest accepted him as Arthur Dillon.

He was free. Honora saw the delight of that freedom in his loving and candid expression. He repressed his feelings no more, no longer bound.

He was gayer than ever before, with the gaiety of his nature, not of the part which he had played. Honora knew how deeply she loved him, from her very dread of inflicting on him that pain which was bound to come. The convent would be her rich possession; but he who had given her and her father all that man could give, he would have only bitter remembrance. How bitter that could be experience with her father informed her. The mystery of his life attracted her. If not Arthur Dillon, who was he? What tragedy had driven him from one life into another? Did it explain that suffering so clearly marked on his face? To which she must add, as part of the return to be made for all his goodness!

Her pity for him grew, and prompted deeper tenderness; and how could she know, who had been without experience, that pity is often akin to love?

The heavenly days flew by like swift swallows. September came with its splendid warnings of change. The trees were suddenly bordered in gold yellow and dotted with fire-red. The nights began to be haunted by cool winds. Louis packed his trunk early in the month. His long vacations had ended, ordination was at hand, and his life-work would begin in the month of October.

The household went down to the city for the grand ceremony. Mona and her baby remained in the city then, while the others returned to the lake for a final week, Anne with perfect content, Honora in calmness of spirit, but also in dread for Arthur's sake. He seemed to have no misgivings. Her determination continued, and the situation therefore remained as clear as the cold September mornings. Yet some tie bound them, elusive, beyond description, but so much in evidence that every incident of the waiting time seemed to strengthen it. Delay did not abate her resolution, but it favored his hope.

"Were you disturbed by the revelations of Mrs. Curran?" he said as they sat, for the last time indeed, on the terrace so fatal to Lord Constantine. Anne read the morning newspaper in the shadow of the grove behind them, with Judy to comment on the news. The day, perfect, comfortable, without the perfume of August, sparkled with the snap of September.

"My curiosity was disturbed," she admitted frankly, and her heart beat, for the terrible hour had come. "I felt that your life had some sadness and mystery in it, but it was a surprise to hear that you were not Anne Dillon's long-lost son."

"That was pure guess-work on Colette's part, you know. She's a born devil, if there are such things among us humans. I'll tell you about her some time. Then the fact of my wife's existence did not disturb you at all?"

"On the contrary, it soothed me, I think," she said with a blush.

"I know why. Well, it will take my story to explain hers. She told the truth in part, poor Colette. Once I had a wife, before I became Anne Dillon's son. Will it be too painful for you to hear the story? It is mournful. To no one have I ever told it complete; in fact I could not, only to you. How I have burned to tell it from beginning to end to the true heart. I could not shock Louis, the dear innocent, and it was necessary to keep most of it from my mother, for legal reasons.

Monsignor has heard the greater part, but not all. And I have been like the Ancient Mariner.

> Since then at an uncertain hour
> That agony returns;
> And till my ghastly tale is told,
> The heart within me burns.

> *   *   *   *

> That moment that his face I see
> I know the man that must hear me;
> To him my tale I teach."

"I am the man," said she, "with a woman's curiosity. How can I help but listen?"

> He holds him with his glittering eye —
> The wedding-guest stood still,
> And listens like a three years' child:
> The mariner hath his will.

> The wedding-guest sat on a stone,
> He cannot choose but hear;
> And thus spake on that ancient man,
> That bright-eyed mariner.

"Do you remember how we read and re-read it on the *Arrow* years ago? Somehow it has rung in my ears ever since, Honora. My life had a horror like it. Had it not passed I could not speak of it even to you. Long ago I was an innocent fool whom men knew in the neighborhood of Cambridge as Horace Endicott. I was an orphan, without guides, or real friends. I felt no need of them, for was I not rich, and happily married? Good nature and luck had carried me along lazily like that pine-stick floating down there. What a banging it would get on this rocky shore if a good south wind sprang up. For a long time I escaped the winds. When they came.... I'll tell you who I was and what she was. Do you remember on the *Arrow* Captain Curran's story of Tom Jones?"

He looked up at her interested face, and saw the violet eyes widen with sudden horror.

"I remember," she cried with astonishment and pain. "You, Arthur, you the victim of that shameful story?"

"Do you remember what you said then, Honora, when Curran declared he would one day find Tom Jones?"

She knew by the softness of his speech that her saying had penetrated the lad's heart, and had been treasured till this day, would be treasured forever.

"And you were sitting there, in the cabin, not ten feet off, listening to him and me?" she said with a gasp of pleasure.

"'You will never find him, Captain Curran ... that fearful woman shattered his very soul ... I know the sort of man he was ... he will never go back ... if he can bear to live, it will be because in his obscurity God gave him new faith and hope in human nature, and in the woman's part of it.' Those are your words, Honora."

She blushed with pleasure and murmured: "I hope they came true!"

"They were true at that moment," he said reflectively. "Oh, indeed God guided me, placed me in the hands of Monsignor, of my mother, of such people as Judy and the Senator and Louis, and of you all."

"Oh, my God, what suffering!" she exclaimed suddenly as her tears began to fall. "Louis told me, I saw it in your face as every one did, but now I know. And we never gave you the pity you needed!"

"Then you must give it to me now," said he with boldness. "But don't waste any pity on Endicott. He is dead, and I look at him across these five years as at a stranger. Suffer? The poor devil went mad with suffering. He raved for days in the wilderness, after he discovered his shame, dreaming dreams of murder for the guilty, of suicide for himself— —"

She clasped her hands in anguish and turned toward him as if to protect him.

"It was a good woman who saved him, and she was an old mother who had tasted death. Some day I shall show you the pool where this old woman found him, after he had overcome the temptation to die. She took him to her home and her heart, nourished him, gave him courage, sent him on a new mission of life. What a life! He had a scheme of vengeance, and to execute it he had to return to the old scenes, where he was more alone — —

> Alone, alone, all, all alone,
> Alone on a wide, wide sea!
> And never a saint took pity on
> My soul in agony.

> *   *   *   *   *

> O wedding-guest! this soul hath been
> Alone on a wide, wide sea;
> So lonely 'twas that God Himself
> Scarce seemed there to be."

The wonder to Honora, as he described himself, was the indifference of his tone. It had no more than the sympathy one might show toward a stranger whose suffering had been succeeded by great joy.

"Oh, God grant," he broke in with vehemence, "that no soul suffers as did this Endicott, poor wretch, during the time of his vengeance. Honora, I would not inflict on that terrible woman the suffering of that man for a year after his discovery of her sin. I doubted long the mercy of God. Rather I knew nothing about His mercy. I had no religion, no understanding of it, except in a vague, unpractical way. You know now that I am of the Puritan race ... Livingstone is of my family ... the race which dislikes the Irish and the Catholic as the English dislike them ... the race that persecuted yours! But you cannot say that I have not atoned for them as nearly as one man can?"

Trembling with emotion, she simply raised her hands in a gesture that said a thousand things too beautiful for words.

"My vengeance on the guilty was to disappear. I took with me all my property, and I left Messalina with her own small dower to enjoy her freedom in poverty. She sought for me, hired that detective and others to hound me to my hiding-place, and so far has failed to make sure of me. But to have you understand the story clearly, I shall stick to the order of events. I had known Monsignor a few days before calamity overtook me, and to him I turned for aid. It was he who found a mother for me, a place among 'the mere Irish,' a career which has turned out very well. You know how Anne Dillon lost her son. What no one knows is this: three months before she was asked to take part in the scheme of disappearance she sent a thousand photographs of her dead husband and her lost son to the police of California, and offered a reward for his discovery living or dead. Monsignor helped her to that. I acknowledged that advertisement from one of the most obscure and ephemeral of the mining-camps, and came home as her son."

"And the real Arthur Dillon? He was never found?"

"Oh, yes, he answered it too, indirectly. While I was loitering riotously about, awaiting the proper moment to make myself known, I heard that one Arthur Dillon was dying in another mining-camp some thirty miles to the north of us. He claimed to be the real thing, but he was dying of consumption, and was too feeble, and of too little consequence, to be taken notice of. I looked after him till he died, and made sure of his identity. He was Anne Dillon's son and he lies in the family lot in Calvary beside his father. No one knows this but his mother, Monsignor, and ourselves. Colette stumbled on the fact in her search of California, but the fates have been against that clever woman."

He laughed heartily at the complete overthrow of the escaped nun. Honora looked at him in astonishment. Arthur Dillon laughed, quite forgetful of the tragedy of Horace Endicott.

"Since my return you know what I have been, Honora. I can appeal to you as did Augustus to his friends on his dying-bed: have I not played well the part?"

"I am lost in wonder," she said.

"Then give me your applause as I depart," he answered sadly, and her eyes fell before his eloquent glance. "In those early days rage and hate, and the maddest desire for justice, sustained me. That woman had only one wish in life: to find, rob, and murder the man who had befooled her worse than she had tricked him. I made war on that man. I hated Horace Endicott as a weak fool. He had fallen lowest of all his honest, able, stern race. I beat him first into hiding, then into slavery, and at last into annihilation. I studied to annihilate him, and I did it by raising Arthur Dillon in his place. I am now Arthur Dillon. I think, feel, act, speak, dream like that Arthur Dillon which I first imagined. When you knew me first, Honora, I was playing a part. I am no longer acting. I am the man whom the world knows as Arthur Dillon."

"I can see that, and it seems more wonderful than any dream of romance. You a Puritan are more Irish than the Irish, more Catholic than the Catholics, more Dillon than the Dillons. Oh, how can this be?"

"Don't let it worry you," he said grimly. "Just accept the fact and me. I never lived until Horace Endicott disappeared. He was a child of fortune and a lover of ease and pleasure. His greatest pain had been a toothache. His view of life had been a boy's. When I stepped on this great stage I found myself for the first time in the very current of life. Suffering ate my heart out, and I plunged into that current to deaden the agony. I found myself by accident a leader of a poor people who had fled from injustice at home to suffer a mean persecution here. I was thrown in with the great men of the hour, and found a splendid opponent in a member of the Endicott family, Livingstone. I saw the very heart of great things, and the look enchanted me.

"You know how I worked for my friends, for your father, for the people, for every one and everything that needed help. For the first time I saw into the heart of a true friend. Monsignor helped me, carried me through, stood by me, directed me. For the first time I saw into the heart of innocence and sanctity, deep down, the heart of that blessed boy, Louis. For the first time I looked into the heart of a patriot, and learned of the love which can endure, not merely failure, but absolute and final disappointment, and still be faithful. I became an orator, an adventurer, an enthusiast. The Endicott who could not speak ten words before a crowd, the empty-headed stroller who classed patriots with pickles, became what you know me to be. I learned what love is, the love of one's own; of mother, and friend, and clan. Let me not boast, but I learned to know God and perhaps to love Him, at least since I am resigned to His will. But I am talking too much, since it is for the last time."

"You have not ended," said she beseechingly.

"It would take a lifetime," and he looked to see if she would give him that time, but her eyes watched the lake. "The latest events in my history took place this summer, and you had a little share in them. By guess-work Colette arrived at the belief that I am Horace Endicott, and she set her detective-husband to discover the link between Endicott and Dillon. I helped him, because I was curious to see how Arthur Dillon would stand the test of direct pursuit. They could discover nothing. As fast as a trace of me showed it vanished into thin air. There was nothing to do but invent a suit which would bring my mother, Monsignor, and myself into court, and have us declare under oath who is Arthur Dillon. I blocked that game perfectly. Messalina has her divorce from Horace Endicott, and is married to her lover. There will be no further search for the man who disappeared. And I am free, Monsignor declares. No ties bind me to that shameful past. I have had my vengeance without publicity or shame to anyone. I have punished as I had the right to punish. I have a noble place in life, which no one can take from me."

"And did you meet her since you left her ... that woman?" Honora said in a low voice half ashamed of the question.

"At Castle Moyna ..." he began and stopped dead at a sudden recollection.

"I met her," cried Honora with a stifled scream, "I met her."

"I met her again on the steamer returning," he said after a pause. "She did not recognize me, nor has she ever. We met for the last time in July. At that meeting Arthur Dillon pronounced sentence on her in the name of Horace Endicott. She will never wish to see me or her lost husband again."

"Oh, how you must have suffered, Arthur, how you must have suffered!"

She had grown pale alarmingly, but he did not perceive it. The critical moment had come for him, and he was praying silently against the expected blow. Her resolution had left her, and the road had vanished in the obscurity of night. She no longer saw her way clear. Her nerves had been shaken by this wonderful story, and the surges of feeling that rose before it like waves before the wind.

"And I must suffer still," he went on half to himself. "I was sure that God would give me that which I most desired, because I had given Him all that belonged to me. I kept back nothing except as Monsignor ordered. Through you, Honora, my faith in woman came back, as you said it would when you answered the detective in my behalf. When Monsignor told me I was free, that I could speak to you as an honorable man, I took it as a sign from heaven that the greatest of God's gifts was for me. I love you so, Honora, that your wish is my only happiness. Since you must go, if it is the will of God, do not mind my suffering, which is also His will...."

He arose from his place and his knees were shaking.

"There is consolation for us all somewhere. Mine is not to be here. The road to heaven is sometimes long. Not here, Honora?"

The hope in him was not yet dead. She rose too and put her arms about him, drawing his head to her bosom with sudden and overpowering affection.

"Here and hereafter," she whispered, as they sat down on the bench again.

"Judy," said Anne in the shade of the trees, "is Arthur hugging Honora, or...."

"Glory be," whispered Judy with tears streaming down her face, "it's Honora that's hugging Arthur ... no, it's both o' them at wanst, thanks be to God."

And the two old ladies stole away home through the happy woods.

CHAPTER XXXIX.

THREE SCENES.

Anne might have been the bitterest critic of Honora for her descent from the higher to the lesser life, but she loved the girl too well even to look displeasure. Having come to believe that Arthur would be hers alone forever, she regarded Honora's decision as a mistake. The whole world rejoiced at the union of these ideal creatures, even Sister Magdalen, from whom Arthur had snatched a prize. Honora was her own severest critic. How she had let herself go in pity for a sufferer to whom her people, her faith, her father, her friends, and herself owed much, she knew not. His explanation was simple: God gave you to me.

The process of surrender really began at Louis' ordination. Arthur watched his boy, the center of the august ceremony, with wet eyes. This innocent heart, with its solemn aspirations, its spiritual beauty, had always been for him a wonder and a delight; and it seemed fitting that a life so mysteriously beautiful should end its novitiate and begin its career with a ceremony so touching. The September sun streamed through the venerable windows of the cathedral, the music soared among the arches, the altar glowed with lights and flowers; the venerable archbishop and his priests and attendants filled the sanctuary, an adoring crowd breathed with reverence in the nave; but the center of the scene, its heart of beauty, was the pale, sanctified son of Mary Everard.

For him were all these glories! Happy, happy, youth! Blessed mother! There were no two like them in the whole world, he said in his emotion. Her glorified face often shone on him in the pauses of the ceremony. Her look repeated the words she had uttered the night before: "Under God my happiness is owing to you, Arthur Dillon: like the happiness of so many others; and that I am not to-day dead of sorrow and grief is also owing to you; now may God grant you the dearest wish of your heart, as He has granted mine this day through you; for there is nothing too good for a man with a heart and a hand like yours."

How his heart had like to burst under that blessing! He thought of Honora, not yet his own.

The entire Irishry was present, with their friends of every race. In deference to his faithful adherent, the great Livingstone sat in the very front pew, seriously attentive to the rite, and studious of its significance. Around him were grouped the well-beloved of Arthur Dillon, the souls knit to his with the strength of heaven; the Senator, high-colored, richly-dressed, resplendent, sincere; the Boss, dark and taciturn, keen, full of emotion, sighing from the depths of his rich nature over the meaning of life, as it leaped into the light of this scene; Birmingham, impressive and dignified, rejoicing at the splendor so powerful with the world that reckons everything by the outward show; and all the friends of the new life, to whom this ceremony was dear as the breath of their bodies. For this people the sanctuary signified the highest honor, the noblest service, the loftiest glory. Beside it the honors of the secular life, no matter how esteemed, looked like dead flowers.

At times his emotion seemed to slip from the rein, threatening to unman him. This child, whose innocent hands were anointed with the Holy Oil, who was bound and led away, who read the mass with the bishop and received the Sacred Elements with him, upon whom the prelate breathed solemn powers, who lay prostrate on the floor, whose head was blessed by the hands of the assembled priests: this child God had given him to replace the innocent so cruelly destroyed long ago!

Honora's eyes hardly left Arthur's transfigured face, which held her, charmed her, frightened her by its ever-changing expression. Light and shadow flew across it as over the depths of the sea. The mask off, the habit of repression laid aside, his severe features responded to the inner emotions. She saw his great eyes fill with tears, his breast heave at times. As yet she had not heard his story. The power of that story came less from the tale than the recollection of scenes like this, which she unthinking had witnessed in the years of their companionship. What made this strange man so unlike all other men?

At the close of the ordination the blessing from the new priest began. Flushed, dewy-eyed, calm, and white, Louis stood at the railing to lay his anointed hands on each in turn; first the mother, and the father. Then came a little pause, while Mona made way for him dearest to all hearts that day, Arthur. He held back until he saw that his delay retarded the ceremony, when he accepted the honor. He felt the blessed hands on his head, and a thrill leaped through him as the palms, odorous of the balmy chrism, touched his lips.

Mona held up her baby with the secret prayer that he too would be found worthy of the sanctuary; then followed her husband and her sisters. Honora did not see as she knelt how Arthur's heart leaped into his eyes, and shot a burning glance at Louis to remind him of a request uttered long ago: when you bless Honora, bless her for me! Thus all conspired against her. Was it wonderful that she left the cathedral drawn to her hero as never before?

The next day Arthur told her with pride and tenderness, as they drove to the church where Father Louis was to sing his first Mass, that every vestment of the young priest came from him. Sister Magdalen had made the entire set, with her own hands embroidered them, and he had borne the expense. Honora found her heart melting under these beautiful details of an affection, without limit. The depth of this man's heart seemed incredible, deeper than her father's, as if more savage sorrow had dug depths in what was deep enough by nature. Long afterward she recognized how deeply the ordination had affected her. It roused the feeling that such a heart should not be lightly rejected.

Desolation seized her, as the vision of the convent vanished like some lovely vale which one leaves forever. Very simply he banished the desolation.

"I have been computing," he said, as they sat on the veranda after breakfast, "what you might have been worth to the Church as a nun

... hear me, hear me ... wait for the end of the story ... it is charming. You are now about twenty-seven, I won't venture any nearer your age. I don't know my mother's age."

"And no man will ever know it," said Anne. "Men have no discretion about ages."

"Let me suppose," Arthur continued, "that fifty years of service would be the limit of your active life. You would then be seventy-seven, and there is no woman alive as old as that. The oldest is under sixty."

"Unless the newspapers want to say that she's a hundred," said Anne slyly.

"For the sake of notoriety she is willing to have the truth told about her age."

"As a school-teacher, a music-teacher, or a nurse, let me say that your services might be valued at one thousand a year for the fifty years, Honora. Do you think that a fair average?"

"Very fair," said she indifferently.

"Well, I am going to give that sum to the convent for having deprived them of your pleasant company," said he. "Hear me, hear me, ... I'm not done yet. I must be generous, and I know your conscience will be tender a long time, if something is not done to toughen it. I want to be married in the new cathedral, which another year will see dedicated. But a good round sum would advance the date. We owe much to Monsignor. In your name and mine I am going to give him enough to put the great church in the way to be dedicated by November."

He knew the suffering which burned her heart that morning, himself past master in the art of sorrow. That she had come down from the heights to the common level would be her grief forever; thus to console her would be his everlasting joy.

"What do you think of it? Isn't it a fair release?"

"Only I am not worth it," she said. "But so much the better, if every one gains more than I lose by my ... infatuation."

"Are you as much in love as that?" said Anne with malice.

They were married with becoming splendor in January. A quiet ceremony suggested by Honora had been promptly overruled by Anne Dillon, who saw in this wedding a social opportunity beyond any of her previous triumphs. Mrs. Dillon was not your mere aristocrat, who keeps exclusive her ceremonious march through life. At that early date she had perceived the usefulness to the aristocracy of the press, of general popularity, and of mixed assemblies; things freely and openly sought for by society to-day. Therefore the great cathedral of the western continent never witnessed a more splendid ceremony than the wedding of Honora and Arthur; and no event in the career of Anne Dillon bore stronger testimony to her genius.

The Chief Justice of the nation headed the *élite*, among whom shone like a constellation the Countess of Skibbereen; the Senator brought in the whole political circle of the city and the state; Grahame marshaled the journalists and the conspirators against the peace of England; the profession of music came forward to honor the bride; the common people of Cherry Hill went to cheer their hero; Monsignor drew to the sanctuary the clerics of rank to honor the benefactor of the cathedral; and high above all, enthroned in beauty, the Cardinal of that year presided as the dispenser of the Sacrament.

As at the ordination of Louis the admirable Livingstone sat among the attendant princes. For the third time within a few months had he been witness to the splendors of Rome now budding on the American landscape. He did not know what share this Arthur Dillon had in the life of Louis and in the building of the beautiful temple. But he knew the strength of his leadership among his people; and he felt curious to see with his own eyes, to feel with his own heart, the charm, the enchantment, which had worked a spell so fatal on the richly endowed Endicott nature.

For enchantment there must have been. The treachery and unworthiness of Sonia, detestable beyond thought, could not alone work so strange and weird a transformation. Half cynic always, and still more cynical since his late misfortunes, he could not withhold his approbation from the cleverness which grouped about this young man and his bride the great ones of the hour. The scene wholly depressed him. Not the grandeur, nor the presence of the powers of society, but the sight of this Endicott, of the mould of heroes, of the blood of the English Puritan, acting as sponsor of a new order of things in his beloved country, the order which he had hoped, still hoped, to destroy. His heart bled as he watched him.

The lovely mother, the high-hearted father, lay in their grave. Here stood their beloved, a prince among men, bowing before the idols of Rome, receiving for himself and his bride the blessing of the archpriest of Romanism, a cardinal in his ferocious scarlet. All his courage and skill would be forever at the service of the new order. Who was to blame? Was it not the rotten reed which he had leaned upon, the woman Sonia, rather than these? True it is, true it always will be, that a man's enemies are they of his own household.

A grand content filled the heart of Arthur. The bitterness of his fight had passed. So long had he struggled that fighting had become a part of his dreams, as necessary as daily bread. He had not laid aside his armor even for his marriage. Yet there had been an armistice, quite unperceived, from the day of the cathedral's dedication. He had lonely possession of the battle-field. His enemies had fled. All was well with his people. They had reached and passed the frontier, as it were, on that day when the great temple opened its sanctuary to God and its portals to the nation.

The building he regarded as a witness to the daring of Monsignor; for Honora's sake he had given to it a third of his fortune; the day of the dedication crowned Monsignor's triumph. When he had seen the spectacle, he learned how little men have to do with the great things of history. God alone makes history; man is the tide which rushes in and out at His command, at the great hours set by Him, and knows only the fact, not the reason. In the building that day gathered a multitude representing every form of human activity and success. They stood for the triumph of a whole race, which, starved out of its native seat, had clung desperately to the land of Columbia in spite of persecution.

Soldiers sat in the assembly, witnesses for the dead of the southern battle-fields, for all who had given life and love, who had sacrificed their dearest, to the new land in its hour of calamity. Men rich in the honors of commerce, of the professions, of the schools, artists, journalists, leaders, bore witness to the native power of a people, who had been written down in the books of the hour as idle, inferior, incapable by their very nature. In the sanctuary sat priests and prelate, a brilliant gathering, surrounding the delicate-featured Cardinal, in gleaming red, high on his beautiful throne.

From the organ rolled the wonderful harmonies born of faith and genius; from the pulpit came in sonorous English the interpretation of the scene as a gifted mind perceived it; about the altar the ancient ritual enacted the holy drama, whose sublime enchantment holds every age. Around rose the towering arches, the steady columns, the broad walls, lighted from the storied windows, of the first really great temple of the western continent!

Whose hands raised it? Arthur discovered in the answer the charm which had worked upon dying Ledwith, turned his failure into triumph, and his sadness into joy. What a witness, an eternal witness, to the energy and faith of a poor, simple, despised people, would be this temple! Looking upon its majestic beauty, who could doubt their powers, though the books printed English slanders in letters of gold? Out of these great doors would march ideas to strengthen and refresh the poor; ideas once rejected, once thought destructible by the air of the American wilderness. A conspiracy of centuries had been unable to destroy them. Into these great portals for long years would a whole people march for their own sanctification and glory!

Thereafter the temple became for him a symbol, as for the faithful priest; the symbol of his own life as that of his people.

He saw it in the early dawn, whiter than the mist which broke against it, a great angel whose beautiful feet the longing earth had imprisoned! red with the flush of morning, rosy with the tints of sunrise, as if heaven were smiling upon it from open gates! clear, majestic, commanding in the broad day, like a leader of the people, drawing all eyes to itself, provoking the question, the denial, the prayer from every passer, as tributes to its power! in the sunset, as dying Ledwith had seen it, flushed with the fever of life, but paling like the day, tender, beseeching, appealing to the flying crowd for a last turning to God before the day be done forever! in the twilight, calm, restful, submissive to the darkness, which had no power over it, because of the Presence within! terrible when night falls and sin goes forth in purple and fine linen, a giant which had heaved the earth and raised itself from the dead stone to rebuke and threaten the erring children of God!

He described all this for Honora, and, strangely enough, for Livingstone, who never recovered from the spell cast over him by this strange man. The old gentleman loved his race with the fervor of an ancient clansman. For this lost sheep of the house of Endicott he developed in time an interest which Arthur foresaw would lead agreeably one day to a review of the art of disappearing. He was willing to satisfy his curiosity. Meanwhile, airing his ideas on the providential mission of the country, and of its missionary races, and combatting his exclusiveness, they became excellent friends. Livingstone fell deeply in love with Honora, as it was the fashion in regard to that charming woman. For Arthur the circle of life had its beginning in her, and with her would have its end.

THE END.

Lightning Source UK Ltd.
Milton Keynes UK
UKHW010633040521
383104UK00002B/64